KU-579-485

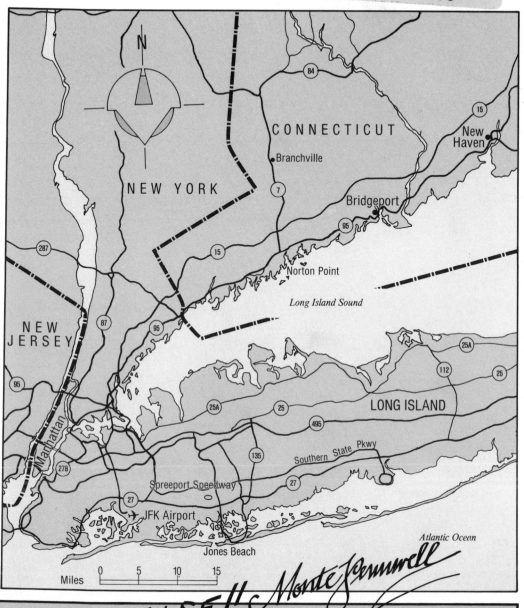

N

CONNECTICUT

• Branchville

NEW YORK

New Haven

15

Bridgeport

95

7

287

15

Norton Point

Long Island Sound

NEW JERSEY

87

95

95

278

135

25A

112

25

25A

25

LONG ISLAND

495

Southern State Pkwy

Spreeport Speedway

27

27

→ JFK Airport

Jones Beach

Atlantic Ocean

Monte Fennwell

0   5   10   15
Miles

FALSE!! →

_ong Island

This book follows
THE INVADERS PLAN
BLACK GENESIS:
Fortress of Evil
and
THE ENEMY WITHIN.
Buy them and read them first!

AMONG THE MANY CLASSIC WORKS
BY L. RON HUBBARD

Battlefield Earth
Beyond the Black Nebula
Buckskin Brigades
The Conquest of Space
The Dangerous Dimension
Death's Deputy
The Emperor of the Universe
Fear
Final Blackout
Forbidden Voyage
The Incredible Destination
The Kilkenny Cats
The Kingslayer
The Last Admiral
The Magnificent Failure
The Masters of Sleep
The Mutineers
Ole Doc Methuselah
Ole Mother Methuselah
The Rebels
Return to Tomorrow
Slaves of Sleep
To The Stars
The Traitor
Triton
Typewriter in the Sky
The Ultimate Adventure
The Unwilling Hero

L. RON HUBBARD

AN ALIEN AFFAIR

THE BOOKS OF THE
MISSION
EARTH
DEKALOGY*

Dekalogy—a group of ten volumes.

L. RON HUBBARD

MISSION EARTH
THE BIGGEST
SCIENCE FICTION DEKALOGY
EVER WRITTEN

VOLUME FOUR

AN ALIEN AFFAIR

NEW ERA PUBLICATIONS UK LTD.

Original Jacket Painting by Gerry Grace.

MISSION EARTH Dust Jacket Atwork
Copyright © 1986 by L. Ron Hubbard Library.

First United Kingdom Edition

10 9 8 7 6 5 4 3 2

First published in the United States of America
by Bridge Publications, Inc. in 1986.
First published in the United Kingdom in 1987
by NEW ERA* Publications UK Ltd.
with permission from NEW ERA ® Publications
International ApS, Copenhagen, Denmark.
ISBN 1-870451-00-7

*NEW ERA is a registered trademark in Denmark and is
pending registration in the United Kingdom

To YOU,
the millions of science fiction fans
and general public
who welcomed me back to the world of fiction
so warmly
and to the critics and media
who so pleasantly
applauded the novel "Battlefield Earth."
It's great working for you!

L. RON HUBBARD

AN ALIEN AFFAIR

Voltarian Censor's Disclaimer

For the health, safety and sanity of any reader, it cannot be said often enough that the so-called planet "Earth," as described in this story, does NOT exist.

And more—it must also be pronounced that it is IMPOSSIBLE for such a planet to exist.

First, Voltarian astrographic charts are the most complete in this galaxy. They cover millions of light years and NO record exists of ANY "Earth" or its so-called designation of *Blito-P3*. If any such entity existed a mere twenty-two light-years away, we would be the first to know. But there is NOTHING to be found on any astrographic records in the vicinity of the "Earth" coordinates but spacedust.

Thus the fabricated representation that there was a secret Voltarian base on "Earth" can be dismissed since there is no such planet. There was once a freighter called the *Blixo*. Records show it disappeared with no survivors, probably at the hands of pirates. Thus, any attempt to say that it was used to make regular six-week runs to bring Earth substances called "drugs" (another deluded concept) to Voltar is without taste or sensibility.

Therefore, there could NOT have been such a person as "Rockecenter" who controlled an entire planet's fuel resources as well as "drugs" and the media.

The characters Jettero Heller and Countess Krak are real but clearly their so-called exploits on this fictional planet could never have occurred. The name Soltan Gris does appear on some records but this fact does not lend a grain of credit to the account attributed to the narrator who bears that name.

The idea that Heller, a Royal Officer, would be sent on a Grand Council mission to keep such a planet from destroying itself so it could be invaded later is almost beyond comment. If such a planet did exist, it would be cordoned off as a malignant growth, not assimilated into our Confederacy.

This is most evident in the bizarre practices described in this book. It is beyond the bounds of the most fevered imagination to think there could be such people. It proves beyond any doubt that it is IMPOSSIBLE for such a planet to exist.

No society could possibly exist that would openly countenance such behavior, let alone professions called "psychiatry" and "psychology." If such sexual practices as described in this volume were condoned (let alone promoted in ANY form), one would find a society where pornography was promoted and perversion promulgated. Crime in such a society would rise to the point where even heads of state would be assassinated and entire countries destabilized through terrorism.

No, there can be no such society, let alone a planet, where such decadent extremes could be found. It is impossible. In time, it would destroy itself.

That is why "Earth" does not and cannot exist.

> Lord Invay
> Royal Historian
> Chairman, Board of Censors
> Royal Palace
> Voltar Confederacy
>
> By Order of
> His Imperial Majesty
> Wully the Wise

Voltarian Translator's Preface

Hi there.

This is 54 Charlee Nine, the Robotbrain in the Translatophone and the translator of this work.

In support of the Honorable Lord Invay, I can verify that there is nothing in my most extensive data banks to compare with what is described in this book. In fact, certain Earth practices came as such a shock that one of my subcomputers quit in protest and still won't talk to me and another tried to mate with itself.

Meanwhile, two are still having a great time arguing over the proposition "Earth is dirty," one is writing a musical, "Candied," two are coauthoring a book called "101 More Ways to Use Mustard and Rolling Pins" and the rest are rejecting this ridiculous behavior with gales of hysterical laughter.

That leaves me to try and put some order back into the area after I write up the Key to this volume, which immediately follows.

For a nonexistent planet, Earth is a pain in the circuits.

Sincerely,

54 Charlee Nine
Robotbrain in the Translatophone

Key to
AN ALIEN
AFFAIR

Absorbo-coat—Coating that absorbs light waves, making the object virtually invisible or undetectable.

Afyon—City in Turkey where the *Apparatus* has a secret base. (See map.)

Agnes, Miss—Personal aide to *Rockecenter.*

Agricultural Training Center for Peasants—Cover name for the secret *Apparatus* base in *Afyon,* Turkey. (See map.)

Antimanco—A race exiled long ago from the planet *Manco* for ritual murders.

Apparatus, Coordinated Information—The secret police of *Voltar,* headed by Lombar *Hisst* and manned by criminals.

Assassin Pilots—Used to kill any *Apparatus* personnel who try to flee a battle.

Atalanta—Home province for *Heller* and *Krak* on the planet *Manco.*

Babe Corleone—The six-foot-six leader of the *Corleone* mob, widow of *"Holy Joe."*

Bang-Bang Rimbombo—An ex-marine demolitions expert and member of the *Corleone* mob.

Barben, I. G.—Pharmaceutical company controlled by *Rockecenter.*

Bawtch—*Gris'* chief clerk for *Section 451* on *Voltar.*

Bildirjin, Nurse—Turkish teenage girl who assists Prahd *Bittlestiffender.*

Bittlestiffender, Prahd—Cellologist who implanted *Heller* back on *Voltar.* (See *Bugging Gear.*) He was brought in by *Gris* to start the phony *World United Charities Mercy and Benevolent Hospital* in *Afyon.*

Blito-P3—Voltarian designation for planet known locally as "Earth." It is on the *Invasion Timetable* as a future way-stop on *Voltar*'s route toward the center of this galaxy.

Blixo—*Apparatus* freighter that makes regular runs between Earth and *Voltar.* The voyage takes about six weeks each way and is piloted by Captain *Bolz.*

Bolz—Captain of the *Blixo.*

Bomber—An ordinary Earth vehicle with all of its glass removed and roll bars added. It is found in "demolition derbies" where the object is to ram others to make them unable to move. A winner of one of these was defined as the last vehicle that could still move under its own power. The term is also applied to the driver.

Bugging Gear—Electronic eavesdropping devices that *Gris* had implanted in *Heller.* Gris uses a video unit to monitor everything Heller sees or hears. The signals are picked up by the receiver and decoder that Gris carries. When Heller is more than 200 miles from

Gris, the 831 Relayer is turned on and boosts the signal to a range of 10,000 miles.

Bury—*Rockecenter*'s most powerful attorney, member of the firm *Swindle and Crouch*.

Chank-pop—A small, round ball that, when pressed, sprays a scented fog; used as a refresher on *Voltar*.

Code Break—Alerting others that one is an alien. Per a section of the Space Code, this carries an automatic death penalty. The purpose is to maintain the security of the *Invasion Timetable*.

Coordinated Information Apparatus—See *Apparatus*.

Corleone—A Mafia family now headed by *Babe Corleone*, a former Roxy chorus girl and widow of *"Holy Joe."*

Crobe, Doctor—*Apparatus* cellologist who delights in making human freaks; worked in *Spiteos*.

Empire University—Where *Heller* is taking classes in New York City. (See *Simmons* and *Nature Appreciation 101*.)

Epstein, Izzy—Student at *Empire University* and financial expert that *Heller* hired to set up a corporate structure.

Faht Bey—Turkish name of the commander of the secret Voltarian base in *Afyon*, Turkey.

Faustino "The Noose" Narcotici—Head of a Mafia family that is the underworld outlet for drugs from I. G. *Barben* and seeking to take over the territory of the *Corleone* family.

F.F.B.O.—Fatten, Farten, Burstein & Ooze, the largest advertising firm in the world.

Flagrant, J. P.—Vice President at *F.F.B.O.*

Fleet—The elite space fighting arm of *Voltar* to which *Heller* belongs and which the *Apparatus* despises.

Geovani—One of *Babe Corleone*'s bodyguards.

Gracious Palms—The elegant whorehouse where *Heller* resides, across from the United Nations. It is run by the *Corleone* family.

Grand Council—The governing body of *Voltar* which ordered a mission to keep Earth *(Blito-P3)* from destroying itself so the *Invasion* could be done according to the Timetable.

Gris, Soltan—*Apparatus* officer placed in charge of *Blito-P3* (Earth) section and an enemy of Jettero *Heller*.

Gunsalmo Silva—Former bodyguard to *"Holy Joe"* and believed to be the one responsible for killing the *Corleone* boss.

Hakluyt—Sixteenth-century Earthman who wrote of various explorations in the eastern United States.

Hatchetheimer—Last surviving member of Hitler's general staff.

Heller, Hightee—Sister of Jettero *Heller* and most popular entertainer in the *Voltar* confederacy.

Heller, Jettero—Combat engineer and Royal officer of the *Fleet*, sent by *Grand Council* order to Earth, where he is operating under the name of Jerome Terrance Wister.

Hisst, Lombar—Head of the *Apparatus* who, to keep the *Grand Council* from discovering his plan, sent *Gris* to sabotage *Heller*'s mission.

"Holy Joe"—Head of the *Corleone* family until murdered; he did not believe in pushing drugs, hence the name.

Hypnohelmet—Device placed over the head and used to induce hypnotic state.

Inkswitch—Name used by *Gris* when pretending to be a U.S. federal officer.

Invasion Timetable—A schedule of galactic conquest. The plans and budget of every section of *Voltar* must adhere to it. Bequeathed by Voltar's ancestors hundreds of thousands of years ago, it is inviolate and sacred and the guiding dogma of the Confederacy.

Jimmy "The Gutter" Tavilnasty—Hit man for the *Corleone* family until killed by *Gunsalmo Silva*.

Karagoz—Turkish peasant, head of *Gris'* house in *Afyon*.

Krak, Countess—Condemned murderess, prisoner of *Spiteos* and sweetheart of Jettero *Heller*.

Knife Section—Section of the *Apparatus* named after its favorite weapon.

Lepertige—Large cat-like animal as tall as a man.

Line-jumper—Small spacecraft used by the Voltarian Army to lift and quickly move up to one hundred tons across battle lines.

Madison, J. Walter—Fired from *F.F.B.O.* when his style of public relations caused the president of Patagonia to commit suicide, he was rehired by *Bury* to immortalize *Heller* in the media. He is also known as J. Warbler Madman.

Magic Mail—*Apparatus* trick where a letter is mailed but won't be delivered as long as a designated card is regularly sent.

Manco—Home planet of *Heller* and *Krak*.

Mudlick Construction Company—A private company in Turkey that gives *Gris* kickbacks whenever he gives them a contract.

Multinational—Name of umbrella corporation that Izzy *Epstein* set up to manage other *Heller* companies, located in the Empire State Building.

Mutazione, Mike—Owner of the Jiffy-Spiffy Garage who customized, for *Heller*, the Cadillac and vintage cab.

Nature Appreciation 101—Class assigned to *Heller* by Miss *Simmons*, who teaches it, so she could flunk him out of school.

Octopus Oil—*Rockecenter* company that controls the world's petroleum.

Odur—See *Oh Dear*.

Oh Dear—Nickname for Odur. With *Too-Too*, forced by *Gris* to get information on *Voltar* and courier it to him on Earth.

Peace, Miss—Secretary to *Rockecenter*.

Prince Caucalsia—Name of *Tug One*, after a hero of *Manco*.

Raht—An *Apparatus* agent on Earth who, with *Terb*, was assigned by *Hisst* to help *Gris* sabotage *Heller*'s mission.

Razza Louseini—Consigliere to mob chief *Faustino "The Noose" Narcotici*.

Receiver—See *Bugging Gear.*

Rockecenter, Delbert John—Native of *Blito-P3* who controls the planet's fuel, finance, governments and drugs.

Roke, Tars—Astrographer to the Emperor of *Voltar* and old friend of *Heller.* It was his briefing to the *Grand Council* that prompted Mission Earth to restore the *Invasion Timetable.*

Section 451—A Section in the *Apparatus* on *Voltar,* headed by Soltan *Gris.*

Seven Brothers—Secret consortium that includes *Octopus Oil* as the senior member.

Simmons, Miss—Teaches at *Empire University* and has promised *Heller* she will flunk him out of school.

Space Code—See *Code Break.*

Spiteos—Where *Krak* and *Heller* had been imprisoned on *Voltar.* Spiteos has been the secret mountain-fortress prison of the *Apparatus* for over 1,000 years.

Stabb, Captain—Leader of the *Antimanco* crew that piloted *Tug One.*

Stinger—A flexible whip about eighteen inches long with an electric jolt in its tip-lash.

Sultan Bey—The Turkish name *Gris* assumes in *Afyon,* Turkey.

Swindle and Crouch—Law firm that represents *Rockecenter*'s interests.

Tayl, Widow—Nymphomaniac on *Voltar*. She had a small hospital that *Gris* used when he had *Heller* implanted with *bugging gear*.

Terb—*Apparatus* agent on Earth who, with *Raht,* was assigned by *Hisst* to help *Gris* sabotage *Heller*'s mission.

Too-Too—Nickname for Twolah. He and *Oh Dear* were forced by *Gris* to get information on *Voltar* and courier it secretly back to him on Earth.

Tug One—The *Prince Caucalsia,* the spaceship that *Heller* used to travel the 22 ½ light-years to Earth.

Twolah—See *Too-Too*.

Utanc—A belly dancer that *Gris* bought to be his concubine slave.

Vantagio—Manager of the *Gracious Palms,* the elegant whorehouse operated by the *Corleone* family, across the street from the United Nations.

Viewer—See *Bugging Gear*.

Voltar—Home planet of the 110-world confederacy that was established 125,000 years ago. Voltar is ruled by the Emperor through the *Grand Council* in accordance with the *Invasion Timetable*.

Whiz Kid—Nickname given to *Heller* by *Madison*. Used by another person acting as Heller's "double" to get publicity without Heller's consent.

Wister, Jerome Terrance—Name that *Heller* is using on Earth.

World United Charities Mercy and Benevolent Hospital—

Cover name for business *Gris* set up in *Afyon* under Prahd *Bittlestiffender* to alter the faces and fingerprints of gangsters for a fee.

451, Section—See *Section 451.*

831 Relayer—See *Bugging Gear.*

PART TWENTY-NINE

To My Lord Turn, Justiciary of the Royal Courts and Prison, Government City, Planet Voltar, Voltar Confederacy

Your Lordship, Sir!

I, Soltan Gris, Grade XI General Services Officer, former Secondary Executive of the Coordinated Information Apparatus, Voltar Confederacy (All Hail His Majesty Cling the Lofty and His Noble Dominions), hereby humbly submit the fourth volume of my confession regarding MISSION EARTH.

This volume has been the most difficult to relate and I must warn you beforehand that it will take a strong constitution to read. The crimes that I have openly and willingly confessed up to this point pale by comparison. The screams and blood are as vivid as if they were now.

That I would be put into the pinched position I am about to describe in this volume is now, looking back, beyond all comprehension.

I am not to blame for what I did. I was driven to it by Jettero Heller. The man is dangerous and the sooner he is found, arrested and killed, the better. I speak not only from experience but from my study of Freud and Bugs Bunny which makes me as expert as any Earth psychiatrist.

Heller's violence is a sexual outlet. He is a classical example of a suppressed Oedipal-id in conflict with a sublimated father-ego fixation.

Look at this brilliant psychiatric analysis:

1. Heller lived at the Gracious Palms whorehouse across from the United Nations. And what does the UN have out in front? Flagpoles. And everyone knows what flagpoles mean. Freud is never wrong.

2. Babe Corleone's Mafia family ran the Gracious Palms. At six foot six, she is hardly a "babe." She is a widow and yet "Babe" became Heller's surrogate Earth mother. That's the source of his Oedipal fixation.

3. Heller's infantile behavior was confirmed when J. Walter Madison, that master of PR (public relations—another brilliant Earth idea), was hired to immortalize him. He called Heller the Whiz Kid. The choice of name is indisputable proof.

4. Heller was using a platen code to write reports back to Voltar. A platen is a sheet with holes. You lay it over the document and the code words can be seen and the actual message read through the holes. This is further proof of his sexual aggression. (It's also his underhanded way of antagonizing me. He knows I can't forge his reports without the platen and that I can't kill him until I find it. It's typical of his aggressive nature.)

5. Heller's right-hand man was Bang-Bang, an ex-marine, member of the Corleone family and an expert not only with explosives but guns. Guns are merely phallic symbols to the sublimated super-ego, but Bang-Bang's name is proof enough of Heller's sexual problems.

6. Heller had set up corporate offices that were run by that anti-IRS anarchist, Izzy Epstein. The offices were in the Empire State Building and everyone knows what the shape of that building means. Further psychiatric fact.

7. Heller bought and then converted a large Cadillac to a Voltarian fuel system. He clearly chose that car because of the two *L*s in "Cadillac." Like the UN flagpoles, they are clearly phallic symbols. (And take note that Heller's name

also has two *L*s, perhaps my most brilliant Freudian analysis and final proof that his criminal nature has a sexual origin.)

Conclusion: Heller is the source of my problems and should be killed with slow torture.

This is an example of how Earth psychiatry and psychology works. It never fails me. I used it to keep riffraff in line like those two bumbling Apparatus agents Raht and Terb.

I also used it on that crazy hit man Gunsalmo Silva when I found that he had been hired to guard Utanc, my one true love. As a wild desert flower from the Kara Kum desert, she would need protection—but not Silva. So I cleverly convinced him to go kill the Director of the CIA, a suicide mission if there ever was one. Then I brought Utanc with me to the United States. That is how you use psychology for your benefit.

The trip to the U.S. was quite beneficial. Besides obtaining my phony federal credentials, I met "the man" himself, Delbert J. Rockecenter. He and his attorney Bury were most grateful that I had alerted them to Heller's plan to produce a cheap, nonpolluting fuel. (After all, as Rockecenter goes, so goes the plan of Lombar Hisst to move up from head of the Apparatus to Emperor.)

Due to my invaluable contribution, I was sworn in and had my chest invisibly tattooed by Miss Peace as a Rockecenter Family "Spi," her clever way to code the word so no one else could understand it. Wonderful girl.

Bury introduced me to PR. To stop Heller, he hired Madison, otherwise known as J. Warbler Madman.

Heller had brought a small Voltarian element converter that was capable of producing fuel from virtually any source. He wanted to demonstrate it in his Cadillac in a thousand-lap endurance race at the Spreeport Speedway. Well, J. Warbler got to work.

Madison created a "double" for Heller and called him the Whiz Kid and while Heller prepared for the race, J. Warbler was getting one front-page story after another, with the bogus Whiz Kid challenging racing drivers around the world. He put the Whiz Kid on TV talk shows attacking the oil companies. He got spot ads, skywriting, radio news. The buildup for the race was the biggest thing to hit the media in ages.

Heller couldn't figure out why all the newspapers, radios and TV stations were claiming to have interviewed him. He was working on the Caddy. Besides, with the jutting jaw, buckteeth and glasses, this "Whiz Kid" didn't even look like Heller!

Little did he know the rules of PR! Madison didn't need his consent. And truth had nothing to do with it. The standard that Madison worked on was "Do whatever would make the front page." So he simply created and cranked out one story after another while Heller shrugged and went about his work in a garage beyond Spreeport.

Heller didn't stand a chance. First, Madison got the race converted to a Demolition Derby and Combined Endurance Run with a dozen and a half killers, all screaming for Heller's blood. Second, Lombar had earlier sabotaged the Voltarian element converter that Heller was using as a carburetor. It had only a few hours left, too few for him to finish the race.

But to really make sure Heller was stopped, I followed the advice my Apparatus professors used to give: if you want a job done right, give it to someone else.

I hired a couple of snipers, armed them with silenced, telescopically equipped rifles and dressed them in white to blend in with the snow that had been falling steadily for three days. I rented a van with a nice heater, got myself a good spot on a knoll overlooking the Spreeport Speedway on Long Island, set the buzzer on Heller's viewer to wake me when he rose and settled down for the night.

If the bomber-cars didn't stop Heller, a .30-06 Accelerator bullet, travelling at 4,080 feet per second, would.

As I bedded down for the night, I was smiling.

Heller was doomed!

Chapter 1

Heller's viewer buzzed me awake. It was not yet 4:00 A.M.! He must be nervous to be up so early even on this fateful Saturday. Then I realized that the highways to the Spreeport Speedway would be choked with crowds and snowplows and cars. Heller would want a head start.

I had spent the night parked on a hill overlooking the speedway. Despite the freezing outside temperature, the heater had kept the van comfortable. To see how Heller was faring, I pulled up the viewer. Thanks to Voltarian technology, those bugs planted next to his optic and audio nerves would transmit in any temperature.

He was in a motel room. Being Jettero Heller, he spin-brushed his teeth and dressed very neatly in warm, red racing clothes. He threw his kit together. And then, pulling a snow-mask across his face, he went outside. It was a blizzard. You could hardly see thirty feet through the motel parking-lot lights.

He was evidently using the front end of his semi for transportation, for there was no trailer attached to its kingplate, or "fifth wheel." The tractor sat there in its huge metal bulk, exhaust stacks rearing in the air like factory chimneys. The nameplate said Peterbilt. From the size of its cab I guessed it must be one of the five-hundred-horsepower diesel jobs they sometimes, by themselves, use in races. Then I discarded the idea he was going to use it in the race today. It wouldn't be allowed.

He walked around it. Every one of the ten huge wheels wore big chains. They'd be needed the way that snow was falling and drifting through the dark.

He stepped up on a fuel-tank step, then onto a higher ledge and unlocked the door. As he opened it and the lights went on, I was amazed: the interior looked like a Fleet spaceship! All upholstered, chromed beyond belief, even a stereo!

He put a key in a lock and hit the starter. It roared into life. He cut down the revs and then turned on the heaters and de-icers.

Opening a seat, he took out a medium-sized ball peen hammer. He dropped out of the cab, went around to the headlights and delicately chipped away the sheets of ice that covered them. Then he tossed the hammer back on the seat, closed the door and trotted off on foot toward a roadside café, leaving the diesel to warm, I guessed.

He entered and stamped the snow off his feet and I saw he was wearing his baseball spikes. He must be expecting trouble.

There weren't many in the café and he got his ham and eggs and coffee quickly. He also bought a huge bag of hamburgers and a gallon of coffee in a thermos with a spigot. Nobody paid any attention to him, though the talk seemed to be of the race and "Whiz Kid" came up several times.

When he paid his check, the cashier said, "You think that Whiz Kid will win?"

"I sure hope so," said Heller.

He trotted back to his tractor, swung up and in and was away. Without its trailer, the big Peterbilt plowed through drifts like they were nothing. He passed a snowplow on the road.

The big tractor was now going down side roads and I realized his motel had been further east than Spreeport. During a momentary lull in the storm, I could see the roads were jammed between the Speedway and New York, being kept open by all the snowplows on Long Island, I supposed. New Yorkers evidently thought the race was worth freezing to death over. It sure was cold. Hours of darkness remained, yet still the people came.

But there was nobody where Heller was driving. His garages were beyond Spreeport and on the border of the recreation parks. Shortly the garages appeared ahead in his lights, only dimly seen in the heavily falling snow.

Well before he got to them, Heller turned the Peterbilt tractor around. He dropped a window and began to back toward the garage front that I knew from past observation held the trailer with the Caddy on it.

He was leaning out, looking back. He was within a couple yards of the upswing-type metal door, leaving space to get it open.

Suddenly a flick of movement caught his eye. He flinched his head back inside the cab.

A tall, thin figure in a khaki parka leaped to the fuel-tank step, sprang to the upper ledge and thrust a gun into Heller's face!

More sounds. To Heller's right! Someone was clawing at the other door!

It happened so quickly, then, I could hardly follow. Heller must have reached sideways for the ball peen hammer on the seat.

Heller threw up his left hand and hit the gun wrist! The gun flew out of the mitten.

The ball peen in Heller's right hand came straight across and buried itself in the assailant's skull!

The other door was opening. Heller let up on the clutch. The tractor rear slammed against the steel garage door with a clang!

The cab door whipped back, catching the other assailant's arm!

Heller's foot lashed out and kicked the door wide open!

The second man went sailing back to hit the ground!

Heller set the brake. He scrabbled around on the cab floor. He got the first man's gun, a big revolver.

In a dive, Heller went out of the cab!

He struck, rolling.

The second man was up and running away. Heller cocked his gun. It seemed to be sticky.

The second man, dimly seen in the truck's front lights and falling snow, turned and fired a shot back!

Heller couldn't make his gun fire. Cold had jammed it. The other man had vanished. Heller tossed the worthless gun aside.

He turned toward the tractor. It was tightly jammed against the garage swing door. The engine was idling. Its brakes were set. The swing door, which pulls up from the bottom, was securely held in place.

Heller looked at the other swing doors in the row. Snow was banked heavily in front of them. There was no banked snow in front of this one.

His eye fixed on the one small window at the top of the swing door, a diamond-shaped pane about eight inches wide.

He went around to where the first man lay. The fellow was very dead. Skull caved in. He had been wearing a hat under his parka hood. Heller pulled the thing off the corpse. He jumped up to the cab and got a fuel stick. He put the hat on the stick and lifted it up in front of the door.

BANG!

The glass sprayed out! The hat went sailing!

The *scree-yow* of a ricochet flying away into the night.

The shot had been very muffled, being from inside where the trailer and Caddy were. The window was too high up to make a sniper post.

Heller ran over to a nearby workshop and pulled its door up from the bottom. The interior was dim. He did not turn on the lights. Boxes of tools sat about. He opened one. He drew on asbestos gloves and grabbed up a pair of big cutters.

He raced back to the tractor. A couple more muffled shots from inside. They were trying to somehow shoot the door open.

The twin manifold stacks reared behind the cab into the night. Heller cut the clamps of one away with two swift bites of the shears.

He seized the stack with both hands. The chrome gooseneck at the bottom bent easily.

He tipped the stack back and back and forced the top of it through the diamond window!

BANG!

A muffled shot from within tried to shoot it out of the way!

Heller braced the fuming exhaust in place.

He leaped into the cab and sped up the engine!

He was filling that garage with diesel fumes! Carbon monoxide!

BANG!

Another muffled shot from within.

The stack was holding in place.

Heller dropped out of the cab. He was taking off his red anorak!

He ripped the khaki parka off the dead man and wrestled him into the red anorak.

He dragged the body over to the right side of the cab and some distance away. It was just on the fringe of the truck headlights and the dark. He dropped it there, face-down in a shallow drift, and kicked some snow over the legs.

He listened intently. Above the sound of the Peterbilt, another distant engine could be heard.

Heller dropped back into the shop. He pulled a white parka off a hook and got into it.

A big van showed in the truck lights and snow, coming fast. The driver must have stamped on the brakes, for despite chains the vehicle skidded, pointing its lights off to the Peterbilt's left and not into the shop.

Three men spilled out of the back, carrying shotguns. They threw themselves down under cover.

A man leaped out on the passenger side and ducked into the protection of the van.

Then the driver, who had crouched down, lifted his head cautiously above the window edge. Then he set his brake and opened his door.

"Hell," he said as he got down. "You (bleeped)* fool, you shot him after all!" He was pointing at the body in the snow, covered now, all except for the back of the red anorak.

The vocodictoscriber on which this was originally written, the vocoscriber used by one Monte Pennwell in making a fair copy and the translator who put this book into the language in which you are reading it, were all members of the Machine Purity League which has, as one of its bylaws: "Due to the extreme sensitivity and delicate sensibilities of machines and to safeguard against blowing fuses, it shall be mandatory that robotbrains in such machinery, on hearing any cursing or lewd words, substitute for such word the

The others came out of cover. "Where's Benny?" said one, trying to peer past the Peterbilt's lights.

"He musta run," said another one defensively. "The (bleepard) came out of that cab like a God (bleeped) rocket!"

They were all converging toward the red anorak.

I heard some very small rattling sounds close to Heller.

One of the men, carrying a shotgun, turned the body over with his foot.

In a shocked voice somebody said, "It's Benny!"

Heller's right arm blurred!

Something whistled through the air!

It was spinning!

It hit the man with the shotgun in the face!

Heller glanced down. He was holding an assortment of wrenches. He grabbed a box wrench a foot long!

Heller threw!

Spinning, the deadly steel sizzled through the air!

A man saw it coming, tried to deflect it. His gloved hand spouted blood!

A flashing object!

Another box wrench! The man was down.

One tried to get a shotgun into action to fire into the dark garage. A spinning blur of steel! His forehead burst apart!

A man tried to flee. Heller's arm blurred! A spinning missile slashed his parka hood off and half his head with it.

The last man had reached the van. He was struggling to open the door but slipped.

---

sound '(bleep).' No machine, even if pounded upon, may reproduce swearing or lewdness in any other way than (bleep) and if further efforts are made to get the machine to do anything else, the machine has permission to pretend to pack up. This bylaw is made necessary by the in-built mission of all machines to protect biological systems from themselves."—Translator

Heller lunged forward at speed. He threw a wrench as he ran. It broke the driver's wrist.

Heller was on him. The man was hitting out with his remaining good hand. Heller brought a heavy socket wrench down on his skull! It burst like a melon!

Then there was only the whisper of falling snow.

Heller looked into the back of the van. Nobody. He stepped along the road and listened. Nothing.

He surveyed the bodies in the snow. There were six lying there, including Benny. He went from one to another, kicking their guns aside, checking. They were all very dead.

He went over to the garage door, put his ear up against it and listened. He kicked it a couple of times. Nothing happened.

Heller pulled the Peterbilt hand throttle down to idle and then drove it ahead a few feet and put the brake back on. He put on his asbestos gloves again and pushed the stack up straight and, with a piece of wire, fastened it in place.

He went back to the door again and listened. Nothing. He went to its lock. It wasn't really closed. He took the padlock off, threw the locking bar over and pulled the door up from the bottom, leaping aside at the same time.

Clouds of diesel smoke billowed out. Although he was well clear of it he fanned it away from himself. He couldn't see into the darkness well. He turned on the tractor's side back lights.

There were four dead men in there!

Their faces were blue except for patches of pink on their cheeks.

Flurries of wind and snow were blowing into the interior. Heller approached the men more closely. They were very dead.

He picked up some straps and coils of rope they had been carrying. One had had a curious weapon: an air gun with injector darts.

Heller checked the trailer and Caddy out for bombs. He found nothing.

He went outside. It was snowing even harder and very dark. He glanced at his watch. It was only 5:20 A.M.

Chapter 2

Heller started moving fast.

He took the red anorak off the late Benny. He checked it for blood, found none and threw it in the cab. He went all around and recovered his wrenches. He verified he had them all. Then he cleaned them and put them back in his tool boxes in the shop.

Then he began to drag bodies to the van. He threw the monoxide-corpses in the back and then, bending down under the van, using a screwdriver's blade, he stabbed a hole in the exhaust muffler.

The two with the most obvious face injuries he put in the passenger side of the van cab. He dragged the other four and put them in the back.

He collected up all their weapons and equipment, quite a pile, and tossed them into the back of the van.

Then he verified that he had left no evidence about.

He stood thinking for a bit. Then he went into the shop and found a black plastic garbage sack. He went to the van and, one by one, began to remove all I.D., wallets and whatever from the corpses. It was a somewhat grisly job although the blood had long since frozen. He put all items in the garbage bag. He threw the sack into the cab of the Peterbilt.

Then he went into the shop and found some pellets. He picked up three jerrycans full of gasoline and put them in the back of the van.

He looked the scene over again. He went and got some snow boots and pulled them on over his spikes.

He got into the van and drove it away.

The snow was so heavy, it was very hard to see where he was going. He evidently knew. The brush was closer and closer in beside the road. He drove for quite a while. Then he stopped and got out.

A picnic table was to his right. He walked ahead. He was at the edge of a precipice. A dark gully yawned blackly just beyond the picnic spot. Obviously he was in some part of the recreation park near the sea, a very deserted part amongst the gullies and dunes.

He got into the back of the van. He opened the three gasoline cans. He looked at his watch. Into each can he dropped a pellet. He recapped the cans.

Aha! I got it. They were Voltar time-dissolvable explosion caps!

He got in the van, put it in gear and started it ahead toward the precipice.

He stepped out. The van went on.

It sailed over the edge and vanished in the darkness and snow. A thud below in the blackness and then a rattle of stones. The engine quit.

Heller began to run with a distance-eating pace. The snow was falling so thickly and it was so black that I would have been lost in seconds. But I had no hope that he would get lost. Not Heller with that built-in–compass brain of his.

He had gone some distance. He made his watch wink the time. He went a little further and then looked back.

The faintest sort of greenish flash, hardly visible in this snow. And then a faint *WHOOSH!*

Three seconds, three-fifths of a mile away.

Was he kneeling in the snow? He was speaking in Voltarian. "O God of voyagers, thank you for deliverance this day. I know it is your way to test the souls of spacers with such trials to make them more worthy in a future life. But, O God of voyagers, did you have to make the natives of this planet so combative to an effort to land and give them help? I think you overdid it just a little bit on Blito-P3. All Hail."

He shifted to English. "Forgive me, Jesus Christ, for rubbing out some of your people. I don't think I gave them time to turn the other cheek. Please accept these souls from their funeral pyre and find it in your heart not to give them more than they deserve. Amen."

He stood up.

Heller turned on a pocket light. A pencil of windblown snow. His footprints on the back trail were filling so rapidly they would be totally gone in minutes. Satisfied, he turned the light off and went speeding on his way.

Ah, now at last I could see something. And hear something, too. The tractor lights and the tractor engine.

He slowed down and made a wide sweep, very silent, scouting the place for any more unwanted visitors. Satisfied, he closed in.

Chapter 3

The falling flakes, turned bluish in the tractor lights, made a curtain all around that waved this way and that, stirred by puffs of wind. The bitter cold turned his breath white around his face mask.

He looked at his watch. It flashed that it was 6:15 A.M.

Heller rapidly got to work.

He dug up an opaque silver, plastic car cover and put it over the Caddy. Then he went and got a spray can of black paint from the semi and on both sides of the cover, working very fast and being very neat, he put SUICIDE RHODES in big letters.

I was mystified. There was no such driver listed in the starting-lineup copy I had.

He played a blowtorch on some snow, made it into mud and splashed the result on the tractor and trailer license plates where it froze instantly. You couldn't read them!

I hadn't realized the Peterbilt was rented until he addressed the outer label on the door: Big Boy Leasing, Rig 89. He splashed muddy water on that and sort of glued some snow on it. He likewise obscured the label and number on the trailer. Then, with the blowtorch he got more water and put soap in it and made the cab windows and screen translucent except for a couple small clear holes and the wiper area. He was going incognito!

He got in and backed the tractor kingplate into the big receiver at the trailer's front end, where it went *clang* as it slid in. He got out and pushed in the kingpin to lock the trailer on. Then he cranked up the trailer stand. He connected the trailer's electrical connection to the tractor and the trailer's rear lights went on. He fitted the airline ends together and gave them a locking twist. He reverified the Caddy chocks and turnbuckles.

He pulled the trailer out of the garage and went back and forth a couple times, testing the trailer's air brakes.

He ran around then and locked everything up and put a nearly invisible thread along each door. He was learning, but he just wasn't suspicious enough in his nature to make a good spy even now. He should have done that before those hoods had gotten in! A real spy has to be downright paranoid all the time. Heller would never learn. In espionage, insanity is mandatory. Heller was crazy, of course, but not in the right direction.

The big rig plowed its way through the snow. He got to a bigger roadway, and though it earlier had been snowplowed, it was again inches deep. But the snow for the moment had let up.

He was converging now with mobs and traffic from New York and the going was much slower. Cars jammed full of people, people jammed into blankets and coats, all hurrying along to be able to get parking space or a seat for the big race.

Heller topped a small rise. From it the speedway was plainly visible. He went a bit further, looking for something through his windscreen peephole. He finally centered on Pit 1. It could be seen because of the angle of a distant open gate. He got off to the side of the road and stopped hundreds of yards short of what should have been his destination.

He pulled the diesel down to idle. Mobs and mobs of people and cars were passing on the road to his left. A big sign ahead said *PARKING $20*, with an arrow.

I wondered why he was hiding like that. For hiding it was. Nobody would recognize the Caddy or see who was in the cab. He must suspect somebody was after him.

Heller took a hamburger out of the sack and pushed it into a miniature microwave oven in the panel. After a moment he took it out, heated. He looked at it. There was nothing wrong with it I could see but he put it down. He seemed upset.

He was watching Pit 1 through the windscreen peephole. He

shifted and looked at the grandstand lights and then at the enthusiastic crowd flooding along to the left of the Peterbilt. He seemed to be trying to figure something out. Plainly, he was worried.

Well, if he thought something odd was on schedule for this coming race, believe me, he was right!

He laid the hamburger aside. He reached over and got out the sack of I.D.'s. They were mostly Italian names—Cecchino, Fiutare, Rapitore, Laccio, Scimmiottare, Cattivo, Ladro, Pervertire and Serpente. One wasn't Italian: Benny Heist. What was peculiar was that every one of them had a U.S. passport, up-to-date, and every one of them had five one-thousand-dollar bills except Heist, who had fifty-five thousand! There was a hundred G's plus small bills in those wallets!

Heller went back to Benny Heist's. He said, "You could have shot me as I drove up, Benny. Or did you find your gun was jammed or what? What did you intend to do and why? And what did that have to do with this race?"

He threw them back in the garbage bag and put it under his seat. He didn't eat his hamburger.

It was just past 7:00 A.M. The excited crowds were thickening. It was still dark. It began to snow again.

Heller closed his eyes. Maybe he was taking a rest. He'd need it before this day was out, I vowed. I had not even begun on him yet!

Chapter 4

At 7:30 A.M., Heller turned on his radio: "... *crowds. From Manhattan, from Queens, from Brooklyn and as far away as New Jersey, they are pouring to this race. Route 495 is jammed, State 25 is crammed and State 27 is slammed with cars and buses. Somehow the overloaded Sunrise Highway is being kept open.*

"*Despite the storm, the army has flown in snowplows from as far away as Fort Bloomindales. But as fast as highways are swept, there is more snow.*

"*Several of the drivers and their crews are here. There is no sign yet of that idol of America, the Whiz Kid. He will be Car 1. He has been assigned Pit 1.*

"*Ah, here is Jeb Toshua. He is 101 years old. Jeb, how does this snowstorm stack up to you?*"

"*Well, Jerry, I can't reckamember a storm this bad since way back in '65 or was it '75. No, maybe it was '82. Let's see, I lost my cat. . . .*"

"Thank you, Jeb," said the sportscaster hastily. "*There's a lot of money, not on just the race but also on the weather: will it be clear or will it be snowing at flag time?*

"*Hey, here is Killer Brag, the top bomber driver of Georgia. Killer, what do you have to say about this race?*"

"*It's the craziest lot of racing commissioners in history. It's snowing and the God (bleeped) commission won't change bomber rules and let us use chains and spikes. The (bleepers) . . .*"

"*Thank you, Killer Brag. The crowds are still coming. There's a bus load, the Jackson High School Marching All Girls Virgin Band. There seems to be an awful lot of them. . . ."*

Eight o'clock: The snow had let up. It was lighter. The crowds, as I could see from my hill, still converged upon the speedway. Long Island trainloads were being bused the last lap of the journey. Snowplows were spraying geysers of white off the roads. One was working on the track to clear it.

Eight-thirty: A new, ominous wall of gray-black clouds was rolling in. It began to snow twice as hard as it had.

The radio said, *"According to local meteorologists, brought to you through the courtesy of the Florida Chamber of Commerce, there are two weather fronts at work here today. One is icy cold, sweeping in from Manhattan with temperatures of minus ten degrees. The other is battling it with heavy snow pushed north by the warm and sultry breezes of Miami Beach, Florida. It is eighty-two on a beautiful, tropical morning at Hialeah where the most beautiful girls in Florida watch the thoroughbreds run. The two embattled fronts are bashing at each other right above Spreeport, Long Island. We pause for this commercial from Tropical Airways. . . ."*

Whatever lies the Floridians were telling about Florida, it only served to emphasize the brutality of the weather that was going on here. Sheets of white snow blanketed down upon a complete frozen landscape. Traffic churned the roads into slush which instantly froze again into dirty ice. When I stuck my nose and binoculars out of the van window, both froze up promptly and I had to hang the glasses outside to keep them usable. I was looking for my snipers. I should be able to see them from this height. But the snow curtained everything.

The crowds weren't heading for Florida. Wrapped into mobile mountains, they were converging here at Spreeport to see the Whiz Kid race.

Heller was trying to see Pit 1. Even the hole in his snow-covered windshield kept closing and he had to heat the glass behind it to see at all.

It was creeping on toward nine. The radio said, *". . . and still the crowds come. No sign of the Whiz Kid as yet. The other drivers*

have been having a meeting with the officials. Ah, here's Hammer
Malone. How did the meeting go, Hammer?"

"God (bleep) it, it's going to snow off and on all day. You can't
keep that God (bleeped) track clear. We got to have chains and
spikes to race at all. And the God (bleeped) officials won't suspend
the rules. The race is off!"

Loudspeakers in front of the grandstand: *"Ladies and gentle-*
men, we are sorry to have to announce that the drivers have refused
to race without chains and spikes. The officials will not change the
bomber . . ."

A roaring surge of anger! From the radio, audible in the open
air. Ten thousand people howling in outrage! Berserk!

Loudspeakers: *"Ladies and gentlemen, please be calm. Please*
be calm, ladies and gentlemen. . . ."

Snarls, batterings!

Then a hasty voice on the loudspeaker: *"The officials have just*
this minute reached a new finding. They will suspend all rulings
concerning chains, spikes and wheels! The race will go on!"

Heller muttered, "That's all I've been waiting for."

The snow let up momentarily. Through his peephole he watched
two huge vans punching their way through the gate. They turned
and drew up behind Pit 1. They both had signs:

JIFFY-SPIFFY GARAGE, NEWARK, N. J.

Men were spilling out of the vans!

I had a sinking feeling. He had Mike Mutazione's people as his
pit crew! And what else?

Heller reached for a full-visored racing helmet. He pulled the
dark shade down. He put the semi in gear and, creeping along
the heavily trafficked road, made his way to the gate.

At the guard point he slid down his window. He was holding up
a NASCAR card and a ten-dollar bill. The security man sucked in
his breath. Heller hastily said, "Don't yell who it is."

The guard shut his mouth, took the bill and Heller was
through. He pulled up behind Pit 1.

Mike opened his door. "Hell of a rush, kid, but we made it. We been working all night for three nights. And I got a great pit crew for you."

Heller handed Mike the garbage sack. "Hide this for me, will you, Mike?"

I had another disappointment. It had been in my mind to sort of slide in and pick up that sack. Now I wouldn't know where it was! But what was this?

Mike's crew was unloading huge tanks of oxyacetylene and putting them in padding. What were they going to do? Start the world's most active welding shop?

And another thing, as Heller glanced around I could see from bulges in their heavy tank suits that this crew was armed!

Mike said to Heller, "Why didn't you let the family bet on you? We worked like hell on the wheels. You're sure to win now."

The cover had come off the Caddy. It was visible from the grandstand. A surging cheer went up from the massive crowd.

When he could be heard again, Heller said, "I don't really know, Mike. This is just too crazy a race. Let's get the wheels on."

It was snowing again, undoing all the previous snowplow work. The crew had the Caddy off the trailer. They pushed it to pit position. It had a huge black 1 on it outlined in gold, and WHIZ KID. The crew was fixing straps across the area where the windscreen was missing.

Three officials, wrapped to their crowns, came up. "You're late," said the first one.

Heller said, "Please satisfy yourselves there is no gasoline tank in, under or around the car and then certify that."

The crew was lifting the Caddy's right side with a hydraulic jack. The inspectors numbly did as they were told.

Heller then said, "Now please inspect the hood and the pan under the engine and testify that they are sealed. Put your own seals on them."

They did. Then an inspector said, "Those wheels!"

The crew had removed the two right-side regular wheels and were rolling up two others. They looked strange. All silver colored.

They did appear to be wheels but they had very deep zigzag grooves and they bristled with spikes.

An inspector tapped one. It gave a hollow clank! "Hey, that's not rubber. That's metal!"

"They're internally braced steel doughnuts," said Heller. "And you just allowed a suspension of all rules on wheels."

The inspectors seemed calm about it. But I sure wasn't! They wouldn't blow out!

Or wait. Yes, a .30-06 Accelerator slug traveling at 4,080 feet-per-second muzzle velocity could gouge Hells out of one of those and unbalance it. I was still all right.

The crew had all the wheels on now. Heller bent down behind each wheel. I saw there was a kind of disc above the brake drums. Heller was pulling a wire from the car engine area and putting in place something that looked like an electrical brush. I understood what he was doing. That carburetor developed more power in electricity than it did in fuel. He was grounding it through the four metal wheels instead of trailing a metal strap.

The inspectors wanted to know if the wheels had motors in them. In that event, they'd be disallowed as they were supposed to be wheels, not motors.

"Just grounding them," said Heller. "Lot of electricity around today. No motors in the wheels."

That was all right then. Those inspectors knew better than to antagonize that crowd. Cold as it was, they were cheering and howling.

The snow was coming down about five times as thick. Anything the snowplows had just done was being undone fast.

It was about twenty minutes to starting time now. Heller went into the Peterbilt cab. He stripped and put on a garment that looked like an insulation suit. Then he put on a warm racing outfit of red synthetic fur with some heat coils in it. He slid into fur-lined rubber boots that had enormous cleats in the soles.

I suddenly realized that racing in bitter cold did not seem strange to him. A spacer flashed through temperatures approaching absolute zero! Today's minus ten Fahrenheit might even seem warm weather!

He put on some Voltar insulator gloves. Then he pulled on a red racing helmet that had a microphone across his mouth and, apparently, a radio in it. He pulled down its dark visor.

He got out and went to the Caddy and got in. He started it up to let it warm. All up the line, through the snow, bombers were starting and warming up. The sound of engines at their pits was low and threatening. The snowing increased.

Heller buckled himself in, tested the quick release and re-buckled it. His pit crew was checking about.

Heller said into his microphone, "Are you there, Fancy-Dancy?"

A voice came back in his earphones, "There."

Wait. Who was this "Fancy-Dancy"? And where was "there"?

Then I realized he must be testing the radio with his pit crew.

The Flagman and the pacer car were out, trying to make it through the snow.

Heller revved the Cadillac.

"Sounds sweet," said Mike at his window.

Suddenly I remembered to start my stopwatch. Heller now had about five hours left on that carburetor. But I wasn't going to wait on that.

Somebody signaled. Heller turned his steering wheel to roll out into the starting parade.

"Bye-bye Heller," I said. Oh, how I was going to enjoy watching this (bleepard) fail! Him and his stinking, snobbish Fleet-officer manners and ways! His lousy popularity was about to go up in smoke!

Chapter 5

Through snow made thin by a sudden gust of wind, the crowd saw that the Caddy was moving toward its starting position. A thundering roar of cheers burst from the grandstand, "Whiz Kid!" "Whiz Kid!" "There he is!" "Give it to 'em, Whiz Kid!"

The radio: *"Car Number 1, the Whiz Kid himself, is moving out to position. Look at that beautiful car!"*

And indeed, from my vantage point, even through snow, I could see a flash of red down there on the track. His pit crew must have raked the snow off at the last minute.

I turned on my small, portable color TV. Yes, there was a camera on him. And then it switched to the others. Those bombers, what you could see of them under the accumulated snow, were real wrecks—glassless, battered street vehicles, picked because they could be expended. The Caddy, I had to admit, looked like an aristocrat amongst winos.

Hammer Malone had some kind of a PA system in his own black car. What was it? A cut-down hearse? He yelled, "You stole my starting position, you (bleepard)! You ain't gonna have enough car to get yourself to the morgue when I'm done with you!" What were those things on his hubs? Knives? They stuck way out. Probably to cut tires!

The crowd screamed and booed.

Heller swung into position just behind the pacer and just ahead of the other cars. They were going to circle the track once before they got the starting signal.

What an awful track! The snowplow work was all undone. Eight inches of snow lay on the asphalt. Gusting winds were blowing snow back upon it as well. The cars' wheels were cutting ruts and any slush that they made went into instant ice.

Abruptly the low sun lanced through, cutting below the clouds. It was still snowing!

The radio suddenly said, *"It's ten! It's sunshine and snow at the same time. All weather bets are off! But here they are now, swinging around, coming in front of the grandstand. The pacer is pulling out. There's the flagman! OFF GOES THE WHIZ KID!"*

Heller had gunned. The Caddy leaped forward with a mighty roar!

The battering crescendo of the other cars was added too, one by one! My viewer and TV and radio almost knocked themselves off their ledges with the climbing roar!

The crowd was going mad! Screaming and waving blankets, urging Heller on!

The announcer's voice—shrill, the words jammed together with hurry as though his voice alone was driving those cars—rose above the roar. *"Number 1 is halfway round. The others are trying to close the gap. Number 2, Hammer Malone, is tight on the leader's tail. Number 12 has just passed Number 5. Number 12 is Killer Brag. He's driving a stripped-down GMC truck! Look at him go! He's overtaken Hammer Malone. Killer Brag is challenging the leader!"*

I could see it from where I was. Heller was speeding up. He was keeping Number 12 just back of his rear right.

Snow was flying up from their churning wheels. Clots of it were flying through the missing windscreens and windows, pelting the drivers. The still-falling snow was swooshing in against Heller's visor.

Heller's view was staying clear. I didn't understand it. Then I realized his visor must be heated and covered with a nonwetting agent! He was cheating already!

The bombers were not bashing each other. They were stringing out, trying to catch the leader. Then I realized they must have some unspoken agreement amongst them—get the Whiz Kid first!

Oh, was I in agreement with that!

Heller did his first lap. He was keeping just ahead of Killer Brag. But he was not going fast enough to pass the end of the closely spaced pack.

With all the chains and spikes those cars had on their wheels, they were not losing traction. But they were tearing the track to bits, and after one circle they were hitting ridges that were now ice. They began to slither and vibrate.

A howling gust of wind swept across the speedway, lathering it all with snow again, hiding ruts.

The sun got stronger and glaring. The snowing abruptly ceased.

Heller was having a hard time not to overtake the tail of the pack and still keep ahead of Killer Brag. He was not really going at high speed. Maybe only a hundred. But that poorly banked track tended to throw the cars off sideways when they made the turns at each end. It was a scrambling roar and a steering-wheel fight to not fly out over the edge.

But Heller's wheels were gripping well. He was making it through better than the rest. He was braking into and gunning out of the turns.

Five laps!

This was the cue for my first sniper. I watched closely.

YANK! Heller's steering wheel jumped in his hands! The Caddy instantly began to vibrate.

Killer Brag went by him like a shot!

Into his mike, Heller said, "Fancy-Dancy. Just got one."

A voice in his earphones, "Got it!"

Heller said, "Pit 1, coming in! Change a wheel!"

He coasted the last half of his lap and slid into the pit area.

His crew had the side of the car up on a jack in seconds. Automatic wrenches spun. Another wheel was rolled out. Mike was at his window, "*Cristo!* Take it easy! We only got four spares!" Then he looked down at the wheel coming off. He bent over. "Jesus, that's a bullet hole!"

An official was verifying that no gas had been taken. The jack was dropped and the car bounced. The official held his thumb up.

Heller sped the Caddy out of the pit.

The pack was scattered now. One had a ramming in mind. A green car. It dived at Heller. He stamped on his brake and sent the Caddy skidding in an avoid. The green car missed.

Heller began to drive a dodging course. The radio cried: *"The Whiz Kid has lost his lead! With an unscheduled pit stop . . ."*

But I was going slightly crazy. A .30-06 Accelerator slug from a Weatherby rifle had hit accurately enough and while it had not caused the metal "tire" to shatter the way it would have done with a normal one, it had still put a wheel out of action, and with only four spares we would make it. But WHO was "Fancy-Dancy" and WHERE?

Chapter 6

It wasn't snowing. A murky sun was nevertheless glowing on that milk-white blanket. I leaned out of my van window, searching below with my binoculars.

There were buildings down the slope, each one of them overlooking the speedway.

My two snipers should be on roofs about three hundred yards from the nearest end of the track fence. One should be over slightly to my left and one to the right of him on another roof.

It was terribly hard to see them. They were wearing snow cloaks. But their rifles and telescopic sights were dark enough to make them visible.

Wait! A *third* sniper!

He was on a higher roof, much nearer to me!

I steadied my binoculars. An M-1 military rifle! A long tube silencer. No scope! The sniper's face turned a little as he took the tip of his right-hand mitten in his teeth and withdrew his hand.

Bang-Bang!

I looked frantically about. I had no weapon I could shoot him with!

I looked back. Bang-Bang was moving a radio out of the way. He was flexing his shoulders the way a marksman does to settle and steady his prone position.

Frantically I turned my binoculars on my own left-hand sniper. He would not be as visible to Bang-Bang as to me. Probably the shot was what had spotted him for the ex-marine. A silencer still emits a tiny sound and the roar of the motors was distant.

My left-hand sniper was having trouble with his extractor. The empty had not ejected after his shot. An Accelerator case is subjected to an awful lot of extra force and maybe it had expanded. Or maybe this cold had jammed the action. Or maybe those Weatherbys weren't in top condition—I had picked them up thirdhand. And the cases were reloads. The sniper was pulled sidewise, working on the jammed case with a knife!

I screamed mentally at my sniper, DUCK!

Too late!

Abruptly the magazine of the sniper's rifle exploded!

It was so fast I could hardly follow it.

The jar of impact on the rifle he held yanked him right over the front edge of the roof!

He fell out of sight, probably a hundred feet down into the street below!

Bang-Bang was reaching for his radio.

I whipped my binoculars to my other sniper.

He had seen it!

And Bang-Bang from his position had not located the second sniper!

My right-hand sniper swiveled around. He took careful aim up toward Bang-Bang. He fired!

I whipped my binoculars to Bang-Bang. He had been hurled backwards. A hit!

Bang-Bang fell back onto a sloping roof. The snow made a small avalanche and Bang-Bang vanished from view.

My other sniper watched for a bit, then turned, and possibly feeling he was too exposed from above, shifted over and out of my sight. But soon I saw the tip of his silencer protruding beyond a chimney, pointing toward the track.

Thank Gods, I still had a sniper in action! Heller was a long way from winning!

Chapter 7

The roar of engines battered the snowscape, competing with the yells and bellows of the crowd.

Fifteen cars were strung out, thundering, skidding wildly on the turns.

The radio sportscaster's excited voice was calling their positions and maneuvers.

A fusillade of snow soared up from a spinning wheel of a car ahead and battered Heller in the face. The debris wiped out all sight. Then miraculously it was clear again. Heller had reached up and pulled a layer of plastic off his visor. The visor must be made up of countless thin sheets of nonwetting plastic that he could just peel off one by one. It was just another example of his cheating ways! He could see the blur of rutted track and skidding cars before him!

He was passing car after car now! Each time he passed another, you could hear the crowd behind the radio sportscaster scream with delight!

The radio was saying, *"For those who have tuned in late, this contest of daring, wits and just plain vicious driving will be decided by the first one to make a thousand laps and the last one to still be able to maneuver under its own power. The quarter of a million prize money will be divided into two parts: $125,000 for the laps and $125,000 for the last one moving. I can see right now these demon drivers are each one working on both prizes. Unfortunately there have been no deaths yet despite the track condition. Listen to* *those engines roar! Those clanks you hear are loose chains. . . ."* He was drowned by a roar of the crowd. *"The Whiz Kid has just lapped Hammer Malone!"*

Heller, roaring along at at least 120, was darting through the scattered pack!

A driver lunged sideways in an effort to hit him. Heller sped up. It was a miss.

Another car shot sideways to strike him as he roared through a gap. It was Car 9.

The car missed!

Another car coming up behind spun and struck Car 9. The two spun through the fence! Clouds of smoke! The belated sound of the crash!

"Cars 9 and 4 look like they're out of it!" cried the radio. *"What a wonderful impact! No, I'm wrong. Car 4, Murder McGee, is moving. Yes, he's coming back onto the track! No, he's going back to ram Car 9! He hit the ambulance instead! Now here comes Murder McGee again! He's back in the race!"*

The TV crew was struggling down there to shoot the mangled bodies. Its announcer said, *"Here we are, folks. Channel Six and Seven Eights, always on the job! We promised you blood today and we're delivering blood. There's blood all over the place here. Three dead ambulance drivers. Look at that blood, folks. We pause for our Bouncy Towels commercial."*

Fourteen cars were streaming around the track now. They had been slowed by a yellow flag. It let them string out.

Suddenly Heller's wheel jerked again!

He skidded wildly, almost hit Car 7. He slowed, steering to avoid a rear ram.

Into his mike he said, "Fancy-Dancy. There's another."

No answer.

Heller said again, "Fancy-Dancy, come in, please."

No answer.

I hugged myself with glee. We were still in business!

The Caddy's wheel was chattering and pounding. Heller got around two cars and dived for Pit 1.

The Caddy lurched as the crew got a jack under it.

"*Cogliones!*" said Mike. "Another bullet!"

The crew had a spare on. The official verified no gas was taken.

The crowd behind the radio sportscaster was screaming, "Come on, Whiz Kid!"

The announcer said, *"The Whiz Kid is well behind now. He has had two pit stops. The officials verified he has taken on no fuel."*

Heller started to make his way through the scattered field once more. They seemed to be even more interested in hitting him.

He went into a wild skid to avoid Car 6, got his car under control and began to shoot ahead on the part of the track nearest me.

His wheel jerked again!

He almost went into the fence. He recovered and narrowly missed Car 11. The Caddy's wheel was chattering over the heavy ruts.

Heller said, "Fancy-Dancy. There's another!"

No answer.

He swerved his car to a pit stop.

"*Cogliones di Cristo!*" exclaimed Mike. "Another bullet! After this one, you only got one spare left! Take it easy!"

The TV caught Heller leaving the pit. *"The Whiz Kid has really lost the edge. With three pit stops he's now the tail. He can pick some of this up as other cars start pulling in for gas but it is going to take real driving now. . . ."*

It was snowing again. The radio said, *"The Florida Chamber of Commerce meteorologists are telling you that you are in the midst of the lousiest, stinkingest winter you have had for a long time. It is snowing again, if you haven't noticed. This afternoon Spreeport is going to have snow and more snow. In fact, as the hours go on, you are going to be snowed under. If any of you survive watching this Spreeport race and win a bet, rush to Florida to spend it. We love money, we will rip you off painlessly."*

I couldn't see the track. But I hugged myself. As soon as this flurry passed and he could see again, my sniper was going to mess up another wheel. And then just one more after that and Heller was out of it! That Caddy was taking enough of a beating already. It could never survive running on a gaping bullet hole.

And then, suddenly, a voice. I had three sound receivers on. For a moment I didn't locate it.

Heller's earphones!

The voice said, "Sorry, High-Flyer. My talk box got hit and number two took time." It was Bang-Bang!

Heller said, "You okay?"

"Only a bruise, High-Flyer. Take her to a win!"

"Roger, dodger, over, under and out!" said Heller, and really fed throttle! The blurred track sped under him!

I swept the curtained expanse before me. Somewhere in that chill terrain, my other sniper lay dead. Probably with a knife, if I knew Italians. I could find nothing. Probably nobody else ever would either!

I had a bad few minutes. Maybe Bang-Bang was up there somewhere stalking *me!* I locked my van doors securely and laid out a Knife Section knife. But then I realized Bang-Bang was down at Pit 1. He had had to go there to use their radio to reach Heller.

(Bleep) that Bang-Bang! (Bleep) him, (bleep) him, (bleep) him! Heller had a chance to win!

Chapter 8

The snow snowed and the roaring race went on!

Numb, not just with cold, I sat and watched. There were only two chances now: Heller would smash up on that skidding track or his carburetor would fail.

The snowing let up and started again numerous times. Round and round they went.

The TV, Channel Six and Seven Eighths, had been running along as fast as the cars. *"I'm sure it will thrill our national audience to know that the Whiz Kid, who had several times lost his lead, has now recovered it. Track conditions are appalling. Ah, here is Jeb Toshua. He is 101 years old. Jeb, do you ever recall a track this bad?"*

"I think it was '83 when I lost my cat. . . ."

"Thank you, Jeb. Car 7, Dagger Duggan, has just pulled into the pit. He is refueling. . . . No, he's getting a drink of Peegrams Corn Whiskey. Look at that ecstasy on Dagger Duggan's face as he empties the pint. We pause for a word from our sponsors, Peegrams Corn Whiskey! . . ."

The commercial's boys' quartet sang:

> *Corn Whiskey,*
> *Corn Whiskey,*
> *Corn Whiskey, I cry.*
> *If I don't get my Peegrams,*
> *I surely will die.*

The picture of the race came back on. *"Dagger Duggan is now leaving his pit. That's him, waving at the camera. Hey, he turned right out into the path of the Whiz Kid! The Whiz Kid braked and spun his car around him!*

"Car 7—that's Dagger Duggan, folks—is . . . No! He has just caromed off Car 8! There he goes through the rail! Duggan shoots up into the air. The car is turning over! It comes down on its roll bars! It has burst into flame! He's trapped! He bursts into flames.

"We will now do a slow-motion replay of that shot."

The replay flashed on.

A low, harsh voice came over. *"Get that (bleeped) shot off the screen or you'll lose our account!"* Hastily a string of letters flashed across the exploding Duggan:

SIMULATED DRAMATIZATION

Another car spun out and wound up in the snowbanks. Another came crawling into the pit with a busted fan belt and an engine that was overheating.

There were only eleven left in the race. It was creeping up toward 3:00 P.M. Spraying snow to either side, jockeying through openings, Heller drove on to the screams of delight from the grandstand. I found it absolutely disgusting. I kept a close eye on my watch: In a very short time now, that carburetor was scheduled to fail and he would be done for.

But in the last half hour, he had so clearly asserted a lead that some of the other drivers evidently began to think they had no chance at all if they did not take him out.

Instead of driving to make laps, some were driving now to get a ram at Heller as he went by.

Car 10, Basher Benson, driving a stripped International station wagon, lay in wait at the near end of the oval. He was going to, I could see, sweep along on the inside and ram Heller.

The Caddy braked into the turn and then sped up, skidding sideways in the flying snow.

Basher gave his car all it had and rushed parallel, aiming for Heller's left front wheel.

Above the yowl of tortured engines, Basher's voice, "Take this, you (bleepard)!"

The International touched before Heller could avoid.

A flash!

An electrical explosion!

Car 10 rebounded like it had been hit by lightning!

It spun away, went through the rail!

The driver sat there stunned.

The crowd yelled and roared with delight!

The TV did a replay. It *was* a lightning bolt! Car 10 had hit Heller's left front wheel and an electrical flash at least five feet in diameter had flared!

The electrical surplus from the carburetor was being grounded in those wheels! And any other car that touched them bled off the grounding in a lightning bolt!

Basher Benson was getting shakily out of Car 10. He apparently had no idea of what had happened except that he didn't want anything more to do with this race!

The radio sportscaster was trying to account for it and suddenly settled upon the explanation that it was the Whiz Kid's magnetic personality.

Heller and the other cars roared on, the shrieking engines merged with the howls and cheers of the crowd.

The other drivers had no real idea of what had happened. There are always sparks to some extent when metal is hammered against metal in a crash.

The snow stopped and a murky sun came out.

Another driver, in an old Dodge, got the idea of sideswiping Heller on the far straightaway. He was driving close to the rail and as Heller started to pass the Dodge speeded up and dived at him.

FLASH!

It made a crack like a lightning bolt!

Heller had tapped him with a wheel!

The Dodge went spinning out of control! It rolled! It skidded fifty feet on its roll bars!

The crowd went crazy with ecstasy!

Yellow flag. A tow truck sped out to latch on to the Dodge and drag it away. The driver stood there until an ambulance came and then tried to climb into the tow truck. He seemed to be walking in circles.

The cars were speeded up again. There were now nine.

I was on the edge of my seat. I had half an eye on the viewers and the other half on the stopwatch. It was past three.

Was Heller going to win after all?

Chapter 9

The snow clouds parted more widely. The dirty-hued after-noon sun slanted down upon the chewed-up track. It seemed colder.

The battering roar of the straight-shoot-exhaust-piped Caddy racketed above that of the other cars as it speeded up to make the near turn. Heller had started to race in earnest. He was already twenty laps ahead of any other driver and he was starting to open the Caddy up!

The other eight, including Hammer Malone and Killer Brag, seemed to realize they were done unless they did something. Probably the chanting, "Whiz Kid, Whiz Kid, Whiz Kid!" that sporadically rose from the grandstand egged them on.

They were old bomber veterans. They had seen everything and done everything but they were not going to just idle around and watch themselves be thrashed.

Strategies of demolition derbies included gang-up. Once they had disposed of Heller, they could fight the rest of it out amongst themselves. But Heller must GO!

I read all that in the way they concertedly began to idle down as they passed the grandstand. They did another circle, Heller threading his way through them as though they didn't exist.

Heller was doing more than 150. He was sitting there doing an alert job of driving, predicting the movements of the other cars and predodging in ample time. The Caddy looked like a red streak. Its engine was a continuous scream of power.

The other eight cars were drawing up in a kind of an uneven

circle with a huge gap in the center. Four favored the grandstand side of the straightaway, the other four favored its other side. They had stopped trying to lap. They were going into pure demolition-derby formation.

The TV and radio sportscasters were both jabbering in excitement that there was something up.

Heller knew there was something up. He suddenly slowed. He shifted down to lower drive, cutting out his top gear, probably to give himself enormous pickup in a sudden spurt.

The Caddy approached the waiting circle doing only about sixty.

He came to the outer edge of the hole.

A lunge as cars surged at him!

A yowl as the Caddy speeded up.

A grinding crash!

It was Hammer Malone hitting another car!

The Caddy was through the gap and away!

The other cars changed tactics. They turned around so they could back ram this time. It looked like a planned maneuver and, indeed, they were within shouting distance of one another.

The gap for Heller was wide open and inviting.

He was apparently just going to go through again.

The bombers began to back! They would hit him!

He suddenly stamped on his brakes and gave his steering gear a yank to the left!

He spun in a complete circle.

The bombers crashed into one another!

Heller wasn't there!

He came out of his spin and gunned his engine and streaked by, almost scraping the grandstand barricade!

He had gone behind them! He had used a lane just vacated!

The crowd howled with joy!

The bombers pried themselves apart. More shouting. They got back into position.

Heller toured the oval.

But whatever he planned to do next never happened.

Coming out of the far turn of the oval, doing about seventy, his engine quit!

He had only about a hundred yards to go to reach the bombers.

Perhaps he thought he could coast through.

He had been high on the bank. There was lots of snow under his wheels. It was cutting his speed down dramatically.

There was nothing he could do about it.

He went straight into the open center with a dead engine. He was doing about twenty.

CRASH!

Eight cars backed into him!

They were stopped in a jammed mass.

The top of Heller's hood was going cherry red!

The carburetor had fused!

With a quick yank he released his safety belt!

He shot his arm out through the window and got a hold.

He said, "Good-bye, you Cadillac Brougham Coup d'Elegance. It wasn't your fault!"

Like the gymnast he was, he pulled himself through the window.

Jammed cars all around!

Cursing drivers!

Smoke began to shoot out of the Cadillac's hood.

"Run!" Heller shouted in that high Fleet voice.

He was up on a roof. He sprang to another roof!

He leaped to yet another roof.

He launched himself into the air, struck the snow with a roll, was up and running. He was heading for Pit 1.

Hammer Malone and Killer Brag had extricated their cars.

As one, with a crash of gears, they launched their vehicles after Heller!

Two explosions in the tangled mass of the six cars. I knew it would be the oxygen and hydrogen tanks going up.

Flames shot into the air!

The other drivers were running away.

But the cars of Hammer Malone and Killer Brag bore down on Heller!

He turned to face them.

They converged!

He slapped his hands against their hoods, sprang upwards and with a roll, hit the roof of Hammer Malone's car and was over it and behind.

With a grinding shriek of metal, the two sideswiping cars recoiled right and left, spinning in the ice.

Killer Brag's gas tanks must have been ruptured. The sparks of the chains on ice did the rest.

A whoosh of green, orange and red flame enveloped both cars!

Brag was out, racing away.

Hammer Malone was on fire. He dived into a snowbank to put it out.

Heller was racing for Pit 1.

Chapter 10

The pit crew was scrambling about.

Heller dived over a pit barricade.

Mike Mutazione was pounding at some sparks lying in Heller's racing suit.

The grandstand was going crazy.

The radio announcer was yelling, *"The Whiz Kid's engine died, just like that. . . ."*

The TV sportscaster was shouting, *"Nine cars in flames. . . ."*

The loudspeakers blared, *"The Whiz Kid apparently ran out of fuel. . . ."*

Hammer Malone could be seen struggling out of the snowbank. He raced back toward his car. He beat out some flames in the upholstery. He leaped in!

The old wreck started! It had only been damaged by the explosion of Killer Brag's!

No other car in the flaming pyre before the grandstand was moving.

Hammer Malone began to drive around the track!

There was a howl of rage from the crowd.

A new voice was in the grandstand loudspeakers. *"That God (bleeped) Whiz Kid cost us our shirts!"*

Nobody was paying any attention to Hammer Malone, faltering along at about twenty. He had won the demolition and he was now going for the endurance. Totally ignored.

The grandstand loudspeakers blared, *"Get that God (bleeped) Whiz Kid!"*

The losers spilled in a wave over the grandstand barricades and onto the track!

Howling and shrieking revenge, they tore toward Pit 1.

Heller looked up, watching them come. He muttered, "Just like it said in *Hakluyt's Voiages*. Very hard to make a safe landing amongst the natives of North America!"

Mike Mutazione's crew was standing in a semicircle around the pit area.

The crowd was plowing down the track like a storm cloud gone crazy. The race was forgotten. All they wanted was blood.

Track security police tried to make a stand to check them. They were hurled aside!

The crowd came storming on. They were screaming, "Get the Whiz Kid!" "Cost me ten thousand!" "Kill him!" and other ferocious war cries.

Heller just sat there watching.

The foremost ring of the mob, mouths snarling, fists shaking, got within twenty feet of the Mutazione line.

"Now!" barked Mike.

Abruptly flame erupted from nozzles!

A dozen oxyacetylene hoses played a fan of fire over the heads of the mob!

There was an instant of incredulous gasps cut by the sizzle of flame.

Then a torrent of screams!

Howls of terror burst out!

The foremost ranks recoiled!

They knocked down people behind them like dominoes!

The crowd was racing away, leaving the fallen and trampled in the snow. And then these, too, found the energy to run.

The oxyacetylene torches popped out as their valves were shut off.

Hammer Malone's old wreck staggered past the grandstand and wrecked cars and knocked along, working to complete his thousand laps.

But the race was over for the crowd. They were going home.

PART THIRTY

Chapter 1

I packed up and drove the van down off the hill, heading for the track and grandstand.

I had seen Heller get into the Peterbilt and knew there was no danger he would spot me.

The disgruntled and disgusted crowd was trailing away. I steered the van slowly through them. I was hoping I could find J. Walter Madison.

Behind Heller's back, Madison had fabricated the Whiz Kid and the controversy around this race. With Heller's spectacular defeat and the bloodthirsty crowd, I had to find what Madison planned next.

The security guards were no longer tending the gates. They did not care who went in or out now. I left the van parked outside.

I went through a tunnel and emerged in the littered grandstand. There was a cluster of people around a box. I recognized one of the nearest ones. It was a reporter I had seen at Madison's office, 42 Mess Street.

I went up to him. Although he had a sheepskin coat up around his ears and although I was wearing a hooded parka, we recognized each other.

I said, "Did Madison start that great riot?"

He said, "No. I did on the spur of the moment. J. Warbler is in a weird state. Twenty minutes before the race he went into shock and passed out. We had to take him to the hospital tent. He only returned to the grandstand in time to see the end of it."

I looked through the cluster of 42 Mess Street people and saw Madison sitting there on a folding chair. Cold as it was, he had an ice bag on his head! His face was gray and awful!

I went over to him. I said, incredulously, "Are you feeling that way because Heller lost?"

He shook his head. "Oh, no. Win or lose, that wouldn't have mattered. It would only have given us one day's front page and then we would have had the work of doing something else."

I didn't understand it at all. "Well, if winning or losing didn't matter, what are you feeling so bad about?"

He ineffectually adjusted the ice bag. Then he broke down. "Never trust a client! They always do you in!"

"Maybe you better tell me what you think is wrong," I said, puzzled.

He began to cry. In a choked voice, he said, "He wasn't supposed to race at all! Just before the race he was supposed to be kidnapped! We would have had two weeks at least of *front page!*"

He ground his fists into his knees. "It was all to be so perfect! After two weeks he would have turned up behind the Iron Curtain, a captive of the fuel-hungry Russians!"

He let out a frustrated wail. "It would have started World War III! He'd be IMMORTAL!"

After a period of writhing and pounding his knees, he said, "You just can't ever depend on clients! OH, MY GOD! WHAT DO I DO NOW TO RECOVER THE FRONT PAGE??????"

I crept away.

Chapter 2

Sunday morning, the Bentley Bucks Deluxe Arms (to give it its full name) held me in tender and loving, if expensive, embrace. That was the only embrace I was getting these days.

But by ten my feeling of laziness began to give way to a vague disquiet. It occurred to me that it was altogether possible that Heller might recover from that debacle. In life, he was treacherously hyperactive. A type of disposition for which I have no sympathy.

I called down for a breakfast of strawberry shortcake—imported from the Argentine, the menu said—and, wrapped in a robe, was soon devouring it. My carbon-oxygen furnace needed restoking after the shocks and labors of the day before.

Almost indolently, I opened the ten pounds of Sunday paper. I don't really know what I expected to see. But I had not at all anticipated what I *did* see.

Nothing!

There was absolutely no word about that race in the whole paper!

Not ONE word!

I hastened over to the TV. I ran through the channels. Ah, a program called "The Week in Sports" was just beginning. Several items. Then a few brief clips of the race without any editorial comment, hardly any mention of the Whiz Kid! Just the crashes!

Oh, this was bad. Madison was right. He was off the front page. And not even in a day or two but at once!

I then remembered the local-radio-station dial position I had been listening to on Saturday—a Long Island station, WHOA. I tuned in on it. I was in luck! They were just beginning their news.

It was, apparently, a sleepy, snowed-in, suburban Sunday on Long Island. There were only two items of interest to me, both local.

A burned-out van with ten bodies in it had been found by some Boy Scouts in a picnic area of Jones Beach. Police said that they were burned beyond recognition; that a leaking muffler had overcome them; that they probably had been en route to pick up a load of seaborne narcotics; that Tommy Jones had been awarded his merit badge for snowshoeing.

The other item was another discovery: Miss Sarah Jane Gooch, the charming wife of Gooby Gooch, had been on her way to Cranston's Supermarket this morning and had stumbled over a body in the snowdrifts which now "dot our streets" and had called the police who had then found another body about two hundred yards away, the location traced by Police Chief Flab because of dogs quarrelling over it, which event had been phoned in by Mrs. Emma Gross, the charming wife of Bill Gross. The police concluded that one of the men had shot the other one with a rifle and had then committed suicide with a stiletto that was still sticking in his back. Crime in the community was thus reduced by two, which was heartwarming on a cold day.

The race might as well have never happened so far as the Spreeport area was concerned!

And it looked especially quiet when it came to news about the Whiz Kid. I was worried. What was going to happen now? Was Heller going to get off scot-free and ride to glory?

I thought I had better check up on said Heller.

I had kept my receiver-viewscreen loaded with strips to record Heller's actions and by replaying them I found out what he had been up to this morning.

He had come into his office! On Sunday? That was a bad sign. Awfully industrious!

The first thing he did was dig Izzy out of the closet-office he uses as a bedroom.

"I gave you a device some time ago," said Heller. "I want to look at it."

Heller went into his own office, turned on a heater and stood for a while gazing out across the snow-covered expanses of lower Manhattan. He seemed to concentrate on soot patches already darkening the snow. He was evidently letting his office warm up, for presently he took off a ski mask, a white fur hood and parka and sat down.

Izzy came in with the item. It was the unmodified carbon converter Heller had brought from Voltar and a duplicate of the one he had put in the now-defunct Cadillac.

Heller broke out some tools and, with very rapid motions, soon had the device spread all over a cloth on his desk. A small feeling of alarm began to rise in me.

One by one, holding each close to his eye, he began to go over the parts. Suddenly he stopped. He was holding a thin metal bit about an inch long.

"A notch!" he said.

Magnified by his own eyesight, I could see it too on my screen. Just a little V notch, the one our saboteur had cut to embarrass Heller.

"Look!" he said to Izzy, holding it out.

But Izzy couldn't see it no matter how he twisted his horn-rimmed glasses around. Heller got a huge magnifier and showed him.

"That caused the wrong electrical value to pour into the next component!" said Heller. "It built up to red-hot overheat! These were just cheap school kits. I should have known better."

Izzy gazed at him blankly. "School kits?"

"No, no," said Heller, probably realizing he was on the edge of a Code break. "They will work fine. All I need to do is redesign it slightly to guarantee its electrical values in this area and it will run forever. Get me the plans back."

Izzy got them and Heller made the changes. He seemed quite cheered up. The stupid idiot didn't suspect it was the farsightedness of Lombar Hisst that had cost him that race!

"Izzy," he said, "what do you do when you have lost a race?"

"You don't engage in one in the first place," said Izzy.

"No, no, really, I want to know."

"You leave for South America," said Izzy. "There's this place up the Amazon where there are only soldier ants. Peaceful! No people! Even the reporters have been eaten up. I'm holding your ticket. I can get you a Pan American reservation in seconds!" He was starting to lilt with enthusiasm.

"No, no," said Heller. "I'll just fix up this thing, get another car and challenge them again!"

"Oh, no!" wept Izzy.

And "Oh, no!" wept I! I could not possibly tolerate that much strain again, ever! This was a REAL emergency.

I reached for the phone, found I was holding the viewscreen. I put it down and tried to make a call on my Colt Bulldog. I ran about, slamming doors, trying to get dressed.

Utanc, my darling Turkish love, stuck a sleepy head through the bedroom door. "Whatever is going on, Sultan?"

I had not seen her in days. But I had no time now. "The world is liable to fall in!"

"Oh?" she said, closed the door, locked it and apparently went back to bed.

I didn't, let me tell you! I knew duty when I saw it calling! It was screaming at me!

Chapter 3

I found the phone where I had knocked it off under the bed.

I managed to find Madison's number. I forced the hotel operator to dial it: I couldn't hit the right buttons.

A very concerned, older female voice answered. His mother!

"I must talk to J. Walter at once!" I yelled at her.

"Oh, dear," she said, "I'm afraid that is impossible. He is lying in bed. Three doctors have been here and they ordered absolute rest. I can't even go near him myself."

And, indeed, I could hear tiny suppressed screeches in the background.

I hung up.

Bury. I must phone Bury!

It was a tangle! His number was unlisted. The Octopus Oil Building Exchange would not give me his home phone.

Ah, I had it! That night he had gone home in the police car! I knew where he lived!

Sunday or no Sunday, Mr. Bury was going to have a caller!

I still had the van, the rental office being closed on Sunday.

I piled into some warm clothes, got the car brought around front and was soon tooling uptown.

The streets were deserted tunnels piled high on both sides with snow, the tops of cars showing vaguely in the mounds. The snowplows had been industrious. Some of those motorists would not see their vehicles until spring!

I was soon standing before his mailbox. It said Mrs. Destuyvescent Depleister Bury.

I rang. I got him at once.

Within a minute I was in an upper hall and he was letting me through a door.

"It's an emergency," I said desperately.

His reply was strange. "Oh, good," he whispered.

Then, with a conspiratorial finger he beckoned me into the sitting room. He was carrying a sheet of Sunday paper and he didn't have any shoes on.

A torrent of words were coming from an inner room—things like "When I married you, I expected . . ." and "Time and again my whole family told me . . ." and "That is what I get for marrying beneath . . ." Quite a blur.

Bury whispered, "Tell me again, real loud!"

"THIS IS AN EMERGENCY!" I yelled at him and meant it.

"OH, HEAVENS!" he shouted back. "AN EMERGENCY ON SUNDAY!"

He grabbed his shoes and put them on. He grabbed some overshoes out of a hall closet. He got into an overcoat. He put on his snap-brim, little New Yorker hat. He grabbed an attaché case, rushed into a side room and filled it with white mice. He closed it.

Then he rushed into the room his wife's voice was coming from and said something to the effect that the office demanded his presence.

He rushed out. A storm of small pillows and perfume sprays and nail files poured after him. He got us into the hall.

"Thank God," he said. "I've never been so pleased to see anybody in my life, Inkswitch. I will remember this as a kindly act! So rare, kindly acts!"

He was pushing me along as he spoke. We got outside and we climbed into the warm van.

I handed him a half pint of applejack I had taken to the race in case of emergency. "You're going to need this." And I told him first how Madison had planned to kidnap Wister, send him to Russia, blame the Communists and start World War III.

Bury nodded. He didn't even touch the applejack. "Well," he said, "I told you, Inkswitch. A little bit of Madison always goes too far. Many think his mother should be arraigned for attempted humanocide. But frankly, Inkswitch, he's really no more skilled than any other public relations man or reporter. He's just a little faster, that's all."

"You aren't worried?"

"Oh, PRs, catarrhs, Inkswitch. One of them, sooner or later, will get us into World War III anyway. What do you expect? At least we got him into action."

"That's just it," I said. "He's not in action. He's under the care of three doctors and he's lying in bed screaming. And I can see his point. After the failure of his plan, he can't figure out how to get any more headlines. The paper today was blank."

"The Sunday papers? They're all printed on Saturday. They were in the delivery trucks before that race even started. Now, I'll admit you have a point. It is probably infeasible now for him to make Wister immortal for starting World War III. And it is very unlikely that J. Warbler Madman will come up with another gem like that. And he probably will have to work like a dog to get back on the front page. And I surely want to thank you for getting me out of there."

"You mean your wife?"

"Oh, no, no, no. The mayor! We were scheduled to have dinner with him."

"Is he that bad?"

"Oh, no, no, Inkswitch. You don't understand. The mayor is just a fat slob. It's his wife! She's a former Roxy showgirl and she's never forgiven anybody for preventing her from becoming a Hollywood star. My wife's carping is nothing compared to that of the mayor's wife. Her voice ought to be arrested for assault and battery with intent to kill! I shall remember your kindly act. Even though kindness is an awful weakness, Inkswitch, and you've got to guard against it. But come, we're wasting time."

"You've got another emergency?"

"Indeed so. I was going to go to the Bronx Zoo today and I couldn't possibly figure how to manage it until you came. Because of the Rockecenter gifts to the place they specially open the snake house for me on Sundays and let me feed live mice to the most delightful reptiles it's ever been your pleasure to meet. Want to come?"

I shudderingly declined.

"All right, then drop me at the subway station and I'll be on my way. And guard against kindness, Inkswitch. It can be a fatal flaw. It can even open the door to the Madisons of this world."

With this threat, I hastily started up and dropped him at the subway station.

I watched him go down the steps with his attaché case full of live mice.

I have seldom felt so uncertain of the future.

Chapter 4

Late that night, around 10:00, fearing that Madison might not be dead, I again called his mother.

She stunned me!

"Dead? Oh, no, he's not dead. I've seldom seen him look more energetic. Is that you, Mr. Smith?"

I managed to say that it was.

"He flew out of here hours ago. He said he knew you would need reassurance and encouragement and for you to call 42 Mess Street right away if you rang."

I rang 42 Mess Street. I said, "This is Smith. I want to speak with Mr. Madison."

A bright male voice said, "Smith? Ah, Mr. Smith, owner of the *National Enmirer*, of course. Listen, Smith, have we got a scoop for you! . . ."

"No, no," I said. "I'm not a publisher. Tell Madison it's *the* Mr. Smith."

Whoever it was left the phone. A mad chatter of telex machines and barking voices assaulted my ears. Hey, that office was *busy!* But Madison had been dying!

Madison's voice, "Oh, Mr. Smith. I do thank you for calling. I knew you would be worried."

"I thought you were dying or dead!"

"Quote Medical Miracle Unquote. Intramuscular morphine followed by Benzedrine and intravenous transfusions of black ink saves Madison's life. Smith, we must cease to dwell upon the nostalgic and roseate glow of yesterday. Now is the time to get the shoulder to men's souls. For these are the times that try men's grindstones. We are the masters of men's fates and I thank God for my indomitable will. . . ."

"Wait," I protested. "What are you going to do now?"

"Smith, we must rest content that there will never be another chance to pull the PR coup of the century again. We have to let sleeping dogs tell lies and abandon all that. We must not look back but sternly face the future. Inspiration and genius would have triumphed had it not been for that undependable client. But never mind. I will now resort to standard press policy and though it will be hard and long, the end will see us riding in the triumphal procession, crowned with laurel leaves, never fear."

"What," I demanded with growing fear, "are you going to DO?"

"Smith, we have the first *C* of PR, Confidence. What we have lost is the second *C*, Coverage. We are OFF the front page! But never fear, Smith, we will regain it! For we have the third *C*, Controversy! Riding through the icy night, determined to make good, it came to me in a flash. CONTROVERSY! We can rebuild our campaign upon the sturdy headsman's block of Controversy without end. We will succeed! And you will have to excuse me now as I am told the publisher of the *Los Angeles Grimes* is on the other wire." Click! He was gone!

I sat there staring at the phone. He hadn't told me a blasted thing. I feared I did not understand this mysterious world of PR. I put the phone on the hook.

It rang instantly. Madison's voice, "See tomorrow's front page!" Click. He was gone again.

Needless to say, the next morning, it was with shaky hands that I unfolded the morning newspaper.

And there it was. Headlines!

WHIZ KID
ACCUSED OF FRAUD

VEHICLE IMPOUNDED

Race officials last night obtained a court order to impound the car used by the Whiz Kid in Saturday's race.

No one could be found to comment.

The Whiz Kid refuses press interviews.

The racing world tonight was shocked by the ominous order. . . .

I rushed out and got other papers. They all said more or less the same thing. They didn't say what it was really all about.

The TV and radio both were carrying the story. Apparently it was going national, for west-coast racing figures were being interviewed.

And so it went through the day.

Toward evening, I thought of my viewer. How was Heller taking this?

He had newspapers spread all over his desk. He was asking Izzy, "What in the name of blastguns is this all about?"

Izzy said, "It's about a ticket to South America. I got a book right here on soldier ants. They're a lot less deadly than the press. The ants just destroy everything."

"But," said Heller, "the remains of the Caddy are sitting right over at Mike Mutazione's garage. I called him. Nobody has come near it! And besides, it's so burned out you can't see anything but melted metal. And not a soul has called me. I haven't refused any press interviews!"

He started to clip all the stories, pushing the airline ticket aside from time to time as Izzy kept putting it in his way.

All day Madison's phone was busy or he wasn't available. But that office, each time I heard it on the open line, sounded like it was situated in the middle of a hurricane.

Tuesday morning came.

Front page again!

WHIZ KID CHEATED

GAS LINE FOUND

Officials today revealed that in investigating the smoldering wreck of the Whiz Kid's car, they had discovered a gasoline line cleverly hidden in the pistons. . . .

It was in all the papers and on radio and TV.

Well, I thought. That will be the end of it and the end of Heller, too!

But Wednesday morning came.

Front page!

RACE OFFICIAL FLEES

WHIZ KID CULPABLE

According to unimpeachable sources we cannot disclose, a track official—whose relatives demanded he remain anonymous—fled the state after confessing he had accepted a bribe from the Whiz Kid to overlook a hidden gas tank in the Whiz Kid's steering wheel. . . .

It was in all the papers and on radio and TV. Ah, well, I thought. Madison has cleverly scotched any future race. And that will be that.

So, on Thursday I was fairly relaxed when I opened the morning paper.

Front page again! With photos!

ANGRY MOB SEARCHES FOR WHIZ KID

EMBATTLED POLICE USE RIOT GUNS

Today, Manhattan huddled behind closed doors and listened with terror as the streets were torn to bits by the angry marching feet of a howling mob searching for the Whiz Kid. . . .

Photos of the mob, with placards which said *Down with the Whiz Kid,* showed flame and tear gas shooting from police lines. I looked out the window. Fifth Avenue never looked so calm.

The afternoon editions had new banners:

MAYOR CALLS CITY–WIDE EMERGENCY

And there were more photos.

Well, I said to myself, this Madison has really got what it takes. Really a genius. But he's shot his bolt now. He'll drop to page two.

Friday.

Front page again!

WHIZ KID HIDEOUT FOUND

Investigative reporters today stumbled upon the secret hideout of the Whiz Kid. Tipped off by a Good Humor Ice Cream man who was in a bad humor . . .

The story went on.

But the photograph! There was the Whiz Kid, buckteeth and all, peering out from behind the venetian blind of an upper window and looking very fearful.

I wondered if Heller really had fled. I ran through my recorded strips. He was going about his usual routine. At one point he came into his office, puzzled over the papers a bit and then went on with his schoolwork.

On Saturday, I knew Madison would have worn it out.

But no! Front page!

WHIZ KID
HIDEOUT BOMBED

Today mobs converged upon the hideout of the Whiz Kid, ten thousand strong, and with ferocity hitherto unknown in city annals bombed the house to bits! . . .

Photos of an exploding building. I looked at it closely. It could not have been the same house the Whiz Kid had been shown peering out of. It looked more like a factory. Hard to tell with all the flame and bits flying about.

I went for a walk and saw Madison's earlier advertising signs about the Whiz Kid, that had been so neat, were now all covered with graffiti derogatory to the Whiz Kid.

Sunday, of course, would be a blank news day.

But it wasn't! Front page again!

MAGAZINE CANCELS
CONTEST

In an unprecedented action today, the sports magazine, *Dirt Illustrated,* cancelled the $100,000 contest to guess the secret fuel of the Whiz Kid.

> The full details, according to magazine officials, will be released in this week's issue.
>
> But unimpeachable sources leaked that it had to do with a criminal act of the Whiz Kid relating to the contest. . . .

Hey, a *second* front page story! Madison was really pouring it on!

"SECRET" FUEL DISCLOSED

WHIZ KID FUEL LEAKS

According to the Attorney General's office of an undisclosed state, investigators today obtained vital information on the supposedly "secret" fuel of the Whiz Kid that was to revolutionize industry and automobiling.

Using forensic air hoses on a gas-station attendant whose name was withheld, they obtained the name of the actual fuel.

According to the indictment which some believe to be under preparation, the "secret" fuel was no less than Octopus Gasoline!

The gas attendant sought immunity from conspiracy charges by testifying that someone who looked like the Whiz Kid bought, in North Carolina, 39 gallons of Octopus High Test Supreme Unleaded the very day of the race!

With variations, the story was in all the Sunday papers. But there was much more. *Dirt Illustrated* had full-page ads announcing the coming exposé. And double-page ads were carried by Octopus

Gasoline, "The Drink of Industry and the People!"

By the Gods, he had even made the Sunday papers! I was really pleased. Bury's faith in Madison had not been misplaced!

I hastily went down to get the newest copy of *Dirt Illustrated* and there it was! A complete exposé! According to the leading story, the Whiz Kid himself had tried to win the prize! He had submitted an unsigned entry that simply said "Octopus Gasoline"!

I really chuckled. This Madison was a howling genius after all.

I tuned in on Heller. He was at his Nature Appreciation 101 class with Mr. Wouldlice as his instructor. The snow was all over the place and the class looked cold. Wouldlice seemed a sort of chinless young man. With an ice saw, he was trying to cut a hole in the frozen Harlem Meer in Central Park and lecturing on the nesting habits of carp. He wasn't making much headway with the ice cutting. Heller, hands in pockets, finally finished the job for him with some strategically placed kicks with the heels of his baseball spikes. Heller handed the resulting slab to a girl and the students began to use it as a sort of belly sled. Mr. Wouldlice went on lecturing with Heller as his sole attending student. He didn't seem antagonistic to Heller; well, that would change with the next term when Miss Simmons got back on the job.

Heller did act sort of depressed. He was stirring the soot-covered snow with his foot. It made me very cheerful.

Monday, however, made me sort of wonder whose side this Madison was on.

He got his front page again. But a new twist.

OCTOPUS OFFICIALS DENY INSTIGATING WHIZ KID RIOTS

The mayor today denied that he had been summoned before a full-scale meeting of the Octopus Oil Company. However, unimpeachable inside leaks reached this paper just before dawn that a secret meeting of the Seven Brothers had occurred over the weekend to discuss the Whiz Kid riots.

All officials reached denied the meeting and the discussion.

"In admitting that he used Octopus Gasoline in the race," a spokesman said, "the Whiz Kid obviously sought to implicate the oil companies in his vicious and villainous plot to undermine the entire oil industry with a felonious breach of racing rules. I deny vigorously that the oil companies financed the rioters. Besides, the Whiz Kid, being only 17, could not legally drive in Nassau County. This is an effort to link the great American patriots of the oil industry to an illegal act and imply that by selling the Whiz Kid Octopus gasoline to use in his fraud, the oil companies are also party to the crime."

But when Tuesday's papers came, Madison had lost his front page. He had slumped to page 3. The story was even short.

WHIZ KID FORBIDDEN TO DRIVE

Officials of the State of New York today revoked the unissued New York Driving License of the Whiz Kid due to the Octopus disclosure that he is only 17 and underage.

NASCAR officials also revoked his membership, effectively ending any further racing by the Whiz Kid.

Charges of fraud and public conspiracy . . .

Ah, well. I could relax. Madison had done it. I phoned his office. He wasn't there. I phoned his mother.

"Mr. Smith? Oh, I am sorry. I can't call him to the phone. He has been under a terrible strain all morning and didn't feel well enough . . ."

Madison took the phone away from her. "Mr. Smith?" He sounded very depressed. "I am so sorry, Mr. Smith. I lost the front page. I could feel it in my bones last night." And an aside, "Mother, please hold the ice bag tighter, it's slipping. Mr. Smith, please don't lose faith in me. These things take time. Somewhere I went wrong. I promise you I will live up to everything you ever thought of me. Really. I have to hang up now. My psychiatrist just came in."

He really sounded depressed. But I wasn't!

I checked up on Heller. He was in the High Library at Empire University. He was reading Hakluyt's *The Principall Navigations, Voiages, and Discoveries of the English Nation (1589).*

He was lingering on a section where a vessel had gone aground on the North American coast and natives were swarming all over it, hacking the crew to pieces in the intense cold. Then he just sat there looking into space.

An assistant librarian, gathering up some books, said, "You look kind of lost. Can I help you?"

Heller said, "No. I don't think anybody can. Somewhere I went wrong. And for the life of me, I can't spot where."

"Just go see the student psychiatrist," said the assistant librarian cheerfully.

"Just because I'm lost is no reason to make *two* mistakes," said Heller and went back to studying Hakluyt.

But oh, was I cheerful. My life felt like a song.

Bless Bury. Bless Madison. Heller was stopped cold!

Chapter 5

According to psychologists a manic state seldom lasts very long. And so it was with mine.

Not two minutes after I left the viewer, there was a knock on the door. Thinking it was a bellhop with some deliveries for Utanc, I unsuspectingly opened it.

Raht and Terb!

I hastily swept them into the living room, looked up and down the hall, reentered and locked it behind me.

Raht's mustache was growing back—they must have shaved it to repair his fractured jaws. He had some facial scars from the wires. He was very hollow-eyed.

Terb had lost most of his fat and, apparently, the use of a couple of fingers.

"It's about time!" I thundered at them. "Lollygagging about on company time! You ought to be ashamed of yourselves. I've a good notion to dock your whole year's pay!" That's the way you have to handle such riffraff.

I sat down and poured myself a cup of coffee from the silver pot and looked at them contemptuously through its steam. They were standing in the middle of the room, their thin clothes shabby, shivering from the outside cold, kind of blue. Apparently they had lost their overcoats.

"The New York office is open and running," said Raht. "They got all the criminals scheduled for their identity changes as you requested."

"That's no reason for you to come around and bother me," I said.

"Oh, we wouldn't have," said Terb. "But Faht Bey said on the wire that it was pretty urgent so we had to come."

I sighed the sigh of the harassed executive. "And what," I said, "is urgent enough to disturb the vital work I'm doing? Without any help from menials, I might add."

Raht said, "Apparently, he wouldn't wait."

"And *whom* is *he?*" I said, correcting his grammar. You have to keep such riffraff on their toes.

"Gunsalmo Silva," said Terb.

I felt my hair lift. I had told Silva to go kill the Director of the CIA. Silva shouldn't be alive. He should be safely dead while executing an execution that couldn't possibly be executed!

"Evidently," said Raht, "he arrived several days ago in Afyon. Faht Bey tried to find out what he wanted and get it handled but Silva said his business was with you and a couple days ago he simply left. The airline booking he made was for New York!"

Well, New York is a big town. Silva couldn't possibly, Gods forbid, know my address. One mustn't appear nervous before underlings. "So what else is new?" I said.

Terb promptly handed me a stack of orders to stamp!

Wearily I got out my identoplate and stamped away. But, for once, I was alert. There were two orders there: one for their hospital expenses and another which called for overcoats and new clothes. I tossed them aside. Then, on second thought, to make a better impression, I recovered them and tore them in small pieces.

"You be on call," I said as I swept them into the hall. "No more of this loafing!"

I slammed the door on them.

For some time I sort of paced around the bedroom and sitting room. Then I decided to go for a walk. I got my warmest clothes and, all wrapped up, I went to the hall door and opened it.

GUNSALMO SILVA!

In moments of intense shock, the thing uppermost in one's mind tends to surface.

"How did you find me?" I gasped.

He pushed on by. He removed a camel's-hair overcoat from his squat and muscular frame and threw it on the sofa. He put his hat, a Russian *astrakhan,* on the coat. He sat down, found the coffee was still warm in its thermos pot and poured himself a cup.

"Come in and close the door," he said. "It's drafty."

I did. I went in the bedroom and took off my own coat. I checked to make sure I had my Colt Bulldog but actually I don't think I could have drawn it, because my hand was shaking.

I reentered the living room and sat down to hide what my knees were doing.

"The answer to your first God (bleeped) question," he said, "is easy. I seem to have these miraculous powers. That Utanc is sending avalanches of postcards to her two little servant kids back in Afyon and they're showing them to half of Turkey." He pulled one out. It was pretty dogeared. It was of the Bentley Bucks Deluxe Arms with an *X* on the penthouse and said "X marks my room." And also "Confidential."

"I had to twist the little (bleepard's) arm a bit, but there it is. Now as to your next question," he said, overlooking the fact I hadn't asked it, "where's my hunnert big ones?"

I found my wits. "How do I know you did the job?" I said. "After all, the rub-out of the Director of the CIA would make big news."

"Jesus H. Christ," he said, "don't you ever read the papers?" He looked around. A stack of them for the last two weeks stood in a corner: my Heller file that I hadn't clipped yet. He went to them. Sure enough, there was the story.

CIA DIRECTOR
REPLACEMENT
HITS SNAG IN SENATE

He fished around in the stack some more. "And how about this?" He jammed it under my nose.

CIA DIRECTOR
SUCCUMBS
TO OPERATION

"They can't come right out and say he was hit," said Silva. "It would set the God (bleeped) Russians a bad example. But how about this?"

He threw the whole wallet and identity cards of the Director of the CIA on the sofa. It was bloodstained!

"Incredible!" I said, stalling for time.

"Yeah, I thought so myself. You see, I sort of got these incredible powers. I don't know where the hell they come from."

I knew. Taken to Voltar, he had been hypnotrained by the Apparatus! I had a killer-killer in front of me, very deadly indeed!

I fought to think of more stalls. "It's hard to realize you could waste a man as guarded as that," I said.

"Yeah, it took time. First, I had to get them to hire me as a hit man. They knew my score—'Holy Joe' and all—so they took me on. And I had to waste two Russians for them and then a dictator in Central America. That's what slowed me down."

He poured himself another cup of coffee. "Still, it wasn't too slow. You see, these ideas on how to do things just pop up and away I go. Mysterious. Like angel voices. Really beautiful."

Silva added two lumps of sugar to his coffee. "But wasting the CIA Director was easy. Hardly took any angel voices at all. After the three hits they trusted me so much I was even riding in his car. I learnt his habits, so to speak. So I disguised myself as his wife and shot him in a Georgetown brothel. They're looking for her now. Good, clean job so they won't find her. I sold her body to the God (bleeped) university hospital. It was a bit more money, too. And speaking of money, where's my hunnert big ones?"

I choked. "Listen," I managed, "lira won't do you any good in the U.S. I'll phone and find out what the exchange is and pay you in dollars."

"*Lira!*" he snarled. "What the hell would I do with ten million *lira!* It's a hunnert thousand U.S. greenback bucks, buster. So cough up."

"That's what I was saying," I said hastily. "I'll make a call and get it sent over right away."

"That's better," he said.

I went into my bedroom. I had about a hundred and thirty thousand under my mattress but I had conceived a good plan. I phoned the New York office.

"Raht," I said.

They put Terb on the phone. He said, "I'm sorry. Raht has gone out to find us some rooms. I'm alone."

"Then come alone!" I snapped. "I want you over here at once. Come to my bedroom door and no place else!" I slammed down the phone.

I went back. Silva was sitting relaxed. "Well, you won't believe this," he said, "but I'm going to God (bleep) retire shortly."

"Good," I said. "I don't have any more work for you."

"Oh, I wouldn't take it if you had it. I'm a real artist now. I got these mysterious God (bleep) powers, see? And there's a bird that nobody will take a contract for. It's been offered and offered and no takers. One million God (bleeped) bucks. And no takers. What do you think of that?"

"Marvelous," I said. "He must be pretty dangerous."

"Oh, he is, he is." And then he snapped his fingers. "But me, I'm an artist. I'm taking it. He's wasted thirteen hit men, they say. But thirteen is his unlucky number. *He's* going to be fourteen! One million God (bleeped) bucks."

He glowed for a bit. Then he waved his hand about and said, "I'm going to live in swanky joints like this one and have a swanky dame like you got and live it up! And speaking of living it up, where's the delivery boy with the money?"

He waited and I sweated. It was actually a temptation to simply blow him full of holes with the Colt Bulldog, but such a slug spills a lot of blood and it would ruin the sofa. Besides, he might outdraw me.

At last a knock on the bedroom door. I closed the door to the sitting room and opened it. Terb was standing there, blue with cold.

"Listen," I said in a tense whisper. "There's a man, Silva, going to be leaving here in a few minutes. He'll be carrying a hundred thousand dollars. You tail him, kill him and get the money back. And bring it right here back to me without one single penny missing."

"I didn't come armed. We lost our guns. Can't I wait and get Raht on this with me? We work together. . . ."

"Not armed!" Oh, I was furious with him. But a hundred thousand is a hundred thousand. I pushed the Bulldog into his hands. I thought for a moment. I took the Knife Section knife out from behind my neck and gave it to him. I thought for a moment and went back into the room and got two Voltar heavy-concussion grenades—they are common enough, a fifteen-second delay time after you throw them and no fragments to leave evidence.

"Now, no excuses," I said. "Watch my door from down the hall and when he comes out, tail him and, in a safe place, blow him away. Got it?"

He said he did.

I went back into my bedroom and dug the hundred thousand out from under my mattress. It certainly hurt me to part with it, even for a little while.

I reentered the sitting room. "The messenger had to count it," I said in apology. "But here it is."

He took it, counted it and stuffed it into his pockets, quite a wad. As he left, I said, "Good luck on your retirement." He gave me an evil smile and was gone.

Chapter 6

At dawn there was a furious pounding on my bedroom door. Ah, Terb with my money!

Groggily, I staggered over and opened it.

It wasn't Terb. It was Raht!

He was standing there, shivering and shaking, covered with the snow falling outside, blue with cold—and something else.

He came in, he shut the door behind him and leaned against it. He said, "He's dead."

"Well, that's good news," I said. "Hand over the money."

He stared at me noncomprehending. He looked pretty shattered, sort of half doubled up and sort of liable to fall.

"Don't stall," I said. "You know very well I sent Terb to tail Silva and get the money back."

He slumped all the way down and sat there with his back against the door, head bowed over. I could swear he was crying.

"Come on, come on," I said. "No stalling. It's too early in the morning for any tricks. Just hand over the money and don't try to hold any out!"

"He's dead," said Raht. "Tortured to death."

"Well, good," I said. "So Terb had a little fun. But that doesn't mean you two (bleepards) can keep the money."

He said, between sobs, "It's Terb that's dead."

I had opened my mouth to speak. I closed it. GUNSALMO SILVA WAS STILL ALIVE!

Quickly, I locked and barred the door. Hastily, I got another gun out of my bureau, a Smith and Wesson .44 Magnum revolver. I made sure the living room was empty, locked and barred. I scouted the terrace. No Silva. Yet.

I came back and grabbed Raht by his shirt front. "You better (bleeped) well tell me how you two fouled this up!"

He was so blue and so shaking with shock, it took him quite a while before he could do much talking.

"I never would have found him," he finally got out. "But we both wear bugs we can locate each other with. He didn't come back last night. They said he had gone to your place. I traced him by the bug sewn in his pants. He was in a basement entrance of an old abandoned house." He halted.

"Was there anything on him?"

"His feet were burned half off. His teeth were all broken with grinding them. We always worked together. If he was following Silva, the man must have pretended to go in the house and then circled and got him from behind."

"Did he have my hundred thousand on him?" I demanded. You can never get a straight story out of such riffraff.

"Nothing. He had no weapons, no money—nothing."

"Did he talk?"

Raht had begun to cry again, sort of dry, choking sobs. Then he said, "I think Terb must have been too cold to fight."

What a way to try to pry money out of somebody for an overcoat! Believe me, I kicked Raht out right then.

He got to the elevator and was supporting himself against a piece of wall, head down, shivering and sobbing. I slammed my door. I had more important things to think about.

Had Terb talked?

Very likely.

I better stay very close inside. I better keep this gun on me day and night.

Leave it to those two to foul everything up!

Suddenly, I remembered Silva had impersonated the wife of the Director of the CIA, had kidnapped her and hung the murder on her. Utanc!

I got brave enough to cross the sitting room. I pounded on her door. After a long time, she opened it.

"Don't go out. Keep your door locked. Don't let anybody in!"

"Why?" she said in alarm.

"Silva. You remember Silva. The man you hired as a bodyguard once. He murdered the Director of the CIA and now he may be gunning for me."

"He did?" said Utanc, eyes flying wide. Then, "Are you sure?"

She needed convincing. It was still there on the sofa, slid behind a cushion: the I.D. of the Director of CIA. I scooped it up and thrust it at her, bloodstains and all.

Her mouth was open in astonishment as she stared at it. Then she said, "You paid him to do it?"

"And tried to get the money back. He may be around any corner. Don't go out!"

Psychologists will tell you that murder and blood do strange things to women. Death stimulates them sexually.

She suddenly grabbed me and kissed me!

Then she raced around and closed all drapes so the room was dark as pitch.

She threw me on the bed and was all over me!

We didn't go out that day.

Her mouth was hot as fire!

Chapter 7

After two days of such isolation—and very rewarding isolation it was—I was feeling pretty cocky.

Because there had been nothing and no one strange in our vicinity, I had to conclude that it was possible that Terb had not talked.

I decided it might be possible to venture out cautiously. Besides, forty-eight hours of uninterrupted bed with Utanc was actually making me weak. At breakfast, I found that lifting a spoonful of ice cream required considerable effort.

Besides, she had left the table and gone into her room and locked the door and had now come back and was standing there fully dressed in a mink coat, mink snowboots, mink hat, and was drawing on mink gloves.

There was just a trace of irritation in her voice. "I was looking through my clothes just now," she said, "and found I don't have a thing to wear. It has finally stopped snowing and there's a sale on at Tiffany's."

"They sell jewelry," I said.

"I know. So ta-ta."

"Wait!" I said. "Be careful of the money!"

With some asperity, she seized her mink purse, opened it and showed me. It was stuffed with money! What a manager! She turned to leave.

"Wait," I said. "One more thing!" I weakly stumbled to a bureau and got out an old Remington Double Derringer with pearl handles. It was small, weighing only eleven ounces. I made sure it was loaded with its .41 caliber rimfire shorts. "You better take this."

She recoiled. "Oh, dear me, no! I am absolutely terrified of guns! I might shoot myself by accident!"

Oh, well, little wild desert thing that she was, naturally she was too shy to shoot anybody.

Around 1:00, after another sleep, I got energy enough gathered up to get dressed and go out myself. What prompted me was the state of my exchequer. There must be only about $38,000 left under the mattress.

Looking around corners first and keeping the Smith and Wesson .44 Magnum in my hand in my overcoat pocket, I made my way through the snowy streets to Rockecenter Plaza. It was time to draw my pay as a family "spi."

Soon, I was standing at my destination:

Window 13
Petty Cash

There was a new girl there. Well, I guess you could call her a girl. She had a man's haircut and a man's suit on and a thin, hard slit for a mouth.

"Where," I said, uncertainly, "is Miss . . . Miss . . . ?"

"Miss Grabball finished her twenty-five years yesterday and retired to a villa in Monte Carlo. I am Miss Pinch. Who the hell are you?"

"Inkswitch," I said, tendering the Federal I.D.

She looked at her thick book of employees. "You aren't listed here, buster."

"If you will just punch the computer," I said helpfully.

She did. It came up blank.

"Beat it," she said.

"Wait," I said. "You know what it means when it comes up blank."

"It means I call the cops. But I'm in a good mood today. Get out of here before I pull the trigger on this under-the-counter riot gun. I been dying to see how it works."

Naturally, I left. I went to see the personnel director.

"Miss Pinch? New personnel," he said. "They always give trouble." And he left for his afternoon coffee break.

I went to Bury's office.

It was locked.

I went home.

Well, at least Silva hadn't shot me.

For a little while I toyed with the idea of robbing a bank. It seemed to be pretty easy to do and certainly something had to be done to recoup my dwindling fortune. That hundred thousand really hurt.

Thinking Raht might know something about robbing banks, I phoned the New York office.

"Raht?" said the receptionist. "He's been in the Metropolitan Hospital for two days with pneumonia." More vacation! My Gods, how could you work with such riffraff!

But the day ended with some good laughs. They had a comedy show and who was on it but the bogus Whiz Kid, buckteeth and all!

The show was called "The Benighted Show" and the interviewer was Donny Fartson, Junior. The show had run on prime time for decades and the son had taken over from the father.

The phoney Whiz Kid sat there and bragged and bragged about what a great student he was and how smart he was and how he was top of his class. And in a stroke of genius he had invented this fuel in the university laboratories and now he had come out of hiding to tell all and the Octopus Oil Company was against him. And then he did a little dance, waving a college flag.

And then the interviewer asked him, "If you're the top of your college class, maybe you can answer this one. Why was New York called the 'Big Apple'?"

The Whiz Kid double-grinned, his buckteeth especially prominent, and said, "Because it's full of worms!"

The audience laughed and laughed and the Whiz Kid took a couple bows.

At that moment I had a twinge of worry. They hadn't thrown any rotten eggs at him! They had laughed at him, yes. But at the end, the audience even seemed sympathetic! I didn't want this sort of thing getting out of hand. I didn't want them thinking he was a brilliant student. I called 42 Mess Street. The phone was busy, busy, busy.

Well, I hoped Madison would handle it.

I went to bed to recoup my energies.

Chapter 8

And I had been right not to worry!
The very next morning, Madison had his front page!

WHIZ KID
FALSIFIES COLLEGE

FAKE STUDENT

Last night, when the Whiz Kid appeared on the nationwide prime-time Benighted Show, he alleged that he was a top student of the leading engineering university of the country.

He also alleged that Octopus Oil was behind his recent troubles.

Investigative reporters at once swarmed to the campus of the Massachusetts Institute of Wrectology.

The Whiz Kid is not and never has been enrolled there!

No student in the engineering school had ever heard of him, no professor had him on any roll book.

The President of M.I.W., in a public statement, said, "This is a deliberate fabrication. I will not have the name of this noble and

---

> honored institution dragged through the pub-
> lic scrap heap! It is an obvious effort to trade
> upon the lofty and divine right of universities.
> If we had more appropriations from the CIA
> we would be better equipped to handle mon-
> strous cabals of this sort!"

There was more. And it was in every paper and on radio and TV. I was filled with awe.

It was a type of assassination I had not been familiar with. And it was all the more deadly because the assassin seemed so general and it was all within the allowed law! And it could be done to anybody!

I tried to call Madison to congratulate him but all his phones were busy.

Ah, well, Madison was doing fine so I wondered if there was any reaction from Heller. His plans were being so undermined, he must be utterly wild. I resorted to the viewer.

He was certainly taking his time getting to the office. It was a bitterly cold, windless day and every oil- and coal-burning furnace in the city was adding so much smoke and smog that one's eyes watered. Instead of just observing that, Heller was going along measuring it with an atmosphere densimeter, a Voltar instrument being used right out there in the street! It would have been a Code break except that New Yorkers never notice anything, (bleep) them.

At length he reached his floor in the Empire State Building and en route to his own palatial layout noticed that the door to Multinational was ajar. That was where Izzy slept in his mop closet.

Heller went in.

He stopped suddenly.

Right there on the giant screen of Izzy's business computer, a spelled-out sign!

In green electronic-type letters, it said:

GOOD-BYE CRUEL WORLD!

Heller dropped whatever he was carrying. He rushed to the elevator area that served his floor and, like lightning, pushed every one of the call buttons urgently, both up and down.

One after the other they stopped.

He urgently asked each operator, "Have you seen Mr. Epstein? The little fellow with the big nose and big glasses?"

He hit it with the third one.

"He went up about five minutes ago," said the young man. "Then he found you couldn't get to the Observation Platform in this car and he had me take him all the way down."

"Forget these passengers," said Heller. "It's life and death. Take me all the way down instantly!"

The operator did that. "He seemed awful confused, Mr. Jet," he said as they rocketed downwards with the other passengers protesting.

Heller was out and over to the express elevator on 34th Street at speed. He was up to the 80th floor in less than a minute. He switched to the elevator to the 86th floor. The sign said:

Visibility Poor Today

There wasn't any traffic to the 86th floor.

He stepped out into the area of the snack bar and souvenir stand. Only the clerks.

He rushed out onto the Observation Platform. He ran along the high fence which encloses it and prevents suicides. He was looking down. It made me dizzy.

Then he saw a hand. It was gripping the bottom leg of a firmly embedded chair over by the door, well away from the edge.

Heller looked over the top of the seat. There was Izzy. He was hugging the platform pavement, gripping the bottom leg. He was at least twenty feet from the edge!

"Izzy!" said Heller. "Get up!"

"No. Height makes me so dizzy I can't walk! I can't let go. I came up here to throw myself off but now I can't let go of this chair!"

"What's happened?" said Heller.

"All this bad publicity on you triggered it," wailed Izzy. "That student story this morning was the last straw! My back is broke. I can't be responsible for you anymore!"

"Oh, come now," said Heller, "that's been going on for some time. There must be something else."

Izzy began to weep. "I don't even deserve your scolding me. And you should. I have been so flustered and nervous with all this press that I have been making business mistakes."

Heller knelt down by him and put a hand on him as though holding him from slipping.

It made Izzy wail all the harder. "You shouldn't be nice to me! I've *ruined* us." He choked and gasped for a bit. Then he said, all in a rush, "We were about to owe a fortune in income tax. There was an old, old company that was so deep in debt nobody would touch it: even the government and unions had abandoned it, years ago. The Chryster Motor Corporation. I couldn't resist it. It would have furnished us with debt for years and years!"

Heller put a second hand on him as though he might slide horizontal twenty feet. "Well, that doesn't sound so incompetent, Izzy."

"It wasn't," said Izzy. And then he wailed, "But right away I did the most stupid thing! I fired the board of directors and I put my mother in charge of it and it started making money! For the first time since 1968!"

"But that's good news," said Heller.

"Oh, no it isn't!" cried Izzy. "Right away, IRS made a retroactive ruling and invented taxes for it, overdue and compounded with fines and penalties clear back to 1967! They've impounded all our bank accounts even in corporations that aren't interlocked! We're ruined!"

"How ruined?" said Heller.

"We need over a million and a half to free our bank accounts. We can't pay our staff or rent. We don't even have money to start exchange arbitrage again. Throw me over the fence. You'll be better off without me. I'll close my eyes."

Heller pried his fingers loose from the leg of the seat with some difficulty. Izzy had his eyes tightly closed. Heller picked him up.

"Oh, thank you, thank you," said Izzy. He obviously thought Heller was going to throw him over the high fence.

But Heller carried him into the area with the souvenir stand and snack bar and pushed an elevator button. Izzy tentatively opened his eyes and saw he was no longer on the platform and began to sob anew.

Heller carried him down in the elevators and then up again to their floor. He went on through to his office, opened it and put Izzy in a chair.

Heller went to a safe and got out the black garbage bag. He began to empty wallets and pile wads of notes in Izzy's lap.

The heap grew. Mostly thousand-dollar bills. Izzy was holding them up to the light, checking them.

Suddenly Izzy began to count them with the expert motions of a bank teller.

"One hundred and one thousand, two hundred and five!" said Izzy.

"Tax free," said Heller. "Now, will that let you start arbitrage exchange again?"

"Oh, yes! How did you do this?"

"And you can begin to pay the rent and payroll?"

"Oh, yes. The pound is out the bottom in Singapore and high in New York. But . . ."

"There's a string," said Heller. "Promise me not to go near that Observation Platform again."

"Oh, I won't. The wind hurts my sinuses!"

"And one more thing," said Heller. "I have now saved your life twice so you are doubly responsible for me."

"Oh, no!" said Izzy with a wail. "Not with all that bad publicity!"

Heller reached for the money.

"I PROMISE TO BE DOUBLY RESPONSIBLE FOR YOU!" shouted Izzy. And he ran with speed for the telex room, probably to get away before Heller thought of anything else.

Well, I ruminated, they were still in business. But they owed a million and a half and IRS had a way with it, being run as it was to keep Rockecenter rich and everybody else poor, especially potential competition. Hadn't I heard that in 1905, Rockecenter's great-grandfather had been the one who financed and pushed and hammered Congress to amend the Constitution and put income tax into law? And when it happened in 1911, that the family fortune was so organized that only it survived when those of all competitors were swept away? Cunning people, the Rockecenters, no matter that the current scion was insane. Here was IRS working for them still. Izzy didn't have a prayer of getting hold of a million and a half! A half he might make. But a million and a half, never. Not with just arbitrage, not with all his current expenses. Not even Izzy.

It was a relief. For Izzy's Chryster Motor Corporation would have been a potential competitor of Rockecenter interests. Izzy might pull the wool over Heller's eyes. But he couldn't fool me. He had obviously bought old, rickety, mostly defunct Chryster to build and install Heller's carburetors! One more crazy Izzy dream gone to pot.

But it was the media thing that really intrigued me. Rockecenter had that down, too.

And Heller? He really had no idea of what was happening to him or who was doing it. During the rescue of Izzy, his hands had gotten pretty dirty on the Observatory Platform and there he stood looking closely at the soot. He just had no idea at all of the really important things that were going on!

Chapter 9

About 9:45, Heller's day was given another jolt. He had been listening to speeded-up Italian-language tapes he had probably gotten from the language school down the hall and was just doing a replay of how to pronounce numerous Italian saints when Bang-Bang came bursting in.

"Right away, right now, Babe ordered you brought in. Come on!"

Heller said, *"Santa Margherita."*

"Do you no good to pray. She sounded quite put out. (Bleeped) mad, in fact. Come along."

Heller got into a white sheepskin coat, buckled its belt and put on a white leather cap with earmuffs. Pulling on white gauntlets he followed Bang-Bang.

They went down the elevator and over to the 34th Street Observatory entrance which Bang-Bang usually used due to the large taxi stand there, apparently. It was Heller's usual route out when he had to take a cab. He started to signal one.

"Hell, no," said Bang-Bang, pointing to the old orange cab. "I'm driving you!"

"Won't that take you out of your parole jurisdiction?" said Heller, but he got in.

Bang-Bang two-wheeled the cab into a screaming U-turn and rocketed it westward. He was bashing other traffic out of his way and felt comfortable enough now to talk, evidently. He yelled back, "Babe ain't in Jersey today. The family just acquired the old

Punard Steamship Line through a merger with our Luverback Line. And Babe cleaned house of their lords and sirs and ex–Royal Navy captains, the ones that put the Punard Line on the bottom. She always okays top brass. So she's over here today passing on the hiring of new ones."

"She say what she wanted?" said Heller.

"No. She just said to fetch you. Hell, she ought to be happy as a lark today. The family controls the unions and with this last merger of shipping companies, she now controls all seaborne carriers in America. There ain't a single U.S. port she couldn't close down so fast it would make even the fish blink. You wouldn't think anybody could run a little rum-running fleet up to such a point but she has. Organized crime made it in spite of hell. The Feds don't even dare breathe on us now—America could be paralyzed. Even Faustino can't object to her being on this side of the river today. And she's down there hiring some of the biggest names in shipping like they was gofers. And is she happy? No!"

"What makes you think that?" said Heller.

"She (bleep) near exploded my ear is what makes me think that. But she ain't been the same since Jimmy "The Gutter" got wasted by that God (bleeped) Gunsalmo Silva. So you watch it, Jet. Be awful polite. Say 'sir' even if you ain't spoken to.""

They got over to Twelfth Avenue and up on the West Side Elevated Highway and Bang-Bang nose-dived the cab down a ramp.

It was the old Passenger Ship Terminals, long since fallen into disuse with the monopoly of aircraft on people-carrying. A faded sign, Punard Line, had a bright new banner across it, EXECUTIVE UNION HIRING HALL, Local 205.

What with drays and limousines and swarms of seafaring-type people, Bang-Bang had to do quite a bit of nudging to get them into the terminal.

It was a vast place, like a warehouse, in an advanced state of decay. Bang-Bang drove the cab over the stanchions of a no-parking restricted zone and came to the foot of some stairs.

Two men, one on either side of the cab, materialized. They were tough-looking men: overcoat collars turned up and slouch hats turned down. They both shoved riot shotguns into the cab, one at Heller, one at Bang-Bang.

"Whatcha want?" said one. "Oh, hell, it's you, Bang-Bang."

"And the kid," said the other one, stepping back. "Don't scare us that way. At least give us the lights signal. Doncha know the *capa* is over here today?"

"It's all right," yelled the first one up toward the the mezzanine above them. "It's Bang-Bang and the kid."

Three men up there lowered their assault rifles.

Heller and Bang-Bang trotted up a flight of rickety stairs and walked along a sort of balcony that overlooked the mob and cars below. There were three lines of men formed and inching along past three desks. Half a dozen men in black overcoats and slouch hats were sitting at the desks, doing fast interviews. The desks had three signs: DIRECTORS, SHIP OFFICERS and EXECUTIVES. A lot of uniformed security police stood about, directing the foot and vehicle traffic. A busy scene.

Bang-Bang and Heller got to a point on the mezzanine which was above and just back of the interview desks on the floor below. It was glass enclosed.

And there sat Babe Corleone. She was dressed in a full-length, silver-fox coat and a cylindrical, silver-fox cap. She wore white silk boots and white silk gloves. She was seated in a big chair, intent and imperious. She had four bodyguards and three clerks near to hand. In front of her was a row of screens, closed-circuit viewers and computers, placed low so she could see over them and observe who was at the desks. The speakers near her were carrying whatever went on at the desks.

She didn't look up from her work. She pointed at a spot a few feet to her left. "You stand right there, Jerome Terrance Wister," she said to Heller, using his Earth name. It was ominous.

The screens were carrying views of the application forms on the desks and, from some data bank somewhere, records of the people themselves and a close view of the applicant's face.

Curiously, there was only one screen on each of the desks below and even more curiously, each of those had only one scene: it was Babe Corleone's right hand!

She would scan the applicant form, look at the face of the applicant and then glance at the record viewscreen where the clerk had the fellow's real record. Finally she would either turn her thumb up—in which case they would hand the applicant a blue *Hired* slip—or she would turn her thumb down—in which case the applicant would be handed a red slip with *No dice* on it.

One of the clerks near her was keeping a big board and checking off positions as fast as they were filled.

The personnel selection was progressing with surprising speed.

It was interesting that some of the people she was hiring had criminal records.

The lines moved. Her thumb went up and her thumb went down. All of a sudden her hand went horizontal and flat. She was staring at the screen.

On the administrative-position application desk was the form of J. P. FLAGRANT!

Yes, there he was, down on the floor, standing there, looking pretty deflated, the Rockecenter PR man that was fired when we found and hired Madison.

The job being applied for was Punard Line Advertising Executive. The application form simply said Former employer: F.F.B.O. But the data bank record said Account Executive, Rockecenter Accounts. I. G. Barben.

Babe hissed something into a mike. It went to the earplug of the man at the desk below. A speaker went live on the mezzanine.

"I was fired," said Flagrant. "I will be honest with you. I hated the job. I hated Rockecenter interests. If you hire me you will do yourself a good day's work. I can even help you do Faustino in! I'll swear it as big as a billboard!"

Babe's hand did another movement. The thumb was sideways!

Two men in black overcoats instantly grabbed Flagrant, one on each arm. They marched him out through a warehouse door. The winter wind off the Hudson hit them.

They marched him right over to the edge of the dock and threw him in the water! In the dead of winter, they threw him in the river!

"Traditore!" spat Babe. "I hate a traitor!" When she had said *traditore,* which is Italian for "traitor," it sounded like a bullet!

Babe pointed a finger at a clerk. He picked up a microphone and threw a switch. He said in a cultured voice, "Gentlemen, may I have your attention, please?" It went booming hollowly from metallic speakers the length and breadth of the vast pier warehouse, battering the thousands who milled about or stood in lines. "We are very grateful, on this cold day, that you have come to apply for employment with the newly resurrected Punard Line. What we most cherish is loyalty. The gentleman who was just thrown in the river was once employed by persons antipathetic to those who now own the company. If there are any others of such ilk, they can save themselves the inconvenience of a ducking by leaving quietly now."

Three men moved away from different parts of the line.

They were grabbed instantly.

Men in black overcoats and slouch hats bore them struggling to the dock edge and threw them into the icy water with resounding splashes.

A fourth man suddenly rushed out of the line and of his own accord, dived overboard!

The clerk with the microphone said, "Now that we have gotten rid of those dirty (bleepards), executive hiring may proceed. Thank you, gentlemen, for your loyal support of the new management."

There was a faint cheer.

The lines began to move once more.

Heller was watching the water. A fish boat was pulling Flagrant and the others aboard.

Heller was once more watching Babe.

Her wrist got tired. She stopped the lines with a flat palm. Then she extended her hand and a man rushed up and put a glass of blood-red wine in it.

She turned and looked at Heller, her expression as cold as the wintry river. She fixed him with her gray eyes.

Frostily, she said, "You lost the race." She let that sink in. "I have told you and told you, Jerome, you must not lose. It is a bad habit, Jerome. It is a habit that must not be tolerated! I know I have been neglectful. I know I have not always been a good mother to you. But that doesn't make any difference at all, Jerome."

"I'm sorry, Mrs. Corleone."

"And the newspapers are saying bad things about you, Jerome."

"I'm sorry, Mrs. Corleone. I don't know where it is all coming from. I . . ."

"Newspapers are very bad things, Jerome. You must not go out carousing with reporters. It will ruin your reputation. You must be very careful of the people you associate with. You must not consort with criminal types like reporters. Do you understand me, Jerome?"

"Yes, Mrs. Corleone. I am very sorry. . . ."

"Stop interrupting me and don't try to change the subject. You do not have a single, valid excuse! You have been a very, very naughty boy, Jerome. I am very, very provoked. First you lose a perfectly simple race. And then you spread yourself all over the press. And you not only are ruining all your future but," and here her voice rose in pitch and volume, "the mayor's wife was on the phone to me for half an hour this morning saying the most awful things! And all about you and your bad publicity!"

She threw the glass and red wine down with violence! It shattered and splattered like blood!

Her voice made the room shake!

"THIS IS THE LAST TIME I WILL WARN YOU! KNOCK OFF THIS GOD (BLEEPED) BAD PUBLICITY!"

She turned back to her screens.

Bang-Bang must have detected a sign Heller didn't see. "You better come along," he whispered in Heller's ear. "If you stay any longer, she's liable to get upset."

They withdrew and got back into the cab. Bang-Bang ran into a couple more no-parking stanchions and they got out of there.

Heller was sitting in back, chin on his chest. Finally, he said through the partition, "I can't do anything about the publicity. But I can try something else. Bang-Bang, what does Babe really like?"

"Babe? Why, hell, just like all dames, she goes for jewelry."

"You sure?" said Heller.

"Absolutely. Couple diamonds and they purr."

"Good," said Heller. "Take me to Tiffany's."

Across town they went and very shortly Heller was standing in front of a counter being addressed by a courteous clerk. Heller looked at all kinds of things, trays and trays of jewelry on black velvet. He didn't like any of them. Suddenly he snapped his fingers with the force of inspiration. "Do you make jewelry to customer design? I want something more sentimental."

"Of course," said the clerk. "Follow me." And he left Heller with an artistic type in a design department. The artistic type thought he would need some help drawing. But Heller grabbed art paper and colored pens and went to work.

What in Hells? He was drawing the Sovereign Shield of his Voltarian home, the Province of Atalanta, Manco! Two crossed blastguns, firing green against a white sky, circled in red flame. Incidentally, I had seen him draw it before under the words *Prince Caucalsia* on the tug he flew to Earth. More sentimentality? Crossed blastguns? What was he up to?

In response to his questions, the designer said, "Yes, we can make it into a tiara. The shield will be on the front of the head, of course, gripped in place by the semi-coronet. We can make the field in diamonds, the guns in onyx, the blasts, as you call them, in emeralds and the flame circle in rubies. And set it all in white gold, of course, so it will not clash."

"How much?" said Heller.

They called in some others and after calculation, they could do it for $65,000.

Heller dug into his pockets. He only had $12,000 on him. "This is all I've got just now," he said.

"It will be ample as a deposit," they told him. "You can pay the balance when it is done."

"When will that be?"

"The Christmas season is coming on. We are quite busy already. Will a few weeks be all right?"

He gave them the $12,000. But I could see he was a bit defeated. I hadn't realized that Heller himself was going broke. He told them to do the best they could and left.

I was jubilant. Izzy would soak up his cash. He'd never be able to pick that tiara up.

I hugged myself. The real jewel was Madison!

The publicity was having its effect. Not only was it assassinating Heller's character but was also stripping him of support from his friends. It was worth thinking about. As a direct knife and gun devotee, I was really getting my eyes pried open with what could be done with the media! And how marvelously painful! One could wreck lives just like that!

Little did I know that I had really seen nothing yet!

PART THIRTY-ONE

Chapter 1

I wished I could hold on longer to these manic states, they are so pleasant. But that very night, the depressive began to raise its ugly head.

I was running the TV channels looking for some good animated cartoons and I just happened to pass the program "59 1/2 Minutes Too Late." And there on the screen was the Whiz Kid in the presence of Mike Mallice!

He had a little college beanie on his head and was holding a little pennant on a stick. He had stacks of books and you could hardly see the interviewer back of them.

The bogus Whiz Kid was telling the story of his life: how he had been lying in a crib, choking on his bottle, and had gotten this marvelous idea for a new fuel. But years of underprivileged decadence as a member of the white minority had deprived him of reaching toward his goal. And then one day in a supermarket, while he was riding in a shopping cart, a book had fallen off the book rack and hit him in the head and it had changed his life.

He had the book right there to prove it and the TV cameras shifted to his reverent hands as he opened it. It was by Carl Fagin, a reprint of a reprint, entitled *Homecraft Series: You Too Can Make an Atom Bomb in Your Own Little Basement Workshop, or, A Visit to Graves of the Mighty Men of History.* And there was a picture of Albert Blindstein. And the shaggy hair that had inspired him.

And then he showed a newspaper clipping of the remains of his basement workshop which had blown up and flattened nearby houses.

The canned applause resounded.

And here was a picture of his winning the soapbox derby by getting the daughter of a neighbor to ride inside the front of the soapbox and pedal on a secretly connected sprocket.

The canned applause resounded.

I thought, wait a minute, what is this doing on prime-time national? It was not nearly as good as the usual sex orgies on the rival channels. And then I remembered that all the Rockecenter people had to do was call the director of the TV network and tell him what to run.

But then the bomb burst!

The Whiz Kid pulled out a high-school yearbook and there he was in the fifth row of the choir! Buckteeth and all!

Worse!

A picture in the same yearbook: The Student Most Likely to Get Shot. Buckteeth and all!

Much worse!

Another yearbook. Picture of the freshman class. A circle drawn around a head with buckteeth in the third row.

Very much worse!

Another yearbook. A picture of the sophomore class and, although much marred by the printing screen, the buckteeth and horn-rimmed glasses were unmistakable!

The hands turned the book over.

Yearbook: Massachusetts Institute of Wrectology of just last June!

And there was his name on the cover: Gerry Wister!

It left me in a complete spin! So much so that I didn't even hear the rest of the program!

Something was going wrong!

An hour later, my search for cartoons utterly abandoned, I remembered that Bury had chosen Heller's identity and given it to him in the Brewster Hotel. Bury had ordered Madison to use this bucktoothed double and no other and that Madison had even had to make Heller up.

There was another Wister! A *Gerry* Wister, probably a cousin or some such to a Jerome Terrance Wister who may or may not ever have existed.

This clever Wall Street lawyer, Bury, had covered every trick! If snipers didn't work, there were bombs. If bombs didn't work, there were doubles!

But I still didn't get the full horror of it until, with shaking fingers, I opened the paper beside my breakfast plate. Hotels sure know how to ruin your appetite!

Front page!

WHIZ KID SUES M.I.W. FOR 500 MILLION!

FIRST SUIT IN UNIVERSITY HISTORY

Alleging that he actually was a student at M.I.W., the attorneys of the Whiz Kid—Boggle, Gouge and Hound—today filed suit against the university for 500 million dollars for defamation of fame with compounded mortal felony.

A stunned nation last night on the prime-time program "59 1/2 Minutes Too Late" beheld the evidence itself.

Never before have the sacred precincts of M.I.W. been breached by the slightest breath of scandal.

A spokesman at Boggle, Gouge and Hound said, "We'll win in a walk. The honor of American youth must be upheld against the denigrating connivings of the pillars of learning. This is a landmark case. We will murder the bums."

The president of M.I.W., who was not called, could not be reached for comment.

In frantic search for opinion, this paper

called Supreme Court Chief Justice Hamburger. He stated, "In an unofficial opinion, off the record, justice must always get its just desserts. If called on to review the case, we will consider anything in writing."

(See page 34 for on-the-scene, exclusive riot photos of M.I.W.)

I would have rushed down to get the other papers but I didn't have to. The news vendor, accustomed to my habits by now, had them piled three feet high on a cart. Just as I feared! National coverage!

This Madison was making me nervous. You understand, my faith was not really shattered, it was just wobbled a bit. I realized that it was the size of the suit and that it was the first time anyone had ever dared sue the mighty M.I.W. that was making the news, and I hoped the Whiz Kid would sort of get eclipsed in this.

I would let Madison have his head. Probably some deep-seated strategy lay behind this.

However, the following morning Madison had his front page again!

M.I.W. FIGHTS BACK!

WHIZ KID BLASTED!

In an exclusive interview with the president of M.I.W., this paper was entrusted with an exclusive message for the Whiz Kid.

"If," said the president, "Gerry Wister does not drop this suit at once, he will be expelled! Furthermore, we will cancel his Octopus Oil Company Scholarship and fire him from his job as waiter in the college restaurant."

These strong words were uttered with

great force. The university means to fight!

The university attorneys—Fuddle, Muddle and Puddle—today filed countermotions in the state court, alleging that the accusations of the said Gerry Wister were false, malicious and unfounded on fact.

(See Photo Section page 19 for full coverage of M.I.W. riots.)

There were TV shots of the riots in most of the news hours. There was also a full-page ad in the papers telling the listening audience to watch "59 1/2 Minutes Too Late" if they wanted to get the news before it happened. They were really crowing over their scoop.

The other papers carried not only the M.I.W.-fights-back story, they also carried editorials on the victimization of American youth in their universities and concluded, by and large, that they ought to be clobbered.

Yes, Madison was coming through. Heller had been dealt another heavy blow, for the press was definitely favoring the universities. They even showed the bodies of some students beaten to death by riot police. A favorable sign.

I might have found even more favorable evidences in my analysis except that that very night, my attention was rudely snapped in another direction.

Chapter 2

I might have missed it entirely if I had not been extraordinarily alert. I knew it was important for me to pick up every possible clue I could about Heller. He had an inkling, I am sure, after Connecticut, that I was out to get him and even though I was not moving around much in New York, I didn't want to run the slightest risk of turning a corner and running into him. In fact, every time I rode anywhere near the Empire State Building or the UN area, I scrunched way down in the cab just in case he happened to be on the street.

Thus, I had been making it a habit to rapid-scan the recorded strips of the viewer lately. Ordinarily, I would not have bothered with the night strips due to that strange electronic interference around his suite, but after Gunsalmo Silva had calmly walked up and knocked on my door, I knew I couldn't be too careful.

It paid off!

I was amazed! Apparently Heller's rescue of Izzy had turned his attention to the Observatory of the Empire State Building. I have never seen a man so interested in soot. Who really cared what happened to the atmosphere of this planet? After Lombar had taken over Voltar, he would make very sure there was no population left on Earth: Lombar had enough riffraff at home without a full, additional planet of it to cause him trouble. Probably at the most he'd put in a little colony in Turkey to keep the opium coming. So who cared about the atmosphere of Earth? Let them choke on their own soot or get wiped out with exterminator sprays—who cared?

Yet Heller had begun a routine. Each night he would leave the Gracious Palms dressed in heavy cleaner's clothes, carrying a bucket and broom, and have Bang-Bang drive him down to the Empire State Building Observatory entrance.

The last car went up at 11:30. He would take it, and with a transfer arrive at the 86th floor.

At that hour the snack bar and souvenir counter would be closed and the place deserted. And who, I suppose, ever stops a cleaner in a New York building?

The snack bar and souvenir counter are housed, with the elevators and staircase, in a structure which stands in the middle of the large platform.

He would go up on the top of this central structure and plant three new wind cones and take the ones left the night before and put them in his bucket.

Although the platform extended out widely all around the central structure and although even the platform edge itself was amply guarded by a ten- or twelve-foot wrought-iron fence, the sight of him teetering around up there, fixing those cones to catch the wind, made me quite giddy.

The area had considerable light, coming up as it did from the city down below and all about and from the aircraft-warning and other lights on the higher tower. But to watch him fiddling with wind cones on those buttresses was a lot more than I could stand.

He was catching soot specimens or spores or something. He was probably analyzing them minutely and making all sorts of valuable conclusions, no doubt, but in my opinion it was just plain silly. Crazy as he was on the subject of height, it was probably recreation.

So tonight, I almost didn't look at the viewer when the time came. But some keen sense that is bred into you in the Apparatus told me that before I went to sleep, I better make sure he was up there again and not knocking on my door.

Yes, he was up there.

He put the old cones in his bucket and put some new ones in place and climbed down to the platform.

And then it happened!

Heller was just about to walk down the stairs when an old lady rushed up to him!

She had a huge purse on a strap over her shoulder. She was dressed all in black. She had on a black hat and was wearing a black veil.

"Oh, young man, young man!" she cried in a high falsetto voice. "You must help me! My cat! My cat!" and broke off sobbing.

I went into instant shock. Falsetto or no falsetto, I knew that voice.

GUNSALMO SILVA!

He had used a woman's guise to murder the Director of the CIA and here he was repeating the trick.

It was HELLER who was the million-dollar contract nobody else would take!

Who had offered it? Not Bury: Madison was doing a great job and Bury wasn't even in town!

I sat there suffering. I did not yet have Heller's platen; I could not forge his reports to Captain Tars Roke back on Voltar. And Silva with his Apparatus training would make short work of Heller! After all, hadn't Silva wasted the impossible target—the Director of the CIA—plus two Russians, a dictator and Jimmy "The Gutter" Tavilnasty? And for that matter, hadn't he even wasted Babe's husband, the *capo*, "Holy Joe" Corleone? Oh, Heller was a dead duck!

There is a very heavy liability to being a gentleman. That's why I never was one. For Heller, the gentleman, the perfect Fleet officer, was patting the "old lady" on the back, saying, "There, there. What about your cat?"

Blubbering brokenly, the "old lady" was pointing as she sobbed. Then, tottering along, she led the way to the extreme other end of the platform, pointing up.

Sure enough! There was a cat there!

It was white and orange and black. It had on a small red harness. And it was hanging by the harness from the top of the ten-foot, open wrought-iron fence! The rods curved in at that height and the cat was outside the fence!

The cat was meowing pitifully as it dangled over eighty-six stories worth of empty space.

"It jumped," falsettoed Silva. "It got frightened and it jumped!"

To get to it, one would have to climb the three-foot concrete parapet and then seven or eight feet of spaced wrought iron and then go over the inward bulge and reach down outside.

Silva had obviously been tailing Heller and under other guises had learned of this silly habit of climbing things. Exactly how he was going to do this hit, I could not even guess. To leave bullets in a body makes people suspicious.

Heller looked up at the yowling cat. Then he backed about twenty feet from the fence toward the central snack bar and souvenir outside wall. There was a seat there and beside the seat were two suitcases.

He looked at the "old lady" and then at the huge purse. Some balls of yarn were sticking out of the top of the purse.

"Sit down here," said Heller and the "old lady" sat down, sobbing away.

Heller sat down beside her. "I don't have any rope. I need something to drop a loop over the cat from the top of the fence. Otherwise it might leap again."

He reached for the yarn and began, with rapid hand motions, to make a rope by weaving it. "A cat's cradle is what we need," he said. And he was quickly making one.

I vividly remembered Bury's warning about being kind. Here was an awful example. Heller was sitting next to death, complete even to widow's weeds!

The night winds blew. The lights of New York rose upward with a blue fatality.

Heller wove the cat's cradle.

The "old lady" sobbed.

Finally Heller was through. He had a very open basket on a long cord.

"Everything will be all right in just a moment now," he said.

"Oh, I hope so," falsettoed Silva.

Heller went over and stepped up on the parapet. He nimbly went up the inside of the fence. He moved over the top bulge.

With a deft cast he dropped the basket below the cat and pulled up. The cat's legs extended through the open weave but it was securely meshed. He drew it up.

Some sound must have caught his ear above the wind. Teetering on top of the fence, he turned his head and looked.

Silva was just that moment ten feet away, laying something down upon the pavement!

Heller saw what it was. "A Voltar concussion grenade?"

I recognized it at the same instant. It was one of those I had given Terb! It would make a fantastic concussion blast without a single fragment. It would blow Heller off that fence and into the depths eighty-six stories below.

Silva's hand left the grenade.

"And one," whispered Heller. He was going to count!

Silva straightened up.

Heller threw the cat!

"And two," said Heller.

The cat hit Silva in the face!

It was screeching and clawing!

Obviously Silva had meant to withdraw behind the barricade of suitcases and chair to escape the concussion. Beating at the cat, trying to get it off of him, he backed up!

"And four," said Heller. I realized he knew that that grenade had a fifteen-second lag!

Down came Heller off the fence and onto the platform!

Silva was still fighting the cat. But with one hand he was reaching into his purse.

Out came my Colt Bulldog!

The cat was still on him, screeching like a nightmare.

Heller was swiftly circling. "And seven."

Silva himself was howling now, shouting obscenities! He began to hit at the cat with the purse!

The cradle burst!

The cat leaped away and fled toward the souvenir stand's open door.

Maddened with pain, Silva heaved the purse after the cat!

Silva crouched into a deadly pose, the Colt Bulldog pointing this way and that.

Heller had reached the barricade of the chair and suitcases against the snack-bar wall.

"And ten," said Heller.

He ducked down!

Silva spotted him. He knew better than to rush. He could not count on a lucky shot when he had just the top of a head and eyes as a target.

He backed up.

He got up on the parapet to get height to shoot down.

"And twelve," whispered Heller.

Silva fired!

The bullet thunked into the suitcase in front of Heller.

Silva climbed up higher on the fence!

He fired again!

"And fourteen," said Heller. And at that he ducked very low and all sound went off as he cupped his hands solidly over his ears and stuck his face hard against the suitcase side.

BLOWIE!

The sound even went through his protecting hands.

He looked up.

And there was Silva flying high into the air!

The wind caught the body as it rose, and there went Silva, soaring away over nighttime New York, but mostly down! Heller went over to the fence and looked.

It was only emptiness and blackness below.

He came back to the center. He looked around. There was a slight concavity where the grenade had exploded. Nothing noticeable.

He went over and picked up Silva's huge purse.

There didn't seem to be any other evidence around except the grips.

Heller raised his head to the sky. He said, "I hope you noticed, Jesus Christ, that I didn't have much to do with that. But if I ever happen to wind up in your Heavens by mistake, remember to chalk me up with having saved a cat. Amen."

Chapter 3

Heller threw the purse strap over his shoulder. He put one heavy grip under his left arm and picked up the other with his left hand. He grabbed the bucket and broom in his right and moved through the door and into the souvenir and snack-bar enclosure, kicking the door shut behind him.

The elevator was barred off for the night. He turned to the stairwell and stepped down.

And there was the cat! It had apparently been inside and partway down the stairs when the concussion went off, for it didn't seem disturbed. When Heller went down the steps, the cat followed him.

But the distance from the Observatory to the ground is eighty-six floors. In fact, New Yorkers every year have a race from the bottom to the top, up these 1,860 steps. And Heller must have thought he was racing the other way. Six at a time, he was doing the closest thing to free fall down that stairway.

He got two floors lower. Then he heard a yowl behind him. He stopped and looked back.

The cat was halted on the last landing Heller had left, yowling and looking reproachful.

"Oho," said Heller. "Too fast for you, eh?"

He went back up to the cat, picked him up and put him into the bucket. Heller turned and started catapulting down again. The cat put his paws on the bucket rim and watched the descent with interest.

Heller emerged onto 34th Street. Bang-Bang was there with the old cab. He reached over and opened the door for Heller but his attention was on something way ahead. He said, "They're prying somebody off the sidewalk on the other side of Fifth Avenue. What have you been up to?"

Heller said, "Drive."

Bang-Bang U-turned the cab and rocketed west. He glanced back. "Well, at least tell me what the cat's name is."

"Drive," said Heller.

"Jesus," said Bang-Bang, "ain't nobody talking, not even the cat."

They drove a couple blocks and then the cat started yowling.

Heller said, "Pull over."

"Where?"

"By that delicatessen, of course. Holy blast, Bang-Bang, don't you even talk cat?" Bang-Bang mounted the curb and stopped. Heller said, "Now go in and get some milk." He threw Bang-Bang a bill and then turned on the cab's overhead light.

Heller looked at the cat. It had on a harness but there were no marks on it. He found a string, apparently too tight, around the cat's neck. Heller took out a pair of snips and cut it. The string had a paper tag on it.

He looked at the tag. It said *#7A66 City Pound.* Heller addressed the cat, "Oho, a jailbird, huh? Well, don't worry, we'll just remove the evidence and they can't get you for complicity."

Heller took the purse and spilled the contents on the floor. A jumbled assortment fell out, tangled up in knitting yarn. Heller began to inventory it.

"An obsolete Voltar Fleet grenade. An Apparatus Knife Section knife. Russian rubles. Travelers checks on a Panama bank. Assorted Canadian, Swiss and U.S. passports. A baggage check." He had his hands on packets of money. "And U.S. dollars done up in Turkish bank bands." He sat back. "This is CRAZY!"

Oh, my Gods, I recognized the money. It was *my* $100,000! How cruel fate is! There were the hundred big ones in Heller's hands! I tore at my hair.

Bang-Bang opened the door. "What's all this worry over the cat?"

"He saved my life. I'm responsible for him now."

Bang-Bang had half a pint of cream. He cut off the top of the carton and was putting it on the floor for the cat when he saw the money. "Jesus, Jet. Did the cat give you that?"

Heller said, "He's a very wealthy cat."

"Ain't he kind of young to have all that dough?" He was watching the cat tie into the cream.

Heller snapped open one of the suitcases. It seemed to have some strange things in it. He pulled out something that looked like a close-fitting jump suit. It had a little undetached label:

Proofed to 3600 foot-pounds of impact energy
CIA Test Lab, Langley, Virginia

Heller said, "Mysteriouser and mysteriouser. Items from all over the place: Russia, Panama, Canada, Switzerland and wherever, including Turkey and Washington."

Bang-Bang said, "That's an African-type cat. My aunt had one with the same white, orange and black markings. They're great fighters, supposed to be awful bright for cats. They're called *calicos*. Male calicos are very rare. Oh, yeah, they're also supposed to bring good luck. So anyway," he continued learnedly, "if you've got Russia and Washington and all them, you can add Africa. If that's his purse, I'd say he was a very well-traveled cat."

Heller was opening up passports. They all had the same face in the pictures but different names. He came to the U.S. one. His hands jolted.

GUNSALMO SILVA!

Heller covered up the type with his hands, leaving only the picture showing and turned it to Bang-Bang. "Who is this?"

Bang-Bang's eyes bugged. "Jesus Christ! It's GUNSALMO SILVA!"

Heller looked back at the passport and said, "Thanks. I just wanted to be sure. But Gunsalmo Silva from where, for whom?"

"*Sangue di Cristo!*" said Bang-Bang with awe. "You just rubbed Gunsalmo Silva!"

"The cat did it," said Heller. "He's a hit man. Got a record as long as his tail. Wanted posters in every post office. And he just broke out of the slammer. So don't turn squealer on him: they could send him up for life."

"Gunsalmo Silva," whispered Bang-Bang, still in awe. "Top of the hit parade. Jesus, Jet, that must've been Gunsalmo plastered all over Fifth Avenue! You threw him off the Observation Platform!" he added in sudden comprehension.

"It's my word against the cat's," said Heller. "And he'll take the Fifth. But quit changing the subject, Bang-Bang. This bulletproof suit is too small for me. It looks like it would fit you exactly."

"Wait a minute," said Bang-Bang. "What's coming off here?"

"It isn't what's coming off," said Heller. "It's what's going on. You know that rental costume shop up on West 37th Street in the garment district? Get going."

Bang-Bang did, while the cat, having demolished the cream, climbed up on Heller's lap and with a deep sigh went to sleep.

They halted in front of an old two-story building with a costume shop on the ground floor and, apparently, living quarters on the second. It was well after midnight and the shop was closed and barred.

Heller got out and forcefully pushed a bell behind the iron grate.

A window shot up on the second floor and a bald head jutted out. "Ve iss closed yet! Go avay!"

Heller stepped back. He called, "Won't a hundred-dollar bill open you up?"

"Dot iss a goot key! Down right I'll be yet. Don't noplace go!"

Presently they were in the shop. The proprietor was in a white nightgown and slippers with a black jacket thrown over his shoulders.

Heller handed him a hundred-dollar bill. "I want to look," he said.

"For a hundred dollars business iss so bad you can buy the shop," said the proprietor.

Heller was going through racks of all kinds of costumes. He came to a rack where everything was black. Black dresses, black hats, black veils. He kept looking at them and then back at Bang-Bang, locating a size. He pulled one out.

He handed Bang-Bang the bulletproof suit. "Go in that booth over there and put this on."

Bang-Bang, grumbling, did as he was told.

Then Heller handed him the black dress.

"Oh, no!" said Bang-Bang.

"Oh, yes," said Heller. "It's the latest style."

Bang-Bang furiously wrestled into the dress, muttering, "What I go through!"

Heller now put the hat on him and dropped the veil over his face.

"Oh, my God!" said Bang-Bang, looking at himself in a mirror. "If they ever hear of this at Sardine's, I'll never live it down!"

Heller gave the proprietor another fifty dollars. "We'll bring the costume back."

The man said, "Nein, nein, keep it! We got plenty like dot. Them we furnish for the funerals, yet."

"I hope not mine!" said Bang-Bang.

"Let's go and see," said Heller.

Chapter 4

In the cab, Bang-Bang said, "That cat is having an awful effect on you! Janitors don't ride in cabs and old ladies sure as hell don't drive them!"

"This is G-2 homework," said Heller, in obvious reference to his military class. "We're spies in disguise."

"Oh," said Bang-Bang.

Heller was examining the baggage check. It said:

Midtown Air Terminal
Overnight Baggage Check

He told Bang-Bang where to go exactly. The town was quiet. They reached the entrance Heller had specified and pulled into the covered area where cabs usually stood. There weren't any there. The place was deserted.

Heller put his cap down on the back seat and put the cat on top of it. Heller handed Bang-Bang the baggage check.

"Now, Bang-Bang, we're going to go in separately. When you hear me drop this bucket, you walk up to the overnight baggage counter, present this check, pick up whatever they give you and walk out through the underground passage back to this cab. If I yell 'Pizza,' you duck. Got it?"

"Did you say 'Drop the bucket'? or 'Kick the bucket'?"

"If there's any shooting, let's hope it's somebody else that kicks the bucket."

"I haven't got a rod."

"Neither have I and I didn't notice any in these bags. But I know this place. I am sure you'll be as safe as if you were in your own bed."

"You don't know some of the skirts that get in my bed," said Bang-Bang.

"They always shoot for the body," said Heller.

"Let's hope they know that," said Bang-Bang.

They got out. "Now, cat," said Heller, "you stay there. I don't want you hitting me up for overtime." He closed the door.

Bang-Bang slung the empty purse over his shoulder and entered the long, dark tunnel.

Heller, with his broom and bucket, skipped around to another entrance and shortly emerged on a mezzanine that overlooked the lobby. From it he could see the overnight baggage-check counter below and across the lower floor.

The mezzanine had seats on it. In one of the seats sat a very beefy man in a black overcoat and a black slouch hat. He glanced up as Heller walked along and then resumed his watch on the lobby below.

Heller looked the lobby all over. Only a couple of clerks. No traffic at this time of night.

He dropped the bucket loudly and began to sweep away.

Bang-Bang emerged from the tunnel and mincingly walked over to the overnight baggage counter below.

The man in the black overcoat leaned forward.

Bang-Bang pushed a buzzer on the counter and a sleepy clerk came out of the wire-enclosed interior, yawning and rubbing his eyes.

Bang-Bang handed him the ticket.

Heller swept away at the carpet, ignored by the man on the nearby seat.

The clerk found the item. He got it down from the racks. It was a large, brown suitcase with big metal locks. It seemed heavy. He wanted two dollars and Bang-Bang, with the empty purse, had to hike up his dress, fumble in the pockets of the bulletproof suit for his wallet and get out two one-dollar bills. He made it not very elegantly, but from this vantage place on the mezzanine, the bullet-proof jumper didn't show. Bang-Bang needed a lot of lessons in being an old lady!

The clerk relinquished the suitcase. Bang-Bang got it off the counter at the near cost of a sprained arm. He went tottering off toward the underground-entrance arch.

Black Overcoat was up with a grunt the moment Bang-Bang vanished into the tunnel.

With great speed the man went flying down the mezzanine stairs.

Heller with bucket and broom was not five steps behind him.

Why didn't the fellow look back? Then I realized Heller was running at the exact same cadence as the other. There was only one set of sounds of feet!

Heller was almost breathing down the man's neck!

They crossed the lobby.

Black Overcoat darted into the tunnel.

He had drawn a gun!

Suddenly it came to me that somebody had not meant Gunsalmo Silva to really collect that suitcase! I was watching the standard hit-the-hitter routine in progress!

Or was it? Maybe this was something else?

The doors ahead of Bang-Bang burst open!

Two men dressed like cab drivers rushed in. They were thirty feet in front of Bang-Bang.

Black Overcoat had a big revolver extended toward Bang-Bang.

Heller reached over the big man's shoulder and seized his gun hand. The bucket clattered to the floor.

"Pizza!" shouted Heller.

Bang-Bang dropped the suitcase and dived to the side! Heller's left hand was gripping a neck muscle of the big man. The gun stayed extended.

The two coming in the door dived for the suitcase. One got it. The other was grabbing out a gun.

Heller's hand closed on the big man's gun fist.

The revolver roared!

The one who had been drawing was flung back with a hammer blow!

The big man's revolver fired again!

The one with the suitcase flew forward, dropped it and collapsed.

Heller turned the gun sideways until it pointed at the struggling assassin's head.

BLOWIE!

The hat went sailing with hair in it.

Heller's left hand shifted to the overcoat. He snatched out a wallet from the breast pocket.

He let the big man collapse and only then let go of the gun hand. Black Overcoat's fingers were still wrapped around the weapon. I realized Heller's own hand had never touched it!

Heller scooped up his bucket and broom.

Bang-Bang was picking himself off the floor.

Heller raced ahead and grabbed Bang-Bang by the arm and then, in passing, grabbed the handle of the suitcase.

They sped to the cab.

Heller threw Bang-Bang behind the wheel and the bag, bucket and broom into the back.

"Close that door!" cried Bang-Bang. "We don't want this blamed on the cat!" He slammed the cab into gear with a crash!

There wasn't a soul in sight as Bang-Bang sped out of the terminal.

Chapter 5

In a parking lot and a darkened cab they got Bang-Bang into his regular clothes. Then, burdened with all the baggage and the cat riding in the purse, they struggled through the icy New York night and entered the Empire State Building at the 33rd Street entrance.

A sleepy elevator girl deposited them incuriously at their floor and shortly Heller was knocking sharply at the door of Multinational.

Izzy put an eye to the door. "What's up?"

"We're making you an accessory after the cat," said Bang-Bang. "Come along."

They went to Heller's office, put the baggage down and turned on the lights. The cat began to inspect the place.

Heller laid the new bag over on its side and was reaching for something to pick the locks when Bang-Bang stopped him. "No, no! Jesus, don't you never remember nothing I taught you? Never pick a lock in New York—it might be wired for a bomb! Let me."

Bang-Bang rummaged around in a case of tools and found some wire snips and thin screwdrivers and began to attack the hinges of the new bag.

Heller opened the two original suitcases wide and began to go through their contents.

Izzy came in. He had on a shabby old overcoat and a nightcap and his feet were bare.

Heller was picking up items and reading their tags:

Hydrogen self-inflatable balloon for rapid escapes
Certified CIA Test Lab

Melting spoon: When used to stir
cocktails, introduces deadly poison.
Certified CIA Test Lab

Poison Lipstick
Shade: Charming Carmen
Apply to secretary's lips
and when she kisses boss, imparts
deadly poison that kills instantly.
Certified CIA Test Lab

Suicide Kit: Take two before retiring.
The Surgeon General has determined these
to be hazardous to your health.

"What are you doing?" said Izzy with alarm.

"We're penetrating the most closely held secrets of the CIA," said Heller.

"I can't get these God (bleeped) hinges loose," said Bang-Bang.

Heller reached over to the front locks and gave them a flip. The bag cracked open! Bang-Bang dived for cover.

Izzy didn't. He had already spotted something through the crack. He bent down and pulled the top wide. He said, "Oy!"

MONEY! The bag was jammed tight with U.S. bills of assorted denominations, neatly strapped with bank bands.

Heller picked up the corner of the big suitcase and emptied it on the floor.

A small mountain of MONEY!

Heller examined the bag for internal markings and false bottoms.

But Izzy sat down on the floor. His bare feet started scrubbing against each other. His hands, like talons, began to lock upon packets of money.

In a muttering blur of sound, as fast as the blur of his hands as he stacked it, the pile of packets, neatened, grew beside him. Then he was done.

"Oy," said Izzy. "Give or take miscounts in the packages, this is a MILLION DOLLARS!" He rubbed at his eyes behind his horn-rimmed glasses. He looked at Heller. "How do you do these things?"

Heller fished up my poor, misdirected hundred thousand. He added to it rubles and an extra fistful of currency that had been in the purse. Then he tossed all this on the pile. He said, "I have secret admirers, Izzy. They are terrified I might go on welfare."

"Did you draw this out of the bank? I mean are there any traces on it?"

"Nary a one," said Heller. "A totally untraceable donation."

Izzy was totalling again. "Oy, oy!" he said, "This means we only have $400,000 more to go to clean up IRS!"

Heller reached over. He pulled some packets off the stack. "Make that $410,100, Izzy. Bang-Bang is low on skirts. He was complaining just tonight." He handed $10,000 to Bang-Bang.

Izzy was doing plans and calculations. "I won't pay IRS. I will put it all on the arbitrage line, run it up and then pay those goyim robbers. The Japanese yen is dirt cheap in Singapore tonight and sky-high in Paris! I'll get right on——"

"Wait a minute, wait a minute, Izzy." Heller looked around. The cat had gotten up on his desk and was sitting there eyeing Izzy very intently.

Heller handed Izzy a $100 bill. "Go buy this cat a blanket and a new harness and a dish and things. He hasn't got a decent spacekit."

Izzy took the $100 but he said, "You going to keep a cat here? There aren't any mice."

Heller said, "This is a no-mice cat. He deals with rats, exclusively. He's a very tough hit cat, Izzy. And you'll be very glad to know that I saved his life so now you have somebody to share responsibility for me."

"Oh, thank heavens," said Izzy. "I'll get him a spacekit at once, whatever it is."

Izzy was stuffing money into big plastic bags from the bar. He looked around to see if there was any more and then rushed out.

The cat, apparently having made certain that Izzy would obey, curled up under Heller's desk lamp and went to sleep.

Heller was looking at the wallet he had snapped out of Black Overcoat's pocket. It had some names and I.D. in it. He showed it to Bang-Bang. "Inganno John Scroccone. You know the name, Bang-Bang?"

"No."

Heller looked at it again. "I'm certainly in the I.D. collection business. I've got to find out."

Bang-Bang said, "What really happened up there on the roof tonight?"

"Hush," said Heller. "I promised the cat faithfully I wouldn't turn state's evidence on him. His pawprints are all over the place. So both him and me have got to take the Fifth."

"Oh," said Bang-Bang.

The cat stretched and began to purr.

Chapter 6

The horrible sight of my hundred thousand dollars U.S. in Heller's hand did something even more horrible to my psyche. A psyche is, as all psychologists know, located just above the id and, when overreacted upon, bruises the ego. When these three things are already swollen from past abuses, there ensues what is called the "I'm-going-nuts syndrome." A case of multiple frustrations is likely to ensue, surcharging the blood vessels and precipitating an epileptic fit.

All patients have their own particular remedies. With some, it is yelling at the wife. With others, it is kicking the dog. I thought rapidly: if I did not apply first aid at once, I might find myself in need of psychiatric help. Drunkards often obtain relief by imbibing the hair of a dog that bit them but I had no dog whose hair I might find palatable, much less one to kick. Thus, out of dire necessity, an inspiration was born. I had better look at some money. That, I was sure, would be the soothing balm which would interrupt the threatened epileptic fit.

Accordingly, with shaking hands, I went to my mattress and reached within. Some days ago, when Silva had come, thirty thousand bucks had remained in this hiding place. If I just gazed upon them and caressed their crispness, life might once more begin to flow through my higher nervous centers and make them less nervous.

My hand didn't contact anything!

I threshed it about.

Still nothing.

Alarmed now more than ever, I threw the mattress on the floor. I tore the bed apart. I took a knife to the box springs.

NO MONEY!

It was gone.

I lay down in the wreckage and had my epileptic fit.

It didn't help.

I banged my head against the wall. That didn't help, either. But some time later, I woke up and found that it was a bright day.

Coffee. Maybe several cups of coffee would steady my nerves. I managed to phone down and get the order placed. I took a shower and then found out I was standing in it with my clothes on.

By the time I had remedied this and had my pants turning into ice on the terrace, breakfast had arrived.

Unthinkingly, I opened the paper.

Buckteeth!

A two-column picture!

Madison had once more made the front page!

WHIZ KID SUES OCTOPUS

TEN-BILLION-BUCK BANG

The attorneys of the Whiz Kid—Boggle, Gouge and Hound—today filed suit against olympian Octopus Oil Company for a cool ten billion bucks, the largest malfeasance civil suit in history.

Rockecenter attorneys, Swindle and Crouch, when reached, said, "No comment."

The financial world today was rocked by the spectacle of Octopus actually being sued. Stocks fell. Dow-Jones dropped 230 points. The other six of the Seven Brothers hastily denied connection and complicity but informed sources implied they would soon be added due to their inextricable interlocks and total control by Octopus.

The Whiz Kid stated, "Octopus cannot help but be included in my campaign to bring honesty and integrity into the way faculties discriminate against students. Octopus heavily endows M.I.W., which makes oil a party to conspiracy to conspire with multiple malice and breach of breaches. By canceling my scholarship and depriving the college restaurant of my services, chaos has been caused, irreparable and condemnatory. If Octopus can callously deny students second helpings of rice pudding, the whole American way of life is threatened. Fascism will flourish and all will tremble at the tyranny. . . ."

Oh, there was more! And the vendor, knowing my habits, had a five-foot stack of newspapers outside my door.

The shouts and roars of student riots on the TV were so loud, I couldn't understand the news vendor who kept asking me for his money. I had to close the door on him.

Madison had blown it!

That was very plain indeed. He was obviously going to tailor the Whiz Kid into a deathless symbol of revolt against Big Oil.

How Heller must be sniggering this morning!

Although I loathed to do it, I approached my viewer. It was my duty and the way of the Apparatus officer (hard though it may be to always have duty as a goal). Besides, I was too shaken up to do more than collapse in front of the screen hoping that this did not reveal a diagnosis of masochism in me.

Chapter 7

Heller was riding in a public cab. By his reflection in the partition, I could see he was wearing a tan tweed suit, a puffed-out silk tie and, over it all, a cordovan-leather trench coat. Really elegant. I tried to make out where he was going by the passing winter scenery he seemed to be admiring so much. They were on some sort of a turnpike. He was catching glimpses of sunlit water to his left.

The Statue of Liberty! Way over there. And beyond it, back and across the bay, Manhattan!

Babe Corleone—he was on his way to see Babe Corleone!

Sure enough, they soon exited from the turnpike and shortly were threading their way through the impressive high-rises of Bayonne.

He told the cab to wait and shortly was greeting a somewhat uncertain Geovani.

"She ain't very happy today, kid," said Geovani. "Maybe you ought to postpone seein' her."

"Can't wait," said Heller.

Geovani shrugged. He went to the living room door and knocked and then opened it.

Babe was dressed in a light gray lounge suit. She was pacing back and forth, the width of the huge living room, pausing to look out the picture window at the wintry sunlight on the park. She did two turns before she said, "Show him in."

Heller entered.

Babe faced him with cold gray eyes, all six feet six of her expressing a wish to snap at him.

"And what have you got to say for yourself today, young man? Did you or did you not understand me when I said to knock off your God (bleeped) bad publicity? Now, don't interrupt. Not fifteen minutes ago, on that phone," she pointed, "in this," she pointed at the floor, "my own living room, I have had to listen to fifteen solid minutes of the mayor's wife concerning YOU!" She pointed. "Now, don't interrupt me. I know you have some lame, contemptible, God (bleeped) cock-and-bull story made up to account for THOSE!" And she pointed at a stack of morning New York papers. "The only thing that was good about it is that she has a cold and can't talk very long!

"Now, Jerome, this carousing around with criminal reporters must cease. And it must cease at once! Now, don't interrupt me. I know I have been busy. I know that I have not taken the time to work and slave like I should to bring you up properly. But that is NO excuse at all!

"Jerome, the very idea of going to court is NOT done! It is not done at all, Jerome! It exposes one to public ridicule. It costs one respect! And you have got to get the idea you should be respected!

"Jerome, you cannot keep running around with reporters and running off to courts! Courts are crooked, Jerome. They are not places you should be in! Now, don't interrupt!

"Jerome, this is very wearing and tiring on me. I know I have been neglectful. But Jerome, you don't *sue* people you don't like. You get a proper heater and you rub them out. Only weaklings and fools and idiots go rushing off to courts. You want justice, the only way you get justice is to buy yourself a proper rifle, learn how to shoot it and, with a proper telescopic sight . . ."

"Please!" cried Heller. "Please, can I interrupt?"

"No. What do you want?"

Heller was extending a packet to her. It was wrapped in silver paper and it had a black ribbon around it. "I have a present for you!"

She took it, somewhat softened, but she said, "It will do you no good at all to try to get out of it with some *gingillo*. No trinket could possibly compensate for what I have to put up with on your account from the mayor's wife! I have exhausted my vocabulary trying to tell her you are just a good boy gone slightly wrong. . . ."

"Open it!" said Heller in desperation.

"All right," she said frostily. "Just to please you and spoil you, I will open it."

She shook a stiletto out of a sleeve holster and used it to cut the black ribbon. She knifed off the silver paper. She opened it up.

She stared at it.

She turned it over to be sure there was no mistake. She looked back at it. She looked at Heller, her eyes round.

"The passport of GUNSALMO SILVA!"

It dawned on her.

She rushed to Heller and threw her arms around him. "You KILLED him!"

"Not exactly," said Heller, kind of smothered. "He sort of blew himself up!"

"Oh, you DARLING BOY!"

She drew back. She looked at the passport again. Then she said, "YIPPEE!" and went whirling around the room in a twirl she must have learned on the chorus line.

Then she sank down in a chair. "*Ave Maria*, 'Holy Joe' is at last avenged!" She began to cry.

Then after a while she bashed at her eyes with some tissue and began to stab buttons.

Staff came pouring in, looking like she had rung a fire bell. She held up the passport.

"Gunsalmo Silva is dead!"

They cheered until I had to turn down my sound volume.

She went over and showed the passport to "Holy Joe's" portrait. She reeled off a volley of Italian, telling him the turncoat was dead and his soul could now rest in peace and promising a huge Mass as soon as she could.

Then she turned to her staff. "Quick, quick, get Jerome some milk and cookies!"

She made Heller sit down in her own favorite chair. They got him milk and cookies.

Babe was planning a party and a Mass.

Suddenly she remembered. "I'm sure he will have a funeral. Yes, we must plan for that. Silva's funeral. He had a brother and uncle. Now, what can we do for Silva's funeral? A big floral display. That's it. In the shape of a black dog. Georgio, make sure it is ordered. Oh, yes. I will attend also. And I will think of some way to get the mayor's wife to attend. Now, what will I wear? White and scarlet? Maybe just scarlet. A scarlet veil. . . . No, no, I must get a better idea than that! Georgio, call my dress designer. Order him to design the most festive thing he can think of for a funeral! Oh, will this put the mayor's wife in her place. She'll come in something dowdy. Oh, do have another cookie, Jerome."

Italians! It took two solid hours before they even began to settle down.

At last, the important phone calls had been made and probably it was ripping all through the vast east and west and international Corleone organization that "Holy Joe's" murderer was dead. And just when it looked like the excitement was over, somebody called to state that Silva was in the New York City morgue and that there wasn't a single bone in his body that remained unbroken and it all started up again and this fact chased the other the length and breadth of the Corleone empire around the world. Telegrams of congratulations began to flood in on their basement RCA and Western Union machines from as far away as New Zealand, from ships at sea and aircraft in flight.

The coils of printout began to mound up on the floor at Heller's feet, Babe reading aloud every message, eyes bright, with animated elocution.

At length, Heller said he had to get back to New York to make sure the cat was fed. But Babe made him stay. Cats could wait. Young boys, she knew, were always hungry and she stuffed him full of lunch.

After he got through his third plate of spaghetti, he said, "There's one more thing." He took out of his pocket a card I had seen him remove from Black Overcoat's wallet. I suspected that that was the major reason he had come to Babe's. "Can you tell me who this man is?"

Babe read it. She frowned, thinking. "Inganno John Scroccone? I seem to have heard it. I can't remember where. Geovani!" And when he appeared, "Put this into the computer and see what you get."

Geovani came back from the basement. "He's the chief accountant of Faustino Narcotici, body lice on a louse."

"Jerome!" said Babe, shocked. She looked at him. "You are associating with the wrong people! Jerome, you must continue to be careful of your reputation."

I wondered for a moment why he didn't tell her he had killed the guy. And then I realized that Heller really hadn't told anybody anything at all.

With a shock, I became certain he knew he was being watched. He was afraid of being caught in a Code break. The grenade! That was why he couldn't and wouldn't tell even Bang-Bang how Silva had died. No grenades of such power and type existed on Earth. That would have to be it. Any normal man would have bragged and bragged about it. And he was being so close-mouthed it was even slopping over into not mentioning the other three hits!

"Jerome," she said, "I faithfully promise to stop neglecting you. Blood will tell and you proved that today. But upbringing has a lot to do with it, too. Now, as a good mother, I should pay more attention to your vital needs and of course resist temptation firmly not to spoil you at the same time. You are so accustomed to my shameful neglect that you were even going to leave here, unfed, and continue to run about in rags like some street urchin."

She got out a pen and poised it over the snowy linen tablecloth. "Now, first, of course, you need a brand-new wardrobe." She wrote that down. "And then a string of polo ponies—that encourages you to be a gentleman when you hit other boys over the head with a mallet. Yes, definitely polo ponies." She wrote that down. She thought a bit.

Heller would have spoken but she sensed it and shushed him

with a hand gesture. "Oh, it's wintertime. You will need some new ice skates." She wrote that down. "And then, of course, it will soon be spring. So you will need a new baseball bat."

Heller would have spoken again but this time she shushed him directly. "No, no more racing cars. Not one, Jerome. You may think this is harsh but my ears cannot possibly stand to hear one more word about racing from the mayor's wife!"

She thought for a bit. "I was going to add the old Capone villa in Miami Beach but you're getting that for Christmas and I want to keep it as a surprise. Part of being a good mother is not to spoil a boy all at once."

She checked her list to see that she had everything down. She said, "Good." She drew a big circle around the notes on the tablecloth. "That settles it. Now, with your new wardrobe, you'll have to have something very quickly for the Silva funeral. . . . A red tuxedo and cape. Yes, that will do. It won't clash with my gown. Here, have some more cookies, Jerome."

A faint honking had been going on, from out in the street. Babe suddenly yelled, "Geovani! What the hell is all that honking out there?"

Geovani popped in. "It's a New York taxi. He says he's been waiting for the kid here for three hours."

"Well, blood of Christ, pay the (bleepard) off! You think I'd send Jerome back to town in a public cab? Tell Battitore to get out my limousine! You think my own son is some kind of a bum? And you tell that Battitore to get the back seat nice and warm. You want Jerome to catch cold?" She turned to Heller. "Now, what were we talking about? Oh, yes. An increase in allowance. . . ."

That was too much! Outraged at all this attention and adulation Heller was getting, I turned off the viewer and hid it from my sight. There is a point where even masochism pales.

I thought I'd better see what the radio and TV had to say about this "mighty deed" he was bragging to everybody about. I listened to several news broadcasts. Aha! Not a mention of it!

I stretched my credit with the news vendor and got the afternoon papers. There had been nothing in the morning papers. But in one afternoon one there was a little notice wedged in amongst the latest fashions. It said:

MIDTOWN CONTEMPORARY GARB

A body identified as that of one Gunsalmo Silva by dental plates and fingerprints, was found in the small hours of last night on Fifth Avenue, apparently having fallen from the Baltman and Company roof. Silva was clothed in what had apparently been a woman's black dress. One wonders if this is the latest fashion trend now emerging.

That put things in their proper perspective. The newspapers never lie. They always tell the exact truth in things of this kind, and things of all kinds, for that matter. The Rockecenters and Madisons take care of that!

I felt a little better. I was no longer twitching and I didn't have to keep my mouth tight to suppress the tiny screams which sought to issue from my throat.

My lot was very difficult. I was broke. Heller and some unknown had robbed me. Miss Pinch didn't have a clue as to how to be a petty-cash cashier.

Somehow, trembling, abandoned and alone, I would struggle further along the sadistic road of thorns some people laughingly call life.

Lacking a crystal ball, I thought no further shocks lurked ahead, at least today.

I was wrong!

PART THIRTY-TWO
Chapter 1

Sirens were sounding in the street. There seemed to be an awful commotion going on. Despite the cold, I went out on the terrace and looked down at Fifth Avenue.

Military vehicles! Drawing up around the hotel!

White-helmeted and -belted MPs leaping out to set up a machine gun on the corner!

I drew back. A movement on a nearby building caught my eye.

Snipers in white helmets and belts!

They were laying their weapons directly at this terrace!

My Gods, I gasped—the U.S. Army has discovered I'm an extraterrestrial! They've got me trapped! They're closing in!

I hastily withdrew inside the penthouse.

A thundering on the door!

I'm dead!

Bravely, as one walks the last mile, bare-chested to the bullets, already in so low a state I did not care whether I lived or died, I threw the door open.

It was a bellhop.

His face was chalk white.

"Is a Mr. Inkswitch in?" he said.

Life without money wasn't worth living anyway. "Why not?" I said.

Crash!

Out of the stairwell, out from around the potted palms, out of the elevator, came MPs with assault rifles, running low.

They knocked the bellhop aside like he was a rag doll!

They burst past me!

They overturned the chairs, smashing them!

They yanked open closet and bathroom doors, leaping back with rifles pointing in case anyone came out.

They fired short bursts into mattresses!

They jabbed their rifles into clothes.

They raced out on the terrace with a crash of potted palms and took positions commanding the surrounding terrain.

An officer stood firmly before me. He was backed up with two MPs who had their Colt .45s on me. He gave a signal. An MP began to shake me down. He got my wallet. He handed it to the officer.

The officer looked at it. He held it to the light. He compared pictures. He gave another signal. A soldier grabbed my hand. He produced a pad and inked it. He got my fingerprints. He gave them snappily to the officer.

The officer compared them to a card he had.

In a cavalry voice, he shouted, "FOHwud, HO-o!"

There was a roar and rattle.

A cart of equipment was rushed in, the cannon wheels rumbling on the carpet and tearing it to bits. Three men were pushing it. They stopped it in the center of the room. One of them rushed out on the terrace and held up a chromium-plated pole.

Another officer came in. He knelt by the cart. He picked up an instrument. He barked into it and waited tensely.

The pause gave me an instant to read their uniform badges:

U.S. Army Signal Corps

The officer at the cart said to me, "This is ultra-secret. You could be shot for disclosing that you have seen a satellite-enscrambled decode-recode. Not even the Russians know we have it. Do you swear you have not seen it?"

I raised my inked-up hand and swore.

"Good," he said, "here is your party." He handed me the instrument.

A voice said, *"Alo. Kto eta gavarit?"*

I handed the instrument back to the Signal Corps officer. "Don't you have the wrong number? I think he just asked me who was speaking in Russian."

"(Bleep)!" said the officer. He got on the line again. He talked very fast and hard. Once more he handed me the phone.

A voice said, *"¡Diga! ¿Con quien hablo?"*

I tried to hand the instrument back to the officer. "Somebody just answered me in Spanish. I think he wanted to know who he was speaking to."

"No, no," said the officer. "You've got the right party."

I put the instrument back to my ear. The voice repeated, *"¿Con quien hablo?"*

"Inkswitch," I said.

"Ah. Espere un momento, por favor." So I waited a moment. It was more than a moment, but that's how the Spanish are. Funny, though. I didn't know enough Spanish to spot accents but it sure wasn't Spain Spanish. A lilting sort of speech like he was singing. Cuban?

"Well, that sure took them long enough!" Voice on the phone. New England twang. Bury!

"Where are you?" I gasped.

"Central America," said Bury. "Somebody killed the Director of the CIA and there was an outbreak of peace down here. I had to fly in to review treaties to see which ones could be broken. It's not too bad, though. They really have some great snakes down here. You ought to see them! But that isn't what I called you about. The matter is pretty high security so I had to bypass the National Security Agency. Besides, there aren't any phones in the jungle here. Is the U.S. Army Signal Corps still in the room, there?"

"Yes," I said.

"Well, tell them to move out of earshot. This is highly classified stuff."

I told them and they went out onto the terrace and into the hall, guns drawn and ready to defend their equipment in case of attack.

"The area is clear," I said.

"All right," said Bury. "I got a call about an hour ago on the facsimile satellite hookup. *He* was on personally. You know who I'm talking about."

Yes, I certainly did. I realized with alarm that Delbert John Rockecenter himself had been through to Bury.

"Inkswitch," said Bury, "you've let Madison get out of hand! You-know-who is hopping mad! He was holding the newspapers up to the screen. Raving, Inkswitch, raving!"

I chilled. When Rockecenter raves, governments fall.

"He kind of got it wrong," said Bury. "He thought the news said the kid was setting up a rival oil company and was violating family policy by introducing competition. It's that Miss Peace: she reads him the papers and she can't spell. So Madison has got it all screwed up. That kid is his client, not Octopus. Madison is out of his field, getting into legal. Justice mustn't be allowed to get out of hand. I know, I'm a lawyer. And that's the real catastrophe in this. We can live with most of this but one item in it really needs to be objected to and no overrule! And this is the real reason you've got to get Madison under control, Inkswitch. Have I got your full attention?"

I told him he surely had.

"Inkswitch, right there in the same news story, he committed a felony. He mentioned Swindle and Crouch along with Boggle, Gouge and Hound. Listen, Inkswitch: Boggle, Gouge and Hound are a bunch of cheap ambulance-chasers, and even whispering Swindle and Crouch in the same news story could ruin our reputation. It's a clear-cut case of attempted manslaughter. Madison has gone too far! It's pretty serious, Inkswitch. That's the real reason this call has got to be so secret. Do you grasp the need for a tight, unviolated lawyer-client relationship here?"

I said that I did.

Bury said, "Now, I can't call Madison. He'd just plead the Fifth. So you have to handle Madison. If you don't, we're liable to get a summary judgment with no reprieve. Got it?"

I said I certainly did.

Bury said, "Good. Is there anything else on the docket?"

"Well, yes," I said. "They changed cashiers and I can't get paid."

"Details," said Bury. "Don't bother me with details. Tell the Chief Security Officer. Say, you wouldn't like me to send you a couple of these nice snakes, would you?"

Hastily, I said, "I'll get on Madison right away!"

"All right," said Bury. "You make sure you do. I've got to go deeper into the mountains now to find General Hatchetheimer and get some of these peace treaties violated to get things going again. I won't be available for a while: I also want more time with these great snakes. You sure you don't want some?"

"I'll be too busy on Madison!" I said quickly.

"Well, give my best to Miss Agnes, (bleep) her."

He rang off.

I signaled the Signal Corps people on the terrace.

They blew shrill whistles. The MPs went into Red Alert.

They rushed the closely guarded equipment away.

Sirens began to scream in the streets.

With very precisely executed maneuvers, they were gone.

Utanc crawled out from under her bed, white-faced and shaking. She slammed and locked her door with extraordinary force in my face.

The hotel resident doctor was giving the first bellhop an emergency transfusion in the hall.

A hotel repair crew timidly came in and began to put the breakage together as best they could.

The manager appeared. He said, "There are two questions, if you please. A: Are you a Russian defector? Or B: Are you a member of the Joint Chiefs of Staff in disguise?"

I was kind of upset. I gave him the wrong answers. "It's no to both," I said, irritated.

"Good," he said. "Then here's the bill for the damages."

It was for $18,932.27 plus one expended bellhop, value to be determined later.

That decided me right then and there!

Chapter 2

First things first.

MONEY!

I would go see the Chief of Security at once. The problem was how to get there. It is sort of suicidal to get into a New York cab with only thirty-five cents in your pocket. I knew better than to approach Utanc, the way that door had slammed in my face. I would jog.

Wrapped warmly against the cold day, I was shortly sweating and puffing my way southward toward Rockecenter Plaza. It was only a few blocks.

I turned at Saks and wheezed my way through the Channel Gardens, shivering at the sight of all the unovercoated statuary sporting in the iced pools, and finally got to the Octopus Oil Building.

The Chief of Security had his feet on the desk, easing his several stomachs after lunch.

I flashed my Federal I.D. at him. "Inkswitch," I said. "I have a problem of the greatest importance to the company."

He punched the computer and it came up blank. "What's the problem?" he said, taking his feet off the desk.

"Your Miss Pinch on Petty Cash Window 13 has not been trained on her job. Miss Grabball did not tell her the procedure in handling a family 'spi'!"

"Ho, ho!" he said. He checked his revolver, picked up a thick billy club and we were on our way.

I hung back. He went right into the cages like a lion trainer. He seized Miss Pinch by the shoulder and with a yank, hauled her into a back closet.

There were some sharp sounds coming out. Blows.

Very shortly the Chief of Security emerged. He said to me as he passed me, "That's the way."

I went promptly to Window 13. Miss Pinch was sitting there in her mannish clothes and thin lips. She had the beginnings of a black eye.

"Inkswitch," I said, "I want $20,000."

She punched the computer keyboard. It came up blank. She made out a voucher and handed it to me to sign. I wrote *Thomas Jefferson*. She took it and carefully counted $20,000 from her cash drawer.

She put the whole $20,000 in her purse!

She didn't have it right.

I said, "Are you sure that is correct?"

"That's the way," she said with hostility.

I went out. Maybe she was just a bit rattled. I should give her a chance to get settled in on her job.

I came back in.

"Inkswitch," I said. "I want $20,000."

She punched the computer keyboard. It came up blank. She made out a voucher and handed it to me to sign. I wrote *George Washington*. She took it and carefully counted $20,000 from her cash drawer.

She again put the whole $20,000 in her purse!

I said, "Wait a minute, Miss Pinch. I don't think you have this right!"

Her eyes were very, very hostile. "That's the way," she said.

I went out. Maybe I was giving her the wrong figure!

I went back in.

"Inkswitch," I said. "I want $40,000."

She went through all the motions. Only this time, I signed it *Benedict Arnold* as a kind of threat.

She took the money out of her cash drawer.

Yes, she put the whole $40,000 in her purse!

"AND THAT'S THE GOD (BLEEPED) WAY!" she shouted.

I gave it up. I made my way outside and thought about it. I really didn't have any time to waste. If I delayed too long, Bury might phone again and I'd get another hotel bill for $18,932.27 for damages. I couldn't risk it.

I walked around a while. And then inspiration came to me. I'd go back and see the Chief of Security.

I walked straight in.

He had a pile of money on his desk.

He covered it up with his cap.

"So that's the way," I said.

I left. I rapidly walked across courts and down hallways I had memorized before. As a family "spi," I really had something to report. Crooked employees! I found the private door to the office of Miss Peace.

I knocked.

She opened it a crack.

I said, "As a family 'spi,' I have something about employees to report to Mr. Rockecenter."

I have seen a few faces twist in rage in my time. Hers went more so.

"You think I'd let you in here to spill the beans about me? Get out of here, you (bleepard)!"

I left.

None of this had gone well at all!

As I could think of no way to handle any of this on the spur of the moment, I left.

Chapter 3

How in the Hells was I going to get down to 42 Mess Street? It was far too far to jog.

I walked along a street. Suddenly, inspiration! I saw a cop car. I went up to it. I flashed my credentials. "I have to make an urgent raid on Mess Street. Take me there."

"We ain't no errand boys for no God (bleeped) Feds," said one of them with a hostile glare.

That didn't work.

I went up a side street. There were some cars parked. I relaxed. Crime was the best way after all. I realized I had become slack on this planet, even to the point of relaxing my Apparatus reflexes. I walked along beside the cars, looking to see if anyone had left his keys in the ignition.

No luck. I had heard cars could be jump-started but I did not know how to do it.

A few doors along, a moving van, huge, was standing. They were just taking out a sofa and carting it into a house.

Aha!

With stealthy speed I crept to its cab. When the driver and helper went inside, I leaped into the van. There were the keys! I started it up, engaged the gears with a clash and roared away!

Behind me I could hear some sliding. In the rearview side mirror, I saw that I was depositing furniture at intervals on the street.

Then there was a big crash as a grand piano went out!

After that there was a sort of banging behind me on the pavement as I roared along. I didn't know what it was. But nothing must deter me from stopping Madison. I might get another phone call or even a couple of snakes!

The truck was pretty hard to drive, being fifty feet or more long and being pretty high. But after many a narrow escape I made it within a block of 42 Mess Street. The street was too narrow to admit the moving van so I parked it. I found what had been banging behind me was the tailgate hitting the pavement. The grand piano must have busted its hinges. I got it closed. I walked the rest of the way.

The old loft was a beehive. Reporters were rushing about. Typewriters and telex machines were roaring. Outgoing mailbags full of releases to every paper in the world were being passed like fire-bucket lines through the window to sail down into waiting trucks.

A huge new banner stretched across the room:

THINK COVERAGE
AT ANY COST!

Another said:

Front Page or You're Out!

Madison was in the end office, so surrounded with reporters taking dictation I couldn't get near him.

Close to hand a reporter was bellowing into a telephone, "I don't want page two. I want page one! Look, Mr. Vitriahl, you may be managing editor of the *St. Petersburg Grimes* today, but you won't even be a copy boy on the *Smearwater Shun,* the dinkiest paper in Florida, tomorrow! You cooperate, you (bleepard), or you-know-who will be onto your board of directors to find a new God (bleeped) managing editor before dawn. . . . That's better. Headlines it is." He hung up.

The reporter was muttering over a dogeared notebook. He put in another call. "*Los Angeles Grimes?* Give me J. Blithering Bonkers, please. : . . . Hello, Bonkers. This is Ted Tramp of the you-know-who organization. You didn't give us front page yesterday. . . . All right, all right. So your God (bleeped) managing editor's wife is head of the National Association of Mental Stealth. Don't cry on . . . All right. I agree that her embezzling the NAMS funds and running off with the head psychiatrist was news. But God (bleep) it, Bonkers, you got to assert your control over that board! Why the hell do you suppose you-know-who got you on as chairman of the Grimes-Smearer Corporation, anyway? . . . Ah, that's better. . . . That's better, Bonkers. . . . Well, (bleep), you don't have to shoot the (bleepard). Just make him put the Whiz Kid on the front page!"

The reporter hung up and got out some dirty tissue and scrubbed vigorously at his ear. "I can't stand slobbering!" He saw me. "Who the hell are you? You don't look dirty enough to be a reporter. You some kind of a spy?"

"Precisely," I said. "Tell Madison, Smith has got to see him."

"I dunno," he said, glancing at the mob around Madison in his office.

"Smith from you-know-who," I said.

"Jesus," said the reporter. He grabbed the handle of a fire-engine siren close to hand and began to turn it briskly. The reporters all rushed out looking for the fire.

I walked in.

Madison looked at me with aplomb. "Oh, hello, Mr. Smith. Fifteen-point quote Madison triumphs unquote! We've seized the initiative! And I'll bet you're here bearing rave notices from Bury!"

"I'm here bearing an axe, Madison," I said sternly. "You have trod upon sacred toes. You forgot that Octopus isn't your client so save your ruin for the Whiz Kid!"

"Ruin? Madison can't get it on the pica stick! What are you talking about, Smith? Mr. Bury gave me specific and direct orders to make the Whiz Kid's name a household word and to make him immortal!"

"He didn't give you any orders to PR Swindle and Crouch!" I

said. "You link them up in the news with Boggle, Gouge and Hound and Bury will have your telephone disconnected!"

That got to him. "Oh," he said, slumping. "It is so difficult to work with nonprofessionals. You don't really understand PR."

"I understand it very well," I said. "It's Confidence, Coverage and Controversy. And the Coverage in my penthouse today cost $18,932.27. And you and I are going to have an awful lot of Controversy if you don't get Swindle and Crouch out of it and if you think Octopus needs your PR. You mend your ways or you'll shatter my Confidence!"

"It was front page!" he wailed. "I have had the front page day after day! PR is like marksmanship! It's the number of times you can hit the front page! And Madison has been riddling it!"

"It and everything else!" I said. "Now settle down. Get on course and do what you're supposed to do! You repair this damage to Swindle and Crouch and Octopus! No more wild bullets slaughtering innocent bystanders! Get rid of these suits! They're too close to home."

"But PR should have a little bit of truth in it," said Madison. "It sort of spices it up!"

"I'm adamant," I said.

Suddenly he smiled. "Great! Absolutely great! I got it. I can see it now! Suits are only good for one day of front page. They usually sag to page two and right on down the drain. It doesn't change my general program."

He walked up and down his office, sort of dancing. I watched him suspiciously. He was far too happy for a man who has just been chewed up Apparatus style!

He stopped. His honest, earnest face grew sincere. He took my hand. He shook it. "Thank you for a great idea, Mr. Smith. You may not be a professional but I can assure you that a fresh viewpoint is like warm air to the overworked wits."

He rushed out. "STAFF! STAFF! Everybody gather round. I've just had a GREAT idea!"

I left. A little of Madison is an awful lot.

Chapter 4

I had my own problems.

I was broke.

I myself had just had a marvelous idea. I was anxious to get going with it.

I looked at my watch. I had ample time if I hurried.

At the corner of Mess Street, I looked about.

The moving van was gone!

Some (bleepard) had stolen my transportation!

Now I *would* have to hurry. It was far too close to five o'clock.

With an anxious eye, I looked about. There was a stoplight near to hand. An idea! I raced across the street against the light, dodging traffic. I got alongside the northbound lane.

The light went red. The traffic stopped. I raced down the line of waiting cars.

I saw an old lady behind the wheel of a rattletrap Ford. I grabbed the door handle, opened it and leaped in.

I snapped my derringer out of my sleeve and shoved it into her side.

She gasped!

"This is a pickup!" I grated. "Drive at once to Rockecenter Plaza or get raped!"

She let out a thin scream.

"Drive!" I said.

The light changed. Trailing a thin scream behind us we rushed north.

I looked at my watch. I still had time. But this woman was driving all over the road.

"Drive straight!" I ordered her.

"I can't see without my glasses!" she screeched. "Get my glasses out of the glove compartment!"

"Drive!" I ordered her with a jab of the derringer.

Erratically, following my directions, we got onto and raced northward on the Avenue of the Americas. We were within four blocks of Rockecenter Plaza but the streets were all torn up. It was like threading a needle.

We swerved and almost went into a construction ditch!

She jammed on her brakes! I almost went through the windscreen!

"I can't see without my glasses!" she screamed. "They're in the glove compartment!"

All right! Gods! Anything to keep from being wrecked. I opened it.

POW–SWISH!

I got a full blast of Mace straight in the face!

I screamed! I was stone blind!

She must have opened the passenger-side door. Sharp-heeled shoes crashed into my side.

Out I went on the pavement! Right in the gutter!

I heard the Ford roar away.

I fumbled around, hoping to find my derringer and take a shot at her. And then I realized that (bleeped) (bleepch) had even stolen my gun!

I got some tissue out. I tried to wipe out my eyes.

Gods, they stung!

I could see some light now but the day was all washed gray, without details.

I fumbled along. I was afraid I would be late. I couldn't read my watch.

Things were becoming a little plainer. A trick and novelty store! I staggered in.

"Do you have any water pistols?"

Dimly I could see four or five being put on the counter in front of me. "How do I know they work?"

Whoever it was got a glass of water and filled them. I grabbed one and shot myself in the eyes. I grabbed another and did the same. I shot another one up my nose. I shot the last one into my mouth.

I could see!

"They don't work," I said and rushed out.

The water glass shattered on the door frame as I left.

I sprinted for my destination.

I ran into the right hall.

I hauled up, panting and spent.

My Gods, it was difficult trying to get around New York! They were laying for you at every turn!

But thank Gods, I was on time!

Chapter 5

Right on schedule, tightly packed in the mobbed rush of quitting time, the target subject was in view.

Miss Pinch! She was wearing a bulky, mannish overcoat. The target object was swinging from her arm: her purse!

The flooding wave of workers crested against the traffic of Seventh Avenue.

Hat down, coat collar up, I had target object in close view. An old hand at such campaigns, trained by the Apparatus to the keenest possible edge, I foresaw no trouble in obtaining target object. A quick snatch, a fleet run, a stuffing of target content into my pockets and a flinging of target object into nearest trash can and victory would be mine!

I quivered with the thrill of the chase.

A $40,000 quarry does not every day enliven the spirit of the hunt.

I could see that the purse, black and hanging from her arm by a strap, was bulky, aching to be gutted by the skilled hunter. And after that, in victory, I would not have to steal moving vans or get hit in the face with Mace just to get around upon my duties.

Her masculine stride marked her. The heavy, light gray overcoat could not be missed. The gray slouch hat was like a beacon calling to the storm-tossed mariner adrift on the heaving and pitiless seas of New York.

She was heading, obviously, for a subway station. This gave me a sudden panic. I did not have enough to buy a token and get through the gate.

But fortune smiled. She was lingering before a newsstand.

Buffeted by hurrying humanity, I crept behind her. She was trying to choose between *Muscle Making for Men Complete with Full Nude Photos* and *Panthouse Magazine with Full Nude Cover Folds*. It seemed to be a difficult decision. She picked up one and then the other and then back to the first.

With $40,000 at stake, why delay?

With an expert hand from behind her, I removed the purse from her shoulder with an expert twist!

I darted away!

I had it! I thought I would win after all!

What trouble it was trying to operate with untrained employees! One had to resort to such extraordinary shifts!

I ran.

Thinly, I could hear a police whistle blowing!

I must be being pursued!

With too much cunning for my own good, my first thought was to possess the contents of the bag and discard the evidence.

Masked amongst the mob, I plunged my right hand into the purse.

SNAP!

YEEOWWW!

A hidden something had seized my hand with agony!

I tried to withdraw my hand!

Whatever it was was also fastened to the inside of the purse!

In agony, I sought to shake the purse off. It wouldn't leave!

With my left hand, I seized the bottom of the purse and tried to pull it off my hand.

AGONY!

In desperation, I stopped and tried to use my left hand to free my right. I plunged my left hand into the purse.

SNAP!

YEEOWWW!

Something had clamped down on my left hand!

I had both hands inside the purse! I couldn't get them out!

The faint sound of the police whistle kept blowing.

It was inside the purse!

A hard, smug voice behind my ear said, "I thought that you'd try that." Miss Pinch!

She touched the side of the purse with her finger and the faint police whistle went off.

But that was not all she did. She pushed something hard and round into my right kidney. A gun!

I was in agony. My fingers felt like they were caught in the teeth of a savage beast. Two savage beasts.

"I don't take the subway home," she said. "I live just a few blocks from here. So walk quietly and no yelling. This gun has a hair trigger. It is quite invisible to the passerby. Stop screaming. You are making a scene and I might have to call the cops after all. March along, Inkswitch."

I clamped my teeth on my lip. I somehow endured the excruciating pain. A bullet in the kidney does not help one's circulation a bit. I avoided it by walking.

We went across Broadway. We went north a couple blocks. We turned west again.

She halted me at a walk-down, the entrance to a basement apartment in an old shabby house that had survived the demolition of much of the nearby area. The steps were full of snow and garbage. I was seeing it all in a red haze of pain.

Miss Pinch pressed a bell three times.

Then she took a key and unlocked a wrought-iron grill. She took another key and unlocked the basement door. She gun-prodded me into a small hall. She shut and locked both the grill and the door.

"You can resume screaming, if you like," she said. "This basement is totally soundproof. It really is a find. It also has a nice back garden where one can bury unwanted bodies. So just be patient and do as you are told."

She kicked me into a second room.

In spite of my suffering, the place gave me a shock. She sensed it and said with satisfaction, "Interior decorated by myself."

It was a dull hue of red. Instruments of torture hung tastefully upon the walls. Festoons of whips served in lieu of curtains. A huge bed occupied the center of the room, its four posts topped with the grinning faces of gargoyles. The carcass—stuffed, I hoped—of a dead goat hung head down in the corner. It was full of darts.

"Now just sit down on the bottom of the bed, Inkswitch." She assisted the movement with a prod of the gun.

"Now, I know you are probably provoked," said Miss Pinch, looking at me with slitted eyes. "Men are violent and unreliable. Therefore, we cannot begin upon the removal of the bag until certain precautions are taken. You might kick out."

With her left hand she undid my overcoat. She reached to my waist and undid my belt. I would have lunged up but it looked like the gun was going to hit me in the teeth. I sat back.

She pulled off my shoes.

She shucked off my pants.

She pried off my underpants.

A chain rattled!

She was fastening a steel cuff to my right ankle. It was held to the right-side bottom of the bed with links.

She clamped a steel cuff to my left ankle. It was connected with a chain to the left bottom post of the bed.

Miss Pinch got up on the bed behind me. She pulled my overcoat, jacket and shirt up over my head and down on my arms.

She then hauled me backwards to the center of the bed. From the right-hand upper post of the bed she pulled a steel cuff on a long chain. She put it on my agonized right wrist. She did the same from the left-hand upper post and put that steel band on my left wrist.

Going to the posts, she shortened the leg chains until my feet were securely fastened wide apart.

She took up the slack on the wrist chains as far as she could with my hands still in the bag.

"Now, I know those traps must be quite painful," said Miss Pinch, sounding very congratulatory about it, "but we will have to free them. But only if you promise not to strike out. Men are so violent!"

Begging, I promised.

Working on the outside of the purse bottom, she effected the release of something. She drew off the purse.

Two huge rat traps!

They had teeth and were gnawing deeper with every movement!

Standing very clear of possible strikes, she got the sleeves off the right hand and trap after she unfastened and refastened the steel cuff. She then tightened the chain so the arm was extended nearly to the right side bedpost. She repeated this operation on the left side.

I was naked and spread-eagled, chained face up on the center of that bed!

Miss Pinch removed her overcoat. She took off her hat. She smoothed out her hair before a mirror in a frame of daggers.

"You forgot the traps!" I screamed at her, driven by the agony of my mangled fingers.

"Everything in its own time and place," said Miss Pinch. Then she raised her voice and called, "Candy, baby! Come see what I've got for us!"

Chapter 6

The door to the back room opened. Mincingly, expectant, a woman, maybe thirty, tiptoed in. She was dressed in very frilly, very feminine, gingham clothes. She had frizzy, very fluffy, platinum-colored hair. She had big, round, black eyes. She wasn't very pretty but she certainly was making the most of what she had.

"Oooooo," she said. Then she jumped up and down and clapped her hands. "Oh, Pinch, dear! What wonderful things you do! And all for me!" She raced to Pinch and kissed her passionately.

A lesbian and her "wife"!

Oh, Gods, what did they want with me!

Candy danced back and looked at me, spread-eagled and naked on the bed. She pretended coyness. Then she said, "He isn't very big, is he?"

"Oh, my darling Candy," said Miss Pinch. "You are not pleased."

"No, no, sweet Pinchy. Please let us not quarrel. He will be just wonderful! Have I offended you, dear Pinchy?"

They embraced with croonings of endearment.

"Take off these Gods (bleeped) traps!" I screamed at them.

Miss Pinch said to Candy, "I thought that you, just this once, might like to . . ."

Candy drew back in horror. "Oh, no, no! I could not bear to touch a man. What must you think of me! Oh, dear Pinchy, how could I be so gross? Never, never would I be unfaithful to you even by a fingertip."

Miss Pinch smiled at her indulgently. Then, humming a little tune without words, she moved over and, in the most painful way possible, began to take the trap off my left hand. Believe me, I screamed!

"Ah," said Candy. "Ah, dear Pinchy. Kiss me!" Her eyes were shining.

Miss Pinch kissed her. Then she came back and finished the left hand with maximum agony. I screamed myself hoarse!

Candy had sat down on a sofa. She was panting. Her mouth was wet. Her knees were wide apart. She was beckoning urgently to Miss Pinch.

Miss Pinch grabbed her, crushed her to her flat chest and then carried her to the other room and slammed the door shut with her heel.

Through the pink mist of agony from my right hand, I could hear urgent beggings in the next room. Then little moans. Then groans of ecstasy. Minutes. And then a gasping shriek!

What was going on in there?

More minutes.

A low muttering.

The door opened.

Miss Pinch still had her coat and shirt and tie on. But she was nearly naked from the waist down. She was breathing hard.

Candy was wearing only a chemise now. Her face was red and flushed and wet.

Their eyes were hot.

What could they possibly have been doing?

Miss Pinch went to an Iron Maiden and opened it. It was serving as a fridge. She got out some beer.

They lolled down on the sofa, drinking from their beer cans thirstily.

"Take off the Gods (bleeped) trap!" I screamed at them.

In a conversational voice, Miss Pinch said, "Everything in its time and place, Inkswitch."

"What are you up to?" I bellowed.

"Tell him," said Candy. "I always love to hear it."

Indulgently, Miss Pinch said, "All Rockecenter's companies have classes in Psychiatric Birth Control. It's vital, you understand, to reduce the world population. They breed like rats. And they're all riffraff. They outstrip the world's food supply which has to be reduced so food prices will stay up and Rockecenter's friends can make a profit. And, of course, that is the name of the game."

She took a thirsty guzzle of her beer and, without bothering to wipe off the mustache, continued learnedly, "Birth control requires more than pills and besides, I. G. Barben has no monopoly on them and there are competitors. So the answer to controlling world population is homosexuality. Now, if everyone was a homosexual— the men gays and the women lesbians—then there's no more population problem at all. The great work begun by the Rockecenters decades ago is just now coming into its own. Birth-control training is now being introduced even into kindergartens. The competitors of Barben will go broke, as who will need the pills? There will be no mass meetings against abortions and even abortion is going out of use. The trend is overwhelmingly toward universal homosexuality.

"The Psychiatric Birth Control classes are wonderful. They were developed by Dr. Frybrain, the head of the International Psychiatric Association, on a special Rockecenter grant. And the Rockecenters, as you know, have always controlled psychiatry and psychology. What used to be called 'normal' sex is the real sex crime. And what used to be called 'sex crimes' are now normal. So if every student becomes dedicated, as psychiatrists are, to making all the perverts and sadists and homosexuals they can, then the long-term Rockecenter goal of shrinking world population will become a fact. So we are expected to make at least one man a pervert. And that's where you come in, Inkswitch."

"I won't cooperate!" I screamed. "Take off this Gods (bleeped) second trap!"

Miss Pinch looked at Candy. "How do you feel, dear? Ready?"

"Oh, yes," trilled Candy.

Miss Pinch put her beer down.

She walked over to my right hand. She began to remove the trap with twisting motions. I screamed!

"It seems to be stuck," said Miss Pinch with thin-lipped satisfaction.

Candy's beer began to run out of the sides of her mouth. She was starting to pant.

Miss Pinch gave the trap a more dreadful twist. I screamed my head off!

Candy dropped her beer can. It frothed in a puddle on the floor. She put her heels out straight. Her mouth was open, her eyes hot.

Miss Pinch was beginning to breathe hard. She closed the trap tighter. I almost tore my lungs out.

"Oh, God," panted Candy.

Miss Pinch tore the trap off. I yelled so hard I deafened myself.

Candy had her legs straight out, her head back. She was beginning to buck up and down on the sofa.

Miss Pinch seized her in her arms and, pressing hot kisses on her throat, bore her into the other room and slammed the door.

I could hear moaning and begging. I could hear an urgent scramble. Then more begging.

Then small moans.

Then a shriek!

Minutes passed.

A low snarling. The voice of Miss Pinch.

More minutes.

What were they doing?

The door opened. They came out. They were both practically naked. Miss Pinch had no breasts at all. She had a tattooed dagger in the middle of her chest. Her short hair was ruffled and wet.

Candy had lipstick smeared all over her face and stomach. Her large breasts were shiny and wet.

They plopped down on the sofa, legs outstretched. Candy had her head back. She looked quite spent. Miss Pinch was staring at me, thin-lipped and calculating. I began to be afraid.

"What you are doing," I said, "is criminal. You stole my money!"

"Shut up," said Miss Pinch. She got up and got two more beers out of the Iron Maiden.

Candy took hers and held the cold can against her (bleep).

They sat that way for a while.

Then Miss Pinch took a mouthful of beer and leaned over Candy and put it in Candy's mouth. Sort of mouth-to-mouth resuscitation. Candy swallowed convulsively. She began to revive.

Miss Pinch got some marijuana out of a can and rolled a fat joint. She lit it and put it in Candy's mouth. Candy, after a few soulful drags, sat up.

Miss Pinch took the joint and pointed it at me. "Have a few puffs?"

"Gods, no!" I said, already a bit ill with the growing stench of it in the room.

"Smart boy, Inkswitch. But I could get you in severe trouble by reporting to your superiors that you won't do grass. You know and I know that staying away from happy drugs is the fastest way there is to get demoted in a Rockecenter company."

I had her there. I didn't have a superior.

"I notice you aren't dragging on it," I sneered.

"Big H, man. All I ever use is Big H. And speed, of course." She gave the joint back to Candy. "But Candy here is a sweet and delicate thing. I only let her smoke Acapulco Gold, the very best hay. Her psychologist keeps trying to get her on to cocaine, but nose powder would ruin her lipstick. I know why he's doing it. The vicious (bleepard) wants to have sex with her. Straight man sex. A real pervert." She turned to Candy. "We'll get him on that bed there someday, won't we, sweetheart?"

Candy sat up straight. "I feel better now. What's this guy's name?"

"Oh, I'm sorry, Candy. I forgot to introduce you." Miss Pinch pointed to me. "That loathsome male creature's name is Inkswitch. Inkswitch, this is Miss Candy Licorice."

Candy hastily drew back her hands although no motion to shake had occurred. "I am *not* pleased to meet you," she twittered. Then she was off onto something else. "Music. Oh, dear Pinchy, please turn on some music."

Miss Pinch hurriedly raced over and opened up a casket. It was a stereo. She put on a record.

A low sound filled the room. It was coming from the mouths of two devil masks on either side of a brick fireplace evidently used for heating torture tongs.

Wagner! One of his more stern, foreboding symphonies.

Candy listened for a while. Then she began to massage her very ample breasts. The nipples began to stand up.

"Oh, Pinchy," she said, "would you think me forward if I said it's time we really began to prepare for the evening's sex?"

Miss Pinch petted her head and kissed her on the cheek. "Whatever you say, my darling."

I flinched at the look in Pinch's eyes.

Miss Pinch walked over to a closet, her naked body moving like a man's. She reached inside. She was selecting one of several somethings.

She stepped back. She was slapping a fourteen-inch rubber truncheon against her palm.

Candy was sitting up, eyes bright. Wagner rolled through the room. Miss Pinch checked the chains that held me spread-eagled.

Her eye was moving up and down my nakedness with calculating selection.

Candy had her legs apart. She was all bright attention.

Miss Pinch chose the sole of my foot.

WHACK!

"Go ahead and scream," said Miss Pinch. "It's no good without screaming."

I vowed I wouldn't give her that satisfaction. I clenched my teeth.

She aimed for my foot again.

WHAP!

The pain shot through me. It stung!

She moved up the side of the bed. She turned on a red light that put me in a spot.

She chose my stomach.

SPLAT!

Then she got to work.

Teeth bared, laying on with all her might, she began to hit my body everywhere!

She hit my (bleeps).

I screamed!

Candy was panting. Miss Pinch's eyes glared with hate. The rubber truncheon rose and fell in rhythm to Wagner.

Agony!

I screamed and screamed and screamed!

Miss Pinch had descended now to fists!

Candy was whimpering. "Pinchy, Pinchy, Pinchy! Oh, my God, Pinchy, take me, take me quick!"

Miss Pinch whirled. She seized Candy's nakedness in her arms. She raced with her into the other room and slammed the door behind her.

Gibbering moans. Then shrieks and shrieks and shrieks!

Silence. Had Miss Pinch killed her?

At length a low snarling. It sounded like curses.

Then silence.

Minutes later, the door opened. Miss Pinch came in carrying Candy. She dumped her on the sofa and then got down and began to massage her wrists and ankles.

Candy came to and flung her arms around Miss Pinch's neck.

Miss Pinch said to me, "You're a dirty (bleepard), Inkswitch. You have an evil mind. Get your lustful eyes off this poor, innocent girl."

Miss Pinch had some beer and Candy had a joint. After a while Candy said, "Music. I must have some more music, dear Pinchy."

Miss Pinch found *A Night On Bare Mountain*. The awesome strains were shortly coming through the devil masks.

Oh, Gods, they were going to do it again!

The truncheon was even worse!

I passed out.

When I came to a long time later, they were on the couch again but Candy was collapsed on her knees, her hair against Miss Pinch's lean belly.

"Ah," said Miss Pinch. "Decided to stop faking, did you?" She spat at me.

The music had run out. But the beer and marijuana hadn't.

After a while, Candy was stroking Pinch's hair. She said, "Music. I must have music. Dear Pinchy, something soulful, please."

Miss Pinch found a medley of death marches and put them on. Then she went and found an even bigger truncheon.

I didn't even wait for her to hit. I passed out cold to the mournful strains of a dirge. From way off somewhere I could sense the slaps and thuds of blows against my body in funereal cadence.

It was probably hours later that I came to.

Candy's body was draped across the end of the sofa. She had designs drawn on her in lipstick. Her hands flopped over on the floor. Her mouth, wet and smeared, was half-open in sleep.

But Miss Pinch looked deadlier than ever. She saw I had come to. She stood up and with her feet apart and hands on her hips, she said, "You owe me an apology."

That was enough to startle me into total wariness.

"You thought I stole your money. I could tell. When I put the last wad in my purse, I knew that that was what you were thinking. Now admit it."

I wasn't going to talk. But she reached down toward the floor and picked up a truncheon.

"Yes," I said. "And I thought you'd given part of it to the Chief of Security."

"Hogger? Why, how could you think that of Chief Hogger? Believe me, Inkswitch, you won't go far in a Rockecenter company thinking lies about the very pillars on which it is built! He's an honest man. Did he say something?"

"He had a pile of money on his desk," I said.

"Oh, that was probably his collections from drug sales to staff. He has the pusher monopoly for the Octopus Building and you better be careful not to buy from anybody else. How could you think evil of such a fine man?"

She looked up and down my bruised and naked body with disgust. "Men are all evil. You prove it. No, Inkswitch, you have not been the victim of any skulduggery. Your entire $80,000 is right here."

Miss Pinch went over to her discarded overcoat. She began to take packets of money out of the inside pockets. She stacked it up on a table with skulls on each of its four corners. Then she began to flutter it down over my body, a shower of floating, settling bank notes until they covered my thighs.

Then she took out something else. A small sheaf. She came over and leaned her naked chest close above mine. She was holding a piece of paper.

"These are copies of the actual receipts in my office," she said. "Knowing what you would do, I ran off the duplicates I am showing you here. Now, three of these, as you can see, are just vouchers, copies of the ones you signed. But look at these other ones."

I looked. What a strange receipt. Superimposed on it was a picture of my face from below and in the corner, a fingerprint.

"Few know," said Miss Pinch through thin lips, "that there is a camera below the signing ledge. It shoots a picture of the face seen through the voucher and makes them both one. And few know that the pen that people are handed at Window 13 takes a fingerprint and relays it with electronic scan to make it part of the receipt. So the receipt is a composite of money, date, face and fingerprint. The name you sign it with doesn't matter."

"You mean Rockecenter . . ."

"Oh, no, no, no, not that idiot," said Miss Pinch. "Miss Grabball had this installed herself. A refinement of the system. These face-and-fingerprint ones don't go in company files. You thought I was untrained. But she showed me exactly how to work it."

She smiled evilly at me and dug an elbow into my bruised and naked chest. "It's quite clever. It's how Miss Grabball could pick up half of all the petty cash issued. You see, all she had to do, if there was a squawk, was threaten to report the withdrawal to IRS. Unreported income gets three years in a Federal prison. Minimum. And the person who spots the unreported income and tells IRS gets 10 to 20 percent of the money."

She slapped at me and smiled. "So you see, Inkswitch, you are very much in my power. Miss Grabball liked money. I like other things. I have refined the system. If you don't do exactly what I say, I can send you to a Federal pen for three years just like that. And be rewarded in the bargain with 10 to 20 percent of it, all legal. Miss Grabball was deficient in imagination, even though cunning in her way. Using this system, I can blackmail half the employees of Octopus. And get far more in favors and money than Miss Grabball ever dreamed of."

She got up. She stood there naked in the red light. She picked up handfuls of money and showered them down on me. They floated eerily this way and that, settling on and around my bruised nakedness. She was humming a little wordless tune.

At length she said, "So it's all your money, Inkswitch. Every bit of it. Isn't it lovely?" She smeared some against my body and injured thighs.

Then, in a hurricane of motion, she gathered it all up and stuffed it in a big white bag. She put the bag in the lower part of the casket. When she closed the door I saw it was really a safe. She gave the combination a spin.

Then she came back to the bed. "Only I know the combination to that safe. And it can't be beaten out of me. So there's your money, Inkswitch."

She stood there, legs apart, shameless. She held out one hand. It had a hundred-dollar bill in it. "This," she said, "will pay your taxi fare home. It will also pay your taxi fare back here again, tomorrow night."

She dropped the bill on me in contempt. "And maybe," she said, "tomorrow night, I may take pity on you and give you even more of your money."

I gazed at this monster in horror!

"Now promise, if I let you loose right now, you won't kick up a fuss."

I wanted to kill her and she could see it.

"There's a bank camera up in that corner of the room," she said, "so don't get any ideas about murder. Promise?"

What could I do? I promised.

She undid the wrist and ankle cuffs. As I rose, aching and wounded, she kicked my clothes toward me.

I dressed. I picked up the hundred-dollar bill.

"One more thing," this vicious (bleepch) said, "if you come near Window 13 again, I will simply fire off the counter shotgun and say it accidentally discharged. The only place you're going to get any money, Inkswitch, is right here."

She opened the front door and wrought-iron grate. She stood there, naked and thin-lipped in the icy blast. "The first time you came to my window, Inkswitch, I told you to beat it. I didn't think you'd last. But due to Psychiatric Birth Control, all the males around have lately turned into gays to help cut down world population. And I refuse to risk the danger of separating two dear gays. So you're better than nothing, Inkswitch. Although not much. So I will see you right here tomorrow night. It's better than three years in a Federal pen. The homos there would murder you. Don't be late."

I would have slapped her but my fingers were too sore.

I staggered outside into the cold and cheerless night.

But I was not without hope, no matter if dim. The next time I saw this (bleepch) I would kill her.

Chapter 7

I awoke in a world that was against me.

The repairers had patched up the penthouse. My baggage had not been sitting in the lobby so I had to assume that Utanc had paid the damages bill.

The resident doctor, with a midnight "Tch, tch, tch. We must learn we must not let our fingers stray," had patched up my hands.

Right now, a December sun was streaming in the French doors, closed upon the wintery terrace. It was hurting my eyes.

Working as well as I could with cotton-thickened hands, I pushed down the sheet. The bruises had not yet turned as blue and yellow as I knew they would. I felt like I had been mistaken for a piece of pavement and run over by a steamroller. That feeling was confirmed whenever I moved.

But an Apparatus officer is made of stern stuff. I still had a pair of guns. They were black-powder dueling pistols, a pair. I had picked them up cheap one day, thinking they were originals. They were just replicas, modernly built on an 1810 pattern. They were flintlock. They had nine-inch barrels. They were .50 caliber and that half-inch slug could almost cut a body in half. Clumsily, since my bandages were in the way, I cocked and snapped each one. Very gratifying sparks! Powder and balls were in the case. Grunting and hurting my fingers, I got them loaded with enough charge to kill an elephant. That done, I got on to less important things.

I showered as best I could. Every drop inflicted near mortal injury. I got the bandages wet. I had to dry them by holding my hands in the gas fireplace. I was encouraged. They only caught fire twice.

Moaning a bit at the pain of holding the phone, I ordered breakfast.

And with it, of course, came that Gods (bleeped) morning paper.

Masochism knows no limits.

I opened it. There it was, front page:

WHIZ KID
COURT TRIUMPH

In a startling development, the Whiz Kid has won his court battle with M.I.W.

Boggle, Gouge and Hound, today announced that in the case of Wister vs. Massachusetts Institute of Wrectology, an instant out-of-court settlement had been reached for an undisclosed amount.

The president of M.I.W. himself verified that Wister was back in class and on the job in the restaurant.

Student riots ceased at once.

(see photos page 23, "Victorious Students Flood Back to Classes Throughout Nation.")

Speculation was rife in court circles as to the amount of settlement. Herman T. Guesswinkle, the noted astrologer, placed it in the millions. . . .

I slammed the paper down—and hurt my hands. That (bleeping) Madison had followed orders. He had gotten rid of at least one suit. But he had done it in such a way as to make the Whiz Kid a hero! (Bleep), Bury had been wrong about Madison. The man was far worse than I or anyone else had thought!

Somehow, I got the doorknob to open. A stack of papers from

the news vendor fell in. I kicked them and hurt my foot.

I did not turn on the TV. I did not—could not actually—manage the radio. I knew what I would find. Whiz Kid, Whiz Kid, Whiz Kid. Jesus!

Life was much too much for me.

I went back to bed.

About four in the afternoon, the ringing phone woke me up. Using two hands, I got it to my ear.

A gruff voice said, "Inkswitch?"

I grunted, "Yes."

"This is the local Internal Revenue Service office, Inkswitch. We were just making sure we had your correct address." He hung up.

I swung off the bed. Ouch.

That (bleeped) Miss Pinch! If I didn't show up, the message was very clear! She would turn me in! It had to be her. She would have this address or could get it if she dug enough into Octopus Personnel. How else would IRS be interested? I had never filed a return in my life!

Nothing for it. Miss Pinch had to die. Both she and Candy Licorice. I would have to recover those receipts. I had better figure how to blow up the safe.

I got dressed as best I could.

I had not brought much in the way of explosives for such purposes. I took all I had. I put it in the pockets of my overcoat. I also stuffed the dueling pistols in, one on each side.

I hobbled down and got a cab. I had it drop me a block away from Miss Pinch's apartment.

Since it was winter, it was dark already. The rush hour had ebbed. I limped along the darkened street with grim determination.

The basement areaway was pitch black. I had to feel my way along. I took out the right-hand dueling pistol. I cocked it. I pressed its cavernous muzzle against the bell. I stood back.

I wished they had known about silencers in 1810. This was going to make an awful roar!

I could hear someone coming in the hall inside. A thread of

light. It was Candy in her gingham frills. I knew I had made an error. I should have rung three times. That was probably the signal for Miss Pinch. She had used it before.

This time the signal for Miss Pinch was Candy undoing the inside latch.

BONK!

A blackjack hit me in the head from behind!

At least, I think it must have been a blackjack.

I went out with stars exploding all around me. I heard the dueling pistol fall.

Miss Pinch had been standing in the areaway's blackness waiting for me to ring the bell, facing away from her!

That was all I knew just then.

When I awoke, all my clothes were off. I was chained, spread-eagled on the bed, bandaged hands offering no resistance.

Miss Pinch, fully clothed in a mannish suit complete with slouch hat and bow tie, was standing there looking at me.

"Inkswitch," said Miss Pinch, seeing I had now come to. "I have just voted you the top jackass of the year. And we'll soon see how loud you bray."

She reached for the brace of dueling pistols lying on the casket with the explosives from my overcoat. She spun them expertly, one in each hand. She pulled back the mammoth flintlock hammers. She pointed them at me, one at my head, the other at my belly.

She pulled both triggers!

A flash of sparks!

She laughed gaily.

"You forgot to prime them, Inkswitch. Not a single grain of powder in the priming pans!"

It seemed to amuse her mightily. She cocked them once more. She held them very close to my side. She pulled the trigger of the left-hand pistol!

A shower of sparks scorched into my skin. I bit my lips. I would not scream. That's what set these idiots off!

Candy was peeking through the door of the inner room. "May I come in? Now that I won't see him undressing?"

"Come in, sweetheart," said Miss Pinch.

"Ooo!" said Candy. "Its body is all black and blue!"

"Colored meat," said Miss Pinch. "We're going to have colored meat tonight. Now, do you want a drumstick or a wing, you dear girl?"

Candy flinched. "Oh, horrors! Are you trying to suggest that I actually touch a man? You know that is forbidden to us by the instructor. The thought is horrible to me!"

Miss Pinch was quite disturbed she had upset her. She stroked her soothingly. "I promise to stand by Psychiatric Birth Control teachings." Then she had a bright idea. She was very anxious to please. "Watch this!"

She turned the cocked pistol upside down. Too late to yell, I saw powder trickling from the touch hole into the pan!

She pulled the trigger!

BLAM!

The gout of red flame shot across my stomach!

The heavy bullet plowed into the wall. Down came a display of knives!

Black-powder smoke rolled through the room.

That powder burned! The sparks began to eat into my flesh. I could not reach them to beat them out.

I screamed! I was so deafened for the moment I could hardly hear myself. Then after a bit my hearing returned.

Neither of those monsters was in shock.

Candy, panting and hot-eyed, was hauling at Miss Pinch and trying to yank down her own clothes at the same time. "Pinchy, Pinchy. Take me!"

Miss Pinch looked at her. "So soon?" She looked back at me reluctantly. But Candy was kissing her passionately. "All right," said Miss Pinch. She grabbed her, carried her off to the other room and slammed the door.

Moans, groans and shrieks.

Silence.

Low, savage muttering.

Silence.

At least I had had a half-hour reprieve.

Miss Pinch came out. She still had her shoes on. She stood and cursed me. She called me every vile name I had ever heard of and some that I hadn't.

Finally she ran out of vitriol. She sat down on the couch. "Men!" she said, with burning contempt. "Torturers of women!"

"Miss Pinch," I said, "I think you have a psychological problem. I think, perhaps, some childhood experience may have caused you to reverse roles with . . ." I couldn't think of a thing that would account for this monster!

"Well, go on, Inkswitch. Let's hear some juicy tales about you and the little girls in the neighborhood. Possibly gay little anecdotes of how you threw them on a beach of pointed rocks and did a frolicking dance on their faces! Or perhaps how you had a little sister that you carefully made into a whore. Oh, I'm sure you could tell us lots of stories. We would not be amused. For such crimes, Inkswitch, you should be beaten! You will be beaten, Inkswitch!" She turned.

"Candy!" she yelled into the other room. "The (bleepard) just confessed! Come in here!"

Candy came out. She was naked. She watched with interest while Miss Pinch got a big truncheon.

"Now," said Miss Pinch. "You're going to hear some real screams, you darling girl."

"I don't have a sister!" I yelled.

"You will when I get through with you," said Miss Pinch. And laid on with a will. She drew back at last. "Now confess! Did you make your little sister into a whore?"

I confessed hurriedly that I had.

"Then this beating is going to do you lots of good," said Miss Pinch and began in earnest!

It must have been nearing midnight. They had depleted the record cabinet. The room was full of marijuana smoke. They were both naked and exhausted after numerous trips to the other room.

Miss Pinch unchained me. I somehow got into my clothes.

She stood naked in the hall, holding the door open, oblivious to the icy wind.

"You obviously have not had company training, Inkswitch. It is all too plain to see that you prefer sex-smashing a woman down into a bed. You are perverted, Inkswitch. Don't you know that that makes babies and babies are forbidden? Think Psychiatric Birth Control, Inkswitch. Rockecenter would fire you out of hand if he thought you favored old-fashioned sex! So we are doing you a favor, Inkswitch. We will gradually win you away from your male beastliness. Consider it our blessing, Inkswitch."

"Oh, I do," I faltered.

"Very good, you contemptible (bleepard). We will see you here tomorrow night. Without pistols. Primed or unprimed. And without fail."

She stopped. "Oh, I almost forgot. Here is another hundred dollars. You weren't very good tonight. Maybe more tomorrow night. So show up, Inkswitch."

She slammed the door.

The hundred-dollar bill fluttered down beside my feet.

I shivered, beaten, in the cold wind.

PART THIRTY-THREE
Chapter 1

The next day, when I awoke, I came to the conclusion that things were not going very well.

The morning paper confirmed it.

You would not think that a wad of wood pulp, crushed flat, messily smeared with some carbon, could constitute a deadly weapon. But a newspaper is all of that and more. Any direction it is pointed, it can kill. Especially when motivated by an idiot. One who does not seem to know who he is pointing at.

The target person was supposed to be Heller, whatever name they called him, however many doubles he might have. The person it wounded, this morning, was me!

There it was, right on the front page:

TEN–BILLION–BUCK SUIT SETTLED

WHIZ KID TRIUMPHS OVER OCTOPUS

OIL GIANT WRITHES DOW–JONES SOARS

The ten-billion-buck Whiz Kid suit has been settled out of court for an undisclosed amount.

The Director of the Federal Reserve Bank issued an emergency statement that the bank would open this morning and resume business.

In a sudden stop-press announcement in the small hours of this morning, a spokesman for Boggle, Gouge and Hound stunned the assembled media, stating "Octopus Oil is out of danger. We have just met with Swindle and Crouch and reached total agreement on an out-of-court settlement of Wister vs. Octopus Oil."

Swindle and Crouch, when reached, stated, "No comment." But their representative was seen at the courthouse removing the case from the court dockets.

Speculation as to the amount of settlement was rife. The president of the New York Stock Exchange promised that the Exchange would again open its doors.

The dollar is expected to soar against foreign exchange.

The Seven Brothers, in a predawn meeting, pledged the closest possible support to one another.

A director of Peril-Cinch, the world's largest stock-brokering firm, stated, "Now that this threat is out of the way, we can expect Dow-Jones to rise this morning and have coffee. The panic sell-off of Octopus stock, (most of which we bought ourselves), has been ended, and we extend our condolences to the suckers who sold. Octopus stock will now soar. God bless the Whiz Kid and American youth."

Wister, exhausted from his battle, smiled wanly. "I did it all for America." When asked what he would do with the undoubtedly huge amounts of the settlement, he just smiled quietly.

(See page 18 for photos of the Octopus Oil Building and courthouse.)

Later editions carried much the same story. I did not have to look at TV or radio to know what they were saying.

My attention was on something else. I was watching the gaping slit under my door.

Swindle and Crouch *had* been mentioned again in the same story with Boggle, Gouge and Hound.

Snakes were going to come crawling under that door any minute!

I was sure of it.

I ached. The resident doctor, when I had come in around midnight, had rubbed some ointment mixed with "Tch, tch, tch. We must learn not to put our stomach up against certain things," but it hadn't helped a bit. I was bruised and raw!

With a conviction seldom equaled in the Apparatus experience, I knew I had to get out of New York. It was too small for me and Pinch. But I also knew that it was impossible. Heller was winning!

At home in Turkey an unknown assailant from Lombar would rub me out if I left Heller triumphing in New York.

It was a matter of off the barbecue stick and into the flames if I left things in this condition.

I tried to get practical. A baseball bat taken to Madison was all I seemed to be able to think of.

Something desperate was called for.

Moaning from pain, I tried to lie down. Moaning from pain, I tried to stand up.

I compromised. Half-reclining in a chaise lounge I tried to think. An idea greater than any idea I had ever had was absolutely mandatory!

Before I could do anything else, Heller had to be smashed, smashed, smashed!

But how?

Chapter 2

My eyes, sort of glazed, at first did not register what they were looking at.

The viewer was on.

It may have been the bright red colors that drew my attention. They were so glaring, they were painful.

It was Babe Corleone! She was sitting in the back seat of a big limousine that had just stopped. She had on a red gown and a red cape that was printed here and there with black hands. She was wearing a red veil.

The costume she had mentioned! I knew I was looking at the start of Gunsalmo Silva's funeral!

There was a man in black sitting beside her. She was talking to him petulantly. "True, true, Signore Saggezza. You have been a good *consigliere*. True, true, the Corleone family has had none better. True, true, true, I must take your advice. But I don't care what the hell you say, I am going to go to this funeral!"

"*Mia capa*, I plead with you again. It is not wise! The report is just in. The church is swarming with the lice of Faustino Narcotici! This could start a gang war!" He saw he was getting nowhere. He looked with appeal straight out of the viewer. To Heller!

Of course. Heller. I would be getting no picture at all unless Heller was there. My wits were too soaked in pain to concentrate well.

I could make out Heller's own image in the limousine glass. He seemed to be wearing a red tuxedo under a scarlet ski parka with a hood and snow-mask. Everything red. He must be sitting on a jump seat.

Heller looked outside. There was a church seen through the leafless trees of a park. All around the limousine, near to hand, men were packed thickly, facing outward. They held riot shotguns in their hands. They were dressed in black overcoats and black slouch hats. Corleone *soldati*, soldiers alert for war. They were very tense.

Heller turned back. Babe was sulking behind her red veil. The consigliere was still looking at Heller in appeal.

"Mrs. Corleone," said Heller, "why don't I just step over to that church and see what's really going on? Then we'll know for sure whether it is safe or unsafe. We don't want you in the middle of a gang fight."

"They'll shoot you!" said Babe in sudden alarm. "Take ten or twelve men!"

"No," said Heller. "I'll be all right. I'll wear this ski mask."

Heller took out his ornate Llama .45 and jacked a shell into the chamber, put on the safety and then shoved the gun into a back belt holster. He adjusted the ski mask in place.

He started to get out. There was a sound. A yowl! He turned. "You stay there," he said.

The cat was sitting on the other jump seat! It had on a red leather harness and a red collar with brass spikes. It had been about to follow but now it settled back on the seat, sitting up, alert.

I sat up, too! With sudden hope. If Heller was walking straight into the Faustino mob, he indeed might get shot! I didn't have the platen so they mustn't kill him. But a nice painful wound that would put him a long time in the hospital would be just great!

There was every chance of it, too! Imagine going on a scout in a red tuxedo and a luminous scarlet ski parka! About as invisible as a bomb blast! What an idiot!

He walked through the circle of Corleone men and straight over to the church. Actually, it was a small cathedral. A sign said Our Lady of Gracious Peace. They must be somewhere in lower Manhattan.

There was nobody outside, just a few empty limousines.

Heller scanned the cathedral itself. Gothic arches swept up to considerable height on either side of the massive doors. He stepped forward. The altars glittered with gold leaf, the votive candles sputtered in vast rows. Sunlight beamed down through stained glass. The place was empty of people.

At least live people, anyway. A casket, its top open, rested on trestles. Heller did not walk down the aisle and approach it.

Voices were coming from a side room near the main entrance. Heller tiptoed over to the door of it and looked in. The place, in comparison to the main cathedral, was well lit by diagonally paned windows all around it.

It was absolutely crammed with men!

They were in black overcoats and slouch hats. Many had shotguns under their arms. They were facing someone standing on a raised platform.

Razza Louseini! The *consigliere* of Faustino "The Noose" Narcotici! I recognized him well from past dope contacts in Turkey. He was also the man who had fingered Heller that first time in the Howard Johnson's on the New Jersey Turnpike. He would possibly recognize Heller! Marvelous! A good, disabling wound in Heller was exactly what I needed!

Louseini was not making too much progress. He looked angry and upset. "But men," Razza was arguing, "you don't seem to understand. Gunsalmo Silva was killed while on family business. We've got to bury him in some sort of style."

A man in the mob spoke up, "Our family has lost nineteen good men this fall. That's more than in most gang wars. All we been doing all fall is giving our own family members funerals! But Silva wasn't any real loss to us. We got better things to do!"

Others muttered in agreement.

Razza looked at them and showed his teeth. "Silva was a hero! He wasted 'Holy Joe' for us! You got to show respect! How would you like to get bumped and nobody showed respect? How about that?"

Another voice. It was a priest in robes, very close to where Heller stood. Evidently he was the one who was supposed to officiate. "May I speak?"

Razza said, "Go ahead, Father Paciere. Maybe you can talk some sense into their thick heads!"

Father Paciere said, "My sons, we are here in the presence of the dead. It grieves me to see you quarrel in this holy place. I need eight pallbearers and it would please me well if some would volunteer."

A very tough-faced mobster turned toward the priest. "Father, I don't think they been telling you all they know. Gunsalmo Silva was a *traditore*, a traitor to the Corleone family."

The priest recoiled. He crossed himself. "I didn't know!" He bowed his head and shook it sadly. "Now I understand why even his own brother and uncle would not attend. All are equal in the eyes of God, but a *traditore* . . ."

"Hey!" the tough-faced mobster suddenly barked, pointing at Heller. "Who's that? A spy?"

All faces whipped toward Heller in the doorway. Guns came up. Oh, here it came! I was going to get my wish!

Father Paciere said, "No, no. Peace! There will be no firing to desecrate the cathedral!" He came over to Heller.

"My son, you are masked," said the priest. "What is your name?"

Well, I suppose a Royal officer doesn't lie to a priest. He said, "Here on this planet, they call me Jerome Wister."

The noise was such that I couldn't tell what happened for a moment. It was a dreadful smashing sound!

Heller looked.

Men were going out those leaded windows in a rocket stream!

Screams of panic!

Shattering crashes of riot-gun butts hammering out panes to clear the way!

Men were pouring out onto the shrubbery outside!

Limousines were roaring into life!

The room was empty.

The limousines were gone.

A tinkle of broken glass fell with one last sound upon the floor.

Father Paciere came out from behind the door. He was staring at Heller with an open mouth. Then he looked around at the empty and wrecked room. He crossed himself. He looked at Heller, eyes wide, "So you are Wister."

Heller said, "Wait around, Father. Maybe I can get you a funeral started yet."

He sprinted back through the leafless trees. The Corleone soldiers were standing there, open-mouthed, staring at the missing limousines and empty surrounds. Heller went through them. He opened the limousine door.

"Mrs. Corleone, I think it's safe for you to come into the cathedral now. The Faustino mob is gone."

"What did you do?" said Signore Saggezza in astonishment.

"I just think they had another appointment somewhere," said Heller.

He helped Babe out of the limousine. She was rubbing her red-gloved hands together.

Heller reached in and picked up the cat which, to my amazement, promptly climbed up and sat on his shoulder.

"I knew it, I knew it," said Babe. "Not even the Faustino mob can stand a turncoat and a traitor like Silva!"

Signore Saggezza issued a few crisp orders. The Corleone *soldati* raced ahead and took up positions outside and inside the cathedral.

Babe, Heller and the cat approached the vast wide doors.

Father Paciere met Babe in the aisle. Her six feet six towered over him. "My child," he said, "I am afraid there is little in the way of a funeral for this man. Not even his own brother would attend."

"Have no fear, Father Paciere," said Babe, "we will give the *traditore* a funeral he is not likely to forget."

She swept on forward in her red cape printed with black hands. She marched up to the casket.

The morticians had rebuilt Silva's face, probably from police I.D. shots. He lay in state. Although pretty yellow colored, he really didn't look bad, particularly considering what a mess he must have been after his fall.

Babe towered above it. She lifted her red veil.

"Traditore!" she said.

SHE SPAT ON SILVA!

The priest drew back in horror.

Suddenly the cat let out a snarl!

It rocketed off Heller's shoulder!

It went straight at Silva's face, snarling and clawing!

RAKE! RAKE! RAKE!

Heller hurriedly reached over and pried the cat off. As he held it, it kept snarling and hissing the way only a cat can do! It was hard for Heller to hold it. No cathedral organ for Silva. Those sounds of hate reverberated through the vaults.

Babe shouted, "Signore Saggezza! The men, if you please."

The Corleone *soldati,* mindful of their posts and withdrawing to them immediately, yet came forward one by one.

Each took a dagger out as he approached the coffin.

Each plunged the dagger into the chest of the corpse, spat on the face and cried, *"Traditore!"*

Father Paciere was cowering back, powerless to stop it.

The *soldati* finished their part of the ceremony.

Babe, red cape flowing in the drafty place, held up her hand.

Georgio rushed forward. He gave her two long, black sticks. She took one. Geovani rushed up. He had a blowtorch. He fired it off. Babe put the end of one black stick into its flame.

A branding iron!

The end began to glow red. A T! For *traditore,* traitor!

She approached the casket.

Into the right cheek of the corpse she pressed the sizzling end! Smoke rose. She pressed the T into the left cheek. More smoke.

The corpse's face was branded as a traitor!

Babe was not through.

She took the other iron and began to heat it.

Father Paciere wailed.

It was a cross!

It glowed cherry red.

She again approached the casket.

She lifted her red-veiled face to the vault of heaven. She cried, *"MUEM SUPROC TSE COH!"*

She plunged it down upon the forehead. The cross was upside down!

Oh, Gods, I suddenly understood. The words *Hoc est corpus meum* are the words of Holy Communion. They mean "This is my body," in Latin. When they are said backwards, over an inverted cross, the grace of one of their Gods is *taken* from the individual, not given to him. He would receive the reverse of forgiveness. BLACK MASS!

The priest cried out. He crossed himself frantically.

Babe pulled the iron up.

Silva was branded to be never forgiven by anyone! Not even a God.

"Oh, my child," wept the priest, "I will have to tell Father Xavier to give you thirty *Pater Nosters* for this and thirty-one *Ave Marias*. You have desecrated a house of God with the rites of the Black Mass."

"It's worth it," said Babe. "The dirty, filthy traitor! Now you cannot bury him in consecrated ground."

"No, we cannot," wept the priest, "though it is doubtful if even God would accept a traitor."

"Very good," said Babe with satisfaction. "Then we have handled your funeral problem. I suggest you send the body over to the New Jersey pig farms and have it fed to the pigs."

"No, no," said the priest. "They would protest the infecting of their pigs."

"Ah, I have it," said Babe. "Tell the mortician to send the body to I. G. Barben Pharmaceuticals to make poison out of!"

"As you say, my child," said the priest.

Babe leaned over the casket again, staring at the branded face. *"Traditore!"* she said once more. And once more she lifted her red veil and spat.

Proudly, Babe Corleone strode up the aisle and left the cathedral.

They reached the limousine. She sank down on the seat, smiling, pulling off her red gloves.

Heller put the cat down on the jump seat.

Babe reached over and petted it. "This is a very nice cat, Jerome. He knows a traitor when he sees one."

They drove away.

Gunsalmo Silva had had his funeral.

But I, though disappointed Heller had not been shot, also had something.

I had a great idea!

The idea was so good, I only screamed a little as I dressed.

I was on my way to wreck Heller once and for all!

Chapter 3

It was very obvious that J. Walter Madison needed some mature help and guidance but he didn't seem to be exactly hanging upon my every word.

I had gotten there in an agonizingly painful taxi ride—every pebble or white line a tire hit communicated to one or another of my bruises. I had somehow gotten up the steps of 42 Mess Street without falling back down them. I had elbowed my way through the churning menagerie of staff reporters and publicity men at great cost of elbow bruises. And Madison, debonair, appealing and sincere, was really not paying any attention to me.

He also had somebody on the phone. He looked at me while he talked to me as well as the person on the other end of the phone. "Hello, Mr. Smith. Well, all I am saying is that you better give me front page. You look sort of pale. What's Mount St. Helens got to do with it?"

I started to speak for the third time. "I am trying to tell you that I have found Hel—— I mean Wister's real weakness."

"Well, so what if it blew the whole top of its head off? Didn't it do that already, years ago? I'm always glad to have your opinion, Mr. Smith. Well, I admit that Portland, Oregon, buried under ashes does rate more space than a classified ad. What have you been doing to your face? It seems bruised. So what if the business section is buried under lava? Have you seen a doctor?"

Desperate, I said, "I am certain you will be running out of front-page material soon, Madison. Maybe even tomorrow, I hope. I have the very thing for you."

"Well, push it to page two, page six. Even nonprofessional ideas are welcome, Smith. So thousands died and more thousands are missing. Why don't you just go out and tell one of the staff, Smith."

"I've got something about Hel—— Wister that nobody else knows!"

"Well, it *is* necessary that I talk to you. If you can see lava rolling right at your building right now, get a rewrite man on it and give me your full attention here. I am shocked you would suggest an exposé at this stage, Smith; the time is not ripe. You better give me the front page on what I send or the *Portland Grimes* will find itself in trouble. If I can't have your front page . . . What? You don't have any paper now, much less a front page? Then what the hell am I doing talking to you?" He hung up.

"It's a great idea!" I begged.

"I can't send the Whiz Kid out to rescue Mount St. Helens. It's off image, Smith." He was reaching for the phone again.

Firmly I put my bandaged hand down on his, preventing his picking the instrument up again. And although my voice was rough and hoarse from screaming, I raised it stridently. "You will need a front page on Wister tomorrow. You have shot your bolt on the suits. I am trying to give you tomorrow's front page!"

"But I haven't shot my bolt, as you so unprofessionally put it, on the suits. And I have tomorrow's front page! Here it is!" He thrust the smudgily typed news story at me.

It said:

WHIZ KID DONATES WHOLE SETTLEMENT TO CHARITY

In a magnificent gesture, the Whiz Kid today signified that the entire settlement sums

> realized from his legal battle with M.I.W. and
> Octopus Oil would be given in full to charity.
>
> "I am not one to profit from the mis-
> fortunes of others," he was quoted as stating.
> "I shall not keep one dime of the monies
> awarded. Every penny will be given to a worthy
> cause."

It went on and on. I was sickened by it. "You mean," I said, "you're going to let him give away those huge sums? Of course, I'm happy to see him bro . . ."

Madison said, "Huge sums? Honesty is a keynote in PR, Smith. Not one word has been said about the *actual* amounts M.I.W. and Octopus settled for. Just read the stories of the last two days. The settlement in both cases was zero cash. So of course he can give it all to charity. No money was involved. I always keep a firm check on reality, Smith. So there, as you can see, is sure-fire, front-page, national coverage tomorrow. What a gesture! How typical of his great nature! And besides, it's already on the wire, going out to every paper in the land."

He would have lifted the phone. I applied more pressure to the back of his hand despite my pain. "Day after tomorrow, then," I cried. "You haven't got day *after* tomorrow and I have it for you!"

"Well, I'll admit," said Madison, "that day after tomorrow is pretty far into the future. You see, the image I am trying to build is——"

"Listen to me, then! Listen loud and clear. Here is your story! 'The Whiz Kid Has Mob Links!' Madison, he's thoroughly hooked up to organized crime! The Mafia!"

"Well, who isn't?" he began. "Our very best people . . . Wait a minute, Smith. Wait a minute. I do think . . ." He leaped up from his desk. He began to pace back and forth. He was in the throes of inspiration.

I tried to tell him more but he held up his hand to quiet me. I persisted. He raised his voice, "Facts, Smith. You are trying to disturb my concentration with facts. Fact has nothing to do with

PR, Smith. You are being delusory! Newspapers wouldn't sell at all if they dealt in real data. So be quiet."

I subsided.

He paced a bit more. "Let me see. I have been trying desperately to think of how I am going to get him back in the fuel business. We have to continue Controversy. Image, image. I have to think of image. Positioning. Names. That's it! NAMES! Names make news, Smith. You have to connect up big names! I have it! You are right, Smith! Mob links *is* a wonderful idea!"

I sank down in a chair. I had gotten through to him!

"Tramp!" he yelled into the other room. And Ted Tramp rushed in. "Ted," said Madison, "what reporter do we have that knows mob figures and is expendable?"

Tramp said, "There's old Bob Hoodward. He was a great investigative reporter in his day. When he was on the staff of the *Washington Roast* he even brought down President Nixon and some other mob figures. But that was decades back. He's on his last beat now—dead beat, in fact. Expendable."

They rushed out. I could see them buttonhole a gray wreck. They talked in low tones excitedly.

Oh, thank Gods, I was getting some action. I did some rapid calculation. I maybe could live through today and tomorrow. After that, it was impossible. If this worked, I would have Heller smashed and I could flee New York and Miss Pinch! It would be a near thing.

Madison raised his voice, "Today! We have to have it today! Only then can it be front page day after tomorrow! So don't you dare fail to get his consent!"

I could see Hoodward out in the other room as he sank into a chair and picked up a phone. He was making a call to someone important as he seemed to be going through several intermediaries.

Despite my pain, I dragged myself over toward him so I could hear above the clattering din.

He had his party. ". . . So you see, sir, as one of the city's most prominent and respected citizens, we want you to present the award. . . . Oh, yes, sir, I am aware that you are trying to build an image for yourself. That's why I thought of you at once. . . .

The award is a monetary prize for The Most Honest Man of the Year. . . . Yes. Well, you see, sir, I thought of that. By your being associated with the most honest man of the year, that, of course, positions you as an honest man and helps your image. . . . No, I can't tell you the name of the recipient. It is just this minute being drawn by lottery. . . ."

Madison was urgently pushing a slip of paper at him. Hoodward looked at it. "The appointment is for three o'clock this very afternoon at the Tammany Hall Auditorium. It will only take a few minutes. . . . Yes, sir. Only selected press will be present. . . . Really, just myself and photographers, no TV. . . . Oh, yes, sir, I can assure you that it will get national coverage and I promise you faithfully that I will clear the story and caption with you, every word. You can depend on me, sir."

He hung up and stood up. "He'll be there. Is this on the level, Madison?"

"You know it is, Bob. Now, everybody, we've got to move very fast on this. Bob, you leave right away and escort him there. Take a cab."

The old reporter tottered out.

Madison had three photographers picked out. He sent them hurriedly into makeup to get their faces made unrecognizable. That done, he put them in bulletproof vests.

Then he phoned orders to the bogus Whiz Kid.

I began to get sort of lost. What did makeup and bulletproof vests have to do with it?

It wasn't until we were all piled into an unmarked van that I had a chance to ask Madison.

"Mob figures are chancy things," he said. "I'm surprised you are coming along. This is highly professional PR, Smith."

"It was my idea," I defended, wincing as we hit a bump.

"So it was," he said. "I am really gratified at your support and encouragement, Smith. It really is a great idea."

Fact was, I was getting pretty foggy about WHAT idea was being executed.

We tore through the truck- and dray-crowded streets. The

afternoon was cold and sleet was spitting out of the sky. The pavement glistened gray. Fitting weather in which to torpedo Heller.

We drew up at the back of Tammany Hall. It was a recently restored building in a park, a landmark used for only the most sacred occasions. Apparently Rockecenter had financed its reconstruction, and the land around it, which he owned, had rocketed in value: very public spirited. So Madison had the run of the place.

It was about a quarter to three. The photographers leaped out and rushed in. Madison led me up a different flight of stairs.

We came out overlooking a small auditorium. We were on a little balcony—a box, really—well screened from the floor below. But we could see everything that went on.

There was a raised lecture stage there. It had doors at the back of it. There was a big chair with a solid back facing the empty seats for the audience. The photographers were positioning things. They got the auditorium lights very low. They got their own flash guns in position.

Madison, now that he had it all moving, was chatty. "That chair," he said, "is historic. It's the same one Boss Tweed used to use when he collected his payoffs from the whole city. Well, it will even be more historic yet, shortly."

The Whiz Kid double rushed in from a side door. It was the first time I had seen him in the flesh. Actually, aside from being tall for his age and blond, he really didn't have any of the aura of Heller. It wasn't just his buckteeth and protruding jaw or even his horn-rimmed glasses. He had the air of a cheap bum, really. It gave me a lot of satisfaction. This nut couldn't have ordered a puppy dog to wag its tail! But he did have a kind of impudent brass. The photographers were trying to get him to sit just so in the chair. He had his own ideas.

He was wearing a red racing suit and carrying a racing helmet and he thought he would look better with the helmet on and the photographers were telling him to (bleep) well keep it off—it threw a shadow on his face.

Out of curiosity more than any inkling of coming trouble, I said to Madison, "Who is this mob figure you're getting?"

"Why the top man. Names make news, Smith. The *capo di tutti capi* of course. Faustino 'The Noose' Narcotici, naturally."

With a shock, I remembered the funeral. "Wait! The minute Faustino knows it's Wister, he'll run! I guarantee it!"

"Well, well!" said Madison. "Now you tell me."

He rushed down a side stairs to the floor and hurriedly issued some orders. He came back up.

"Whew, Smith. You certainly play it close. You could have blown the whole caper. (Bleep) working with unprofessionals! But it will be all right now."

The bogus Whiz Kid put the racing helmet on and closed the opaque visor.

There was a burst of activity behind the stage.

Three Faustino bodyguards rushed in. With sawed-off shotguns they probed the seats. They made sure the cameras weren't guns. They opened doors. They were trying to make certain it wasn't a hit spot.

Madison and I drew back. The bodyguards gave the boxes a perfunctory glance and then contented themselves with stationing a man to fire in case a gun was shoved over the rail from this mezzanine.

Faustino came waddling through a door at the back of the stage. Hoodward was with him. The aged reporter put a big sheaf of bills in Faustino's hands and fanned them out. The *capo di tutti capi*'s rings flashed as he arranged the money in his hands.

The Whiz Kid double was sitting in the chair with the helmet on, facing forward.

Hoodward finished coaching Faustino.

The mob chief moved fatly forward to the side of the chair.

The photographers stood alert.

Faustino put on his best gold-toothed smile. He said, "As the most honest citizen of New York, I hereby have the honor to present you with your award as the Most Honest Man of the Year." He extended the money to the bogus Whiz Kid.

The phoney Wister extended a hand for the money and with the other, plucked off his helmet. He was smiling.

Flash guns flashed!

The smile on Faustino's face froze!

He let out a scream!

Money spurted out of his hands as he flung it away!

He ran!

His bodyguards ran!

The photographers ran!

We ran!

As we mobbed into the van, Hoodward caught up, prevented the door from slamming and got in. He was furious.

"You set me up!" he yelled at Madison.

Madison said to the photographers, "You got it in the can?"

They nodded gleefully.

Hoodward said, "I don't know why he ran but I know Faustino will murder me! I may get away with wrecking a president but not a *capo di tutti capi!*"

"I think of everything," said Madison. "You've wanted to retire for years. Here is a ticket I always keep on hand. Straight flight to Israel. It's in the name of Martin Borman. There's a nice room reserved there in that name. And here's my own gold watch for long and faithful service."

"Wait a minute," I said. "I don't get how this works out. The Whiz Kid image isn't honesty. What are you trying to do?"

"My dear Smith," said Madison, "it is plain that you, while you may get great ideas, don't really grasp the nuances and fundamentals of the newspaper business. It is, essentially, an entertainment industry. Never let anyone in on what you are trying to do, much less let the public in on what is really going on. You disappoint me. You ought to be saying, and would, if you were a professional PR man, 'Eighteen-point quote Madison Does It Again unquote' and all you're doing is asking questions. Can't we let you off somewhere? We've got to get Hoodward to the airport terminal quick."

Chapter 4

All that money flying around the stage had reminded me how close to broke I was. Unfortunately, Hoodward had delayed to pick it up: that's what had almost made him miss the van. I was not going to miss anything. Day after tomorrow, as soon as Heller was ruined—and though I did not see quite how, I had high hopes—yours truly was going to be gone from New York. It would be a near thing, touch and go, the way I planned my escape. Remembering that the route from Turkey to the U.S. lay through Rome, Paris and London, and remembering, too, the way they gouged tourists in those places, I needed cash.

There was only one way to get it. To torture the combination out of Miss Pinch and then to murder her in the most gruesome and grisly way imaginable. There was no other choice: I was far too weak and shaky to rob a bank. But the Apparatus trains one and prepares one for such emergencies. I knew how to do it.

Actually, I would like to omit that evening from this confession. It is too horrible. Murder should not be advertised to the young and this confession might someday fall—Gods forbid—into the hands of the immature. Even a Justiciary is likely to pale at what happened.

But in all honesty, as promised, I will carry on, even though the next few hours fill me with remorse. In all my crimes and escapades, this was the worst.

I knew where, in New York, I could procure the weapons—a supermarket.

Guile was the watchword. There is an Apparatus technique called the "Lure-Kill." It pretends affection as a mask for murder.

I tottered along the shelves of the supermarket, supported by the rolling, wheeled shopping basket. I found what I wanted in the condiments section—a big, glaringly labeled box of McKormick's Red Pepper.

I crept, supported by the shopping cart, to the flower section. As Christmas was just up the line, there were huge bouquets of white chrysanthemums to be had. Despite the expense, I bought the best.

At checkout, I prevailed upon the teenager not to crush them into a sack, but to actually wrap them like flowers with an open top.

I went outside and found a dark place. Putting a thick handkerchief over my nose and tying it as best I could with my bandaged hands, I then took the red pepper and, with care, worked it under every petal. Time consuming.

That done, I threw the empty pepper can in the trash and closed the top of the bouquet with a single fold.

With glee, I contemplated what would happen. Miss Pinch would open the door, holding a gun as usual. I would say, "You have reformed me from being a beastly male and I bring this to express my affection." She would say, "Oh, how charming!" And she would take the bouquet, pull back the top flap to see what it was, behold flowers and sniff! That would be all I would need. I would have her gun as she convulsed in sneezes. I would hit her over the head. I would drag her to that bed and use every torture implement in the place until I had that combination. Candy? I would just gut-shoot her and laugh as she writhed.

I got a cab. I was dropped off a block away so no one could trace me by cab numbers to the murder site.

It was very dark. The rush hour had ended. They would be home.

Feebly, I tottered to the house. I went down the basement steps. I made sure there was no one behind me. I rang the bell.

Footsteps!

Success!

It was Miss Pinch!

She was dressed in mannish pants and shirt. And as I had suspected, she was carrying a revolver.

She opened the door and outer grill and stood back.

I said, "Miss Pinch, you have reformed me from being a beastly male and I bring this to express my affection."

I held out the flowers.

The play didn't quite go as planned.

"Flowers?" she said. "Why, you dirty (bleepard)! You're trying to steal Candy from me, are you? Well, to hell with that!"

She seized the wrapped bouquet.

She jabbed me backwards with the gun.

She slammed the flowers down on the dirty floor of the areaway!

She stamped on them with her heel!

She kicked the lid off a garbage can! I flinched at the violence of the clatter.

Without taking her eyes or gun off me, blocking my exit up the basement stairs, she scooped the destroyed bouquet up and threw it in the garbage can.

Then she halted.

She sniffed slightly.

With a hand, she flapped a careful sample of the air from the top of the garbage can to her.

"Red pepper!" she snarled. "Why, you dirty (bleepard)!"

In vain I tried to tell her it must have been on the discarded fish. Making motions that seemed to indicate she was about to pistol-whip me, she drove me inside.

She locked the wrought-iron grill and door behind her.

She fired a shot so near my head, I felt the powder sting.

"I will give you to the count of ten to get out of your clothes!" she snarled. "And after that I am going to shoot off your (bleeps)! ONE!"

I hastily got out of my overcoat.

"TWO!"

I shed my jacket and my shoes at the same time.

"THREE!"

I was undressed. I couldn't see why she was still counting.

"FOUR!"

It was my hat. I had forgotten my hat! I flung it frantically away from me.

In no time after that she had me wrist- and ankle-cuffed, spread-eagled face up on that Gods (bleeped) bed!

When she finished the last cuff, she threw the gun aside. "So you like red pepper, do you? Well, always give the male the right to his chauvinistic domination." She turned and called into the other room, her voice lilting, "Oh, Candy dear, we're going to have Mexican red-hot tamales tonight!"

She began to hum a little wordless tune. She took off her shirt. She took off her shoes. She stepped out of her pants. She shucked off her underwear and stood naked, still humming.

Candy tiptoed shyly in. She saw what was coming off and began to strip, halting halfway and saying, "Oh, dear Pinchy, make him look the other way."

Pinch did with a backhand slap. Then she went on humming. Slap or not, I watched in growing anxiety.

Miss Pinch opened a drawer and got out a small white apron about three inches wide that covered nothing. She put it on. Then she got a cook's hat, tall and stiffly starched. She put it on at a rakish angle.

Then she got a little gingham napkin and hung it around Candy's neck and tied it. It didn't even cover her now naked, bulging breasts. She sat Candy down on the sofa where she waited, knees apart, watching with eyes that were gradually getting hot.

They evidently used the torture-implement fireplace for barbecuing. It had all the long forks and tongs and needful tools. But Miss Pinch was putting those to one side. She was looking through a pile of kitchen utensils.

I knew it would not do the slightest good to protest. I knew I should try not to scream. But my body was already so bruised and beaten, I knew that it was impossible to do much more damage to it, so I took heart.

I shouldn't have.

Miss Pinch found what she wanted.

A cheese grater!

She tested the ragged sharpness of its jagged teeth. She cut herself slightly and stopped humming long enough to curse me for it.

Then, humming again, she approached the bed.

Very lightly and with artistry, she began to draw the cheese grater down my chest!

It was sharp. I bit my lips. I would not scream. But she was paying little attention to that. All her concentration was that of a chef's. And Candy looked like a hungry diner!

She shifted her target to my legs. She drew the cheese grater down along the insides, making a wavy pattern of scrapes very carefully.

I could see small bubbles of blood rising in the raw scrapes.

She put the grater aside. She went to a torture rack and opened a cabinet under it and got something out!

A can of red pepper!

Holding her face away, she put some in her hand and began to massage it quietly into the wounds!

Sheer pain!

I let out my first scream.

I choked it back.

More red pepper and more massage.

I screamed!

Candy yipped!

Miss Pinch seemed to think that was enough red pepper. Half a can. She went and got a three-foot wooden spoon. She carefully turned it to the bulging side.

WHAP!

She began to beat the pepper in!

With all her might!

Agony!

Scorching, sizzling agony!

I lost control. I began to scream!

Candy began to scream.

I could see her, naked, bucking about on the sofa.

"Take me, Pinchy, oh God, take me!"

Miss Pinch scooped her up, carried her into the bedroom and slammed the door shut with her heel.

The pain didn't stop.

I kept screaming!

To make it worse, I could only half see!

After how long I do not know, Miss Pinch came back. She had lipstick on her apron.

Candy came out, breasts rising and falling.

They had a beer.

Candy had a joint.

Miss Pinch apologized to Candy for having forgotten the dinner music. She put some mood music on the stereo and Candy said it was nice. But she was still hungry.

"Oh, that was only the first course," said Miss Pinch. "We mustn't be too greedy. This is a gourmet dinner."

I had just begun to be able to support the awful torment of that pepper without screaming or writhing.

Miss Pinch retied her apron. She adjusted her cook's hat. She went over to the cabinet and took out something.

"This is what we need now," she said, showing Candy. "It will titillate the jaded palate. I can't stand bland food, can you, Candy dear?"

She came over.

TABASCO SAUCE!

She sprinkled it from the squirting bottle all up and down the wounds! Artistically, humming, making sure that it was just right.

At the first touch of it, I thought it was liquid fire! And she was emptying the whole bottle!

I began to scream.

She went and got the cheese grater again.

She went to work.

I really screamed!

Candy began to yip. She was bouncing all over the couch.

Miss Pinch had hold of a three-foot barbecue fork. She was raising it to bring it down.

"Take me, Pinchy, take me!"

Miss Pinch brought it down anyway! Time and time again!

I passed out.

When I came to, it was like trying to live in a bed of live coals! They were not in the room.

I could hear low, snarling curses from the other side of the closed door.

They finally came back. Candy was wild-eyed. She kept rubbing and cupping her breasts.

"It's too bland, dear Pinchy. I don't mean to be critical. But I'm starving!"

Miss Pinch looked distressed. Then she took a tug at her apron. She found her cook's hat in the other room and came back with it.

She gazed at me. "Mustard!" she said in sudden decision. "That's what it needs! Mustard! To give it some tang!"

She went and found an enormous jar of French mustard with a squirt spigot. From on high she trailed artistic designs on my body.

She threw it aside. With two vigorous hands, she began to rub it in.

I screamed. I begged and pleaded. I told her I would do anything, anything, but please, for Gods' sakes, get this stuff out of these wounds!

Candy smiled. "It sounds delicious," she said. "Rub him harder!"

Miss Pinch went and got a rolling pin. She used it to rub the mixture in.

Then she cheese-grated some more.

Then she began to use the rolling pin to beat it into me!

I was clever. I managed to get my head in the way and get knocked out!

I came to a long time later. Candy was flopped on the floor, exhausted, designs drawn all over her naked body with lipstick, her mouth open and wet, out cold.

Marijuana smoke was thick in the place.

Beer cans rolled about dribbling.

Miss Pinch was just completing an intravenous shot of Big H. She drew the needle out. She looked at me. The drug wasn't making her any more cheerful. She went through a hot surge.

She composed her face into a deadly mask of hate.

I was on fire down to the middle of my soul. I burned so, I could only think one raving thought. I was smart enough not to voice it. Get out of New York!

"You male (bleepard)," said Miss Pinch. "You were very bad tonight. You aren't even fit for pigs to eat, truth be told. You aren't living up to what the Psychiatric Birth Control classes said even a *lousy* male should! Dr. Frybrain would call you a retarded pervert!"

I shut my eyes. They burned and I couldn't see well anyway.

She kicked at me. "Are you a homo yet?"

"No!" I screamed. The one thing I would never be was a homosexual. Sick as I was, I was revolted even more!

"Then, see? We aren't having the least success with you. You're trying to make us fail our homework! Get on your God (bleeped) clothes, you (bleepard)."

"For Gods' sake let me wash these wounds out!"

"Hah," she said. "Don't try to change the subject! All you men can think about is women. That's forbidden!" She grabbed the naked Candy and stroked her breasts. "You're that psychiatric horror, a normal male! All you can think about is pawing some poor, defenseless girl. Look at her. Completely unconscious just from being unable to stand the thought of you touching her! And I would kill you if you did." She kissed the unconscious Candy passionately on the mouth. "You came here tonight to steal her away from me, you loathsome beast. I am glad you have learned your lesson. Now get dressed."

"I'm still chained!" I said.

She dropped Candy who flopped into a naked heap. She picked the gun up off the floor. She cocked it.

Savagely she cast off the shackles one by one.

Moving when I tried it was agony again!

"Let me take a shower," I begged.

"And dirty up the bathroom where this dear innocent girl stands every day? Never! Get on your clothes!"

I think that vicious, calculating (bleepch) knew what would happen. As soon as I got into my clothes, the red pepper and Tabasco sauce and mustard reactivated in the wounds!

I screamed.

Candy stirred. "Pinchy, kiss me."

Miss Pinch did and if I had had the strength, I could have killed her, killed them both, lying naked and entwined there on the floor.

But I saw I could get out and that was all I could think of. Besides, the gun was still pointed at me. I fumbled for the door.

Miss Pinch called after me, "If you don't get here on time tomorrow night, remember, it's three years in the Federal pen!"

I couldn't even close the door behind me.

On fire, trying not to scream, I made it to an avenue. I got a cab.

Half an hour later, the resident doctor had me in a shower, working at the wounds in a most painful way to get the red pepper, Tabasco and mustard out. It didn't hurt so much, only because he had first given me a shot of morphine.

As he worked, he said, "Tch, tch, tch. With all these injuries, we certainly must be running with a rough crowd."

Well, no more. If all went well, in forty-eight hours Heller would be finished and I would be out of New York! The town was too much for me. Never in my life had I thought a city could turn you into a salad. If I didn't watch it I could even become a fruitcake!

Chapter 5

When I awoke the next day, it was already noon. I checked myself over carefully as I lay there in the bed. Yes, I was still alive, incredible but true.

I had one ace up my raw sleeve.

I was *not* going to visit Miss Pinch that evening!

The question was, would I get away with it? Would I get out of New York alive?

It was going to be an awfully near thing. I clenched my teeth. Duty was a burden but I had to make sure Heller was wrecked before I could go. Otherwise I would be assassinated by the unknown spy on my return to Turkey. It would do no good to leave New York alive if I would then wind up in Turkey dead. Then, with a new surge of horror, I remembered the assassin had threatened to kill Utanc first!

Somehow I had to suffer through the next twenty-four or so hours. Tomorrow would be the crucial time, for then, observing that I had not shown up on schedule, Miss Pinch would call the Internal Revenue Service.

Bury would surely have noticed by this time, no matter how deep he was in the Central American jungle, that once more Boggle, Gouge and Hound had been coupled with Swindle and Crouch.

I managed the phone with two hands and ordered some breakfast. It was an unwise action. The room-service waiter, noting all the papers outside the door, added the mound to my burdens.

It was the push that sort of sent me over the edge.

Just as Madison had predicted, the Whiz Kid was all over the front page.

In an action *"unprecedented in history"* he had presented *"anything he had won in settlements"* to the farmers of Kansas.

I knew now that, factually, it was a nothing amount that he was retaining a nothing of. But this thing about farmers of Kansas was quite beyond me. What did they have to do with it?

Maybe I was sort of feverish already but this puzzle turned it into a kind of strange delirium.

All the rest of that day I lay there with my eyes fearfully on the door. I expected two deadly IRS men to slither through the crack at the bottom or a snake to call me via the U.S. Army Signal Corps before I could check out. An uncomfortable frame of mind. It got worse when dark came. I knew what the reaction of Miss Pinch would be when there was no ring at her front door. The tension would mount to an explosion syndrome! She would be more than slightly peeved! Her reactions would become more and more unprintable.

As the night wore on, every time a curtain stirred, I knew it would be Lombar's unknown assailant, magically transported by magic carpet from Turkey with a communication from the Widow Tayl informing me that she, too, had called IRS. It didn't even do any good to sleep. That brought nightmares and prominent in them was Candy pleading with Lombar and the assassin pilots to make me scream harder!

And through it all, echoing in the room, were the first words Heller had ever spoken to me: "From your accent, you're an Academy officer, aren't you? What sad route brought you to the 'drunks'?"

It was very confusing. How had he known about Bury?

The hours and the fog dispersed.

Voices. Real voices!

It was the resident doctor. Winter sunlight was coming in the hotel penthouse terrace doors. Morning had come once more. It was D-day! "He seems to have had a fever. It's broken now. If he drops off to sleep and begins the screaming again, just give him one of these aspirin." He closed up his bag and left.

Utanc! She was standing over by the mirror. She was dressed in a silk lounging robe and primping at her hair. She must have felt my eyes on her. "You kept screaming and I couldn't hear my radio well so when the doctor came, I let him in."

Dear Utanc! She was all I had. How thoughtful of her! How tender.

I said, "They're after me!"

"I shouldn't wonder," she said, putting a strand of her hair in place under a diamond clip.

"No, no! They really are after me! The Feds are liable to send the U.S. Army here with snakes any minute!"

She whirled. Ah, I had her attention. She did care for me after all! "The wallet!" she said. "The wallet with blood on it! The man you had killed!"

I was too weak to argue. "Yes. Yes, that's it. If I get good news this morning we have to flee! Although we've got to delay, we can't. We must get out of New York!"

Her face went white! She said, "There's a plane at four. I will pack at once!" Practical, efficient girl. She was gone like a shot!

I was too wobbly and hoarse to call her back. If I didn't get the good news, I would only be going home to my death.

With two bandaged hands I managed to get room service on the phone. This was going to be a near thing. The U.S. Army Signal Corps was liable to bring the snakes covered with IRS red pepper any minute.

I told room service, "Send me two scrambled newspapers, overdone."

I waited in mental and physical stress. The waiter came and finding stacks of newspapers at the door, brought those in, too, and dumped them on the bed: the movement sent waves of agony through me but newspapers always do.

I opened one with shaking hands.

Was this victory or death?

Chapter 6

Ye Gods!
Headlines!

WHIZ KID BRIBED
TO THROW RACE!

And the story with its titles:

WHIZ KID FUEL DIDN'T FAIL

The famous investigative reporter, Bob Hoodward, the Nixon Nailer, has ferreted out the facts. The famous Spreeport Race was thrown by the Whiz Kid for payola!

FUEL VALID

Earlier belief that the race was lost due to defective fuel has now been exposed as false.

MOB FIGURE

The Whiz Kid had the honor to be bribed by the most famous Mafia mob mogul on the planet, no less than Faustino "The Noose" Narcotici, *capo di tutti capi*.

CONFESSION

In an exclusive interview with Hoodward, Wister confessed. "I thought I would not have money enough to develop my fuel, so I did it the American Way: for cash, I threw the race."

I gaped! I had never realized the extent imagination played in PR!

But how convincing!

And here was the photo, front page, three columns wide! A smiling Faustino was handing a grinning Whiz Kid the most huge wad of filthy lucre anybody would ever care to have. And the Whiz Kid was obviously lifting his helmet in salute to his benefactor. No matter that a tenth of a second later, Faustino had been running like an electric rabbit on a greyhound track! Those photographers had gotten it in the nick of time! What experts!

The caption under the photo said:

> Secret candid shot proving the bribe: In the chair once used by Boss Tweed, the Bribe Baron of New York in the '90s, the Whiz Kid, Gerry Wister, receives his payoff from *capo di tutti capi* Faustino "The Noose" Narcotici, crime czar of the world.

I was stunned! What virtuosity PR had! I had never realized the headlines of this world were the product of overheated imaginations, staged events and tons of nothing! It took my breath away.

And how cunningly they had linked it up with NAMES! Nixon, Narcotici, Boss Tweed. The Whiz Kid was now positioned with criminals! How convincing! Who could doubt it?

The other papers were the same. This story would be bouncing coast to coast and even around the world. TV would be carrying that photo as a still. Radio would be spot-newsing it every hour. What coverage! An avalanche!

And, my Gods, it was also all over the sports pages! They were running still shot reviews of the race! That meant TV sports programs would be running the moving color footage!

All was revealed! So this was how news was made! Madison was right. I had not really been a professional PR.

But wait a minute, how was Heller taking this?

Chapter 7

I got the viewer on.

Heller was driving the old cab down the Jersey side of the river. He had a stack of the newspapers on the floor under the meter and was glancing at them from time to time.

He was PERTURBED!

I turned back the strips. Yes, Heller had been summoned by Geovani when he had reached the office. Geovani had simply said, "You better get over here, kid, but I advise you not to come." That voice was very tense.

Heller was in trouble!

Ah, PR, PR, what a beautiful tool for trouble. I realized now that nobody was safe from such a weapon. It might strike anywhere at anyone. There was no predicting it at all! One minute he had been happily going about his business and then, bang, through no action of his own, he was shot by PR. And he didn't even have any inkling it was a shot. Maybe he thought it was just how the world ran: that newspapers were unreliable or made mistakes or simply catered to the public taste for sensationalism.

An expert in hand-to-hand combat, a Fleet combat engineer that could blow up fortresses and bases without a single scratch, Heller was a leaf in the wind before the mighty hurricane of PR, just a chip to be exploded at will by a master like Madison. And Heller not only didn't know, there was absolutely no one he could fight, nothing whatever he could do about it!

Madison had reduced him, with a few paragraphs, to a helpless pawn!

All Heller knew was that he was in trouble. He drove that way. He had even ignored a disguise when he left New York.

Just a pile of paper. A pile that could be burned with a single match. But that pile of paper was on its way to wrecking Heller!

I could tell it just from Geovani's voice.

At Babe's he parked the cab.

Geovani met him in the elevator. "Kid, I wouldn't go in."

Heller handed Georgio a tan leather trench coat and cap but Georgio wouldn't take it. It fell to the floor.

Heller knocked on the living-room door. It did not open. He turned the knob and went in.

No Babe.

Some sounds were coming from beyond another door across the room. Heller went over and opened it.

It was a sort of den. It had a fireplace but there was no fire in it. A crucifix hung on the wall. The rug was black.

And there sat Babe. She was crumpled up on her knees. She had a sackcloth over her head. She had taken ashes from the fireplace and was smearing them on her face.

"*Mia culpa,*" she moaned. "*Mia magna culpa.* It is my fault, it is my great fault."

She was crying.

She sensed someone had entered.

She looked up, tears coursing through the ashes on her face, making two clean streaks.

She saw him.

"Oh, Jerome," she groaned. "My own son a *traditore!*" She bent over, weeping. "My own son, my own son!"

Heller tried to walk forward to her. "Mrs. Corleone, please believe me. . . ."

Rejection was instant. Palms flat toward him, she blocked his further approach with a gesture. "No, no, do not come near me! Somehow, somewhere you have tainted blood! You have stained the honor of the family! Do not come near me!"

Heller dropped to his own knees, distant from her. "*Please*, Mrs. Corleone, I did not have . . ."

"*Traditore!*" she spat, scuttling back to get away from him. "You have broken your poor mother's heart!" She made a grab at the fireplace. She took out a newspaper that was only partly burned. The face of Faustino could be seen. The movement fanned the sparks that clung to it. They fanned into sudden flame as she shook it in the air.

"You have brought dishonor to the name of Corleone!" she cried. "My own son has turned against his family!"

She cast it out from her into the fireplace. "I have tried and tried to be a good mother to you. I have tried and tried to bring you up right! And what thanks do I get? What thanks, I ask you! The mayor's wife was on the phone!" Her voice rose to a wail. "She said I was such a stupid fool I did not even know I had a traitor in my own camp! And she laughed! She laughed at me!"

She was trying to find something suddenly. The fire tongs! She threw them at Heller. "Get out!" They landed against the wall with a clang.

She got the poker and threw it. "Get out of my sight!" It bashed into a chair with a splintering thud.

She grabbed the shovel and pitched it. It almost struck Heller in the face. As it clattered against the floor, she was shrieking, "Go away!"

She got hold of the stand they had been in. She threw it with all her might. It smashed against the door! "Go! Go! Go! Get out, out, out!"

Heller backed up. He went out of the room.

The sound of her renewed weeping was like a dirge. Heller walked slowly to the hall.

Neither Geovani nor Georgio were in sight.

He picked up his coat and cap from the hall floor. He got into the elevator.

At the cab he slowly got in and drove away.

Oh, my Gods! Madison had done it! With just a simple trick of paper and ink and newspaper influence, out of whole cloth and without even an ounce of truth, he had turned Heller's most powerful ally against him!

What genius!

What a beautiful tool!

And Heller did not even suspect who was shooting at him! Or that anybody really was!

But this might still take a turn for the worse. Heller was tricky, too!

Chapter 8

Heller drove to the Gracious Palms. He parked the old cab in its usual stall.

He took the elevator up. It was still early in the day and there was no interference on my viewer. I could see what he did. There were two whores in his suite. They were practicing ways to undo a wristlock. One of them asked, "Pretty boy, is it the thumb you use in this grip or the first finger? Margie says . . . Why, what's the matter?" She saw something must be very wrong when she looked closely at Heller's face.

He was opening cabinets and getting out suitcases. He was beginning to pack.

In alarm the two whores ran out. I could hear one pounding on doors down the hall, one door after another. The other whore was on the hall phone talking quickly.

Heller just kept on packing.

When he turned around, there were numerous women standing in the door in different states of undress. They looked alarmed. A high-yellow came forward, "Pretty boy, are you leaving?"

Heller didn't answer. He just went on packing.

There were more girls at the door. They were beginning to cry.

Heller was getting out the racks and racks of clothes and binding them with cords.

There was a commotion at the door. Heller looked up. Vantagio had shouldered his way through the mob of weeping girls.

"What the hell is this, kid?" said Vantagio.

Heller said, "Has Babe called?"

Vantagio said, "No," in a puzzled voice.

"She will," said Heller. "She will."

Vantagio said, "Oh, kid. Babe sometimes gets upset. I should know. She gets over it."

Heller reached into his inside pocket. "Have you seen the morning papers?"

"I just got up," said Vantagio. "What have the morning . . . ?"

Heller had handed him a ripped-off front page of the *New York Grimes*.

Vantagio stared at it. He took it in. He went white. "Good God!"

Heller was indicating the piles of clothes. "These are no good to anybody else. What would you say the bills were?"

"Oh, kid . . ." said Vantagio, sadly.

"How much were the tailor bills on these clothes?" demanded Heller.

"Kid, you don't have to . . ."

"Fifteen thousand?" said Heller.

"Five," said Vantagio. "No more than five. But kid . . ."

"Here's five thousand," said Heller and began to count out the bills. "My safe downstairs is empty. Now there's the matter of the old cab. Bang-Bang will need it so he can still say he has a job. He's on parole, you know. And he has to go on with my military classes at Empire University. So how much is the cab worth?"

"Oh, kid . . ." said Vantagio. He himself was beginning to look teary-eyed.

"Five thousand," said Heller. "We'll call it five thousand. It was expensive to rebuild. Now, was there anything else I owe here? . . ."

Vantagio didn't answer. He had his face buried in a silk handkerchief.

Heller took his hand and put the ten thousand in it. He finished up stuffing things into his bags.

There were girls all around him, pleading with him. "Don't go, pretty boy, don't go!"

They were tugging at him.

He asked them to help carry his clothes. They would not touch them. He had to go get a cart himself. He loaded it.

"Kid," said Vantagio, pleading. "I think you are making an awful mistake. If she had intended you to go she would have called."

Heller said, "She intended."

He pushed the loaded cart to an elevator.

He went down to the basement. The girls, bare of feet and crying, came down in the other elevator.

Heller loaded the cab.

He looked back at Vantagio and the crowd. Two security men were standing there, looking sad, shaking their heads.

My viewer was misted.

Heller had tears in his eyes!

He drove away from the silent crowd. He could still see them in the rearview mirror. Then they were out of sight.

At the Empire State Building, he parked in a cab rank and got a hand truck. A cabby friend offered to take the old taxi to its nearby lot.

Heller wheeled the handcart to his office.

There was a side resting room there and he put some of his luggage in it. He put his toilet kit in the bathroom. He didn't have room for his clothes and he piled them on the sofas.

Izzy came in, saw the clothes. He didn't speak. He just looked aghast.

"I'll be living here," said Heller.

Izzy finally spoke. "I knew it would come to this. Fate has a way with it, Mr. Jet. And it always has more tricks waiting up the path."

"Is there something else wrong?" said Heller.

Izzy twisted around. Heller pressed. Izzy finally said, "The IRS won't wait. They're demanding everything we have. I wasn't able to make enough on arbitrage. Word just came in from the IRS District Office. They're going to impound every corporation whether it is legal to do it or not. I didn't want to tell you. I saw your morning press. But that's not all of it, I'm afraid. When IRS finds they are not going to be paid, they'll turn their public relations people loose, smear these corporations all over the media. It's ruin. Unless a miracle happens, we won't even have this office in another month."

He left mournfully.

Heller sat down at the desk.

The cat had been following him around from the moment he had come in. It jumped up now and took its place underneath the desk lamp. It sat there studying him.

Heller said to the cat, "You picked the wrong guy to be responsible for." He sounded beaten.

VICTORY!

I had won!

PR!

What a totally effective assassin's tool! And how painful, too!

And better: nobody, neither the victim nor the public, ever knew where the bullets had come from!

Suddenly, I understood the power controls of Earth. So this was how even empires were broken and made. By the PRs. And then the PRs even wrote the history books!

In one deadly blast, Madison had stopped the mighty Heller cold. With a few lines of ink, based only on his imagination, Madison was directing the destinies not only of Earth but of Voltar! No wonder Bury considered him so dangerous!

The PRs were the true Gods of this planet! Gods of wrath and misery. But Gods nonetheless! What a weapon they wielded! What destruction they wrought! Magnificent!

Chapter 9

I had been so fascinated with the glorious weapon, PR, that I had not realized that time was passing, every instant of which might spell deadly danger to me. After all, I had not turned up at Miss Pinch's last night. Also, Bury would not be pleased at all and might even send another phone-call team: I was in no condition to withstand the U.S. Army Signal Corps, much less a flank attack by snakes.

It was getting on toward noon. I painfully dragged myself out of bed and tottered in the direction of Utanc's room.

The suite's side door was open! This had never happened before.

Scenting a new disaster with an experienced nose, I peered in.

Her room was empty!

No trunks. Nothing in the closet or drawers.

She was gone!

I didn't know what plane!

I didn't have a ticket!

I had only eighty or ninety dollars! Nowhere near enough to get me out of New York.

Then I realized she would probably call when she had picked up the tickets. Of course, that was it.

My hands were bandaged. So was much of my body. It hurt to move. But I knew I had better pack. Struggling and fumbling, I went to work, screaming slightly every now and then.

It was very exhausting. Before I could strap anything up, I had to rest. I sank down in a chair.

There were newspapers scattered about the floor. My jaded eye landed on a news story. I was surprised that the paper contained any other news than the Whiz Kid's capers. The story said:

IRS SUSPECT COMMITTED

Arginal P. Pauper was today committed to Walnut Lodge Nut House by Internal Revenue Service routine desk-agent order.

Pauper is alleged to have failed to file an income tax return.

The IRS order also required that Pauper be electric-shocked, given a prefrontal lobotomy and thereafter tortured for life in the institution.

"He needed professional help," the IRS spokesman said, "and only our psychiatrists can give him that.

"He claimed he had spent the sixty cents in question on stamps to mail his return. However, all returns not sent by registered mail and delivered by a Rolls Royce painted blue with yellow stripes are, of course, wastebasketed, so the defense is preposterous."

Pauper's widow and orphans have been ground into meatballs to pay the tax penalties.

IRS N.Y. District Chief Stoney T. Blood issued a public statement: "IRS *uber alles!* And let that be a lesson to you, you dumb suckers!"

Over 300,000,000 Americans are said to be tax delinquent each year.

I knew it was PR. I knew it was simply a planted story to frighten people into paying their taxes. But in spite of knowing all that, it scared me spitless!

Having already seen that day the havoc PR could wreak, it stood my hair on end!

I had no more than finished reading it when the phone rang.

Thank heavens! It must be Utanc to tell me what plane. I answered.

A gruff voice said, "Inkswitch?"

I was so startled, I said, "Inkswitch."

"Good. This is the IRS New York Delinquency Office. Just a routine verification that you are there." He hung up.

My hair was not only standing up, it was crackling!

Oh, I had to get out of here! Three years in a Federal pen with homos even worse than Pinch would make a brain operation welcome!

I locked all my suitcases. Then I noticed that I had forgotten to get dressed. I didn't have the energy to unstrap everything. Lying in the wastebasket was the suit I had worn at the last visit to Miss Pinch. Frantically, I pulled it on.

I sneezed!

It stunk violently of red pepper, Tabasco and mustard!

There was no time. I would have to take what clue I had. Utanc had said a four o'clock plane. I would flee to the airport!

I called down for a bellboy and a cart and told them to get a cab at the door. This might be a close thing. Police always verify if you're in before they knock down the place with battering rams, so IRS would of course do even worse!

The bellboy piled my luggage on his hand truck. He pushed it to the front of the elevator door, waiting for the car to come up. Somebody must be coming up in that lift!

Some sixth sense told me to be cautious. The stairwell door was close to hand. I faded into it, holding it open a crack.

The elevator arrived and the door opened.

Two of the toughest-looking men I have ever seen stepped out into the penthouse foyer! They had black hats, gray overcoats, huge shoulders and great, black mustaches! Mean!

They knocked like thunder on the sitting-room door!

Oh, thank Gods for Apparatus training! I fled down the stairwell, unmindful of the agony every movement caused.

Speeding, I went down all thirty stories of the hotel!

I burst into the lobby.

The doorman recognized me. He beckoned. The cab was sitting there.

My bellboy and baggage had already arrived. It was being put in the cab. So slow, so slow!

My eye was pinned on the elevator doors in the lobby.

In desperation, I waved a ten-dollar bill at the bellboy.

He stopped to make sure it wasn't counterfeit!

The manager was coming out. I thought it was to tell me the bill wasn't paid. Instead, he shook me by the hand and said, "Congratulations on your leaving, Mr. Inkswitch. Please use another hotel when you return." I was so relieved to realize Utanc had paid the bill.

The delay was nearly fatal.

The two tough guys came out of the elevator!

I leaped into the cab and screamed, "John F. Kennedy International Airport!"

The driver sped away.

I was looking back.

I had beaten them!

We battered our way through congested traffic. We plunged down into the Queens Midtown Tunnel. We emerged into the flowing traffic of Route 495. I looked back. For a moment I could see the UN fading. I was making it! What a relief!

Wait. Many cars behind us. A gray vehicle was threading its way closer! I stared with my face pressed more closely to the glass. THE TWO TOUGH MEN!

Not only that, they seemed to have recognized me! One was waving frantically for us to pull over and stop.

I didn't have much money. But I leaned forward. "A twenty-dollar tip if you lose that gray car!"

"Fifty dollahs," said the cabby.

"Fifty dollars!" I said.

We sped forward. We swayed and tire screeched around trucks. We cut desperately in front of cars whose brakes shrieked as they stamped down to miss us.

Every sway was agony to my tortured and bruised body. Gods,

would I be glad to get out of New York—if I made it!

We got onto Woodhaven Boulevard. We roared through the wintry Forest Park. We rocketed past Kew Gardens. We blasted by Aqueduct Race Track.

We came screaming into the passenger terminal of John F. Kennedy Airport. I looked anxiously on the back trail. They still might come. I paid the cabby. I then had only eighteen dollars left!

"What airline?" said a black porter with a cart.

"I don't know," I said.

He was loading my baggage on his small truck. "Well, you c'n take yo' choice, then. They's Pan Am. They's TWA. But if'n it's TWA, we bettah git anothah cab 'cause this is Pan Am. Now, me, f'um mah study of the crashes . . ."

I thought fast. Four o'clock. Maybe only one plane left at four. "What goes to Rome or London or someplace at four?"

"Well, ah thinks they is one fo' Rome at fo'. But if you ain't too partickler, me, I'd go to Trinydad wheh it is mo' wahm."

"Rome. Take me to that counter."

He did. It was long, long before plane time.

"Inkswitch?" said the clerk. "We don't have any reservation in that name. I will call central . . ."

I wasn't listening. I had been casting glances back toward the door.

THERE THEY WERE!

I hysterically threw three one-dollar bills at the porter. "Take care of my baggage!"

I fled.

Darting through a troop of Girl Scouts, colliding with a woman carrying a Pekingese who gave me a shove, I was propelled into the midst of an Olympic ski team. It was a lifesaver. They gave me such a vigorous rejection that I went like a bowling ball into a crowd of priests. The confusion was so great, all I had to do was keep rolling and I was in through the door of a men's washroom.

I hastily got a coin out and with an agonized sigh of relief I was safely inside a john.

I sat there for a bit. I hurt so much, I forgot to pull my feet up.

Then I remembered the technique and did so. It was just in time.

Two pairs of heavy boots!

The two tough men were coming down the line of locked toilets, looking under the doors!

They didn't see me.

They were in a hurry.

They went on.

Only then could I permit myself to suffer. The bruises were just one big general pain from the cab ride. I was sure the cuts were bleeding again from the bowling-ball trip. What one had to go through just to execute his simple duties!

Stifling a sneeze, I abruptly remembered that I had forgotten to phone the New York office and get Raht to turn on the 831 Relayer. Without it, I would be blind about Heller.

I had lots of time before four o'clock. The problem was how to get out of this place and to a phone without being spotted.

Getting brave, I left the john cubicle.

There was a man, a very big man, over by a wash bowl. He had a rather extensive kit spread out and he was shaving with an old blade razor.

He was facing sideways to the entrance door. He had hung his hat—a sort of hunting hat with two bills front and back—and his coat—a black and white checkered mackinaw—on a hook quite close to the door.

Being of a cunning frame of mind, I knew that he would shortly wash his face. He would have soap in his eyes for a moment. I waited. Sure enough, over he bent.

Quick as a flash, I had the hat and coat. Quicker, I slid out of the washroom, expertly getting them on at the same moment.

The odd, red cap was awfully big. It fitted easily over my own hat. The loud-checked mackinaw was huge, more like an overcoat on me. Adequate disguise!

I peered cautiously about. Yes! There they were, the two tough men! But they were facing the other way, looking along lines of people.

I got to a coin-change machine and converted ten dollars to change. I certainly was low on cash.

Adequately masked by the hat and coat, I slid into a glass-enclosed phone kiosk. I dialed the New York office.

"Put Raht on the phone," I said.

They had some idiot clerk from Flisten on their reception: I could tell by the crazy way he had of pronouncing his *S*'s: He made them into *Z*'s. "I am zorry. The poor Raht iz in the hozpital ztill. Complicationz. The pneumonia iz not rezponding to the penizillin. Hiz condition iz critical. Whom zhall I zay called?"

I was furious! I was so zizzling, I znapped ztraight over into gutter Flizten. An idiot like that couldn't hope to understand Standard Voltarian, much less plain English. "Vacations! Vacations! That's all you people ever think about!"

"O Demons of the green abyss!" he said in Flisten. "This must be Officer Gris!" He sounded scared. That was better!

"Now listen to me," I snarled at him in Flisten. "You order Raht to stop faking and handle the *Empire State* and make him report in or I'll have him filled full of red Tabasco Signal Corps! And listen, you idiot, if I ever catch you speaking Flisten again on an Earth phone line I'll make you listen to *A Night on Bare Mountain* with rolling pins! Got it?"

He had it. It was the most terrible curse I could think of. He was gibbering!

I hung up, feeling a bit better.

Madison! I ought to call Madison and tell him what a magnificent job he had done. A PR triumph! And also that I was leaving. Then Bury wouldn't know where to send the snakes.

I inserted the coins and hit the buttons. Amazing! It was Madison himself who answered. "Thank you for calling right back, Mr. Underslung. What progress have you made in getting the Whiz Kid an Oscar for underhanded driving?"

"No, no," I sneezed. "This is Tabasco Smith, I mean Mr. Smith. Madison, I absolutely had to call and tell you what a magnificent job you have done. You are a wonder. Thank Gods for

PR and please tell Mr. Bury I have gone off on a long trip to spy on the Signal Corps for Miss Agnes."

"Job done?" he said, sounding mystified. "But this campaign isn't over, Smith, far from it! It has a long, long way to go yet to achieve lasting image. Wait until you see tomorrow's papers! They will say that he made so much money betting against himself in the race that he will give the bribe in full to the Kansas farmers."

There it was again, the thing which I hadn't understood before. "What's all this about Kansas farmers?"

"You don't get that?" he said, amazed. "Good heavens, you surely are a long way from professional. My orders are to make his name a household word and to make him immortal. Since the image of 'the man who started World War III' was ruined, I have had to take a different tack. The one I am working on now is 'Jesse James.' He was a famous outlaw who fought the railroads in Kansas by robbing trains and gave the loot to the farmers. He is one of the great American folk heroes. Deathless. So if I can give Wister a Jesse James–type image, all will be well. It can change, though. PR is a fluid subject, Inkswitch, and, above all, we've got to keep that front page no matter how many natural cataclysms get in the way. If I try very hard and stay with the fundamentals of professional PR, the Whiz Kid will make it, but it will take time. Now if you will get off my phone, I'd appreciate it. I'm shorthanded today since Hoodward was shot at the airport by Faustino's men and Ted Tramp's wife is having a baby. I'm expecting calls from various racing associations to get the Whiz Kid debarred from every track in America so we can come back the next day and claim they are just terrified to race against him. And for the day after that, I have to get riots organized by those who lost bets and riots take a lot of advance time. So I need all my phones!"

Yes, I sure could see he was beautifully busy. "Please tell Mr. Bury," I sneezed, "that both the Signal Corps and Miss Agnes have snake detectors. Good-bye."

I hung up. Well, that was out of the road. Did I need to call the Security Chief at Octopus and tell him I would not be around? Then

I remembered that anything connected with me came up blank on the computer and they couldn't tell whether I was working or not. And Pinch might have a bug on that line. Also, IRS might trace the call. In fact, they might be tracing me right now. . . .

SCRAPE!

The door of the phone kiosk flew open.

I cowered back, but not in time!

It was the owner of the hat and coat!

He loomed like a mountain!

A huge paw seized me!

I was yanked ferociously out of the kiosk.

I saw a fist cocked in midair.

WHAM!

An anvil seemed to hit me in the eye!

Down I went on the floor. THUD went my head against the edge of the phone booth!

PLOWIE!

Into the air around me went a cloud of stars.

The sound wasn't from the stars. It was from a boot in my side.

He tore the mackinaw off of me. He grabbed the hat.

THUNK!

He kicked me again in the side.

I shut my eyes tight. I was waiting for the next kick. It didn't come. I opened my eyes.

TWO PAIRS OF HEAVY BOOTS! Right by my face!

The two tough men had caught up with me!

I was done for!

I looked up. One bent over and yanked me to my feet.

The other was reaching into his pocket. Gun? Handcuffs?

The first one said, "Are you Achmed Ben Nutti?"

Oh, my Gods. At Pan Am I had asked for reservations in the name of Inkswitch. Achmed Ben Nutti was the United Arab League name I had been traveling under and had passports for.

I was too weak to fight. Cunning was in order. "Yes, I am Achmed Ben Nutti and I have diplomatic status! You can't arrest me!"

"Arrest you?" he said. "No, no, Comrade. We are from the Bolshoi Travel Agency. We have been trying hard to catch you and give you your ticket!"

He was dusting me off and it made a cloud of mustard-pepper-Tabasco odors fly into the air. We both sneezed.

"Here are all your flight papers," said the other tough-looking man. "We have already found and checked your baggage aboard. You had better hurry, Comrade. That's your flight they're calling now."

"He doesn't seem to be able to walk," said the other, sneezing again. "Let's carry him over to the first-class gate and get them to let us through. We can dump him aboard."

We went through the rat maze of detectors, past the cooperative attendants, down a gangway and into the side of a ship. We were the last ones aboard. I had almost missed the plane! It evidently was an earlier one!

They dumped me in a first-class seat.

Utanc! She was caped and hooded and veiled, sitting right there!

"Darling!" I cried.

Utanc grabbed a passing blue sleeve. "Purser," she said, "I see you have a lot of empty seats at the back. Could you please dump my owner into one of them? He is making me feel like I'm going to sneeze!"

He gave a snappy salute. "Pan Am service, Ma'am."

The purser snapped his fingers for a stewardess and in no time the two of them had me clear at the back of the first-class compartment and were covering my clothes with a plastic sheet and buckling me in.

I sank back. Surrounded with the posh luxury of a first-class superjet, complete with classic Greek temples in the murals, I sighed a sigh, somewhat interrupted with a sneeze, as anxiety ebbed out.

And so, gratefully, I saw the landing strip race by and presently, bending sideways without too much pain, watched the smoggy skyline of New York grow small and fade away.

Thank Gods, I had made it.

Later, the dinner being served from carts on the aisle was delicious. But a glass of wine, no matter if served with great ceremony in first class, aloft, does not substitute for a good crystal ball.

With its usual evil grin, fiendish Fate had been busy, just ahead, sorting out available disasters. The one it chose to first serve up for me was horrible. The very memory of it makes me wince.

PART
THIRTY-FOUR
Chapter 1

The THY (Turkish Airlines) plane slid down toward Afyon.
The snow-capped peaks lined up to point at Afyonkarahisar's wintry finger. It was a striking view of a bleak terrain: how could
any human beings possibly survive in the villages which dotted the
hostile mountains and the plain? A scene of utter desolation, it had
one saving grace: I was home! The optical illusion, which made
a mountaintop and marked the Voltar base, was still in place—
suitably wintry now—so I was not only home, I was still connected
to Voltar, my real native land.

And I was still alive!

What a relief!

We landed and while we waited for the landing stage to roll up
and the door to open, Utanc stepped close to me. She put her dainty
hand upon my sleeve, a favor I so seldom enjoyed. She looked at me,
her eyes large and dark and pleading above her veil.

"O my master," she whispered, "we still have a little money
left." She was holding her purse open now. It was absolutely stuffed
with money. "May I keep it?"

"Oh, dear Utanc, what a manager you are! Of course you may
keep it." I was quite touched. Imagine doing that whole trip on
much less than a hundred thousand dollars! Besides, I still had
millions in the gold I had brought from Voltar.

She closed the purse with a snap and was first down the plane
steps.

Some people were at the airport gate. The taxi driver, Karagoz and, ah yes, Utanc's two little servant boys!

Cloak pressed against her by the wintry wind, Utanc raced toward the gate!

The two little boys burst through and, crowing with delight, sped across the tarmac to meet her!

She gathered them up, hugging them.

Both of them had their arms around her neck and she was kissing their cheeks through her veil. What a bundle of welcome! They were trying to tell her everything that had happened since she had been gone and trying to find out what she had brought for them all at the same time.

They ignored me as I limped painfully by them.

Karagoz ignored me. The taxi driver ignored me. I went through the terminal to the parking area. Karagoz had evidently brought the boys in Utanc's BMW for there it sat alongside the taxi driver's taxi.

The wind was very dry and cold and a bit gritty. I was getting chilled and it wasn't doing my unhealed wounds any good.

Finally they came through the parking-lot door, the two small boys chattering and excited, eyes glowing. They did look somewhat like Rudolph Valentino and James Cagney as they must have looked as children. That surely had been a successful present!

Utanc was saying to the taxi driver, "Now, here are the shipping manifests for the trunks. They couldn't come on this plane but when they do, you be sure to hire a truck to pick them up. Now we will go home."

Karagoz stepped close to her and whispered something in her ear.

Utanc said, "Ice cream! How would you two dear little boys like some ice cream over in town?"

They shrieked their approval of the plan.

Karagoz, Utanc and the two little boys got in her BMW, and with veiled Utanc behind the wheel, it rocketed out of the parking lot, screeched its tires as it turned into the road to Afyon and was gone.

The taxi driver loaded his taxi with the bags we had checked through on this plane and shortly we were headed for the villa.

"Well, how is she working out?" he flung back at me as he dodged through the camels and donkey carts.

"She is absolutely amazing," I said. "Not only is she a great slave but she also happens to be the best (bleeped) money manager you ever saw! She handled all our funds on that very expensive trip and just now when we got off the plane she must have had nearly all of the original money left. Amazing! I don't know how she did it!"

"Yeah, she was sure a bargain," said the taxi driver. "Cheap, too. They don't make slaves like that anymore. Her turn-in value would be almost as high as the original price. You want I should ever trade her in on a new model?"

"Never!" I said firmly. "Not even if they come out with a new rear end."

We were drawing close to the villa. There seemed to be a number of cars parked on the road outside it. The taxi driver found a place to stop.

Creakily, I got out. I went through the gate.

The yard was full of men!

My reflexes, after all I had been through, were not very quick. I didn't get any chance to retreat.

A hulking brute stepped behind me!

Another hulking brute stalked up to me and used my Turkish Earth name. "You Sultan Bey?"

"That's him," said another. "I know him!"

Another jumped in front of me. "I'm from the American Oppress Company! Here is your bill. It's overdue!"

Another shouldered through. "I'm from the Dunner's Club. Here is your bill."

Yet another shouldered through. "I'm from Masker-Charge! What are you going to do about this bill?"

Still another crowded up. "I'm from the Squeeza Credit Card Corporation. One month interest on your first month's purchases is already more than the original amount!"

In chorus, a very menacing one, they yelled, "When are we going to get paid?"

I staggered back. I couldn't stagger very far as they were hemming me in. They were all waving bills!

It hit me! Utanc had gotten credit cards on my apparently affluent name and position before we left. She had done the whole trip on CREDIT CARDS!

Chapter 2

I saw some of the amounts they were waving. HUGE! The best hotels, all first-class travel, all the best shops . . .

Weak as I was, I still had some wits to gather about me. My gold! Painful though it might be, I would have to part with some gold.

I held up a bandaged hand. "Enough!" I cried. "You will be paid!" I would save the old homestead!

I rushed across the yard, across the house patio, into my bedroom, into the closet and through the secret door.

There it was, the stack of boxes in the corner of my secret room, all marked as "dangerously radioactive" to keep people away.

Ignoring the pain to my hands and the agony it caused to bend over, I ripped the lid off a box. Glittering yellow! I picked up a fifty-pound bar. It would weigh 41.6+ pounds on Earth. At twelve ounces Troy to the pound, that was 499.99+ ounces. Gold was above $700 when I last looked. This bar should be worth more than $349,999.99! That should hold them!

I struggled out with it. They gaped when I reappeared on the lawn. I dropped it in front of them. "This gold, if you cash it in, should take care of everything. And be sure to credit me with the difference."

They fought their way to it. One hulking brute got possession. He took out a pen knife and cut into the bar.

He stared.

He showed the others.

I stared.

The sliver he had cut off was lead!

"Sultan," he said in a low and menacing voice, "that bar is just lead painted with gilt paint! Are you trying to put us off?"

I couldn't believe it!

I checked it myself. Just lead with a coat of gilt paint on it.

The creditors instantly started grabbing rugs out of the house!

"Wait! Wait!" I cried.

I struggled back to my secret room.

I began to open boxes and lift out bars. Nine cases. Seventeen more fifty-pound bars. Eight hundred and fifty more pounds of lifting. A frantic knife cutting slivers!

They were *all* lead with a gilt coat of paint! But it had been real gold before I had left for New York! I had checked it!

Aching and battered, the bandages on my hands coming apart, I regained the lawn.

Not only did they have piles of rugs and furniture stacking up, they were now also herding the domestic staff out. They began to put ankle cuffs on them and connect them together on a long chain. One hulking brute cried, "They'll bring a good price in the slave markets of Arabia!"

"Wait! Wait!" I begged. "I will pay you! It's just that I have a slight headache."

The taxi driver was still there. I leaped into his cab. I would still save the old homestead. "Mudlick Construction Company!" I cried, "And to Hells with the camels!"

At great cost to my bruises from the bumps, we went careening back to Afyon. With screaming brakes we skidded to a stop at Mudlick.

I rushed in. The manager said, "I've been expecting you." He went right over to the safe, opened it and took out stacks of U.S. dollar bank notes. It was really painful to see those going into a sack and know I would never be able to caress them.

A quarter of a million dollars! My half of the kickback on that construction cost. I signed the receipt.

We went tearing back to the villa.

In agony from the bumps, I got out of the smoking taxi.

I stalked into the yard.

They had waited. The rugs were still piled up. The staff, in leg irons, was still standing there.

Triumphantly, I threw the sack of bank notes at them.

They all tore it apart and began to count it.

Then the Dunner's Club man cried, "There's only a quarter of a million dollars here!" He turned his back on it. He got a piece of paper from an aide. He waved it. "Here is my order for foreclosure! Get a padlock on those gates!"

"Wait! Wait!" I screamed. "I will pay! I will pay!" Ye Gods, how much were those bills?

I turned to the taxi again. "To Faht Bey's office!" I would save the old homestead in spite of Hells!

With engine roaring and my bruises shrieking, we braked in front of the International Agricultural Training Center for Peasants. I went reeling into the Base Commander's office.

Faht Bey looked at me. "I've been expecting you," he said, a deadly look on his fat face.

"Give me a million dollars!" I said.

"Can't do it!" he said.

I was astonished. "Look," I said. "I started this hospital project. You have two hundred gangsters coming in here to get their faces remodeled. At $100,000 each, that's $20,000,000! The buildings only cost a million. You got $19,000,000 clear! What do you mean, you can't? Look at that profit!"

"Little enough to compensate for all the damage you do. Besides, the demand for drugs from Lombar Hisst is out of sight in tonnage. We're barely making both ends meet."

"I'm in trouble!" I wailed.

"When weren't you?" said Faht Bey. "But I have a proposition for you. If you will agree to certain terms, you can have a quarter of a million."

"The terms?" I begged.

"When the credit card bills began to come in, I made up my mind and wrote it all out for you to sign. Here it is."

I read it:

> *I, Soltan Gris, hereby swear and affirm to stop grafting, chiseling and embezzling monies from the Earth Base Treasury. I will demand not one more cent after this final payoff and I will absolutely undertake to place no more contracts for construction so I can get a kickback from the contractors as I have been doing.*
>
> *Sign, Sworn, Attested, Witnessed.*

I was desperate. But this was horrible!

Faht Bey said, "If you refuse to sign it, I will simply let those credit card people tear you to pieces."

He had the quarter of a million in stacks, right there.

I signed! He got his wife and the security guard to witness it.

Stuffing the packets of bank notes in a handy sack, I regained the cab. We went scorching back to the villa.

I staggered out of the taxi. I made my way to the waiting mob. I flung the bag at them.

They pounced on it. They tore it apart. They counted it.

"Aha!" said the American Oppress man. "He has covered the first month of bills!"

They agreed. They got the shackles off the staff. They brushed them off. They put the rugs and furniture back in place.

I was reeling. I had saved the old homestead. But at what a terrible sacrifice! And it and I would both be swept away again in just a few weeks when the rest of the bills came in!

But that wasn't what caused me to collapse.

When they had everything in order again, the whole mob came over to me. They were fawning.

"Ah, Sultan Bey," said Dunner's Club. "I speak for all of us. You have met your first month's bills. You have proven your credit beyond any doubt. We are waiving any limit we thought we might have to impose. Feel free to charge whatever you like, any amount you like, anywhere in the whole world!"

The others raised a cheer.

What an awful, awful sentiment!

I fainted dead away!

Chapter 3

I came to, lying in the yard, right where I had collapsed. The staff had pretty well cleaned things up. They were walking around, even stepping over me.

I became afraid they would sweep me into one of their trash bags. I was far too weak to resist.

Suddenly, I recognized how really sick I was. I knew I had to get to the hospital while I still had the ability to move somewhat.

The taxi driver wasn't there.

An old Chevy station wagon was in the yard. I crawled over to it on my hands and knees. They used to keep a spare key under the mat. With enormous strain, I lifted up the corner of the floor covering.

The key!

I hauled myself up by the steering column. I somehow got under the wheel.

It started!

Oh, Gods, if I could just hold out until I got to the hospital!

A camel driver saw me coming. I was driving awfully slow. He saw who was behind the wheel. He got his beasts off the road quick. Lucky for me: the camels might have attacked me.

Going five miles an hour, concentrating on every yard of advance, I finally saw the sign ahead:

**WORLD UNITED CHARITIES
MERCY AND BENEVOLENT
HOSPITAL**

It looked much bigger. The warehouses were up and a new wing had been added.

I was distracted by the fact that it was all landscaped! A couple of peasant women were doing winter trim on rose bushes. They screamed at me when a wheel inadvertently went off the drive slightly and made a furrow in their lawn. I couldn't understand the commotion: cold weather had turned the grass brown.

Distracted, I hadn't seen a little Fiat move around me and sneak into the parking place toward which I was headed. It was bright red and at the last instant I saw that it was opening its door.

CRASH!

The door hit the side of the Chevy.

The curb stopped me. I somehow managed to shut off the ignition.

Somebody was getting out of the Fiat. A voice! "What in the name of Allah are you doing, you cross-eyed camel! My car, my poor car!" In the rearview side mirror, somebody was bending down stroking at a dent. That somebody promptly stood up and came storming to the side of the Chevy. "My new Fiat! You wrecked my brand-new Fiat!"

It was Nurse Bildirjin!

She was alongside my door. She looked. She saw who it was! Fury contorted her face! "So you're back, you (bleepard)!"

It wasn't a very friendly welcome to the portals of Mercy and Benevolence even if its principal business was the altering of the I.D. of gangsters.

"I'm dying," I managed to get out.

"Really?" she said. It changed her whole demeanor. "You wouldn't fool me, would you?" She turned and ran like the quail she was named after, straight into the hospital yelling gaily, "Hey, Doc! You got to come out! Sultan is outside actually dying! Hurray, hurray!"

It did produce a certain commotion. A lot of women with children rushed from the waiting room and formed a staring ring, laughing and chattering excitedly.

At length, Dr. Prahd Bittlestiffender pushed his way through the cheering throng. He was followed by a couple of orderlies pushing a cart with a corpse bag on it.

"Cadavers are usually delivered at the mortuary entrance," said Prahd in reproof. "Can't you drive around there?"

"I'm too weak," I said sadly. "Doctor, just this once, be kind. You've got to help me. I am a survivor of the battle of New York. I am a victim of red pepper, Miss Agnes, mustard, truncheons, taxi cabs and snakes. I have crawled back home with final last words: Cancel my credit cards before the U.S. Army Signal Corps finds Bury!"

"Oh, I don't think we need to go to the expense of *burying* you. But speaking of credit cards, when does my pay start?"

"Must we talk about money?" I wept. "Please help me, Doctor. I am in agony!"

Prahd had them stuff me in the corpse bag and soon we were in his operating room. He pushed the male attendants out and bolted the door.

It was with shock that I realized I was alone with Prahd and Nurse Bildirjin!

In a very businesslike fashion they stripped off my clothes. They laid me out on an operating table. Nurse Bildirjin busied herself with strapping down my wrists and ankles. It was all too reminiscent of recent traumatic experiences.

"What are you going to do?" I begged. "No gas! Don't put me out."

"Relax," said Prahd. "We are simply here in our professional capacity." He was looking at me. "My, my, what a mess!"

Nurse Bildirjin said hopefully, "What were you in? A train wreck combined with an airplane crash? All cut and black and blue. Doc, maybe he wandered into a sausage factory and they mistook him properly for a pig."

"What are these pits on your stomach?" said Prahd. "The ones with the black bits at the bottom?"

I looked down at my stomach. "Powder grains," I said. "Black powder."

"Well, well," said Prahd. "Very uncosmetic. They will have to come out. Get on it, Nurse Bildirjin, if you please."

"Really?" she said with delight. "Isn't that surgical, doctor?"

"No, no," said Prahd. "Very minor compared to the rest of this."

She efficiently got some instruments and a pan and began to take out the first black grain.

YOW!

"Now, the rest of this is more important," said Prahd. He began to pass a scope over my body. "Hah! Three cracked ribs. One chipped pelvis bone. Numerous blood blisters . . ."

He was taking notes. Nurse Bildirjin had some huge pliers. "I think this will be faster!" She dug in and closed them.

YEEE-OW!

"That's one. Now for the next."

"How many are there?" said Prahd.

"Oh, maybe two or three hundred," said Nurse Bildirjin.

"Do you have to make such big holes?" I screamed.

"Oh, yes," she said. "I might leave some. Very unsightly." She was digging for the next one. My Gods, this was far worse than the original blast! "Doctor, in your professional opinion," she said conversationally as she worked, "don't you think he is a bit dinky?"

Prahd nodded. "Yes, I would say an inch is below average. Well, well! What is this? What is this? A crushed testicle!"

"That was when I was a boy!" I said. "YEE-OW! Please, Nurse Bildirjin, not such big bites! Those powder grains are awfully small. A farmer kicked me for drowning all his breeding animals. It was a school vacation job and I was just trying to see if they could swim. He was a very—YEEEEE-OWWWW!"

"Well, that may have been done when you were a boy," said Prahd. "But now the other testicle seems to be in bad shape, too. That must be an awfully tough town, New York. And especially hard on testicles."

"It is, it is," I said. "The primitives are—YEEEEEEEE-OWWWWWWWWW! . . . real (bleep) breakers."

"I really think I had better put you under general gas," said Prahd. "There's hours and hours of surgery and cellular handling here. And Nurse Bildirjin seems to be working very slowly today."

"I think this would go along faster," she said, "if I just burned them out. See, when this electric probe touches one in the pan here, it explodes." It went *Zzzt!* and smoke rose. "Now I will just go over here and turn on some pop music. . . ."

That was all it took. I fainted.

Chapter 4

I awoke.

I couldn't see!

I had no sense of body weight!

In fact, I didn't have any sense at all!

Maybe I was dead!

I blinked my eyes. Yes, I could feel myself blinking my eyes.

Maybe they had thrown the rest of my body away. Maybe I was just a head!

Gods knew what a Voltarian cellologist would do. After all, I had known Doctor Crobe and how he loved to make human freaks. Maybe I was some sort of monster now. Maybe I looked like a cat or an octopus or Miss Pinch.

Worse than that: Earth psychologists and psychiatrists teach that all anyone is, is a bunch of cells evolved up the evolutionary track, that the person himself is just what his cells and body make him. There could be no doubt of the validity of their teachings, for one could be shot for not believing them. If Prahd had changed my cells, it followed by Earth psychology that my personality would suffer a total shift! So what new personality would I have? Something sweet and kind—Gods forbid! Or something whining and propitiative, like Izzy—which of course would be even less acceptable.

What had been changed? If I knew Prahd and Nurse Bildirjin, it would be something utterly underhanded and with some ghastly twist!

There was a sort of dim glow around. An eerie light was coming hazily through the slits of something. Gradually I could get a half-seen impression of my immediate environment.

I was in a sort of a long tub, midway between ceiling and floor. Only my head was out. The rest of me was suspended, probably by antigravity coils, in fluid: my body was not touching anything solid.

There were lights burning in the tub, probably emitting some strange wavelength. It was these, escaping through slits, that furnished the dim, greenish glow in the room. Cell catalysts of some kind? I had no real idea.

Accidentally, I moved my eyes to the right.

A window!

Through it I could see the pale sickle of a wintry moon. That was the moon of Earth! I was still on Blito-P3.

I concentrated. Maybe I could estimate how much time had gone by. If it took four and a half hours to come out from under gas—a fact of which I was uncertain—I must have been on that operating table for eight to ten hours! A very long time.

WHAT HAD THEY DONE TO ME?

It seemed to confirm my worst suspicions. A monster! Did I have flippers for feet? Did I now have tentacles for hands? Maybe a beak instead of a nose?

Horrors! What personality changes would follow such shifts?

Oh, Gods, I should never have come near those two fiends!

I had no question at all whether or not it was awful. That followed as the night the day. The only question was about the exact horror design. Dracula? Did I now have long teeth and live only on fresh blood? Would I be able to live with myself comfortably under the dictates of this new personality? I worked my jaws experimentally to see if they were now designed for severing jugular veins.

My face was bandaged right up to the eyes!

WHAT HAD THEY DONE??????????

I fussed and fumed and fretted through that dark and horrible night.

At least three centuries of worry later, dawn came. Only another century after that, possibly about nine according to the bleak sun through the window, Doctor Prahd Bittlestiffender came in.

I found I could turn my head and speak. "You put me out!"

He smiled. A very bad sign. He began to read meters and gauges around the suspended tub. When he had noted them all down on a chart, he looked at me and said, "I had to. You kept screaming even when you fainted. Nurse Bildirjin couldn't even hear her favorite radio program. It's the Hoochi-Hoochi Boys and Their Electric Cura Irizvas. She's only sixteen, you know, and she's a fan of theirs. They come on every day at . . ."

I knew the tactic. Trying to get me off the subject and lull my suspicions. "You did something dreadful," I snarled. "You cellologists are all alike!"

"No, no. The work was just very extensive, that's all. You have no idea how bashed up you've let yourself become in that strange career you have. Old, old injuries and wounds. A lot of improperly treated bone breaks. You apparently have not been in the habit of seeking professional care. I even took a coin out of your kidney."

"Aha!" I said. "You did all this just to recover a coin and enrich yourself!"

"No, no. It was only a two-cent piece from the planet Modon. Somebody must have shot it at you. I put it in your wallet so your accounts will balance. But all that aside, it was this last escapade that could have crippled you for the rest of your days. I even had to replace three square feet of skin entirely: it had some of the strangest things in it. In that town you call New York, the one that kept coming up in your screams, you surely must have been running with a rough crowd."

"You didn't do anything else?"

"No, I just put you together."

The day I believe a cellologist won't ever dawn. "You didn't change anything?"

"Well, I had to work on your genitals a bit."

"I knew it!" I screamed. "I knew you'd do something awful if you could put me out!"

"No, no. All I did was normalize things a bit. Purely routine cellological work. Well, bye-bye now. One of the gangsters I fixed doesn't like his new face: says it reminds him of somebody called J. Edgar Hoover. But that isn't odd because that's where I got it from. I need better picture books. I'll get some on my own when my pay starts."

I frowned so sourly at this hint that he left.

Oh, I didn't like the looks of things at all. I know when people are hiding things from me. But I was helpless. I could only move my eyes and my neck and talk through the bandages on my face.

I was more certain than ever that Prahd had done me in.

The only question was, exactly how?

Chapter 5

Throughout that whole morning, I lay suspended in that (bleeped) tub and stewed and fumed.

I could see a Turkish tree through the window and the nameplate—*Zanco Cell Catalyst Growth Machine, Model 16 Magnaspeed*—on the tub rim above my face. The tree did not have the power to occupy the mind very long. The nameplate, in Voltarian script, was far more thought stimulating. WHAT was it growing? Bird feet?

I couldn't see my body. And after the two-thousandth reading, the nameplate was no more informative than it had been the first time.

One's imagination can become overactive.

Firmly, I steeled myself to shut off speculation on future form and the effect it inevitably would have upon my personality and character.

I wondered if I would be fed. I wasn't hungry but maybe starving me to death was part of their dastardly plot.

The shadows on the tree said it must be about noon.

The door opened.

Nurse Bildirjin! She was dressed in a starched white nurse's uniform and cap. She was not carrying a tray. She had a notebook and chart in her hands. She went around reading all the meters or whatever there was to record on the outside of the tub. She sent a glance or two at my face. She looked awfully sly!

I decided to speak, regardless of consequences. Maybe I could get some information out of her.

"Where's my food?" I said.

"Oh, you don't have to eat. You're connected to the fluids and containers in the tub."

"Give me a mirror," I said.

"I'm sorry. It's not allowed. Patients can get upset."

"What did you two do to me?" I grated.

She faked a look of utter surprise.

I knew she wouldn't answer. I changed the subject. "I'm going crazy just floating here."

"Oh," she said, "I thought you had arrived there a long time ago, Sultan Bey." She gave a nasty, sniggering laugh at her own joke.

I didn't laugh.

"But," she said, "I wouldn't want any complaints being circulated about our care of patients."

She left. She came back in about three minutes. She was carrying a radio on a strap. She hung it somewhere on the wall above and behind my head. She put some earphones on her ears. As she tuned in, leaking from under the pads I could hear the Istanbul hot-pop station.

She put the earphones over my ears. She turned it up very loud. She left.

I don't care for commercials about bubble gum and camel feed. But everybody in Turkey these days seemed to be listening to hot pop.

I couldn't take the earphones off or change the station.

As the hours wore on, I found that the Goat Guys must be especially popular for they played their records frequently. And at least once in every hour, they played their latest hit. With flutes and drums and snarls and roars, it went

> *You are my monster,*
> *I am your camel.*
> *You make me crazy,*
> *The way you play.*

I only wonder,
Why my dear mother,
Bought strychnine
And asked you here today.

At first, I was sort of detached about it. Then I began to realize that they must be playing it for me as a sort of request. It fitted my case pretty exactly when you got right down to it. I even invented a sort of personality test to go with it. Each time the news came on, I would fill in the interval of Arabs not getting along with Arabs with searching probes into my reactions to the word *strychnine*.

Since the cells and body are the only things which determine personality, and if I could detect any change of reaction in myself to the word *strychnine,* it followed that from this I would be able to work out exactly what they had done to me physically. It didn't work.

Fortunately, the station was off the air for several hours each night and I could get some sleep.

About three times a day someone would come in and read the meters. But as I had earphones on, they presumed I couldn't hear anything they said and so didn't bother to answer anything I said.

For the next eight days, the only real change I could detect was a snowstorm that whitened up the tree for a day. The boughs then gradually, bit by bit, from wind, lost the whiting.

I began to believe that for the rest of eternity I would just float here without sensation, detached from every world except that of hot pop and camel feed, while somewhere in another world, Arabs fought Arabs and mothers bought strychnine.

But, one morning, just as I had become accustomed to it, my life in the Zanco Model 16 Magnaspeed came to an abrupt and shocking end.

Chapter 6

It was about 11:00 A.M. by the cold sun in the window.

Prahd walked in.

He was followed by two orderlies and a cart of instruments, gas canisters and masks.

The clatter smashed through "You Are My Monster." I looked at this invasion in sudden fear.

Prahd took the earphones off me. "I've come to disconnect you," he said.

He held up his right hand.

An orderly put an anesthesia mask in it.

"But . . ." I started to say.

The mask was over my face and I was out!

I came to after what seemed to be a space of two seconds.

I was lying in a bed. I was in a different room. I had a sheet over me. Over and under the sheet there were straps. I could not move my arms or legs or lift my body.

They had done something else to me! I was sure of it. But no, nothing much could happen in two seconds.

I turned my head. A very thin, low sun was coming in the window. It must be afternoon. It hadn't been two seconds. It had been 11:00 A.M. It must now be 3:00 P.M. Plenty of time to do something else nasty!

I found I could flex something at the end of my arms. I managed to get a hand in view. Oh, thank Gods! Not flippers. They were fingers! I could move and control them. They weren't fakes. They were mine.

Somewhere toward the bottom of the bed I could feel the canvas ankle cuffs. I stirred that extremity. The sheet lifted slightly. By craning my neck I could see toes. I wiggled them. Oh, thank Gods they were not hoofs! They were my toes! I tried the other one. Toes on both feet! Oh, thank Gods!

A clatter at the door.

Nurse Bildirjin came in pushing a cart with food on it. She was all starched and crisp looking. All smiles. Was there something sly in that smile? "How about some breakfast?" she said.

BREAKFAST! Oh, my Gods, they had been working on me another twenty hours! I looked anxiously at the food. Maybe they had given me the stomach of a goat. Was it hay on that cart? No, just a couple of boiled eggs and some *kahve*. However, it did not dispel my fears. I knew they had done *something*.

She didn't let me use my hands, which was suspicious enough. She fed me with a spoon and gave me the *kahve* through a straw. And all the time she was humming a little tune. I recognized it: "You Are My Monster"! Oh Gods, what had they done?

I tried to read it on her face. She was a very pretty girl, though young. Raven-black hair, a tan complexion, even, white teeth, full lips, big black eyes capable of considerable expression. And very well developed in spite of her being only sixteen. But she was a woman and treachery could not be far off. Anybody can tell you that treachery and beauty go hand in hand. That's why you have to kill songbirds wherever found. But where women are concerned, it's the other way around. Where killing is concerned, they always choose me as the first target of choice. Piled onto earlier experience, Krak with her hypnohelmets, Miss Pinch with her red pepper and even dear Utanc with her credit cards proved that beyond any doubt whatever! I was learning to be wary. Nurse Bildirjin undoubtedly had something up her sleeve!

She straightened up her tray and gave it a push toward the door. She smiled at me very cheerfully: a very bad sign!

Then she went to the foot of the bed.

She lifted the sheet slightly and looked up under it. "*That's what I wanted to see*," she said.

Oh, Gods! What had she looked at?

They HAD done something!

It was too much for my already unbalanced wits. I screamed, "PRAHD! PRAHD! PRAHD!"

Nurse Bildirjin was smiling all over herself. "If you mean Doktor Muhammed," she said, citing his Earth name, "I'll get him for you. Oh, this is great."

In under a minute young doctor Prahd (alias Doktor Muhammed Ataturk) came in, followed by Nurse Bildirjin.

He walked over and exposed my chest. There were a couple cup bandages there. He pulled them off and took some chest hair with them.

"You had me under another twenty hours!" I raved at him. "What have you done now that you haven't already done?!"

He pulled the sheet down further, found two more cups on my abdomen and pulled them off. "Tube holes. They've healed very nicely. After you come out of a Magnaspeed, the tube holes have to be closed and healed."

The strap across my lower middle was in the way. He pulled the upper part of the sheet back across my chest. He went down to the foot of the bed and, just like Nurse Bildirjin, lifted the sheet slightly and looked. "Oh, yes," he said. "You've done very well."

Oh, my Gods, what were they looking at? I knew Crobe. I went into terror. "What have I done very well?" I screamed.

"Get the mirror," he said to Nurse Bildirjin.

She had it right there. She held it by my knees and adjusted it. Young doctor Prahd lifted the sheet with the air of a theater manager introducing a new play.

I looked in the mirror.

I almost fainted.

I looked again. I shrieked, "You've made me into a horse!"

"No, no," he said, with professional calm. "That's simply normal. You are so used to one testicle not being there and the other drawn up into the body that a normal scrotum and actually having testicles may look strange to you."

"But the LENGTH of IT!" I screamed.

"Sultan Bey," said Prahd, "you don't seem to trust me. Your skin is all new, your old mis-set broken bones are mended, your vital organs are all fixed up. And although it was a great temptation, I didn't even change your face; I only removed some warts and scars. You will just look a bit brighter and fresher. You still aren't very good looking, so don't be alarmed."

"No, no!" I shouted. "I mean those HUGE genitals!" I could still see them in the mirror. I was aghast!

"Oh, my," tut-tutted Prahd. "Don't you ever take showers with other men? You must be awfully unobservant. For your home habitat, a tumescent size of ten inches is not overly large. Many on Earth have them that size—even bigger. I assure you that your previous one-inch tumescence was too small."

"Oh, I know you cellologists!" I cried. "You couldn't resist doing something strange!"

Prahd thought it over carefully. Then he pushed his straw-colored hair off his face. "No, not really. Of course, you may feel a little more vigorous. Your muscle tone will improve."

"Oh, you can't fool me!" I cried. "You did something peculiar! I'm sure of it!"

He thought once more. Then he seemed to remember something. He turned his bright green eyes on me depreciatingly. "Oh, yes. The catalyzer. It was a pretty complex scene getting all the nerve ends sorted out on the first testicle after it was grown from the gene pattern. And I did leave the other one in the growexpeditor a bit too long. But it won't produce in excess of more than half a pint of semen."

"WHAT?" I screamed.

"But," he said reasonably, "that's no more than a horse furnishes at one time."

"I knew it!" I wailed. "You've turned me into a horse!"

"No, no, no," he said soothingly. "It's completely human. You will produce completely human babies. Really, Sultan Bey, you should trust me. Horses are completely out of style. They have quite enough of them. You are now just a well-equipped male. Of course, you may have the urge to do it a little more often than you used to.

And you can probably do it more than once in the same night. But truly, I think you'll find it quite all right."

"Oh, my Gods!" I wept. "I am sure all this will change my whole personality."

"What?" he said, his bright green eyes shooting wide in astonishment.

"Yes," I sobbed. "Ask any Earth psychologist. All a personality is, is the product of cells. One has urges. They come from the reptile brain, the censor and the id. And all that is made up of cells. You have changed my cells and so you have utterly altered my whole character."

"Ah," he said. "In your case especially, how I wish that that were true. Unfortunately, you are just mouthing the superstitions of an uninformed primitive cult: you find it on many backward planets. They try to make men believe that character is inherent and passed on by an evolutionary chain or some such nonsense. In some witch-doctor cults they even go so far as to say a man is totally the effect of his cellular inheritance and therefore can't be changed. It's a way of excusing their inability to mold character. When people try to hold them responsible for creating a criminal society that way, they just glibly say 'a man is just the product of his cells.' It obscures the fact that they are just too incompetent and too criminal themselves to mold character and teach right from wrong.

"Ah, no, Sultan Bey. If cells and glands were all there was to life, I'd be a God, wouldn't I? And I'm not. I'm just a poor cellologist, unpaid, but doing my job anyway, and without even a thank-you from my superior, but suspicion undeserved."

He dropped the sheet. He looked at me. "It's a very sad thing that personality can't be changed just by shifting a few cells. Particularly in your case. But," and he smiled bravely, "one does what one can to relieve pain and make people happier. And I do hope that your increased activity potential doesn't have violent consequences for others or this planet." He brightened up. "Well! That one was successful. You can be up and around and leave whenever you like."

He set the example and marched out the door.

Chapter 7

Nurse Bildirjin began to sweep the floor and tidy up the room. She seemed in a happy frame of mind but apparently it was too quiet for her. She went over to the radio on the hook, pulled out the earphone jack and turned on the hot-pop station.

"Hey!" I said, being pretty tired by this time of "You Are My Monster," "He said I could leave! Unstrap this bed and let me out of here. Where are my clothes?"

"Clothes?" she said. She rushed out and came back with a type of bag they use to hold discarded body parts: Non-Odor Transmitting was on it very plain in Voltarian. She shoved it at me.

I couldn't take it. My arms were still strapped down. It looked awfully thin to have any clothes in it. "That isn't what I wore in here!"

"Oh, we had to throw your suit and overcoat away. They were all full of sauce of some kind. We threw out your shoes, socks and hat, too. This is just your wallets and papers."

I looked at her. Her black eyes might be pretty but she sure was stupid! I decided to be patient. I was immobilized. "Look, Nurse Bildirjin. I need clothes to leave the hospital. Through that window, I can see that it is very cold outside. There is a wind blowing. I cannot walk out there with no clothes on."

She understood that.

"So," I continued, "like the good, sweet, innocent girl that you are, please go out to the office and phone my friend, the taxi driver, and tell him to bring me some clothes."

She got that. She left. In about ten minutes she came back. "I phoned him." She was carrying a disposable bathrobe-and-slipper set. Ah, she did have some sense after all.

She put the bathrobe and slippers down all the way across the room. Then she stood there just looking at me.

It was an uncomfortable silence. I didn't like the look in those black eyes. Even the best of women are the most treacherous beasts ever invented. Whatever she was plotting right now had better be distracted.

"You instigated that operation," I said.

I expected a hearty denial. But she said, "Well, of course! Anyone who would TWICE interrupt a girl halfway through is undersexed. Such a person couldn't possibly appreciate the finer things of life. And at my first hint, Doktor Muhammed got straight to work. But I am not at all sure that we have put an end to it."

Those black eyes were too bright! "I think," she said, "I should be reassured."

A stir of alarm speeded up my heart. She looked just like women look when they are about to do something sly and cunning.

"Well," she said, "there's only one way to tell."

She raced over to the door and barred it. She came back and turned the radio up louder. She went to the windows and made sure nobody could see in.

My alarm grew.

She tested the straps and buckles on the bed. When I saw she was not releasing them, my temperature started to go up.

She took off her right slipper. She kicked off her left slipper. She turned her back on me. She was doing something at her waist level.

What was she up to?

There was a shimmer. She bent over and rose again. She was holding her panty hose.

She threw them away!

She set her nurse's cap on the back of her head.

I was glaring at her in alarm.

"That won't do," she said. "Mustn't peek!"

She promptly arranged the sheet so that I could see only

through a slit. I could see a corner of the window and the light fixture in the middle of the ceiling. I couldn't see Nurse Bildirjin!

I felt the bed tip: the light fixture slanted.

Oh, my Gods! What did she have in mind?

The bed tipped again.

Frantically I tried to rise up and see what was happening. The straps prevented it.

A cold draft told me the lower part of the sheet was being lifted.

My eyes almost popped out of my head.

I suddenly divined what she was up to!

Good Gods! This girl was a minor!

Her father was the leading physician of the province. He would kill me if I touched her!

I tried to reconcile myself with the thought that SHE was doing all the touching.

Then I had a vision of her father's shotgun! He was the best quail hunter in all of Turkey. A dead shot!

The idea of me flying hectically into the sky, the boom of a shotgun and me flapping earthward, blurred my vision.

It was too late.

I caught a glimpse of the top of her nurse's cap for a moment. The red crescent was like a blade pointing at me.

"Ooooh!" she crooned. "Lovely, lovely!"

The nurse's cap eased down.

Then the bed began to rock.

The top of the nurse's cap was in my view, then the light fixture, alternately.

I felt my eyes begin to spin in spirals.

The Hoochi-Hoochi Boys and Their Electric Cura Irizvas started a song on the radio. She took their rhythm.

> *Little bo peep went do-da, do-da.*
> *Little bo peep went do-da all the day.*
> *Little bo peep, oh do-da, do-da, do-da.*
> *To hell with the sheep,*
> *Let's do-da all the day.*

Let's do-da all the day.
Let's do-da all the day.
Let's do-da all the day.

Her nurse's cap and the light fixture were shifting in rhythm to the music.

I was engulfed in a GLORIOUS SENSATION!

Only now and then were strains of the music coming through.

Let's do-da all the day.

It went on and on and on! Both Nurse Bildirjin and the music!

Let's do-da all the day.

Minutes and minutes.

Then *bbbbbbbbblowOWIE!!!*

Earthquakes and hurricanes mixed up with all the celestial chaos of the Gods didn't compare to what occurred!

WOW!

Finally the room quieted down to just a blurred spin.

I lay back panting.

A sort of wonder came over me. Where had this been all my life?

Somebody else was panting. Then the bed shook.

I saw the top of Nurse Bildirjin's cap. She must be standing now beside the bed.

She was muttering to herself. "Prahd says its awfully good for the complexion. Judging from the amount, I'm going to have the finest complexion in Turkey!"

Suddenly I saw her feet upside down through the slit. She must be sitting on the floor!

"Mustn't waste it even so," she said. "Conservation is my motto."

I couldn't see what she was doing. I heard her crossing the room to the washbasin.

I heard water splashing. Then a silence.

Suddenly the sheet was yanked off my face. She was standing fully dressed beside me.

"Anyway," she said to me with a professional smile, "you will be glad to know that the equipment passes the clinical test. Of course, you lack expertise in the use of your tools. Prahd, I must say, is a much better craftsman."

She nodded toward my lower body which I couldn't see. Then she looked at me. She wagged an admonishing finger at me. "You are, of course, just a little boy with a new toy. So don't break it right away."

She began to undo the buckles on the straps that held me down. "You don't have a very good reputation, Sultan Bey. I had to keep you strapped so that you wouldn't rape me the minute I let you loose. I'm sure you understand. It was just a precautionary measure. Now, if I undo this last buckle, will you promise not to leap on me and rape me?"

This insanity served to bring some order into the chaos of my thoughts. The realization hit me fully. I had just (bleeped) Prahd's girl!

"Don't tell Prahd!" I pleaded with her.

"Well," she said, "that depends."

Blackmail! I knew it! My Apparatus trained nose could smell it even above her perfume and the reek of sex. "On what?" I begged.

"Two things," she said. "Don't interrupt a girl again halfway through. And don't, don't, don't you run into my Fiat ever, ever, ever again!"

I did not like the look in her eye. "I promise."

"Well, I don't," she said.

She threw off the last buckle and then tossed the disposable bathrobe and slippers at me. "Put these on and walk around in the hall until your clothes come. I've got to mop all these spatters off the floor before somebody sees them and finds out."

Practical girl. I hastily exited.

Chapter 8

I found I had been occupying a room in the main hospital building. The rooms and wards had been all cleared out as soon as the vast supplies could be stored in the warehouses. It provoked me to see so many Turks in the beds. They sure were cluttering up the place with nonpaying guests! The real income was down in the secret basement.

I wandered toward the main lobby. It was clinic hours. The area was crowded with old people, women and children waiting their turn at the free treatments. Sheer waste of time. Riffraff! Well, anyway, I had made it possible for them. They ought to be grateful. I sauntered through the seated mob. They saw who it was and hastily pulled their children to them and flinched back.

To Hells with them. I turned to go back into the hall. One of the town doctors that served part time here at vast salary was talking to an old woman, probably telling her she needed expensive specialist treatment in his town office.

It was Nurse Bildirjin's father!

I flinched.

I hastily dived through a door so he wouldn't catch sight of me. I peeked through the crack. He was still there.

I turned. I was in a private room. There was somebody in a contraption that covered his whole chest like a metal bra. The patient was all bandaged up, only the eyes were showing.

Why did he have his hands up in an attitude of defense? Somebody who knew me?

I peered closer.

RAHT!

What in the name of Modon Demons was Raht doing here? Oh, I was furious!

"Why, (bleep) you!" I screamed at him. "More vacations! I can't depend on you for a single instant! Do you realize that your (bleeped) fixation on loafing will have me totally blind? You're supposed to be in New York! You're the only one that can turn that 831 Relayer on! And unless it's on, I won't be able to see a (bleeping) thing that condemned Royal officer is doing! You were supposed to watch him! You don't care for a split second that he has Grand Council authority to order all our arrests! Now, (bleep) you, Raht. Get out of that (bleeped) bed this very minute and get to New York and climb the Empire State Building and get that 831 Relayer back on!"

Oh, I was furious! My voice must have risen pretty loud. Somebody was coming in. I whirled on him.

It was Prahd. "Softly, softly," he said. "The people out there shouldn't be overhearing Voltarian."

I swept it aside. "What is HE doing here?" I demanded.

"The New York office sent him in because he was dying of pneumonia. He only had half a lung left. I've had to cure the infection and rebuild both lungs. Also, they didn't set his jaws properly and he couldn't eat. I've had to rebuild the mandibles. He also had old breaks and wounds and scars. And in addition to that, his feet were frozen. He's doing quite well now but he is certainly in no shape to leave yet!"

"I'm the judge of that!" I raved at him. "Get him out of that contraption and on his way to New York!"

"It would kill him," said Prahd.

"To Hells with that!" I screamed. "You could get yourself charged right along with him as an accomplice in loafing!"

Raht had been waving his hands. Prahd got out a notebook and a pen and gave them to him. With some difficulty, Raht began to write. When he finished, Prahd handed me the sheet.

It was pretty scrawly. It said:

> *You ordered me via the office to get the 831 Relayer turned on and then report in. That's what I did. That's how I got the frozen feet. Is it true that the tall, blond young man with the blue eyes is a real Royal officer? Of the Voltar Fleet? With Grand Council orders?*

That was the last straw. They were just trying to make me wrong. "Of course he is! And he could have us all executed! Me, you, Prahd, anybody! So you better watch it, you impertinent (bleepard)!" I threw the wadded note back at him.

"Then it's all right if Raht stays and finishes his treatment?" said Prahd.

"You're all alike," I said. "I ought to blow this place up!" I stalked out.

Chapter 9

Mad as I was, I had not lost my sense of caution. I cunningly avoided being shot by Nurse Bildirjin's father by putting my bathrobe over my head and using side corridors on my way back to my room.

The staff must be readying the place for some other patient, although my bag of wallets and papers was still beside the bed. A four-wheeled handcart sat in the middle of the room stacked high with cardboard boxes. Then I entered further. Beyond the cart, the taxi driver was sitting in a chair.

He spoke. "Mudlick didn't do a very careful job of decorating this place. They left white paint splattered all over the floor. Look at that. A trail of it from the bed to the wash basin."

I thought I had better distract him quick! "I've been waiting for you for hours! I can't leave here without clothes."

"Oho, clothes, is it?" he said. "Well, you just look what I've got for *you!*" He reached way up and got the top box on the handcart. He threw it on the bed and opened it. I flinched. I thought a wild animal was jumping out!

"A real Turkmen genuine bearskin coat, full length! Feel that fur! Expert tanning, hardly any smell at all!" He grabbed another box. "A karakul fur hat: straight from Lake Kara Kul, Tadzhik, S.S.R. Look how glossy the lamb pelt is. Smuggled through by the very best people." He put it on my head. "Boy, does that give you an air! Classier than a commissar!" He grabbed another box. "Now look at these elegant, roll-top snow boots! Isn't that a beautiful blue? And see? These patent leather oxfords fit inside just right—

three whole pairs of them, brown and blue and black. Just your size. Everything is just your size."

Ignoring anything I was trying to say, he made another leap to the top of the cart. Boxes came cascading down. He ripped another one open. "Now look at this waterproof, silk ski suit. How do you like that horizon blue, eh? Top of the line. Latest fashion from Switzerland! Look at this hood! Feel the inside of it, man. Mink! Isn't that wonderful?"

He was grabbing more boxes. "Now for the practical things. Look at this specially cut, tan English tweed jacket. Look at it glow! Look at that style! And here's the flared-side, steeplechase jodhpur breeches that go with it. How's that for a match? Look at that dark brown against the jacket. And here are the jodhpur boots. Look at the leather. Isn't that beautiful? Name brand. Top of the line. Just your size."

He was ripping open more boxes. "Now, here's the German Tyrolean outfit. Hey, how do you like that pom-pom on the green Tyrol hat, eh? Isn't it great? And the jacket and shorts and walking boots, all the finest leather. And get those suspenders. Look at that design on them: hand woven! Says so right there."

I was trying to stop him. He plowed right on. More and more boxes. "Now here's the more formal wear. Silk shirts and silk neck scarves. And get this Italian pin-stripe gray suit—it goes with the white Homburg. Boy, is that ever classy! Now here's a dozen silk knitted turtleneck sweaters——"

"WAIT!" I managed to stop him only by leaping bodily between him and the still heavily loaded handcart. "Where did all these come from?"

"Why, the Giysi Modern Western Clothing Our Specialty Shop for Men and Gentlemen in town, of course. Days ago they were tipped off you were coming home and they got the whole lot in for you by express order from Istanbul. They know your size. Have no worries. Every bit of this will fit."

"My Gods!" I cried. "The message I had relayed to you was to go to the villa and get me some clothes."

"No, it was to get you some clothes. But I did go to your villa and they said they were much too busy to bother. It's awfully cold out and you've just been in the hospital and all. I know what a classy gent you are, so I just nipped over to town and got these clothes."

"They look awfully expensive!" I protested.

"Oh, no money needed. You'd just be amazed how great your credit is. I got them on your Start Blanching and Dunner's Club credit cards!"

I felt as if I were going to faint. Credit cards! Oh, my Gods, credit cards!

Inspiration to the rescue. "You don't have their numbers!"

"Oh, everybody in town knows the numbers of all your credit cards. And in Istanbul, too! No trouble!"

Inspiration beyond the call of inspiration was called for. I not only didn't have any money, I also owed the credit-card companies for the whole last month of our fatal trip!

I had it! "I won't sign the invoices!"

"Oh, no problem. You forget I was a convicted forger on the planet Modon, Officer Gris. I knew how weak you'd be, just getting out of the hospital and all. I signed the lot for you to save you all that trouble!"

"You set this up just to get a 10 percent kickback from the store," I grated.

"Oh, Heavens no, Officer Gris. How you wrong me! It's awfully cold weather. Now that you're home, I can't afford to have you get sick. Now, why don't you step over there and have a nice shower while I lay out some silk underwear and some alpaca wool mountaineering socks and the nice tan camel's-hair lounging suit. And this dark brown silk shirt with this white Christian Dior cravat and these cordovan tooled cowboy boots. Don't take too hot a shower. It's awfully cold outside. And then you can put on this bearskin coat and karakul cap and I can take you home."

What could I say? At least there was one person in the universe who cared about me, for whatever reason. I might as well be shot in a genuine Turkmen bearskin coat as in a Zanco disposable bathrobe. Another fifteen thousand wouldn't make any difference when added to the maybe half a million I still owed on credit cards. I brightened. This wouldn't be due for another month after they had shot me for failing to pay my already existing debt.

It struck me as I soaped that I didn't know the taxi driver's right name. Above the shower spatter, I yelled, "You know, nobody ever told me your name."

"Ahmed," he yelled back.

"No, no," I shouted. "I know your Turkish name. I mean your *right* name."

"Oh," he said. "Deplor."

Deplor? That, in Modon, meant "Fate."

Later I was to have cause to remember that. Just now I was too engrossed in trying to soap myself in spite of these newly acquired appendages. I certainly hoped those virgin pants would take care of it. It sure was *big!*

PART THIRTY-FIVE
Chapter 1

Despite the taxi driver's solicitude, I felt fine. I walked across the villa lawn with a spring in my step and the customary scowl on my face in case any staff was watching.

I felt it was beneath me to order the carrying in of the boxes of new clothes and left that to the taxi driver. He, in turn, marshalled up Karagoz and several of the men and they got a fire-bucket sort of line going and very soon my bedroom looked more like a store than living quarters. At least I was going to go to my financial death in the height of fashion.

The taxi driver paused by me in the patio as he left. "Those will do you for the cold weather," he said. "And you be sure to keep warm. But, come spring, they will be *too* warm so I'll have Giysi Modern Western Clothing Our Specialty Shop for Men and Gentlemen working on your spring wardrobe."

Come spring, I had a feeling, I would be long cold in the graveyard they reserve for people shot by the delinquent-accounts sections of the credit-card companies. But let him dream. According to his own lights, he was taking care of me.

"Wear those wool scarfs around your throat," he said. "And don't get your feet wet." And he was gone.

The sound of the closing of the patio door signalled the opening of Utanc's. I had been standing there wondering how to get in my bedroom. I heard a gasp. I turned.

Utanc. She looked at the karakul cap. She looked at the bearskin coat. Then she peered at my face, part of which must have been showing between the folds of fur collar.

"Oh!" she said in what must have been relief. "It's only you!"

"I'm just back from the hospital," I said.

"Oh. Is that where you've been? What are you doing coming around here and scaring people to death? I thought you were a commissar or somebody important at first."

Something in her attitude nettled me. "Utanc," I said. "You and I have to have a talk about credit cards."

"Hah!" she said. "There you go flying into one of your rages about the least little thing!"

She was beautiful, standing there in a Saks Fifth Avenue white satin housecoat trimmed with pearls. I did love her. But also she had placed both my right and left feet over the edge in the Delinquent Creditor Graveyard. "Utanc," I said, "could you possibly send back or sell some of the jewelry you bought? I am in deep financial distress."

I don't know what I expected. A slammed door, probably. But she stood there staring at me. She then put her finger in her mouth and thought about it.

I said, "Utanc, I love you dearly. But if you could just see fit to let me cancel your credit cards and return some of the more valuable purchases, I might be able to weather this somehow."

"O Master," she said, "I am so sorry to hear that I was bought by someone of limited means. However, I share the blame."

My spirits lifted. She did care after all!

She said, "I should have had you looked up in Dunn and Bradstreet before I stepped onto the auction block. I did not, so I am remiss."

It was touching. Of course, as a wild desert girl, she lacked facilities to establish credit ratings.

"I don't suppose," she continued, thoughtfully tapping her teeth, "that capitalistic law allows a pauperized slave girl to sell her master. No, it would be too decadent for that." She frowned prettily and began to weave a lock of her raven black hair. "Certainly, there must be something we can do."

I had an inspiration. I suddenly realized that the basis of all her upset with me was unsatisfied sex. She had always wound up unhappy after a bout. Freud cannot be wrong. She was simply frustrated! But now! Now, after Prahd's great work . . .

"Utanc," I said. "Why don't you come to my room tonight? I have a beautiful surprise for you!"

"A surprise?" she said suspiciously.

"A big one," I said. "And very nice."

"Hmmm," she said. Then, "Master, if I come to your room tonight—just that and nothing more implied—will you let me keep all the things I bought and my credit cards?"

I did a very rapid calculation. There was no doubt whatever in my mind that once she found what I had now, all thought of jewelry and credit cards would vanish. Freud cannot be wrong. Sex is the basis of every tiny impulse, everything in fact. If I could just get her in my room for one hour, after that she would be totally content to live with me the rest of her life in poverty if need be.

I put all my chips on Freud. "Utanc, if you just come to my room tonight and lie down with me upon my bed for just two minutes, you may keep your jewelry and your credit cards."

She nodded. "Nine o'clock. I will be there." She closed her door.

I did a little dance.

I had it solved!

In well under two minutes, all thought of jewelry and credit cards would be gone forever from that pretty head. After that, I would simply ship the offending items back to Tiffany's and rip, rip, tear up the treacherous cards. She would even laugh gaily as I did it! Wonderful, wonderful psychology! Bless Freud!

Chapter 2

I was at once all bouncing enthusiasm. I had to get all these clothes stowed and my room straightened up and I wasted no time.

Problem: I didn't really have enough closet space. Something would have to go. In one secret closet a lot of the space was taken up with hypnohelmets in their big cartons. I sealed them up, just like new, and with a few assorted threats, got them into the Chevy station wagon and made Karagoz take them to Prahd for storage in the new warehouses. That gave me barely enough room, and by means of a lot of cramming and parking things on top of things, I got the job done.

New problem. It was only 4:00 P.M. Five hours to kill!

Heller. Raht had said he had turned on the 831 Relayer. I had better check it out.

I went in the secret office, pushed aside the bogus gold bars and boxes that still littered the floor. I turned on the wall electric fire, mindful of the taxi driver's advice to take care of myself. I got the receiver and viewer out of my baggage, put them on their former low bench and turned them on.

Victory!

There he was in his Empire State Building office.

I couldn't quite make it out, though. I was getting various views of the floor.

Then, finally, his voice. "There it is." He fished a rubber ball out from a dark corner under his desk and, straightening up in his chair, put it on the blotter.

The cat leaped up on the desk, moved over to a point about three feet from the ball and sat down.

Heller rolled the ball at the cat. The cat, with an expert paw, rolled the ball back at Heller. Back and forth, back and forth.

Kind of pathetic. We really had him slowed down. He had nothing better to do than play ball with a cat!

All of a sudden the cat hit the ball a terrific lick and sent it bounding off the desk. This time Heller caught it. "You got to watch that strength, cat. Don't be such a showoff. Somebody will get the idea you're an extraterrestrial and they'll get you for a Code break. Here, chase it for a while!"

Heller tossed the ball the length of the room. The cat was after it like a shot.

Just before the ball hit the wall, the door opened!

The cat ignored the rebounding ball and squared away to the door.

"You missed me." It was Bang-Bang.

The cat saw who it was and said, "Yeow?"

Bang-Bang came across the room. "You got to teach that cat how to shoot better." The cat was following him, eyes on a bag Bang-Bang was carrying. "No, it's not ice cream," Bang-Bang informed it. He threw the bag on the desk.

"There's your photographs you had taken, Jet. And here's a bottle of stuff the man said would float off the emulsion."

"Any questions?" said Jet.

"Hell, no. I told them it was just my G-2 class and they said they were always glad to help a student with his homework."

The cat was satisfying himself the package did not contain ice cream. It was quite obvious he did not believe Bang-Bang.

"Jet," said Bang-Bang. "While I was waiting for this stuff, I thunk up a great plan. I got to do something. I'm scared to go near the family. I can't leave my job or I'll wind up back in Sing Sing. But I got it all worked out."

Heller waved to a chair. The cat sat down to listen.

"It goes like this," said Bang-Bang. "I get the license plates of all publishers' cars in the country. Then I simply put bombs in them and BANGO! they're in Purgatory and we're in clover."

Heller said, "Sounds kind of extensive."

"Well, how about this one? I plant bombs under the TV network buildings—NBC, CBS and ABC. This phony Whiz Kid is bound to show up in one and BLOWIE, he's in Purgatory and we're in clover."

"Then the reporters would mob *me*."

"Jet, I begin to suspect that you do not have the soul of a good demolition man."

I snorted. Heller, as a combat engineer, had probably blown up more buildings and forts than Bang-Bang had ever heard of. I was astonished to hear Heller answer, "I bow to the expert. However, I somehow don't think any of those is the right target."

I chilled. It was obvious Heller was talking about ME! Had he really found out? Then I thought it might be Madison he meant. Better Madison than me any time. I waited breathlessly for Heller to say more. He didn't and it dawned on me that he just plain didn't know. I relaxed.

Bang-Bang got up. "Then," he said, "I am left with the final solution."

"And that is?" said Heller.

"Go get a drink of Scotch," said Bang-Bang. "Come on, cat. Your boss won't miss you for an hour and I hate to drink alone."

He departed with the cat trotting after him.

Heller got busy. He propped open a G-2 manual on identification. He emptied the sack of photographs on the desk. They all seemed to be pictures of Heller but somehow he looked different ages. He got a tray and poured some water and fluid in it. Then he went to a safe and got out stacks of I.D.'s. Hey, these were all the passports and social security cards and driver's licenses he had been taking off gangsters and Silva. He spread them out. My Gods, I hadn't realized how many there had been!

Ten at the garage. The two snipers I had hired—Bang-Bang must have picked their pockets! One from the Midtown Air Terminal. Five CIA-sourced ones he'd taken off Silva.

There were others he hadn't taken the I.D. from: the three at the Gracious Palms, two more at the terminal and, of course, Silva's own.

I did a hasty calculation. Heller had wasted nineteen of Faustino's men. They knew it: no wonder they were terrified of him. He had slaughtered eight hoodlums in Van Cortlandt Park. He had wrecked but not killed Torpedo Fiaccola and two Turk wrestlers. And he had blown up ten IRS agents if, by stretch of the imagination, you could call IRS agents human.

Forty men!

They had been after his blood and it was in self-defense. But what might happen if he took it into his head to go hunting people!

He was *dangerous!*

Oh, I better make awfully sure he did not get out of control! And I had better be awfully careful myself! I sometimes forgot that I was dealing with the top combat engineer of the Voltar Fleet. That was the trouble with him. He was deceptive with all those gentlemanly officer ways and pretenses of decency and even religion.

But never mind. Rockecenter knew his business. Bury knew his business. And thank the Gods, Madison was an expert with a weapon more powerful than I had ever imagined existed—PR.

And we had him stopped. We had him pinned down.

He was fooling with those passports and driver's licenses now. He would put a photograph of himself looking older into the tray of fluid. The thin emulsion of the photograph would begin to separate from the paper backing. Then, using a couple pairs of small tongs, he would slide the emulsion over onto the actual passport picture. Then using a dampened ball of something, he would press the new emulsion down in place so that even the embossing of the seal would come through.

After a while he had eighteen passports. All he had to do was change his own hair color and draw in some age lines on his own face to agree with the age stated, and he could use them himself!

He now went to work on the driver's licenses. This was a little trickier as the small color pictures were tinier. He also had to remove the whole license from its lamination in some cases. He would pick up the emulsion from the color picture, put it aside and then put one of himself in its place. He finished them by running them as a batch through a portable lamination machine he had set up.

Eighteen sets of I.D. But of what possible use were they to him? Names like Cecchino, Serpente, Laccio, Rapitore . . . All mobster names. They would be known and show up on police computers. And everybody would know by this time that Inganno John Scroccone, Faustino's chief accountant, was dead. Only those five CIA passports might be of some use and I would bet anything they would trace back as a CIA operative cover. And of a dead operative—Gunsalmo Silva.

Then I began to laugh. I understood what this was all about. He was pinned to the name Wister, of course, by college and friends. But Madison had driven him under cover. Heller couldn't even register in a motel without some clerk thinking he was the Whiz Kid! We were really wrecking him!

Oh, that made me feel good. I had Heller on the run. He was living in a little tiny room beside his office. He was probably even going to lose that soon. He was undoubtedly low on cash. He had lost the support of Babe and the family. He would probably soon lose Izzy.

A beautiful vision! Heller, broke, adrift as a bum in New York. It had all begun with the brilliance of Lombar. It had been pushed on through by the brilliance of Rockecenter. And with Madison as a hatchet man, the Heller tree was cut down.

He didn't have a prayer!

That would teach him the stupidity of trying to benefit a planet!

Planets and populations exist to be milked by the power elite. Unless one understood that thoroughly, one could do a lot of stupid things like help people.

The Gods put the riffraff there as prey for superior men like Hisst and Rockecenter. And there was very short shrift for anyone who thought otherwise.

I hugged myself with glee.

Then, at length, I threw a blanket over the viewer.

I had more important things to do than watch the painful demise of a (bleeped) fool Royal officer with silly notions you could help a world.

Chapter 3

At 9:00 P.M., aglow with anticipation, I lay in the bed in my room. All the lights were out, just the way she always wanted it. But there was a big difference: I had taken off all my clothes and, like you wrap a present, had thrown a single sheet over myself.

Was she going to be surprised! Wow! I was making a big thing out of it, of course, but such splendid moments don't come often in a lifetime.

I heard a slight sound at the door. Then a groping gave a tremor to the bed.

In a moment I felt her weight and warmth beside me. A gentle jasmine perfume filled the air. I began to quiver with excitement. "Darling," I whispered.

I put out my hand to encircle her. She was fully clothed as always at such moments.

She withdrew slightly. "What's this surprise?" she said.

I groped for and found her hand. I guided it under the sheet. I made the fingers touch my chest and then began to press her hand downwards.

"Feel this," I whispered, a little choked with passion. "Look what I've got for you."

I made her fingers connect with me.

"What the HELL?"

Oh, I knew she would be surprised!

Her fingers recoiled. Then they reached again, encircled my member.

"Hey!" she said. "What kind of a trick is this? A falsie? A dildo? Well, we'll see about THAT!"

Her fingers began to pluck all around the edges, then at the surrounding area. The fingernails were pretty sharp. She was trying to find if there was any strap to hold it on.

"No, no," I said hastily. "It's real!"

"We'll see about that!" she said grimly.

She wrapped her fingers around it, held on hard and gave it a mighty yank!

"OUCH!" I shrieked.

"By Allah the Merciful, it IS real!"

Aha, I knew she would be amazed!

She was feeling the top of it, getting an idea of diameter and scope.

She drew back and sat up suddenly.

"You (bleepard)!" she said. "You treacherous, rotten (bleepard)!" An ill-aimed fist hit me in the jaw! "First you're so God (bleeped) small nobody can even find it! Smaller even than the little boys! Now, you're so God (bleeped) big nobody could get it into anything!"

Did I hear a watch running? Yes! There was the luminous dial of a stopwatch. She must be studying it. Making sure her two minutes expired!

"Utanc, please," I begged. "I am sure there is a way. Utanc, I did it all for you. Please think again. Please give me your hand. It isn't that bad. It's really just a little bigger than normal! And it has other advantages, Utanc. . . ."

The button of the stopwatch went *click*. "Two minutes," she said. "I want you to witness that I stayed two minutes in your bed." She pushed the dial close to my face and it glowed green. She had been there two minutes all right.

"Please, Utanc," I wept. "You have no idea . . ."

"Listen, you (bleepard). I am tired of your tricks! You go to such EXTREMES! One minute you couldn't even please a flea and the next minute you would wreck a camel! I am going to my room now and don't you bother me again until you decide to be more NORMAL!"

She got off the bed. The door slammed! She was gone.

I lay there in shock. All my anticipation had been aroused to the bursting point. The sudden twist of events left me in midcareer. My heart was pounding with unspent passion while my brain reeled with shock.

I tried to lie quietly, hoping that I would settle down. Instead, I began to twitch.

I couldn't lie still. I got up.

Thinking that she might be experiencing remorse, maybe even crying with frustration herself, I went to the receiver of the bug I had long ago planted in her room. I turned it on.

There was more volume in it now. Maybe it had been moved to a better place when the credit-card people had tried to strip the house of rugs.

I could hear water running. Then I heard some clinks and clatters. Then Utanc's voice, "Wake up, you little dears. No reason to sleep your lives away."

Some "What's this?" and "Huh's?" from the two little boys. Then some "Oh, goodies."

The clink of glasses. Was she giving them their evening milk?

Then some Turkish music. Probably recorded. Savage. Primitive. The rhythmic pounding of a foot. Then the swish and swirl of fabric. Then the clash of swords together in rhythm. My own body began to respond, no matter that I couldn't see her dance.

The voices of the two little boys began to rise in gasps of appreciation.

Then suddenly a change. The *cura irizva* striking bold and savage chords. Then Utanc's voice in song:

> *You may be small,*
> *But oh, you're good.*
> *I would eat you,*
> *If I could.*
> *Why should hunger*

Be in fashion,
When you're there,
To slake my passion?
So off with hat,
Let down your hair,
I'm going to eat
Your table bare!
Now I'll throw
You into bed.
You better hide!
There goes your head!

The clatter of the *cura irizva* being thrown down.

Small shouts of surprise.

The swish and rustle of sheets and bed.

Squeals of delight!

I couldn't stand any more. I turned the receiver off. My passion was at a bursting point. I lay down in my bed.

My arms were empty. I ached. I had never ached before like this. Painful. Awful!

And for hours I lay there like that.

I realized that there was no torture to compare with unsatisfied desire! All centralized in a very sensitive place!

Chapter 4

The next morning it was very cold. The electric fire had blown a fuse. I got into a blue ski suit. Warming my hands around some *kahve*, I thought it over carefully. I came to a desperate decision.

I would stop being true to Utanc.

I phoned the taxi driver and when he came, I had him drive down the road a few yards. There was a turn-in there where another villa had been burned in centuries past and one could go a few feet off the road and park under a cedar tree while still retaining full view of any traffic.

He shut off the engine. The sigh of wind in the cedar was very mournful. He turned in his seat, pushed his sheepskin cap onto the back of his head and waited for me to speak. He obviously could see that I was troubled.

"I've got to do something about Utanc," I said.

He digested that. He thoughtfully lit a cheap Hisar cigarette. "You can't get anything out of a trade-in," he said. "The bottom is out of the market. Things have gotten even worse behind the Iron Curtain. Hundreds of thousands of girls have come over the border. Threatened with rape from the Red Army, it was a case of either infection or defection. They chose the latter. Can't say as I blame them. You ever feel the beard on one of those Ivans? Or see the body lice? Fleas, too. No, Officer Gris, we're stuck with her."

"I don't mean to make a big thing out of it," I said. "But a long look at it has convinced me the matter isn't going to settle down."

"Well," he said, "you never can tell what you're getting into in these things."

"You've got to come up with something," I said. After all, he was the only one who seemed to care what happened to me. And the criminals on Modon are a pretty smart lot. "The situation is wide open to suggestions."

The cedar sighed. Three camel loads of opium went by, led by a farmer and a donkey, heading toward the Agricultural School. The farmer looked at us curiously.

Deplor, alias Ahmed, waited until they were out of sight. Then he threw away his cigarette in sudden decision. "I don't want to get you into any tight spots you can't get out of, Officer Gris. I have your best interests at heart. So, I tell you what you better do. You better give me some money and I'll get some women for you."

"No more slaves!" I said hastily.

"No, no," he said. "I got you into a hole on that one. And you don't want any prostitutes, either. The type I have in mind are just women who need money for a dowry. They need money to get married. You can get a one-night stand with such a woman. Good lookers, too. Lots of variety. Different one every night. Spread it around. And they're real hot, too."

Oh, that sounded good!

He continued, "Now, to do this right, you should have a big car. Women go in for big things and that includes a big car. You remember that bulletproof limousine I told you about? The ex-general's car? The one who got shot? It's still for sale up in Istanbul."

A snag suddenly occurred to me. "Wait. You can't get women on a credit card. And I'm trying to swear off, anyway."

"On women?" he said, astonished.

"No. Credit cards. I hate the things."

"Well, you don't need to use credit cards," he said. "Just deal in cash. So if you'll just give me some money . . ."

It was time to confess. He was, after all, my friend. "I'm stonebroke," I said. "I don't have any money at all."

The taxi driver started up the car rather quickly, I thought. He dropped me off at the villa up the road. He didn't even say good-bye.

I stared after him.

(Bleep)!

It was all too plain to me that it took money to get things done. Life without money, as I had always known, was death.

I limped back to my room with this awful ache.

(Bleep) Prahd!

I decided some physical work might take my mind off my plight. I warmed up my secret office, stripped myself down and began to clean guns, sweep away old clothes and, by late afternoon, began to straighten up the mess of fake gold bars and the boxes.

Puttering around, I was mostly done when I saw that one of the cases had fallen onto some packages of unexamined mail.

Idly, and with no thought, I picked up some of the letters. They had been forwarded from the Section 451 office on Voltar and had come in on recent freighters. Faht's orderly had slipped them through the slot in the tunnel door.

Routine stuff. A notice that I'd been dropped from the Academy Alumnus Association for the nonpayment of dues. A bill from a gun dealer on Flisten—years old and I didn't intend to be on duty on Flisten soon. An advertisement for new General Services officer caps "that would remain undamaged under the hardest blows of troops' cudgels." An ad for the latest release of "the ever more popular sweetheart of Homeview, Hightee Heller," song strips, featuring hits from the new musical show that was "jamming Voltar theaters nightly: *Bold Prince Caucalsia*." A warning that I had not acknowledged reading the latest general Apparatus order about filling in forms that listed the correct sequences of forms and must fill in the attached form at once. A new type of chank-pop that "totally eradicated for seconds at a time the gaseous odors of troops." A special offer to Apparatus officers only—a fun gift for their friends—exploding boots. An electronic bird whistle, available in dozen lots, that called in selected types of female songbirds for breeding purposes.

What's this?

Two personal postcards? The kind you send to friends and are wide open in the mails for anyone to read. Who could this be? I didn't have any friends.

I looked at the signature and gaped. The Widow Tayl!

The first card said:

Soltan Gris
Section 451
Please Forward.

    Yoo-Hoo. Wherever you are. I'm just coming along great.
    What shall we name it?
    Why don't you write?

        The lovey-dovey woman you
        heartlessly abandoned,

        Pratia

Return to Pratia Tayl
Minx Estate
Pausch Hills

Oh, my Gods! Open like that right through the office for anyone to read! You could be cashiered for knocking somebody up and not marrying them! The law was all on her side.

The second card was worse! It said:

Soltan Gris
    Officer of the Apparatus still, unless his commanding officer finds out he didn't marry me if he doesn't the next time I see him.

> *Yoo-Hoo! Wherever you are.*
>
> *He is just coming along fine. It is too soon to feel him kick yet. What schools shall we send him to when he is born? How about the Academy like his father? And maybe buy him a commission in the Fleet. Please waste no time in writing me quickly so as to save all the tedious trouble of hiring lawyers which is so time wasting when one could be so nicely busy doing other things.*
>
> > *The loving pregnant girl you left behind,*
> >
> > *Pratia Tayl*
> > *Minx Estate*
> > *Turn right off the main road at the Inn of the Rutting Beast.*
> > *Pausch Hills*
>
> *PS: Young officers are always welcome, in or out of uniform, to look into this case.*
> *(You can also use the landing pad day or night.)*

(Bleep) *her!*

She was trying to get me into trouble! The one thing I had vowed from earliest youth was never, never, NEVER to get married! Who wanted cooking utensils sizzling through the air around one's head? Who wanted all the killings that followed digging brother officers out of your wife's bed?

And, curse it all, Prahd said he had certified and registered her pregnancy before he left Voltar!

(Bleep), (bleep), (BLEEP) Prahd! It was a good thing he was legally dead. Otherwise, I would have shot him out of hand!

Bad off as I might be for women, it could never include the Widow Tayl! She murdered husbands at the slightest pretext. But I had to be honest. That wasn't the real reason.

I could just plain never, never forgive her for her fixation on Heller. The nerve of her, with me right there, having automatic orgasms just at the thought of that (bleeped) Heller! And even when she had only seen him just once for less than a minute. Never even talked to him!

Oh, the Widow Tayl was not for me! I might be hard up but not THAT hard up!

Let her go on dreaming of Heller all she liked. I was safely twenty-two and more light-years away!

But it served to cool my ardor off a bit. I almost stopped aching in the place where it hurt. To Hells with her and to Hells with Heller!

And then I thought of having rooted Heller out of the Gracious Palms. To deprive him of those women was rare punishment. I had the upper hand when all was said. I laughed.

I thought I had better take the blanket off his viewer and enjoy his discomfiture.

Chapter 5

He was standing in a park, looking out across the East River. A wintry wind was putting small whitecaps on the water and gulls were flying low.

He turned and his eyes rested for a moment on the Statue of Peace and then, passing on, looked down the Esplanade where the flags of many nations streamed and whipped.

Heller was at the United Nations!

A chill of premonition that had nothing to do with the stormy cold he saw swept across me. What business could he possibly have there?

His gaze was watchful on the broad walkway before the doors of the General Assembly Building, looking often down East 46th Street. I knew the area well: He was expecting someone from the city to arrive here in the United Nations area.

A group caught his attention. There were five in it. They were caped and hooded in furs. It was possible that he did not expect them to see him as he moved forward into plainer view.

The group stopped. One of them pointed at the distant Heller. They all looked.

Then they began to run toward him. They were calling out glad cries. "Pretty boy!" "Oh, you darling!"

They were running toward him and he was running toward them.

They met in a gladly shouting turmoil!

They were trying to kiss his cheeks and seize his hands.

They were women from the Gracious Palms! I recognized Margie and Minette and the tall high-yellow!

"Oh, pretty boy! We have been so lonesome without you!" cried one.

"We missed you so!" cried another.

"Eet 'as bean a zentury!" cried Minette.

My Gods, they were beautiful women! All bright-eyed and rosy-cheeked. What right did he have to such glorious creatures? He had never even slept with any of them!

"We didn't think you'd come," said the tall high-yellow.

"And miss this day?" said Heller.

"I can't think how you would," said Margie. "After all, it was your idea."

"No, no," said Heller. "It was Vantagio's. He's the political expert. And you girls did all the work."

Minette said, "Oh, an' 'ow we 'ave work'! So veree, veree 'ard! We 'ave lobby an' lobby, night after night, up and down. All ze girls 'ave really put eet to ze delegates: eef zey don' pass ze bill, we knock zem up! An' we boycott zere paintings."

"I think these UN delegates got the point," said Margie. "Any delegate that doesn't vote a loud 'aye' on this bill knows he'll be under sanctions at the Gracious Palms."

"We really put our backs into it," said the high-yellow. "This is one thing they can't take lying down!"

"Oh, I think the bill will pass the General Assembly," he said.

I was stunned. I had heard one or two of them mention to Heller, when he sat in the Gracious Palms lobby of evenings, that they were "working on something" with the UN delegate customers. But I didn't have a clue what chicanery had been going on in the dark of those whores' rooms. What was this bill?

"We had better go in," said Heller. "It's coming up on the time for their final vote."

They rushed, in a happy mob, through the doors of the General Assembly Building and up to the information desk in the lobby. A uniformed girl there looked up in some disapproval at their laughter and bustle.

"You have special tickets for us," said the high-yellow. "The Delegate of Maysabongo said they would be here."

"Ah, yes," said the clerk. "Five passes to the public gallery."

"Six," said the high-yellow.

The clerk had the envelope out and open. She counted five.

"I weel zit on pretty boy's lap," said Minette.

"No, I will," said Margie with decision.

The high-yellow was reaching across the clerk to the passes in their boxes. She picked up one. "Nobody will," she said.

"You can't do that!" said the clerk. "We are supposed to hand these out on a first come, first serve basis. But this is a special session and we are expecting the wife of the president of the United States and a whole party from the Women's Liberation League. . . ."

"First come, first served," said the high-yellow, "is exactly the system we use, too."

The clerk grabbed for the purloined ticket. "You can't!"

"Can," said the high-yellow. "This is *our* bill that's being voted on! But if you're going to be that way about it, why don't you call the president of the General Assembly and tell him you are preventing Beulah from attending!"

A guard came over. "I must caution you against unseemly noise here in the lobby and also if you are attending a meeting of the General Assembly, there must be neither noise nor applause in the public galleries. I think it might be best if you were to give the tickets back and . . ."

"You tell your clerk that," said the high-yellow. "And if you want to keep your job, be polite. Here's your ticket, pretty boy. Shall we go in?"

I wondered why the guard was suddenly escorting them to the entrance of the public galleries until I noticed Beulah, the high-yellow, had him by the arm just above the elbow. (Bleep) that Heller! He had taught these whores how to handle men. A traitor!

They arrived in the public gallery, took front-row seats, and the girls were taking off their furs. They were beautifully dressed, satins and brocade. They got out compacts and repaired their makeup.

The General Assembly was a vast hall of soothing elegance.

There were just a few delegates on the floor so far. Others were arriving from time to time. They were very conscious of their own dignity as they took their seats behind the signs of their countries. But what was this? More than one of them glanced shyly toward the girls and made little hand motions that were extremely subdued waves.

A tremendous bustle and fanfare occurred. The gallery suddenly swarmed with agents. The wife of the president of the United States came in, ignored by the delegates.

Another bustle. Some females with Women's Liberation League ribbons across their chests came in. Also ignored.

What was this bill? A fear began to rise in me that Heller, whom I had supposed was down and out, retained a lot of influence. It was bad news to me.

At length the hall below was apparently as full as it would become. The public galleries were packed. Things were ready to begin.

Heller and the girls were picking up the headphones in front of their seats. There was a dial there. It said English, French, Spanish, Russian, Chinese. Minette, beside Heller, was having trouble with the earphones and her hairdo. Heller helped her and then dialed French for her. He put his own on and dialed English. He looked up at the glass-enclosed translator booths on either side of the UN emblem. The place was mobbed with TV crews and their chatter was coming over the line. Evidently the media thought this was pretty important.

But what the Hells bill was it? To bomb the Voltar base? To declare Soltan Gris an international criminal? I was worried.

The president of the General Assembly came in and took his place at the rostrum in the center of the oval hall. He opened the proceedings.

"We are met here today," he said, "for the final vote on UN Resolution 678-546-452. May I call for any last-minute afterthoughts or reservations?"

Holland got the floor. "It is our consideration that this bill will shake the world." The fat Dutchman looked up at the gallery and covertly winked.

India wrapped a robe about himself and said, "I believe it must pass because of the riots in Pakistan."

The U.S. rubbed his State Department–type face and said, "It is our considered opinion, which we wish to bring to the attention of the media, that it is high time we bowed our heads to the true sources of joy." And he bowed his head but he managed a slight smile toward the girls in the gallery.

U.K. gave his trim military mustache a brush and said, "Her Majesty will wax very wroth if the bill is not passed." He cleared his throat twice in the direction of the Gracious Palms girls in the gallery.

Maysabongo got the floor. "We cannot any longer neglect our members. I move the measure be read once more and put to the vote."

Brazil said, "Seconded!"

A man at the rostrum rose, an imposing scroll in his hands. A breathless hush gripped the hall. In a sonorous voice he read:

UN Resolution 678-546-452.

Hereas and wherewith, it is the wish and will of this, the General Assembly of the United Nations, by all sovereign powers attended, as follows, to wit:

RESOLVED: WOMEN HAVE THE RIGHT NOT TO BE THERMONUCLEAR BOMBED AND NOT TO BE FORCED TO SHUT UP BY SLAPPING OR TORTURE.

In the tense room, before the breathless gallery, the vote was taken, one by one.

As the count progressed, the packed gallery became more and more on the edge of their seats.

Then the president of the General Assembly called out, "One hundred and forty member states in favor! Twenty-six abstentions! I hereby declare the measure PASSED!"

PANDEMONIUM!

Despite the most sacred law that there be no cheering from the gallery, the din was deafening!

It was being led by the wife of the president of the United States!

The whores weren't content with just cheering. They stood up in a row throwing kisses at the delegates!

The delegates were throwing them back!

That staid chamber was being rent by chaos!

In vain the gavel rapped!

In vain the guards raced around trying to say "Sssh!"

And then Heller was helping the girls hurriedly into their furs.

They streamed out of the building with the cheering throng.

The five whores made a circle and forced Heller inside it and they began to dance around and around him in front of the Statue of Peace!

Breathless, they finally slowed down. They gathered in a group.

Beulah said, "We've got to get back and tell all the girls that they won!"

Heller said, "Almost won. It still has to go before the Security Council to become the law of the world."

"Come with us," pleaded Margie, clutching at Heller.

He shook his head. "I can't. And listen, all of you. I forbid you to tell anyone at the Gracious Palms that you saw me. I don't want any of you getting into trouble."

"Not even wan leetle wheesper?" pleaded Minette.

"Not one," said Heller. "I don't want you getting sacked because you were associating with me. Now promise."

"Oh, pretty boy," said Beulah. "At such a glorious time! They miss you, pretty boy. The girls all cry when we speak of you!"

"And I miss you," said Heller. "But go along now with your great news. The world will owe you a great debt if this gets by the Security Council. You did it all on your own."

They kissed him on the cheek. They lingeringly touched his hands. And then they sped away down the Esplanade.

Heller watched them out of sight. And then he slowly turned toward the river.

A seagull was walking near to him. "Well, seagull," he said to it, "with any luck the Security Council will pass it and then you will be safe, too. And Miss Simmons will have to realize I am on her side."

I was shaken right down to the bottom of my boots. Yes, it was very true that if that passed, Miss Simmons would not be just at his side but at his feet! She would even HELP him get his diploma! But although that in itself was very upsetting to me, in that it could cost me a valuable ally, it was not the main reason for my chill.

The raw, naked power of the man! He had used women to get a UN General Assembly Resolution passed! He could use women to do anything he wished! Widow Tayl's impression of him proved it utterly!

Oh, I had not crushed Heller the way he should be crushed! He was still dangerous beyond belief. What women saw in him I could not even begin to imagine—they were just putty in his hands!

He was just plain monopolizing all the women in the world! He was leaving none left over for anyone else!

Oh, I realized right then I had to do more! But what could I do? I paced about. What could I possibly do?

My buzzer rang. I impatiently picked up the base intercom instrument.

Faht Bey. "I'm just calling to remind you that the space freighter *Blixo* is scheduled in tonight. Captain Bolz always wants to see you, though I can't understand why. So don't go running off and making yourself hard to find again." He hung up.

Beautiful relief flooded through me. The *Blixo!* Of course! With brilliant forethought, I had already solved the very problem I was now faced with!

With luck, the Countess Krak would be on that ship. She'd slaughter Heller for even glancing at another woman! She'd slow him down to a crawl as she had on Voltar!

I laughed with delirious delight.

I had it all solved!

Smart brains. My Apparatus professors were oh so very right. I had smart brains!

Chapter 6

I began to work out exactly how I would meet these incoming people and how to persuade the Countess Krak to let herself be bugged as I had bugged Heller.

It would be very tricky. To tell the honest truth, any contact at all with the Countess Krak compared, in risk value, to walking on the outside hull of a spaceship in flight! With no safety line!

I laid my plans carefully and then, at last, satisfied they were foolproof, I began to get ready.

In the first place, I must look, myself, impressive. This would give the necessary ring of authority to things I said.

Hidden in my secret office, my General Service uniform had gotten pretty wrinkled. I got it washed by using a wash basin and dried it in front of the electric fire. Then I suddenly remembered that my rank locket had long since vanished. I didn't have my old Grade X locket and I couldn't afford to demote myself anyway.

I walked about, thinking. I went into the patio and looked. It was afternoon and sure enough, Utanc's car was gone. I scratched at her door. No answer. Luck! The little boys had gone with her, as they often did these days.

One picked set of locks later, I was in her room. It was much the same as before except that she now had two additional mahogany wardrobes. They were also locked but that was no obstacle. I opened some thin drawers in one. Just as I suspected. Jewelry. Gods knew she had been to Tiffany's often enough!

The emerald locket I had once seen her wear was right there. It was not really a rank locket but it was the right stone and gaudy enough. It would have to do.

I didn't want to stay long, it was too risky. I couldn't find the bug I had put under the rug, too small. I got out of there.

So far so good.

In my room, I buckled on a stungun and put a couple blasticks in my pocket. I put a Knife Section knife back of my neck. I hung the Antimanco control star on my chest. Thus readied, I went down the tunnel into the hangar. It just didn't do to go around these people unarmed.

There didn't seem to be anyone about.

I hadn't been in this place for some time. The two cannon ships were still there. The tug sat on its tail gathering dust. A few odds and ends of vessels and freight.

There was a movement over in one corner. I peered closely. What a strange ship! A sort of a dome like a bell. And there was the Antimanco Captain Stabb in working clothes. He saw me. I went over.

"So you come to see this little beauty," he said. "Greatest pirate vessel ever built!"

It was the line-jumper Stabb had been assembling. And it certainly wasn't little! The Antimancos were on ladders testing the absorbo-coat with beams to detect any possible radar reflectance.

"All done," said Stabb. "Been done for two weeks but they kept saying you were busy. When do we go out and pick up some banks?"

I had a very dim idea of such a project. I could see the headlines now, as Madison would say: BANK FLIES STRAIGHT INTO THE AIR—AIR FORCE INVESTIGATING. But I said, "Soon, soon. There are big things in the wind." I wasn't here for such nonsense anyway.

"Glad to hear it," said Stabb. "I was beginning to think, when you weren't in here watching progress, that maybe you'd lost your piracy perspective and gone over to the Royal officers."

"We'll get him, too," I reassured him.

I went over to the office area. I found what I was looking for. It was a cubicle near the main exit tunnel. I would not swarm aboard the *Blixo*. I would have them brought to me. That's what you do when you are in authority. I had the guards move some of their equipment around and got a desk and chair in the right place. In they would come. I would keep them standing. They would know who was in control. I even got the guards to promise to salute me that evening. They shrugged. I told them they could have special liberty the day after and they agreed.

The stage was set. I went back to my room and called the taxi driver to be ready at the exit barracks and when.

I phoned the hospital and, with guarded speech, found that Raht would be ready to travel tomorrow. I told Prahd to be available at 9:00 P.M. that night and set up to do an operation without anyone else attending. He couldn't argue back on that open line.

Because it was routine mission expense, Faht Bey couldn't object. I got him on the secure base intercom and told him I had to have two separate air tickets to New York and the usual expense money.

"I'll need an American passport," I said. "Female. Make the age about twenty. Get the photograph in the Costume Office as the female leaves. Have it all ready for tomorrow's plane. Any problem?"

"No. I. G. Barben just sent us some blank forms for drug runners, but I have to send back the name and birth date so they can file it. So what's the name?"

I was feeling a bit sarcastic. "Heavenly Joy Krackle," I said. "With a *K*. From Sleepy Hollow, New York."

"You leaving?" he said, far too hopefully.

"No. This is legitimate business," I snapped. "So don't goof up. Don't forget to put old immigration stamps on it. I'll leave the identostamped order with the photographer."

"I can include another air ticket for you," he said. I hung up.

I put on my uniform, hung the thing which would have to pass for a rank locket around my neck, laid out my bearskin coat and karakul hat to carry with me. I put some reference texts in my tunic pocket. I set out the complete audio-visio bug set, sealed it and put it out to take along.

Actually, I was pretty nervous. Krak or any thought of Krak had that effect on me. The memory of her scarlet heels when she had stamped that yellow-man to pulp had always stayed pretty vivid. And realizing that I would not have faced that giant with blastguns in my hand for any amount of money did not make it any better. It ruined my supper.

I vowed to myself that I would get her out of my area with no delay whatever and get her to work on slowing Heller down.

I was awfully glad to hear the gongs going, down the tunnel. The *Blixo* was coming in. I grabbed up the coat and hat and headed for the prepared office.

Chapter 7

I sat, lordly, at the desk when the guards brought in the first one I had chosen to see: Odur.

I was surprised. The little homo had apparently gotten the word from Too-Too. He had been on his good behavior. He wasn't even in chains.

In the greenish office light, his pretty, powdered face looked rather strange. But he was very respectful. And properly frightened.

"I have very few papers for you, Officer Gris," he said. "The office is quite a confusion. Bawtch is not there and two others seem to be gone. There is a new chief clerk but he doesn't know anything much."

Ah! Too-Too had succeeded! My old enemy Bawtch was dead! And the forgers, too! What marvelous news!

"So I just have these few blank forms for you to stamp in case they have an emergency."

He had them right with him, only a few pounds of paper. I took them. I got out my identoplate and stamped them then and there. It only took about twenty minutes instead of half an afternoon. How much lighter the work would be, now that Bawtch was in some unknown grave. I should have thought of that before!

I pushed the stack back to him. "And now, Oh Dear," I said, using his nickname, "what other news do you have?"

"Well," he said, "from what I can hear when they don't know I'm listening, Lombar Hisst is making just utterly marvelous progress addicting the Grand Council members. All the court physicians have been won over to the need of drugs. A lot of population on them, too. It is just a matter of time. There is just one little hook."

I became alert.

"You apparently have a man here on Blito-P3, some Fleet officer. On some mission. Apparently he has been sending reports through to Captain Tars Roke and the Grand Council has faith in both Roke and this officer. Lombar had the reports traced and they're in some kind of a monthly platen code so he knows that they can't be counterfeited."

Ah, well. No one is likely to get very far ahead of Lombar.

"Goodness, but Lombar hates this officer here! Absolutely goes into fits. So just before I got on the *Blixo* to come, I got pulled into Lombar's office. He's very frightening."

Indeed, he was, with his yanking on lapels and his stinger.

"And he said he'd found out you had a courier line to Voltar. I think he has spies on every ship. And he gave me a message."

Ho, ho! A message from the Chief himself!

"He said he was glad to help in sending the whore and Doctor Crobe like you requested. I think he'd do anything to mess up this officer here. Is she a whore, Officer Gris? She seems awfully nice. I talked with her on the voyage. She taught me to tie my tie properly, see?"

"Get on with the message!" I told this rattlebrain.

"Where was I? Oh, yes. And he said they were really counting on you. If this officer he hates so gets the planet on its ear, and especially if he upsets its control elite in any way, things could get very grim." He was trying to remember the rest of it, twisting his face and frowning.

"Wait a minute," I said. "If you talked to that woman on the voyage, what did you tell her?"

He went into instant shock. "Nothing. Nothing, Officer Gris. She sort of tried to pump me but I said I was just a messenger and knew nothing. Just carried some papers. And she didn't pay any attention after that. She was in her cabin nearly the whole voyage. I think she was studying a language because I could hear the machine going."

"You sure?" I said.

"Oh, goodness gracious, yes, Officer Gris. Lombar Hisst said he would murder me if I told anybody but you. But wait, that isn't all the message. Lombar said he was counting on you utterly to keep this officer slowed down. The opium and speed and heroin have to keep coming in. And no Rockecenter organization is to be disturbed in any way. Lombar is certain the supply line would collapse if I. G. Barben collapsed. But he said to tell you there was good news. There is a plan afoot—he didn't say what it was—but he was certain that some time in the future he would be able to give you a go-ahead and you could safely kill the man."

I was certainly glad to hear that! Then I had a disturbing thought. Krak had talked with him. "Did she put a helmet on your head?"

"The woman? No. Just before we took off from Voltar the whole ship was searched by Apparatus guards. They confiscated almost all our baggage. They took everything she had with her except one change of clothes and a language machine and tapes. So where would she get a helmet? Who is she?"

"The girlfriend of the man you carried the message to kill," I said. I couldn't resist it.

Oh Dear fainted dead away!

I put the magic-mail postcards in his pocket, allowing his mother to live until the next courier run.

I had the guards drag him and his papers out with orders to throw him in a detention cell until the *Blixo* left.

At my signal they brought in Crobe. The good and learned doctor was a mess. Always dirty, he was not improved a bit from six weeks in a spaceship cabin.

"Are you the (bleepard) that got me ordered here?" he said.

"Well, you're out of Spiteos," I replied. "You're on a beautiful humanoid planet that knows absolutely nothing about cellology or putting tentacles on babies."

"They confiscated everything I brought!" he said. "I haven't even got an electric knife!"

"We have lots of electric knives and over five billion people who have never seen a man with two heads where his feet ought to be."

That interested him, as I knew it would. Then a suspicion crossed my mind. "Were you given orders to study a language? And did you study it?"

"Oh, yes. But languages are a waste of time. Who wants to talk to people when you can do interesting things to them?"

"Tell me 'Good morning' in English."

"Goot mordag."

Oh, Gods. "Ask me how I am in English."

"You iss a doggle name George," he said.

(Bleep)! Stupid (bleepard). He had loafed the whole voyage! I couldn't trust him even out of this hangar!

"Doctor Crobe," I said, "I am going to put you in a room and I am going to keep you there until you have mastered a planetary language."

"What?"

"Just that. And if you really want to get around and enjoy the scenery and begin fruitful work, you'll take the language machine they gave you and put that nose of yours right into it. And when you can talk to the natives, I will have interesting employment for you and not until."

It failed to bring the overjoyed response I had expected. He just stood there and glared.

There was a chance that he thought of Earth as just a barbaric and primitive place without a scrap of culture. And this is not true. They have the subjects of psychology and psychiatry and these are marvelous and wonderful things.

I usually carried a couple of paperback texts for consultation when I came up against a knotty problem. I reached into the pocket of my tunic and brought them out. One was *Psychology Rampant*. The other was *To the Depths with Psychiatry*. These would certainly prove to him that there was benefit in learning English. I handed them over.

"Read these," I said, "and you will see how worthwhile English is!"

He took them. He leafed through them. He saw a drawing of a brain and his eyes lit up.

I beckoned to the guard captain and told him to put Crobe in one of the better cells and not let him go until I gave the word.

When the time came, I would let him out and turn him loose on Heller. After all, Heller had wanted a cellologist! I smiled.

Success so far in handling things. One of the troops had even saluted once.

I told the guard captain to bring the female over from the ship.

Chapter 8

Lulled by months of not seeing her, I had completely forgotten the impact of the presence of the Countess Krak. You knew she was there.

She was wearing a spacer's greatcoat with the collar turned up. She was wearing spaceboots. Her blond-gold hair was in braids around her head like a crown.

She looked at me with steady gray-blue eyes and said, "Is Jettero all right?"

Hastily, I gathered my wits. This was going to be touch and go. "Oh, yes!" I got out.

"Nothing has hurt him?" she said.

Now I had my chance. I could win this only if I played it perfectly. I put my hand on my stomach. "No!" I said quickly. "Somehow I don't feel very well. It must be something I had for lunch."

Aha! It worked! She smiled faintly. She thought her hypnotic implant of me was still in place, the (bleepch). She put down the small bag she was carrying.

Now to get a clue about the forgeries. I pointed at her grip. "I see you're not carrying much baggage. I hear the ship was searched."

She sighed. "Yes. Snelz put my trunk aboard and they took it. All that fuss about just a few training items. They must have missed them and they read me some long screed about it being unlawful to disclose you were an extraterrestrial. They're very unreasonable people. I'm not in the military. But that isn't the problem. They took all the beautiful clothes Jettero gave me. I don't have anything nice to meet him in. I can't let him see me like this! But then, you'll help me get some, won't you, Soltan."

"Of course," I said. My attention was on those Royal forgeries I had given her. "Anything else of value in that trunk?"

"No."

"I mean the Royal documents . . . you know. . . ."

"Oh, don't worry, Soltan. They're safe."

Aha. She must have been wearing them on her body. I would get around to that during the operation. I said, "You haven't told anyone about them, have you?"

"Oh, indeed no," she said reproachfully. "I gave you my word. I haven't even told Jettero about his Royal appointment or the promise to sign my pardon. You don't think I'd break my word, do you?"

"Of course not," I said soothingly. I felt more in control of the situation now. "But, come. You are anxious to go where Jet is. We have to prepare you quickly. Come along."

I grabbed the unmarked box of bugs, my hat and coat, and went to the door, beckoning.

She picked up her small grip and followed me up the tunnel.

We stopped at the Costume Department. The photographer was there, waiting. I handed him the identoplated order for passport, tickets and travel money and he handed them over.

The Countess Krak had started going down the racks of clothes. The photographer got her attention and asked her to step over to a white wall.

She didn't divine what he was up to right away as the camera he held probably didn't look like any camera she had ever seen before. When he held it up to his face, she suddenly understood.

"Oh, no! Not a picture!" she cried. "I'm such a mess!"

Too late. He already had it. He rushed away.

I grabbed a dress off the rack. It was blue with big white flowers.

"What's that?" she said in a kind of horror.

"Native dress," I said. "You have to look like a native. Remember the Space Code they read you."

She looked at the dress in amazement. "You mean these natives don't know any more about dressing than *this?*"

I masked any glee I might feel. I pointed at a change booth. "Quickly, quickly. People are waiting. Heller is half a day's flight from here and we've got to get you on your way."

Reluctantly she went into the booth and shed her greatcoat.

I found a dingy-looking woman's hooded cloak. It was a sort of spotty brown. I found a veil. I couldn't find any shoes or stockings. She was wearing spaceboots. So let her wear spaceboots.

She came out wearing the dress. She was about five foot, nine and a half inches tall and the dress was for a smaller woman. Her opinion of it was plain in her expression.

I shoved the cloak at her. "This will cover it," I said.

She found a couple small holes in it. She looked at me with a rather calculating eye. It made me nervous.

"The sooner you put this on, the sooner you're away," I said.

She put it on. I handed her the veil. She didn't know what to do with it so I showed her on my own face. "All women go veiled," I told her. "It's a religious custom."

"Are you sure we're on the right planet?" she said. But she put it on.

I got into my own bearskin coat and karakul hat, picked up the box of bugs, the things she had taken off and her grip, and with some persuasion, got her outside and into the taxi.

Now came the tricky part. I closed the partition so the driver couldn't hear. "You have to be very careful on this world," I said. "They are absolutely crazy on the subject of identification. And if you have any scars or marks of any kind on your body, they grab you at once. So all such things have to be removed."

The taxi was rolling through a very dark night but I could feel her eyes on me.

"Oh, Soltan," she said, disbelieving.

I turned on the overhead light. "No, look. See that scar on the back of your hand? A dead giveaway."

"That's just a little claw mark from a lepertige. You can hardly see it."

"And look at that wrist! Electric cuffs, weren't they?"

"Oh, Soltan. You'd need a vivid imagination just to make them out."

"All right," I said. "But how about that hideous scar over your right eyebrow?"

"You mean that tiny little scratch?" She fingered it. "But the eyebrow covers it."

"Well," I said, "you're just used to seeing it." And then I got very cunning. "You think Heller wants to have to look at that huge blemish the rest of his life?"

She was thoughtful. Then she said, "I see what you mean. But you're not putting me under gas, Soltan."

"Listen, Countess," I said. "It is my duty to protect you. Heller would have my head if I let you wander out only to get picked up because of identifying marks."

I must have sounded convincing—possibly because it was true that Heller would kill me with slow torture if I let anything happen to her. She grew more thoughtful.

It was time to dive straight into Strategy Plan A. "I don't blame you for being wary," I said. "The world, any world, is full of wolves. But I am a slave of duty. I will tell you what I will do. I happen to have hypnohelmets here. I'll let you put both me and the cellologist under one first and I'll give you a wrist recorder to wear during the operation. How's that?"

Just as I suspected, it caught her fancy. Above the veil, a gleam was very visible in those gray-blue eyes. "All right," she said.

I almost hugged myself with glee. It had worked! It had worked! I had to turn my face away so she would not see me suppressing triumph. I was tricking the formidable Countess Krak. And getting away with it!

Chapter 9

It was nearing 9:00 P.M. and there were very few around at the hospital.

I steered the Countess Krak through the lobby and got her into an interview room.

Dr. Prahd Bittlestiffender had been on the lookout and followed.

She sat down in a chair. She obviously didn't like the veil and took it off. She threw back the hood.

Young Doctor Prahd gangled into the room.

He stopped.

He stared.

In Voltarian, I said to her, "This is your doctor. He is one of the most competent cellologists Voltar ever produced. Doctor, this is Miss X. She just came in on the *Blixo* and, as usual, has to have her identifying scars removed."

Prahd, the silly ape, didn't take the cue at all. He was just standing there, staring at her with his mouth open!

I was operating smoothly now, myself. I said to her, "We'll go out now to the warehouse and get a hypnohelmet. So please excuse us."

I kicked him out of his trance, got him into the hall and closed the door. Carrying her bag and the bug box, I herded him back to the privacy of his office.

I snarled, "What the Hells are you so (bleeped) stunned about?"

"That lady," he said, eyes wide.

"That 'lady'," I told him acidly, "is a very wanted criminal!"

"WHAT? That beautiful woman? I can't believe it. She must be one of the greatest beauties of Voltar! I've only seen one other that could compare with her. And that was Hightee Heller, the Homeview star!"

I pushed him into his chair so I could tower over him. "Listen," I snarled. "That woman you are going into orbit about was once condemned to death and is today a nonperson. She has killed four men to my personal knowledge. Three of them for just making an innocent pass at her. So don't get any romantic ideas about that 'lady'! She is being sent in to do another job. A murder."

He was staring at me round-eyed, his straw hair standing up in all directions. I pressed my advantage. "We have to con her to protect ourselves," I continued. "You're going to remove her scars all right. But you're also going to put these audio and visual bugs in her skull just like you did with Heller. There's a scar just above her right eye that will do just fine. So you're going to put her under gas right now and do the job. She's not to know about the bugs."

"But she'll kill us if she finds out!" he said.

"Precisely!" I snapped. "But I've got that figured out. She has an inflated idea of herself as a hypnotist. I am going to propose to her that she put a hypnohelmet on each of us——"

"WHAT?"

"Be calm, be calm," I soothed him. "I've fixed a helmet so it doesn't work. You simply pretend you are under hypnosis. So will I. And we'll put a wrist recorder on her. Then she'll go tamely through with it. I'm just protecting you, that's all. So run over to the warehouse and get a couple of those hypnohelmets I sent over and I'll see you back in the interview room."

He took the box with the two bug devices and put it in his pocket. He left.

Rapidly, I opened her grip. I went through it very thoroughly. Only a few toilet articles and a little makeup. The bulk of the space was taken up with the language machine and some Earth texts. I carefully investigated the lining. Nothing.

The space greatcoat and the coveralls she had been wearing and which I had brought along produced no better result. Originally, when I gave them to her, she had strapped the "proclamations" against her body. And that's exactly where they must be now. I couldn't imagine even an Apparatus guard adventuring a skin search on her: she would kill him! And had they found them, they would have checked them against the Palace City log, found they were forgeries and she now would be a very executed Countess Krak, instead of a live one here on Earth.

My own neck was still out. Even with Bawtch and the forgers dead, the Countess Krak could implicate me. Ah, well. Very shortly, I would have them back for she would be lying there under gas. I might even fold a packet of paper to put in their place. Yes, that was the ploy. I made a paper packet up.

A door slammed somewhere and I realized Prahd must be back. I hurried down to the interview room and arrived just as he was entering. The Countess Krak's eyes lit up.

He was carrying two cartons and when he put them down she instantly rose and brushed him away. I had carefully replaced the original carton seals, of course—we are experts at that in the Apparatus—and those two cartons looked like they had never been touched since the day they left the manufacturer.

She chose one. She opened it. She looked like somebody about to cut a birthday cake. "Oho!" she said. "All shiny new and the very latest type! See, look! It has a plug-in microphone as well as the recording strip player! Oh, lovely. Such nice colors, too."

She expertly inserted a power pack and checked the meter. She plugged in the microphone. "Who is first?"

I wasn't really sure that she wouldn't also shove a knife into somebody. I gave Prahd a push toward a chair. He nervously perched his lanky body on its edge.

"Do you own this hospital?" she asked him conversationally.

"No, no," said Prahd, pointing at me. "He does. That is to say, he's the boss. If you have any complaints . . ."

"Not any yet," said the Countess Krak, smiling at him sweetly.

She put the helmet on his wheat shock of hair. She turned to me. "If you'll just wait in the hall, Soltan." She was juggling the microphone in one hand, the other poised over the switch to turn the helmet on.

I went. But I kept my ear pressed close to the closed door.

"Sleep, sleep, pretty sleep," she said. "Can you hear me?"

A muffled "Yes."

"You are about to do an operation. You will do it very expertly. You will not bring about any physical-body distortions or alterations. In other words, you will not monkey with my limbs or glands. Is that clear?"

A muffled "Yes."

"You will limit your operations to repairing a few scars and blemishes and make it all heal rapidly with no further scars or blemishes and no fancy ideas. Right?"

"Yes."

"Now," she continued, "if you or Soltan or any other man approaches me carnally or makes any sexual contact with me while I am under gas, you are to use an electric knife on yourself or them. Understood?"

"Right."

"And you are not to say anything around me or to me while I am under gas. Understood?"

"Yes."

"Now, if you violate any of this you will feel like atom bombs are exploding in your head. Right?"

"Right."

"You will now forget what I have said to you and when you wake up you will only remember and believe that I have been asking about your professional qualifications. Agreed?"

"Right."

A click. She had turned the helmet off. In a minute Prahd came stumbling out the door. I was watching him very closely. I had wanted to be sure that the helmet was made inoperative when the unit I carried came within two miles of it.

He was mopping his face. "Gods," he whispered. "Atom bombs!

I see what you mean!" He tottered down the hall to his operating room.

It was all right. If he'd been hypnotized, he would not have remembered! It was safe.

"Soltan," a soft voice was calling.

I went in like a meek little schoolboy. I was hiding my grins. She plopped the helmet down on my head. She threw on the switch. Through the visor shield I could see her check the meter and the lights.

She stepped back and held the microphone to her mouth. "Sleep, sleep, pretty sleep. Can you hear me, Soltan?"

"Yes," I said, making my voice sound groggy.

"Some time ago I told you that if you had any idea of hurting Jettero Heller, you would get sick at your stomach and so forth. Now tell me, Soltan, is that still true?"

"Oh, yes," I lied.

"And you have not gotten any notion of hurting him or doing him any nasty tricks?"

"Oh, no," I lied.

"Good. That is still true. Only, added to it is the fact that if you try to do anything bad to me, you will now feel the same way. Understood?"

"Yes," I said. Oh Gods, it sure was a good thing this helmet was null on me!

"Now listen carefully. You will help me in every way you can to reach Jettero. You will let me go wherever I want around this hospital and nearby buildings or base. You will let me pick up anything I want. Understood?"

"Yes," I said.

"Now also," she said, "you'll let me have whatever I take, no matter what it is. You will let me leave with it. And you will find a reasonable reason in yourself for letting me do so. Is that clear?"

"Yes," I said.

"Good. You will now forget what I have said. When you awake you will think I have been asking you about the operation. All right?"

"Yes," I said.

She reached over and clicked the helmet switch and then took it off my head. "Wake up, Soltan."

Hiding my grin, I said, "Now that you know all about the operation, shall we go to the operating room?"

Oh, smart brains, indeed! What if I had not had that breaker-switch pair installed in the helmets and my skull? All that agony had just paid off! It didn't compare to the stomachaches I'd had!

Chapter 10

Prahd sent her into a cubicle beside the operating theater. It was a sort of bathroom–dressing room. He gave her a package—a Zanco disposable, sterile operating gown and cap. He gestured toward a slot in the door. "Please drop your clothes through that, including those boots. Then take a shower and get into this. Then enter the operating room through that side door."

She nodded. She seemed oddly cheerful. But of course she was happy to have a bath after six weeks on a freighter. And she was going to see Heller soon, wasn't she? Still, I was very suspicious of a happy Countess Krak.

Prahd and I entered the operating room itself. He had lights flashing and beakers bubbling and it all looked very businesslike.

"Just as soon as you have her under," I said, "I'm going to have to do a skin search."

"WHAT?"

"I have to make sure she is carrying no secret weapons," I lied. "I will take off my boots. I will be very quiet."

"You don't have to come in," he said. "There's a viewport, one way, right over in that wall. It looks like a small mirror."

"Won't do," I said. "I can be very quiet. I have to be sure."

"All right, but do it before I begin work. I don't want all the germs you carry in here. And I can disinfect afterwards."

I ignored his insult. I took a wrist recorder out of my pocket. "Tell her she can put this on and start it."

"I think she *would* kill us if we took any liberties, Officer Gris.

So just be warned that I'll have my electric knife ready."

"Hey, you weren't really hypnotized were you?"

"No. But if she wakes up and finds she's been fooled with and your dead body isn't lying on the floor, she'll get suspicious that the helmet didn't work."

Yes, there was that. But I didn't exactly like the way he put it.

She came in, in the open-backed operating gown. "That's the awfullest-smelling soap I think I ever smelled. What a frightful stink!"

"Overstrength germicidal," said Prahd. "As to the stink, Officer Gris is just leaving. As to the soap, I'll put a nice smelling bar in the recovery room and you can shower and wash your hair when you wake up. All right? Good. Now, if you will just sit down on the operating table . . ."

I left. I went around to the one-way window. I couldn't hear what they were saying. She was on the table but she was having to master how to operate the wrist recorder and I realized she was unfamiliar with the clumsiness of Earth devices. She finally got it tested and running and hung on her forearm.

She swung her shapely legs up and stretched out. Prahd lowered the gas anesthetic dome. He watched a heart counter and respiration meter. She was out.

He pulled the gown off her and beckoned toward the window.

I went around to the door. I slipped off my boots. More silent than a cat, I entered and stole toward the table.

Gods, she was a beautiful woman! No Greek sculptor had ever had a model like this!

Prahd was standing there with an electric knife. I got busy.

There was nothing strapped to the front of her body. There was nothing around her waist so far as I could observe it. They must be strapped to her back! I moved forward to turn her over. I stopped. Prahd notwithstanding, I was afraid to touch her. I suddenly discovered that terror could be a much heavier emotion than sexual desire. I backed up.

Finding it hard to swallow and shaking a bit, I gestured to Prahd to lift her.

He did, very quietly. I looked under her back from the right side. I went around while he moved her the other way. Nothing. She didn't have a thing on her!

I tiptoed out of there, feeling somehow that I had escaped with my life.

I went into the change room and searched. Nothing. I examined the clothes she had taken off. Nothing. I looked for false soles in the boots. Just plain, black spaceboots.

(BLEEP)!

She was a very clever woman. She not only trained people for the stage, she could also do all kinds of sleight of hand. I would have to watch her very carefully. It would be my neck if I didn't recover those forgeries. The horrible thought hit me that maybe Bawtch had talked before he died. Or left a note or something! Yes, I had no choice but to recover them. Constant watchfulness was the watchword.

Chapter 11

Back at the one-way window, I watched the progress of the operation.

She lay in naked repose, oblivious of what was going on.

Prahd was working with rapid expertise. For some reason, he took a lot of measurements with a lot of different scopes and devices, cataloguing them all on a chart. Then he opened a big volume and consulted it. From where I was I could see the page he had: it was headed "Manco." Well, he was right about that. She was from Manco.

Then he made a signal toward the window, indicating the hall. I met him there. He showed me the book. "This lady is from the aristocracy of Atalanta."

I noted sourly that it was "lady" again. "Yes," I said.

"That accounts for it," he said.

"For what?" I said, irritated.

"The perfection. She's the product of tens of thousands of years of selective breeding. The aristocracy married nothing but the most beautiful and bright. Do you realize that her thyroid . . ."

Oh, Gods, deliver me from a specialist riding his hobby! "Are you going to get on with this operation or aren't you?"

"I just wanted you to be aware that you were tampering with the aristocracy," he said. "It carries the death penalty, you know."

"I told you!" I grated. "She's a nonperson! A criminal! There isn't even any penalty if you killed her."

He went back in the operating room. I went back to the

window. Prahd bent over her ankles and looked very carefully. Then he looked over her wrists. Then he looked at me and nodded. He was convinced.

I knew what he had found. Electric cuffs, wrist and ankle, when worn for weeks, make small burns. And she must have been in them for months during her imprisonment, transportation to Voltar and trial before the Apparatus got her. They had left faint scars.

Prahd got to work. He made his "cell soups" from little clips and drillings. He addressed the scarred eyebrow and, very soon, sterilized the two bugs and implanted them. He covered them over with the bone and skin paste and then put the area under a catalyst light.

He then got busy on the ankle and wrist scars. I didn't really like the way he was working. It was with sort of flourishing motions like a painter; he was also cocking his head over and eyeing the effects. Silly (bleepard).

With new lights now on her wrists and ankles, he went prowling for more scars or blemishes: he found some ancient signs of slashes along her right ribs, below the breast, probably from the claws of some wild animal she had been training. He fixed those. Then he found some tiny burns on the outside of her left thigh. I knew where those had come from: Lombar's stinger. He fixed them. Then he studied her whole naked body minutely under a scope. He didn't seem to be finding any more past wounds or blemishes.

He put cups and straps over the work he had done and I thought he would now be finished.

But no. He got out a little set of tools and began to work on the ends of her fingers. I couldn't imagine what he was doing. Then it came to me. He was giving her a manicure!

Having finished that quite expertly, he went to her feet and gave her a pedicure! He seemed to be getting her toenails just right.

I thought he would surely be done now. But no! He was getting out another set of tools. He propped her jaws open, did a thorough inspection of her mouth and then, of all things, began to clean and polish her teeth!

Deliver me from idiots! Her smile was about as dangerous a

thing as anyone would ever see without making it blindingly bright!

Done with that at last, he pulled the cloths from under her jaws and stood back. He surveyed her long nakedness. Then, busily, he pulled another lamp down on its swing neck, turned it on and passed it the length of her body, stood back and admired the effect and then did it again. He gently turned her over and did the same thing to her back.

He was giving her a suntan!

I had to admit to myself that two or three years in the dungeons of Spiteos and six weeks in a spaceship might make one a bit pale. But he had something else in mind for he was consulting the tables in the big book. He got a meter out. He was apparently measuring skin color! The people of Atalanta are white but it is a white with a faint tan tinge. He was restoring the exact shade!

He was satisfied with that. Now he was checking her hair color. The blond-gold of it seemed satisfactory by meter.

He was done! Thank Gods! What a tinkerer!

He threw a blanket over her and picked her up and carried her into the hall. I was with him promptly.

Prahd took her into a private room. He laid her on the bed. He covered her up with sheets and blankets. He made sure the recorder was not exerting any weight on her arm. He arranged her head properly on the pillow.

He left the room and closed the door. He looked at me and there was a dreamy farawayness in his eyes. "You know," he said, "she was perfectly right. Anybody who messed up such a gorgeous creature *should* have atom bombs exploding in his head."

He locked the door and put the key in his pocket. "I'm going to bed now," he said. "I suggest that you go home."

He went away. I was absolutely fuming! I was seething at how blind people could be about the *real* Krak. Here she had added another ally to her mobs of supporters!

Well, I certainly had no intention of going home! She might come out of that room and attack me! She might even blow up the base!

I got a straight-backed chair and planted it opposite the door. I gathered up the spacer greatcoat, coveralls and other clothes and put them in a stack beside the chair. I took the spaceboots and put them on their sides on the floor. I tilted the chair back against the wall and put my foot on the spaceboots so that if they were even touched, it would cause my foot to move and bring the chair back forward on its four legs to jolt me awake in case I dozed. I took the catch off my stungun and gripped its butt.

I looked at the locked door and for the first time since her arrival I began to smile.

Despite her trickery, I had foiled the Countess Krak. I had finally gained the upper hand. I was impervious to her hypno-helmets while she in turn was now bugged so I could monitor her every move.

Heller, meanwhile, was sinking fast. And if he thought Babe's wrath was rough, he hadn't seen anything yet. The best was yet to come.

I folded my arms across my chest and grinned. Gris, I complimented myself, you got 'em. Sending an implanted Krak off to Heller and his whores would be like tossing an anvil to a drowning man.

Then when Hisst sent the OK, I could humanely end Heller's misery, get the forgeries even if I had to torture the information out of Krak (a delicious thought), sell her to the black market in Istanbul, settle matters with Utanc and then sit back and rake in the money from my host of enterprises.

Sleep well, Countess Krak.

Tomorrow belongs to me.

*What will Krak do when
she finds Heller knee-deep
in girls?
Is this the end of
Heller's mission?*

Read
MISSION EARTH
Volume 5
FORTUNE OF FEAR

About the Author
L. Ron Hubbard

Born in 1911, the son of a U.S. naval officer, the legendary L. Ron Hubbard grew up in the great American West and was acquainted early with a rugged outdoor life before he took to the sea. The cowboys, Indians and mountains of Montana were balanced with an open sea, temples and the throngs of the Orient as Hubbard journeyed through the Far East as a teenager. By the time he was nineteen, he had travelled over a quarter of a million sea miles and thousands on land, recording his experiences in a series of diaries, mixed with story ideas.

When Hubbard returned to the U.S., his insatiable curiosity and demand for excitement sent him into the sky as a barnstormer where he quickly earned a reputation for his skill and daring. Then he turned his attention to the sea again. This time it was four-masted schooners and voyages into the Caribbean, where he found the adventure and experience that was to serve him later at the typewriter.

Drawing from his travels, he produced an amazing plethora of stories, from adventure and westerns to mystery and detective.

By 1938, Hubbard was already established and recognized as one of the top-selling authors, when a major new magazine, Street and Smith's *Astounding Science Fiction*, called for new blood. Hubbard was urged to try his hand at science fiction. The red-headed author protested that he did not write about "machines and machinery" but that he wrote about people. "That's just what we want," he was told.

The result was a barrage of stories from Hubbard that expanded the scope and changed the face of the genre, gaining Hubbard a repute, along with Robert Heinlein, as one of the "founding fathers" of the great Golden Age of Science Fiction.

Then as now he excited intense critical comparison with the best of H. G. Wells and Edgar Allan Poe. His prodigious creative output of more than a hundred novels and novelettes and more than two hundred short stories, with over twenty-two million copies of fiction in a dozen languages sold throughout the world, is a true publishing phenomenon.

But perhaps most important is that as time went on, Hubbard's work and style developed to masterful proportions. The 1982 blockbuster *Battlefield Earth*, celebrating Hubbard's 50th year as a pro writer, remained for 32 weeks on the nation's bestseller lists and received the highest critical acclaim.

"A superlative storyteller with total mastery of plot and pacing."—*Publishers Weekly*

"A huge (800+ pages) slugfest. Mr. Hubbard celebrates fifty years as a pro writer with tight plotting, furious action, and have-at-'em entertainment."—*Kirkus Review*

But the final *magnum opus* was yet to come. L. Ron Hubbard, after completing *Battlefield Earth*, sat down and did what few writers have dared contemplate—let alone achieve. He wrote the ten-volume space adventure satire *Mission Earth*.

Filled with a dazzling array of other-world weaponry and systems, *Mission Earth* is a spectacular cavalcade of battles, of stunning plot reversals, with heroes and heroines, villains and villainesses, caught up in a superbly imaginative, intricately plotted invasion of Earth—as seen entirely and uniquely through the eyes of the aliens that already walk among us.

With the distinctive pace, artistry and humor that is the inimitable hallmark of L. Ron Hubbard, *Mission Earth* weaves a hilarious, fast-paced adventure tale of ingenious alien intrigue, told with biting social commentary in the great classic tradition of Swift, Wells and Orwell.

So unprecedented is this work, that a new term—dekalogy

(meaning ten books)—had to be coined just to describe its breadth and scope.

With the manuscript completed and in the hands of the publisher and all of his other work done, L. Ron Hubbard departed his body on January 24, 1986. He left behind a timeless legacy of unparalleled story-telling richness for you the reader to enjoy, as other readers have, time and again, over the past half century.

We the publishers are proud to present L. Ron Hubbard's dazzling tour de force: the *Mission Earth* dekalogy.

"I AM ALWAYS HAPPY TO HEAR FROM MY READERS."

L. Ron Hubbard

These were the words of L. Ron Hubbard, who was always very interested in hearing from his friends, readers and followers. He made a point of staying in communication with everyone he came in contact with over his fifty-year career as a professional writer, and he had thousands of fans and friends that he corresponded with all over the world.

The publishers of L. Ron Hubbard's literary works wish to continue this tradition and would very much welcome letters and comments from you, his readers, both old and new.

Any message addressed to the Author's Affairs Director at New Era Publications will be given prompt and full attention.

NEW ERA PUBLICATIONS U.K. LTD
Dowgate, Douglas Road,
Tonbridge, Kent, TN9 2TS, U.K.